AVA HUNTER
BABYMOON OR BUST

Babymoon or Bust
Copyright © 2023 Ava Hunter

ISBN: 978-1-7374743-7-1

All rights reserved. No part of this publication may be reproduced, distributed or transmitted in any form by any means, or stored in a database or retrieval system, without the prior written permission of the author.

Babymoon or Bust is a work of fiction. Characters, names, places, angst and incidents are a work of the author's imagination and are fictitious. Any resemblance to real life events or persons, living or dead, is entirely coincidental and not intended by the author.

Cover Design: Sarah Hansen/Okay Creations
Editing: VB Edits
Formatting: Champagne Book Design

ALSO BY AVA HUNTER

Babymoon or Bust

The Nashville Star Series
Know You More – a Prequel
Sing You Home
Find You Again
Love You Always – Sal & Luke's Novella
Need You Now
Bring You Back
With You Forever – Lacey & Seth's Novella

Runaway Ranch Series
Tame the Heart

Dedication

This story goes out to anyone trying to walk that fine between motherhood and woman, sanity and struggle. Motherhood is hard, so let's fuck it up, and find that happily-ever after you deserve.

Playlist

Hotel Key | Old Dominion
Sand in My Boots | Morgan Wallen
Some Nights | Fun.
Stars | Grace Potter and the Nocturnals
At the Beach | The Avett Brothers
I Saw the Light | Hank Williams
Galway Girl | Steve Earl
Water Me | Lizzo
Waves | Luke Bryan
Toes | Zac Brown Band
Girl from the North Country | Bob Dylan & Johnny Cash
C Sections and Railway Trestles | The Avett Brothers
The Mother | Brandi Carlile

Foreword

Hi! I am so excited to bring you a special edition cover of *Babymoon or Bust*! Isn't it gorgeous?

I wanted something fun that screamed beach vibes and tropics, but also something simple with stunning typography and gorgeous colors! And man, oh, man, did my designer deliver! It makes me want to just kick back on the beach with a piña colada in my hand.

I love it so much, and I so hope you love it too. Happy reading!

Psst.
The next page contains trigger warnings.
Please skip if you wish to avoid spoilerish content.

A Note from Ava

Dear Reader,

This book contains a descriptive traumatic childbirth scene as well as brief references to the past death of a spouse by accident and to the past death of a parent to cancer.

If you're sensitive to subjects such as these, please use this warning to make an informed decision about whether to proceed with the story.

But I always promise a happy ending and a growling mountain man.

With big love and all good wishes,
Ava

ba·by·moon
/ˈbābēˌmoon/
noun

INFORMAL
1. a relaxing or romantic vacation taken by parents-to-be shortly before the birth of their baby.

"on the eve of the third trimester, two strangers are stuck together among the whispering palm trees of Mexico for a torturous week-long babymoon"

- a critical period of time after childbirth where the new parents run on madness and caffeine while establishing a bond with their newborn.

"a babymoon is regarded as a special time for the mother and father to fall in love with their baby. . .and each other"

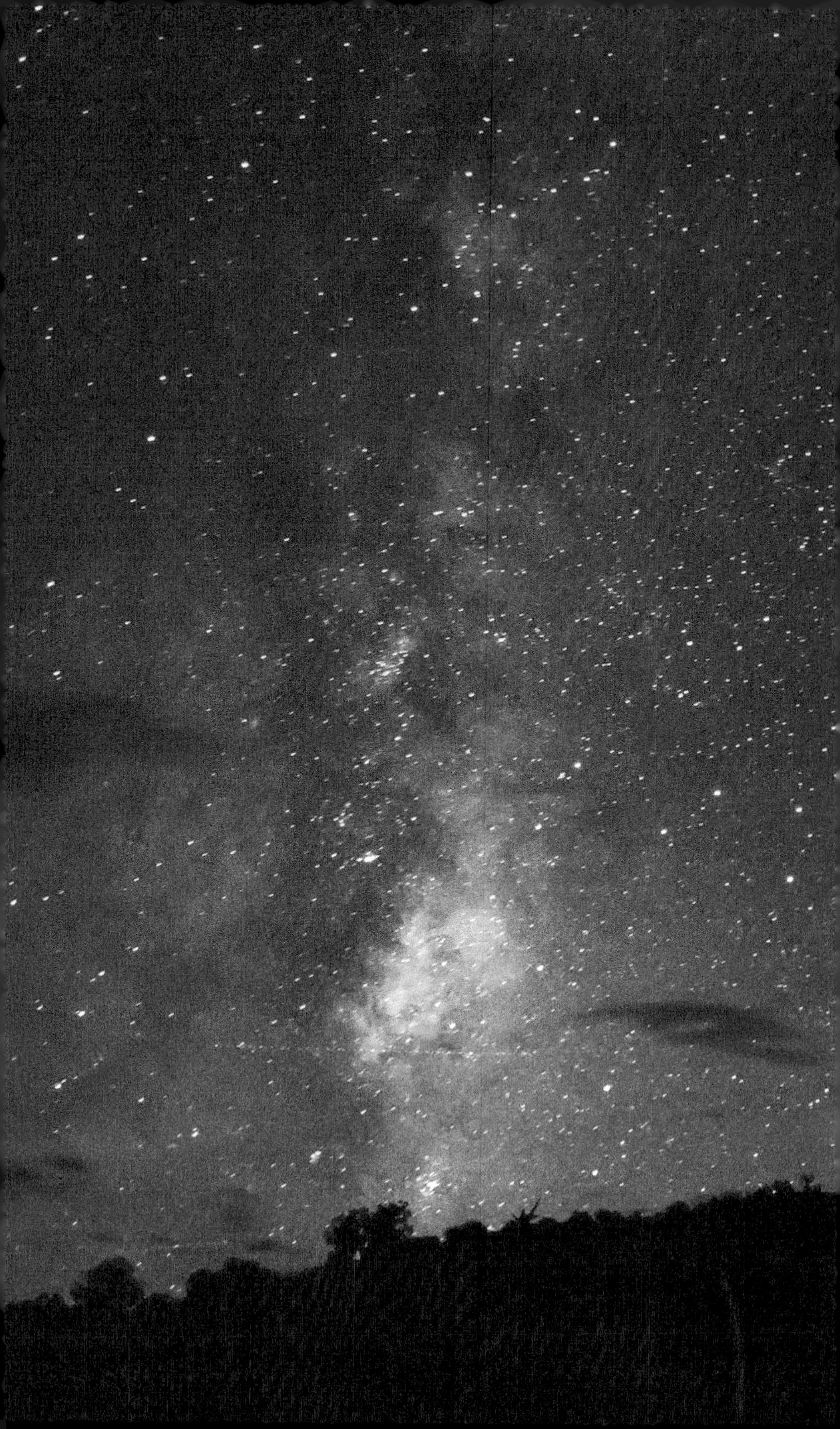

I.

Chapter One

GET LIT, GET LOOSE, GET LAID.

Tessie Truelove lives to cross out each and every item outlined in her carefully planned agenda—three priority tasks a day. But this specific request doesn't make the cut.

As much as she'd like it to.

Tess shuts her planner on tomorrow's lengthy to-do list. Exhaling a determined sigh, she swivels on her barstool to survey the dank Tennessee bar the locals call the Bear's Ear. She can appreciate dive. Hell, she was raised in a dive. Dives can give lessons in bold clashing patterns and thinking outside the box. Automatically, her mind goes to prettying up the surly space. She can't help it. It's ingrained. The walls could use a coat of paint. She'd nix the antlers. Small furry beasts of burden. Get rid of the wooden beer cooler. Add black horseshoe booths for smooth lines. Keep the loud music. Funky country with a beat.

Locals and tourists alike face off over beers and booths. A bachelor party, the men pounding shots with masculine exuberance, roars in the corner. A singer on the jukebox croons about whiskey and the way his ex-wife slugged him with two rounds of lead back in fifty-three. Tessie squints at the plaque behind the bar proclaiming Bear's Ear a must-visit destination.

Drink.

She needs a drink.

And maybe a tetanus shot.

Pushing herself up on her stool, she lifts a hand to the bartender. "Excuse me. Do you have a wine list?"

He scowls, pulling drafts with reckless abandon. "Beer or liquor, blondie. That's all we're servin.'"

She holds his hard stare. "The name is Tess, and yours?"

He sighs.

She presses her palms together in a prayer pose. "I *really* need a glass of wine."

Another sigh. "Tequila okay?"

Inhaling a breath, ready to ramble, ready to work her best no-nonsense magic, she leans across the bar and locks eyes with the man. "Listen, I didn't work a seventeen-hour day and get lost on these dusty back roads to shoot piss-poor tequila shots in a dive bar with nudie calendars on the wall and an eardrum-shattering jukebox. No offense. After the day I've had, I deserve a glass of wine."

The bartender's jaw twitches.

"Please." She lifts her chin. Narrows her gaze.

He stops. Wipes his rag along the bar. Tilts his head. Then a sigh of defeat. "Red or white?"

She smiles. "White, please. With ice."

A curl of his lip. "Don't push it."

He Hulk-smashes a hand into the ancient fridge and fumbles around until he retrieves a dusty bottle. The wine is a translucent white with peach undertones. She doesn't need to pull her Pantone book out of her bag to know which color she'd assign to the drink.

Swatch 9180.

She lives by Pantone colors. They are blissful order. Neat squares that tell a person exactly what to expect. No surprises; no chaos.

Tess jumps as the bartender slams the bottle of wine onto the bar top in front of her with a hard stamp of disapproval.

"Thank—"

Tess is midsentence when he hurries off to surlier patrons. At least he left her the bottle.

"You," she mutters, eschewing etiquette and propping both elbows on the lacquered surface in front of her before dropping her face to her hands.

Even the bartender hates her. And why wouldn't he? She's terrible.

Terrible Tess.

She scowls. Fucking Atlas. He's the one who saddled her with the awful nickname after the whole carpeted wall debacle years ago.

Usually, she's content donning the Terrible Tess moniker because it means she gets the job done for her clients. And rather than her interns, *she* takes Atlas's wrath.

But tonight, that means she's in the boonies celebrating. Alone. Per usual.

Rallying optimism, Tess closes her eyes and inhales deep, doing her best to focus on her big accomplishment of the day.

The newly opened Grey & Grace Hotel in Nashville is the highlight of her portfolio. A popular country singer opened a bar on Broadway and selected her as head designer. A two-year long project finally finished. If this doesn't clinch her promotion at Atlas Rose Interiors—an internationally renowned celebrity interior design firm—nothing will.

After the big reveal and the client walk-through, Tessie offered to buy her junior design staff a round of shots.

They looked at her like she was off her rocker.

"Get a life, lady," one of the interns had grunted before the group of them trudged off.

She opened her mouth to snap, "I have a life," then just as abruptly, she shut it. Sven the intern was right. She doesn't have a life. She has a job and an angry boss and her mood boards and Pantone chips. She has her records and a bubble bath and a glass of wine when she finds the time.

Who could blame them?

Who'd want to hang out with her after she'd barked orders all day?

She barely wants to hang out with herself.

It was that heart-twisting, face-slapping realization that had her spiraling. That made her grab her rental car keys and punch the gas and drive. Just drive. Away from the city and onto dusty country back roads.

In search of a reprieve. A second to be the so-very-not-uptight, not-so-terrible Tess she'd come to be.

And she found a bar where she doesn't have to be herself. A city where no one knows her. A night she doesn't have to hide behind her professional façade. Where no one will call her terrible.

Maybe her cousin Ash's words of wisdom—*get lit, get loose, get laid*—are worth considering.

Because tomorrow, she goes back to the rat race that is Los Angeles

Tomorrow, she'll be Terrible Tess once more.

She examines her gold-tipped nails and drains the remainder of her wine. Refills the glass with a hearty pour.

She loves her job.

But for one night, she wants to forget.

Make mistakes.

Have fun.

Tessie never expected to put her entire life into a job. But here she is, thirty-two years old, and it's exactly what she's done—it's what she's good at. Sleeping alone. Working sixteen-hour days. Keeping acquaintances, not friends. Spending all her time in showrooms, lugging heavy containers of tile and fabric samples, scrambling to appease her clients. Tearing out the most beautiful parts of ancient houses to make way for depressing gray floors and the same boring open concept floor plans. Kissing Atlas's ass and refilling his Xanax prescription for a chance to make it as a senior designer.

She chugs her wine.

God help her, if the hotel she single-handedly designed doesn't get her the Penny Pain account, she'll fling herself into the Cumberland River. She'll float her way back to LA, her perfect makeup ruined. A gorgeous corpse, but a dead, jobless, bloated corpse, nonetheless.

Still.

Her job might not love her back, but it doesn't break her heart.

Work is her life. Because Tessie can count on one hand the number of people who have left her. And if she folded all those fingers down, she'd make a fist. And fists fucking hurt.

Her own money. Her own life.

Indestructible.

Except tonight.

Tonight, maybe she could work in a smidge of destruction.

Excitement. That familiar electricity snaps in her soul. The old Tessie surfacing. The gutsy girl who waited tables for two years to make ends meet after college, who hunted old records and medicine bottles at antique stores when she started staging model homes. Not Terrible Tess, who screams at the interns when they forget to fluff the pillows before a client visit.

Tessie rolls her eyes at the ape-like noises coming from the bachelor party, then glances down at herself. She's not dive enough.

She shrugs off her blazer, leaving herself in a black silk tank top and the ripped jeans she changed into before heading out for the night. A quick flick of her wrist, and she lets down her golden hair, placing the French hair pin beside her wineglass.

Freedom.

She surveys the drink in her hand.

And alcohol.

If Ash were here, she'd give Tessie a quick slap on the ass, and she'd repeat the marching orders she gave her before she boarded her flight at LAX.

Get lit, get loose, get laid.

Tess chews her full bottom lip.

The thought is tempting. She hasn't been laid in what? A millennium? At the very least since open floor concepts were a thing.

But before she can talk herself out of it, a boisterous laugh sideswipes her thoughts. Tipping forward, Tessie peers down the long bar top. Six seats down, a man with sandy-blond hair hoots like a hyena, and beside him...

Her eyes light on the beast of a man sitting stiffly on a barstool. His rugged face is pained, and he glowers into space like he craves an escape hatch, looking just as uncomfortable as she feels.

But aside from that, he's... hot.

Damn hot.

She narrows her gaze. Zeroes in. Appreciates.

Her brain short-circuits as she drinks him in. He's tall, even hunched over the bar top, his body built and broad. He wears a black buffalo plaid flannel shirt, black logger boots, and faded jeans. His black hair's roguishly messy, longer in the front and trim in the back. The sleeves of his flannel are shoved up to the elbows, exposing massive, corded forearms dusted with dark hair and violently colorful tattoos.

As he shakes his head at his friend, he taps along to the beat of the country song.

Tessie goes soft all over.

Her mom would like him.

She scowls at the intrusive thought.

And then she laughs, the memory of the dive bar where her mother worked coming to her.

She would sit in that grimy booth, her legs dangling over the edge while she did her homework. Her mother cleaned tables and poured beer, singing along to the jukebox about cowboys in faraway places. She brought home a record player so they could listen to their own cowboys on vinyl. Late at night, they'd sit beside the record player, and her mom would pull out album after album. She knew them all: George Jones. Waylon Jennings. Merle Haggard. Hank Williams. Old-school cowboys.

This man, though. He's not a cowboy.

She gives him a thorough once-over. That beard. Close-cropped, trimmed neat. How very mountain man. Gruff. Rugged.

She bets he's the type of man who works with his hands. Who has callused fingertips but a soft touch. And kisses like a dream.

A fantasy.

Lifting her glass to her lips, she drains her wine. She could go for a fantasy.

What does his voice sound like?

A rumble of thunder? Sandpaper? She shivers at the thought.

The music, the wine, the sight of the mountain man have Tessie loosening up, relaxing, ready for fun, wanting to dance. Gyrate like a fool on her barstool to the hard pump of hillbilly rock pulsing through the bar.

Everything inside her is bright and buzzy. A slosh of emotions. She doesn't want to play it safe. Just for one night.

A curve on her lip, she considers the jukebox with appreciation. She could do it. She could dance. Become a feral dance floor woman. No one knows her here. What's the worst that could happen?

She slugs her wine.

Get lit.

She smiles as she kicks off her red-soled pumps.

Get loose.

Chapter Two

Solomon Wilder's dead wife is telling him to get laid.

Clear as day, Serena's voice resonates in his mind. After seven years, he may not remember every pretty angle of her face or the deep cobalt color of her irises, but her steady voice has never left him. Always pushing when he needs a good kick in the ass. Urging him to move. Even when he doesn't want to.

"You're scarin' the girls away, Sol." A low drawl sounds in his ear. "You got that frown on your face, man."

He grunts as Howler claps a hand on his shoulder. His best friend angles closer, waggling lascivious brows. "Loosen up."

Twisting the wedding ring on his scarred knuckle, Solomon says, "We're supposed to be doing research." He lifts an amber bottle to his lips. Drains it. "Looking at girls doesn't count as research."

Howler groans loud enough to be heard over the music. "Why are you like this? I finally get you out of the house, and you got me flying solo here."

Solomon smears a hand down his face. His friend's got some goddamn nerve asking him to leave his cabin and his dog and his mountain. Talking him into an eight-hour flight to Nashville when he hasn't left his small town of Chinook, Alaska, in fifteen years.

Reconnaissance Howler called it.

For their busted, broken-down bar.

Howler's Roost.

Housed in an old silo, the pair opened it when they were in their early twenties. The bar looked dive from the outside, but inside, it was unlike any other establishment in their little town of Chinook. Upscale food and drink for locals. Both men wanted to flex their creative muscles *their* way. Howler made craft cocktails. Solomon created locally sourced pub food. And they flourished...until Serena died.

Originally, they'd intended it as a hangout for locals, but once Howler got behind the bar and experimented with cocktails, the tourists started pouring in. Called it the best kept secret in Alaska.

Then, six months ago, a famous country singer from Nashville put Howler's Roost on the map. He was stranded after a concert, and when he'd returned home, he declared to *Food & Wine* magazine that the bar had the best damn cocktail he'd ever tasted.

The attention they've received since has created nothing but chaos. It's made Howler's Roost a destination people fight to get to. Has them hopping planes from Anchorage just to try the signature cocktail, the Redheaded Stepchild. Has Howler stockpiling product so he doesn't run out.

After a blizzard damaged the roof last year, his best friend jumped at the chance to finally give Howler's Roost a much-needed renovation.

Which is where this Nashville trip comes in. Scouting bars as inspiration for their own remodel. Bear's Ear bar is a side-of-the-road pit stop known for its microbrews and burgers.

Sure, Solomon has been out of the restaurant business for a while, but letting his bar crash and burn isn't an option.

Even if that's why the bar fell into disrepair in the first place. Because he wasn't there. Story of his goddamn life.

Howler lets out a tormented sigh, bouncing on the barstool. "You're killin' me, dude. I get you off the mountain for the first time in years, and all you do is glower."

Solomon crosses his arms. "I glower in Chinook too."

"Don't I know it." Howler waves at the plate of egg rolls between them. "What do you think of the food?"

"Great."

"Ain't yours." He circles a finger, signaling for two more shots of whiskey. "You're doing me a favor by being here. We can write this off as a business expense; a cranky ex-chef who needs to have a damn good time." Pushing off the counter, he tips back and surveys the room. "How about her?"

Without turning his head, Solomon says, "No."

"Her?"

"Howler."

"Listen, I know your flirting skills are rusty—"

Solomon snatches up his whiskey and brings it to his lips. "Dead and buried."

"This is an excursion, a celebration. Your dick's last resort." Lowering his sunny voice, Howler leans in. Serious now. "Dude. You've atoned long enough."

Yeah. He has.

He spent the first few years figuring out who he was without her. Now, what used to be love is duty. Guilt. Obligation. A hardscrabble stubbornness to put Serena first in death, because he didn't in life.

"Serena would understand," Howler says.

He grinds his molars and traces the wood grain of the bar top. He didn't come here for a quick lay.

He's here to do research, to help his best friend get their bar back together, and then it's back to Chinook.

"How 'bout Goldilocks?"

With a grunt, Solomon slams his whiskey down and glares at his friend, ready to tell him to shut the fuck up, that they've been here all night, that they've got an early day tomorrow. But the wolfish smile on Howler's face makes him spin on his stool.

There, in the middle of the bar, is a lone girl who's made the floor her personal dance club.

He can't help but stare. Dancing along to the croon of George Strait, she has no rhythm. She's clapping off the beat, but still, she's shaking her hips, swinging her long blond hair, and laughing like a gorgeous, dancing wild thing.

Damn beautiful.

His mouth goes dry. It feels like he just struck gold. The girl looks like it too.

Tossing his head back, Howler cackles and rubs his hands together. "She's a hoot."

"Don't laugh," Solomon orders and gives his friend a glare. "She's having fun. Let her." The girl's in tune with the music, swaying with carefree abandon. Stem glass in her hand, wine sloshing over the rim and onto the floor, oblivious to the raised brows directed at her.

She's not tall, but those legs. And those fucking eyes. Big, brown, and lined with a fringe of long, dark lashes.

She's barefoot, uncaring about the dusty planks beneath her, the spilled beer, the crushed peanuts. Her black tank top dips, exposing the curve of her breasts. Her ripped jeans are practically painted on, showcasing her ass perfectly. She's tan—probably a tourist. But a goddamn gorgeous one. She's magnetic, drawing his gaze and holding it captive. He hasn't stared at a woman like this since Serena. His wife's face is a blur. But this girl's isn't. There's something about her. A fun, flirty, carefree pull that has him aching to know her.

Women. Interaction. Aside from his mother and sisters, it's been seven long years.

Serena's voice whispers: *It's time, Solomon. Move your butt, you bearded fool.*

But before he can stand, a pretty boy from the bachelor party in the corner saunters toward the girl. Solomon tracks him like a shark. He knows that look. Popped collar. Wolfish sneer. On the prowl. He's scared off enough losers sniffing around his sisters to know this kid's only interested in taking advantage of her.

Then, to his friends, the bachelor boy makes an obscene gesture to the girl's backside. Without touching her, he traces her figure with his palms, pretends to grip her hips, and then thrusts his crotch in her direction.

Solomon sucks in a sharp breath, his blood boiling. His fingers curl around his whiskey glass, and his knuckles turn white.

"Chill, man." Howler groans.

He slips off his stool.

Burying his face in his hands, Howler spins on his stool to face the bar. If the fists fly, he's got plausible deniability.

Solomon draws himself up to full height and cocks a brow at the boy. All that's needed. A look that says one more step and he'll rip his fucking head off. Gulping hard, the boy tucks tail and retreats to his bachelor party.

Oblivious to her retreating suitor, the girl spies Solomon before he can back away, her attention halting him where he stands. High cheekbones, full lips, wide-set brown eyes that sparkle like dewy earth. He takes a breath in hopes of slowing the freight train rattle of his heart.

"Hi," she says, the words devoid of any accent. She hops up on the balls of her feet, her toenails sparkly pink against bronze skin. She grasps his forearm, her voice hopeful. "You come to dance, mountain man?"

"I don't dance," he says, the words coming out gruffer than he means.

Behind him, Howler lets out an exhausted sigh, followed by *dude.*

Fuck. That was surly as hell.

Her pretty face creases in disappointment, those once sparkling eyes now dim. "Oh."

He groans inwardly and scrapes a hand down his beard. What the fuck is his problem? She wants a jukebox and a two-step, and he sure as shit should be the man to give it to her.

"You want a drink?" he asks, rallying, praying he can keep her in his orbit a little longer. It's unnatural. His voice. His offer.

She watches him from under those dark lashes, her chin dipped low. "Yes, please." Her tone turns husky. Flirtatious.

Christ. He fixates on her lips. Pink as a glazed donut. Plump.

With the girl following after him, Solomon moves to the bar, ignoring how tight the crotch of his pants feels. "Wine?" he asks over his shoulder.

"What're you drinking?"

"Whiskey."

"Then same."

The bartender wipes the lacquered wood surface with a rag and says, "Hey, boss. What you need?"

The girl glowers. "Oh sure. He says hello to you."

"Two Blanton's," he says. "Neat." As they wait for the whiskey, Solomon rests his hand on the counter so he can nab the tab before she can. A harsh suck of air. Solomon sees it the second realization hits her face. Her good time flatlined.

Her eyes widen, then narrow as her gaze lights on his wedding band. "Are you married?"

Fuck.

"No." It's all he says. All he can say.

She cranes her neck to look at Howler on his other side. In response, he raises his whiskey. "Scout's honor."

"C'mon," Solomon suggests, wanting to explain. "You want some air? Let's go out back."

After a second of hesitation and a scrutinizing once-over, she nods. "Okay." She arches a brow. "But I have mace."

"I appreciate that." He fights the urge to smile, liking her sass.

Whiskey in hand, he holds out an arm, gesturing for her to go first. His heartbeat a steady thump in his ears as she strides to her stool, gathers her purse, and slips on her heels, instantly gaining five inches.

Howler gives a thumbs up, and he scowls in return.

They step out onto the unlit back porch and descend the stairs. Fingers brushing close, breaths held, they wander into a forest of tall evergreens. The girl shivers and shrugs her blazer on to protect herself from the biting March wind. As they move deeper into the trees, the harsh rush of traffic is overtaken by the chirp of crickets. The Bear's Ear bar may be on the outskirts of Nashville, but it's still too city for Solomon's liking.

"So," she hedges, her brows drawn and a small frown playing on her lips. "You're really not married? Because if you are, I'm not looking to be that girl. At all."

The need to be honest fills him. Because here, in this unfamiliar bar with this strange girl, he feels like he can be himself.

It feels like a new beginning.

"No. I'm not. She's been gone a long time." He dips his chin, twirls the gold band around his finger. "It's never felt like the right time to take it off."

She's quiet for a moment. Considering his admission, gauging whether he's an asshole who'd lie about a dead wife.

"I get that. Moving on is hard." Her soft, sad tone tells him she's lost someone too.

"Where are you from?" he asks, searching for a way to fill the silence.

The second the words leave his lips, he curses himself. Cliché chitchat that has him wincing.

Fuck.

Howler's right. He's rusty as hell.

"No." She puts a hand up, keeps her attention on the stream sparkling in the moonlight. "Let's make a deal. No specifics." When he cocks a brow, she elaborates. "Tonight, I'm not me and you're not you."

He nods, appreciating her offer. Liking that he can pretend to be someone else. A man who didn't lose his wife seven years ago. Who hasn't been celibate for just as long. They'll keep it light, even though a hundred personal questions race through his mind.

What's her name? What does she do? Why is she out here? How'd she get to be so damn beautiful?

He nods. Sips his whiskey. "Sounds good to me."

Her smile makes his knees weak.

Christ. Howler was right. He needs to get out more. A smile shouldn't send him to the grave.

She props herself up against a tree and picks at the bark. She takes a long swig from her whiskey, easily breathing through the sting. Then she tilts her head back, flutters those gorgeous lashes, and gasps.

"What is it?" he asks, following her line of sight.

"The stars." She scans the sky. "I can't see the stars where I'm from. Not like this."

It's what he thought. She's from a big city.

"No light pollution," Solomon explains, lifting his drink to his lips. "I know a better view."

She lifts a brow, curious, but she remains silent.

"My hometown is one of the best places in the world for stargazing."

"Really?" she asks, turning her head to watch him, her hair swaying, sending a waft of her scent his way.

"Yeah." He moves closer to her. She smells like she's been dipped in sunlight and vanilla. "One personal question. But keep it vague and slightly uninteresting." He can't help it. "Why are you here tonight?"

She shifts her stance to face him, her pretty face open and vulnerable in the darkness. With that move, the strangeness between them dissipates. Leaving only the comfortable quiet of two people who've known each other forever in its wake.

She releases a breath and focuses on something just over his shoulder. "Is running away an acceptable answer?"

"Could be." He shrugs and takes another sip of whiskey.

"I work too much," she starts softly. "I don't have a life." She looks away, like she's embarrassed by the admission, then back to the sky. "Or love. I don't have stars. My mom would always say, *find your stars*, but I don't have any. I never did."

The sadness in her voice cracks open his chest. "You sound lonesome."

"I'm always lonesome," she breathes, turning her attention to him again.

Her eyes flash, water, as if to say *save me*.

Take me.

And he does. He can't help it.

Solomon steps closer, cleaves her in his arms, and presses his mouth to hers. He wants the scent of her on his skin. In his beard.

She whimpers, sliding her small hands up the wide expanse of his chest as she deepens the kiss.

Long-buried lust snaps inside him, clawing at the edges of his seven-year drought. His hand has been his only companion in all that time. As if reminding him of how much of an idiot he's been in his monk-like devotion, a ragged groan leaves his mouth. Goddamn, there's no comparison to these sweet lips on his, a beautiful girl in his arms, her warm, soft curves pressed against him on this cool night.

She's small and so damn gorgeous. He just might be losing it.

This girl. His.

The thought's a train wreck. A sucker punch.

Tightening his hold on her, he moves his hands to her face, her hair tangling between his big fingers. It's torture. His dick's a steel rod in his pants, and he wants more. He wants more, but she's—

Shit.

He tears away from her. Takes a step back, holding her steady with his hands around her upper arms.

A gasp leaves her lips at the loss of his mouth on hers. "What's wrong?" She blinks at him, her puffy pink mouth open in confusion.

"You're drunk," he grunts. He didn't bring her out here to fuck her. "Can't do this." Even though his dick screams otherwise. He's got three sisters. Some guy took advantage of them? He'd fucking kill them.

She laughs, a melodic lilt that sends flames of desire licking up the walls of his chest.

"Oh, I may have a very fine wine buzz going, but I have my wits about me. I'm not drunk." She palms the scruff of his cheek, the touch like a snap of electricity. "Swear it. I can say my ABCs backward."

And she does.

He laughs out loud for what feels like the first time in forever. "You still haven't convinced me."

"Don't be such a gentleman." She sniffs. Her full lips curl as she pushes herself to her tiptoes and presses into him. "Kiss me, you handsome idiot."

Jaw set, Solomon shakes his head, even as lust and caution war within him.

That's when he sees it. Her expression. Blazing brown eyes. The pout of her lips. The pink flush staining her cheeks. If he sends her back into that bar, she'll find someone else.

Hell if he's letting that happen. He wants to kiss her more than he wants air.

Leaning closer, he slides a hand into all that silky blond hair and captures her mouth with his. The kiss is hungry and tender and steals his breath.

Fuck.

He's in danger of losing it. Of boiling over. An embarrassing as hell moan rattles out of him.

The girl breaks the kiss, breathless. The look on her face is wild, ravenous, radiant. "You live around here?" she asks, eyes heavy lidded.

"I have a room. At the motel around the corner."

"Take me there." She lunges for his lips again. "Show me all the stars."

The girl pulls his face to hers, and he pulls her into his arms, holding her tight against him. Like if he lets her go, she'll disappear.

He'll answer this woman. Hell, he'll give her everything she wants and then some.

One night, no names, two heartbeats, and all the stars in the universe.

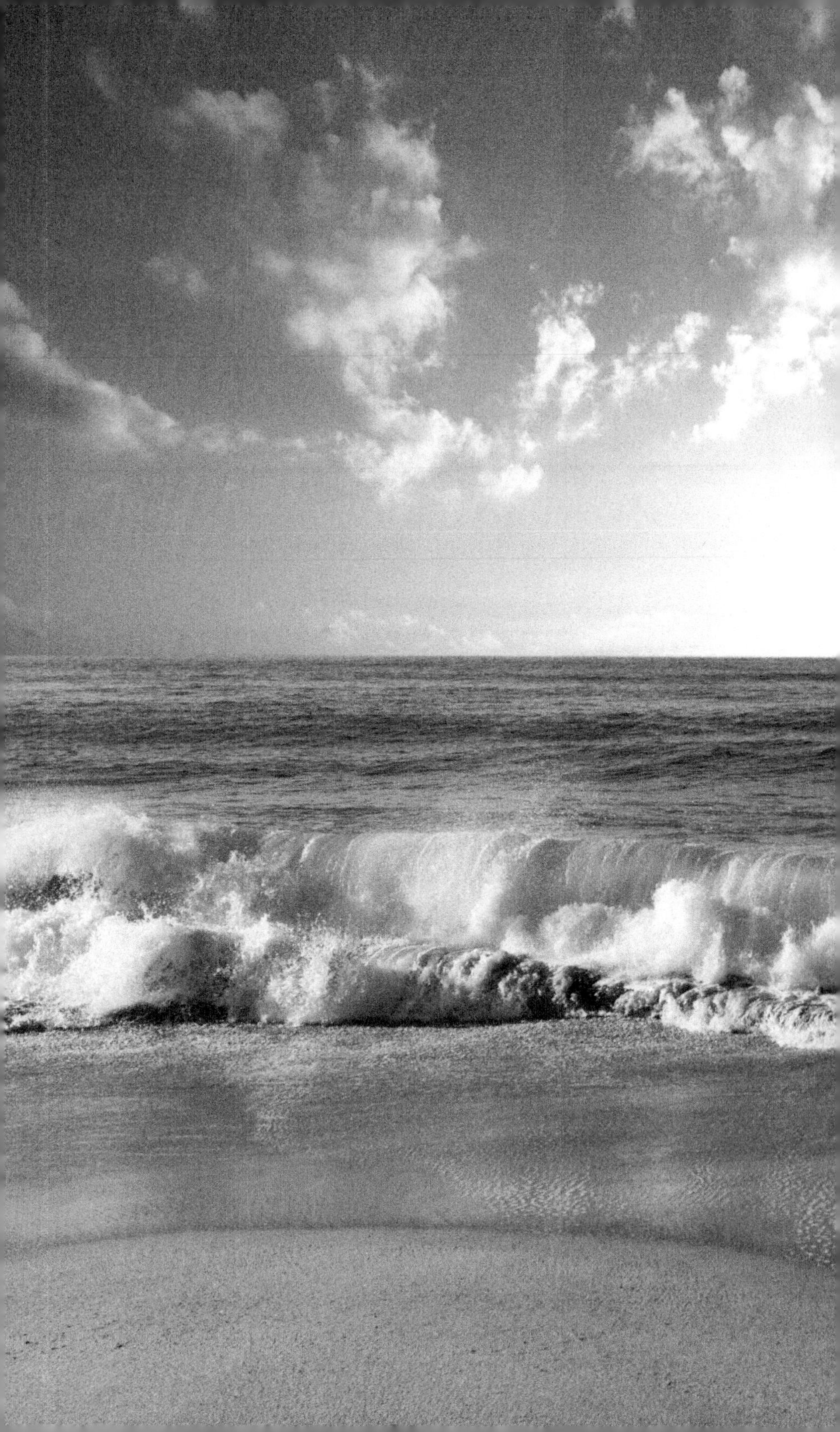

II.

Chapter Three

Six Months Later

IT'S BEEN NINE MILLION, ONE HUNDRED AND SIXTY-NINE days since Tess Truelove last had sex.

Or at least that's what it feels like.

One hundred and eighty-two, approximately.

The roar of the spider crane's engine drowns out the rush of LA traffic as the operator lifts a gigantic concrete statue into the garden of Penny Pain's penthouse. She's been told it's a sculpture of three satyrs dancing merrily—Tess narrows her eyes and cocks her head—but to her, it looks like a phallus.

A penis.

A cock.

Big dick.

She bites her lip.

Big hard bearded—

The whine of the crane jerks her thoughts out of the gutter.

"Careful!" she shouts, throwing her arms in the air like she's a football ref. She shoots a glare at the unconcerned operator. "That statue costs more than your rent." Her withering gaze drifts to a lanky intern. "Slurp your coffee one more time, Ian, and I will unhinge your jaw."

Inhaling a calming breath to control her skyrocketing blood pressure, Tess waits while she oversees the safe deposit of the statue into the garden and then begins her final walk-through of her client's home, a gloriously gaudy penthouse in downtown Los Angeles. Her heels click-clack on the Moroccan tile as she examines her final touches. She inhales. Silk. Sunlight. Smog. Pauses at the fainting couch to finger the velvet texture of a pillow that reads KEEP CALM AND DIE HERE. Dipping as low as she can, she adjusts the small winged skull and hourglass gravestone used as a coffee table centerpiece.

A cacophony from above has her glancing up at the staircase. Penny Pain, hot pink hair flying behind her, runs toward her. "I love the house; I love it!"

Tessie laughs as Penny pulls her into a quick side hug. She may be exhausted, but the smile on her client's face makes all the hard work and lack of sleep worth it.

Finally, she got her promotion. She has the Penny Pain account. An A-list scream queen who's starred in a variety of successful slasher films. The project is a literal dream come true after years of putting in the hours and kissing Atlas's ass and scraping by on pitiful accounts that barely paid for groceries, let alone her rent.

Penny flits a hand toward the bay window, where a crew of TV trucks sits. "*Access Hollywood* wants to film me from my right side, and you know that's my bad side. You take the interview, Tessie. You don't have a bad side. And you know the house better than I do."

She does.

She poured every ounce of herself into preserving the historic Spanish-Colonial Revival penthouse, instead of demolishing it to make room for boring garbage gray walls and white lights. The home is all kaleidoscope color, whimsy, and straight lines, keeping with her design philosophy that a space should be part reality, part fantasy, part risk.

"I'm on it," Tessie says, trading air-kisses with Penny.

As she struts through the penthouse, blowing past her small junior design staff, she ignores the judgmental eyes on her. She knows what they're all thinking.

She's a bitch.

She can't do this.

She's spent her whole life walking a safe, rigid line, but she steps out one night, and the rest is history.

Well, the rest is *his*.

Tessie gathers her bag and swatches at the front door. Glancing down, she palms the high swell of her belly.

When she found out she was pregnant, she screamed. Then she cried. Then she breathed into a paper bag that smelled faintly of crab angels from her favorite Chinese restaurant and called her cousin Ash.

She and the bearded mountain man had used a condom. They were careful, but apparently, careful didn't cut it.

Two pink lines firebombed her carefully crafted world. Could have ended it. But no. She's Tess Truelove, and she doesn't get knocked off balance.

She can do this.

She has to.

She and Ash discussed her options. It's not like she was a sixteen-year-old girl staring at a pregnancy test in a CVS bathroom. She was thirty-two. A woman with a career and a decent bank account balance and a semi-steady head on her shoulders.

A family one day? She wants it. And sure, this isn't what she expected or when she expected it, but being a single parent doesn't bother her. Her mom did it, and so will she. Any other option is off the table. She won't do to this baby what her father did to her—leave or abandon it.

She'll keep it.

Never mind that she's a control-freak and this is the exact opposite of control.

She wants it. With everything she has.

"Find stars in everything," her mom always said.

This baby, this is her star.

A family of her own, a love that sticks around.

Besides, a baby is irrelevant to her career. She won't let this unexpected setback sidetrack her life.

She can juggle a career and a baby. She's good at juggling.

Or breaking.

Whichever comes first.

"Truelove," comes a sharp snap of a nasally voice. "Details. I need details, and I need them fast."

Tessie turns, catching sight of a short, stocky man gliding her way. Thick silver coif of hair. Cocaine in blue suede shoes. Her hyperactive micromanager of a boss, Atlas Rose. As he settles in front of her, she rips the hand away from her stomach. The last thing she needs is Atlas thinking she has a maternal instinct. Not when she plans to continue down her highly demanding career path. Sickness, babies, puppies are like the Ebola virus to Atlas. They make him bleed rectally.

She thinks back to when she was early in her pregnancy. Sick as a dog, barfing her brains out in a bathroom stall, then crawling into a meeting and plastering a smile on her face. She's come so far, but she still has so far to go.

A slow curl of panic, squeezing her chest until she can hardly breathe, has Tessie closing her eyes for a moment. Pulling in a deep breath.

Already, she loves this beautiful little baby, but she's so damn scared.

And then she's back, locking a smile to her face and snapping open her eyes to focus on Atlas.

"The space is finished." Her voice is clipped. Professional. Icy. "I'm stepping in for Penny's interview, and then I'll stick around to make sure the contractors clean up like they promised." Tess tosses her long golden hair over her shoulder. "That puts everything on schedule and tidied up before my vacation."

Waiting for it, her entire body goes stiff. If Atlas complains about her taking time off, she'll scream bloody murder to the high heavens.

Atlas's Botoxed brow tries to wrinkle. But without complaint, he flits a hand. "Crush this interview, Truelove. Remind Los Angeles why we, and not Nova Interiors, are *the* premier design firm."

Tessie keeps a straight face at Atlas's bloodlust and nods. Nova Interiors is their fiercest competition in the Los Angeles market. "I'll be sure to mention it no less than five times."

Atlas spins on his heel without another word and disappears down the hall, barking orders at frazzled interns.

With a sigh, Tessie lugs her bag onto her shoulder, grabs her heavy book of swatches, and exits through the front door, stepping out into the sunlit courtyard.

For a long second, she goes dizzy. Dark spots dance in her vision, and she teeters in her high heels like a newborn fawn, but a hand wraps around her arm, steadying her. "You really gotta stop wearing heels, preggo."

"Don't blame the heels, Ash," she gasps. "Blame low blood sugar."

"Are you even supposed to lift twenty pounds?" her cousin shoots back skeptically.

"The doctor says it's fine."

"It's fine, but it's killing you." Ash gestures at a planter. "Sit."

Following her cousin's marching orders, she exhales a tired breath. She scans the courtyard. The television crew sets up on the sidewalk. The roar of LA traffic fills the air. In the distance, the tall buildings of downtown glitter in the warm September sun.

Already digging through her large tote bag, Ash perches beside her. "What do you need? Smelling salts or granola bars?" She holds both out in one hand.

Tessie frowns, looking from the items to her cousin. "Why do you have smelling salts?"

"People faint at funerals and weddings all the time."

Grateful, Tessie takes the granola bar, her first meal of the day. During the first six weeks of her pregnancy, all she could keep down was Sour Patch Kids and olives. Curiosity piqued, she cocks her head. "Why weddings?"

"Nerves. Locked knees. Bridesmaid slept with the groom." She shrugs. "Shit like that."

Tessie laughs, her nerves easing at the appearance of her cousin. Her opposite in every way. Where Tessie looks like she was shot out of the sun, Ash was scraped out of the LaBrea tar pits. With her long tumble of jet-black curls and blunt bangs, Ash resembles a modern-day Cleopatra in combat boots. The chill to Tessie's uptight. Rough versus polished. Her best bad influence and partner in crime since Tess went to live with Ash and her Aunt Bev after her mother died.

Ash crosses slim ankles, tattooed thighs peeking out of her skirt. "How's Bear?"

Palming her belly, she smiles. "Slowly crushing my bladder but thriving." She bites into the granola bar, the sweetness giving her a much-needed energy boost. "Who died today?"

"Some old guy who used to date Marilyn Monroe. I actually threw myself into the grave, per his request." She waggles her brows. "It was very old Hollywood."

Having dropped out of college after discovering she could cry on cue, Ash launched her own business as a death doula/wedding interrupter. Tessie's still surprised how much people will pay for a stranger to cause chaos or to comfort family. But she shouldn't be surprised; it is LA, after all.

"You about ready to roll?" Ash asks.

"Can't. I have to walk *Access Hollywood* through Penny's house."

"Make sure to show them the statue that looks like a gigantic penis." Ash nudges her shoulder. "Speaking of dicks, did you find the Giant Bearded One yet?"

Tessie flushes. "No. I stopped looking months ago." She turns her attention to the sun-drenched street. "You know that."

She tried to find him.

She did.

After discovering she was pregnant, she called the Bear's Ear bar and asked around for the large mountain man who knocked her up. Maybe not in those exact terms, but she did look. She even put up posters.

He needed to know. She couldn't keep that from him.

But she had nothing to go on. No name. No number. All she had was his shirt, which she had stolen when she woke up that morning and slunk out like the walk of shame that she was.

Even now, the memory of that night has warmth curling through her.

The stars. The bearded mountain man. Her philosophical ramblings about her deepest, darkest thoughts. She told him things she's never even admitted to Ash. Admitted to herself. It was the moonlight. The alcohol. The handsome man doing things to her brain.

That night, that one perfect night in Tennessee, was like a drug. A nice memory she comes back to when she needs peace and calm.

She feels so far away from the Tessie she was that night.

Wild.

Carefree.

Happy.

Ash groans. "You should find him, Tessie. He needs to know."

Nerves flare in her belly, and she crosses her arms. "I did my best. Besides, I'm doing him a favor. I doubt he'd be leaping at the chance to play daddy." At the look Ash gives her, guilt floods her chest. "What am I supposed to do, post a notice on Craigslist?"

A shrug. "You could. You liked him."

Suddenly, Tessie's mouth's as dry as a bone.

"I liked him for a night," she says stiffly, refusing to give her cousin ammunition. Refusing to dwell on the V of his muscular back. The dark beard that tickled her as he kissed a line down the curve of her spine. The safe haven of his muscled arms and the way his voice was like a slow wade into molasses.

"Holy shit." Ash gapes at her.

Damn it.

Tessie flushes, realizing she's said the sentence aloud. She blames pregnancy brain. "Shut up."

Ash cackles and spreads her hands. "Like the Great Molasses Flood of 1919."

Tessie can't help but join in with laughter. "God, you're morbid."

"And you're in love."

She scoffs. "I don't do love. You know that." She palms her bump, making smoothing circles on her belly, and dips her chin. "Only you," she tells Bear. She turns to Ash, knocks shoulders. "And *sometimes* you."

Despite her last name, Tessie doesn't believe in true love. All she knows about love is disappointment. That it leaves. Her dog ran off in third grade. Her mother died of cancer, quick, painful. Her father left when she was still a baby. He knew she was his, had held her in his arms, and still he had walked away from her and her mother.

The only love Tessie's keeping close is this sweet baby in her belly.

Her son.

She'd never admit it to Ash, but deep down, she can't help but feel relieved that she never found the bearded mountain man.

People leave. And letting some random man get close to her child, only to have him walk out? Absolutely not.

It's easier to go it alone. No one gets hurt.

Besides, she's got a career to hold on to and a baby to raise. She's not interested in true love. She likes that steel wall around her heart, thank you very much.

"Truelove!"

Atlas's shriek has both women glancing over. He's waving a T-Rex-like arm, motioning for her to move her ass over to the waiting cameras.

"Kill that guy," Ash mutters, biting into a granola bar with violent intensity. Crumbs scatter across her lap, but oblivious to the mess, she shakes her head vigorously. "Atlas is working you to death."

Straightening up, Tessie squares her shoulders.

"He is, but I'm only four months into this new position. I have to show him I have the chops."

"You're taking great care of that baby and your job, but what about you?" Ash asks, lifting her dark sunglasses to pin her with a knowing look. "You need to worry about Tessie. *You* need to be first." She growls. "Atlas doesn't even care about your wellbeing. You could go into labor, and he'd ask you to stage a room before you left for the hospital. Has he even looked your stomach in the face?"

Tessie needles her brow. "You know what? I can't with you." She inhales a stoic breath. "Don't worry about Atlas. Worry about vacation. And packing. Because God knows you haven't done it yet."

Ash grumbles.

Tessie smirks.

In two days, she and Ash will be on their way to sunny Mexico. Her babymoon. One she planned for and paid for herself. She may not be married, may be an out-of-wedlock disgrace, but she still deserves one last hurrah with her best friend.

At twenty-eight weeks along, she finally has some energy. She's horny as hell. Her smell is supersonic. All she wants is a massage. And maybe a slice of brie, even though according to baby.com, it will absolutely make her go into labor.

She needs this vacation. A beach. Sunshine. Sand between her toes. A mocktail in her hand. No Atlas. No Terrible Tess. No patterns or swatches. No interruptions. Just a champagne dream of a vacation with Ash.

Paradise.

"*Truelove!*" Atlas shouts.

Tessie winces, her skull thudding with the reverberation of his screech.

"We go live in one minute!"

Ash curls her lip in disgust. "God, he's practically frothing at the mouth."

Vacation, Tessie thinks, directing her mind away from murderous thoughts and onto happier things like pineapple man drinks and bronze tan lines and the reflection of the moonlight off the ocean.

And stars.

Always stars.

Ash loops an arm around Tessie's waist, giving her a boost up. "Go before my empath heart cannot resist the urge to murder this guy."

She wags a finger. "No murder. Mexico, remember?"

With a wobble, Tessie turns. She inhales a breath and sweeps her palms over the stomach of her silk mini dress. "Alright, you ready for this?" she asks her belly. Her heart squeezes when there's a kick against her palm. She and Bear—they're in it together.

Just the two of them.

Chapter Four

HE SHOULD DINE AND DASH.

That's Solomon's first thought after taking a seat at the bar at Howler's Roost. Instantly, he's hounded by a waitress who doesn't want his drink order but wants to say hello. She's replaced by his dad's best friend, Grant, who launches into a story about the bear he caught behind the bar two weeks ago. Then his sister Jo's art teacher from twenty years ago. According to her, his aura is green, and he was a Viking in a past life.

When he's finally alone, Solomon drops his hand, letting his old hound dog, Peggy Sue, lick his palm.

He should have gone straight home after he left his sister's. Making the thirty-minute trek into town was a mistake. All he wanted was a drink, not a goddamn interrogation.

As he scratches Peggy's ears, he takes a half-hearted sip of his Maker's Mark and rolls his shoulders, letting the tension melt out of him.

But he gets what he gets. He did it to himself, staying holed up in his cabin for the last seven years. Annoying as it is, they mean well. The entire town of Chinook wants to make sure he's okay, that he's eating enough. They want to tell him they're proud of him for finally coming down off the mountain.

He's been coming to Howler's Roost once a week for the last six months. Dipping a toe back into civilization. Life.

"My craft cocktails put this place on the map, and you order a bourbon straight?"

He grunts, sips his drink, as his best friend's disapproving face floats into his line of vision.

"Hell, I'll take it." Howler whips a rag off his shoulder. "Only time we can get you off the mountain is for a drink."

"That and when Melody has a flat tire."

"Ah, the old little-sister-has-a-flat-tire trick." Howler grabs a beer glass and scrutinizes a smudge, his lips turned down. "You know she's doing it on purpose, right? To get you out of the house. To see you."

Solomon sets his whiskey on the bar top, annoyance curdling inside him. He's not in the mood for another lecture about why he should be eating dinner at his ma's and not Howler's Roost. To change the subject, he nods at the pile of wood in the corner of the room. A broken floorboard the servers have to step around. Mishmash décor: retro neon signs and dollar bills attached to the wall. Rickety wooden tables on their literal last legs, with matchbooks propping them up.

"Place looks like a shithole." He considers the television mounted above the bar. The local news switches over to a sleazy tabloid show that grates his nerves. "I thought you were gonna get rid of that."

Howler crosses his arms and props himself up on the counter behind him, a boyish smirk playing on his lips. "Sure, we'll start there."

"When are you gonna get on the refresh?" Solomon rubs a hand down his dark beard. "The bar needs a theme. We did a whole damn reconnaissance for it. You got the insurance money. You had blueprints drawn up."

Howler splashes whiskey in his glass. "When I get my right-hand man back in the kitchen."

"I told you. No." Solomon fights the urge to glance at the door to the kitchen. Tries not to look at remnants of the pathetic excuse for a frozen pizza he had for dinner. Boring food that can't come close to comparing to the bar bites he used to whip up. Food as local as him. Scotch eggs. Potato leek fritters. Salmon nachos.

With a groan, Howler drapes himself across the bar. "It's time, Sol. I don't got a good chef. I'm feeding people chips from a bag."

"I like chips from a bag just fine."

Liar his friend's hard stare says.

Sitting back on his stool, Solomon frowns. "I thought that road trip you dragged me on lit a fire under your ass to get this place in shape."

There's no good reason for the disarray. No matter how much he tells himself he doesn't care, he can't care, he sure as shit does. The bar is his. Theirs together. To leave it like this is a goddamn travesty. It's just like Howler to get worked up about a project, do the research, make the plans, and let it drop. After thirty years of friendship, he knows the guy's lazy ass has never been the one to see a project through.

Howler cracks out a laugh. "If you want to talk that trip, think it was you who got a fire lit under your ass."

Solomon keeps his attention focused on the TV above the bar, giving nothing away. Not one ounce of ammunition for the sonofabitch to crow about.

Swiping up crumbs, Howler pauses to glance over at the sticking jukebox. Two weather-beaten old-timers slam palms against the hazy glass to get Johnny Cash off repeat. He leans in to Solomon. "Thinking about Goldilocks? I liked her too. A blond with brown eyes." He grins. "Hot."

Solomon grits his teeth and shoots the asshole a sharp look. "Shut the fuck up."

Lifting his hands in a don't-shoot-me gesture, Howler says, "Relax. I'm thinking about all the ways I can thank her."

"For what?"

"For waking you up. Spurring you to rejoin our fine Chinook

society." He presses his hands against the bar and angles closer, his face, his voice, softening. "You took your ring off, Sol."

Studying his hands, his bare ring finger, Solomon makes a fist. Releases it.

He did.

Six months ago, in fact.

The day he woke up to an empty bed after the best night of his life.

A night as unforgettable as the girl he shared it with.

At least once a day, either at his work bench or in his yard, his mind conjures her out of the blue. Hitting him with a bittersweet ache he can't chase away, no matter how hard he tries. The blondest, brightest, most beautiful woman he's ever seen.

Saddest too.

I'm always lonesome.

He still remembers the way her face looked when she said it.

Open, earnest, so damn sad he didn't even have the words. He just kissed her. And it was enough.

He had been rusty, falling all over the place to put the moves on her, but she didn't seem to care. They tore up that bed, her body burning up in his arms. Solomon craved her as badly as she craved him. Everything about her was too good to be true. Heaven. For one night, he had held fucking heaven in his arms.

The next morning, he woke up alone, his shirt gone. As he scanned the empty room for her, the old feeling of panic crept over him. Even now, he hates that she snuck out without a goodbye. Without leaving her name. Without a way for him to make sure she got to her destination safe and sound.

It wasn't his job to worry, Howler reminded him again and again. She was a fling. The first lay he'd had in seven years.

A one-night stand? A fucking fling? No, he wanted *her*. He wanted to find her and thank her for shaking him awake, for tearing off the grim cloak of darkness he's worn for the last seven goddamn years.

He held a shooting star in his arms for one night. Searing, the feeling so intense he'd do anything to keep it, but before he could, it burned out completely.

He misses her. And the peace she gave him.

Still, it's better she left. After Serena—after what he did—love, a relationship, isn't something he deserves.

It's something that should stay far, far away from him.

Head cocked, Howler grins. "Stuck in your head, ain't she?"

"Howler," he says, taking a swig of his bourbon, then patting Peggy Sue on the head. The basset hound licks his hand, gives a low woof of contentment, and goes back to sleep. "When I want your opinion, I'll fucking ask for it."

His best friend hoots, juggling a bottle of Rittenhouse Rye in his hands. "You need a reset," he says, pouring the rye into a rocks glass. "Do what I do and take up with a tourist." He nods, singling out a perky redhead reading an Alaska guidebook. "Take 'em upstairs to my place, rock their world, and in the morning, they leave."

Solomon shakes his head. Love 'em and leave 'em—that's his best friend's default setting.

Howler cocks his head, pulls a contemplative face. "Guess you did that in Tennessee, didn't you?"

Solomon growls and plants his hands on the bar, ready to tell Howler to fuck off, when a bright blast of a voice catches his attention.

"Tell me, Ms. Truelove, Ms. Pain's vibe is very eclectic, isn't it?"

"Absolutely. If you follow me, I'll take you to her screaming room."

"Screaming?"

Solomon looks up, frowning at the crooked TV. A leggy blond in high-as-hell stilettos is giving a tour of a gothic-looking penthouse. *Fucking LA.* Everything about that town screams phony as hell. Not like Chinook and its salt of the earth folk. People who'd give a person the shirt off their backs and the last dollar in their accounts if they needed it.

The woman pauses to open a door. Behind her, a bright pink neon sign blasts the word DEATH. "As you see here, Ms. Pain's space is inspired by a New Orleans mausoleum, but on a luxury scale. Her screaming room and studio have been accented with feline wallpaper, an iconic example of how to liven up a small space." Then she turns to the camera in a close-up and smiles.

All the breath leaves Solomon's body.

Christ, it's her.

The girl from the Bear's Ear bar.

"Holy fucking shit," Howler says, though his voice sounds hazy, far off.

Peggy Sue lifts her head, a low woof of concern rumbling out of her.

Access Hollywood logo in the corner of the screen. The ticker at the bottom reads: *Tess Truelove, Interior Designer to the Stars*

His lips curl. He finally knows her name. *Tess.*

Solomon gapes at the TV like he's conjured her up. Jesus, she's beautiful. More beautiful than he remembers. And damn, does he remember. The lush body he ran his hands over, the way he gripped the curve of her hip and made her moan. His eyes travel from her bee-stung lips to her bright white smile to her breasts to the tight black dress hugging her—

The camera zooms out, the frame focusing on her lithe form and a room that resembles a dungeon.

Vision blurring, Solomon grips the edge of the countertop. An awful what-the-fuck feeling fills his soul, and his stomach drops. He zeroes in on the tiny bump riding low on her belly. The setting sun behind her only accentuates her golden glow.

Fuck.

The world scrambles.

Pregnant.

It's the girl from the Bear's Ear bar, and she's pregnant.

"Oh, hell no," Howler mutters. He snatches the remote off the back counter and snaps off the TV.

Solomon rises. "Turn it back on. Now." His growl leaves no room for rebuttal.

With a pained expression, Howler does.

The segment's ending. Mouth close to the microphone, the girl says, "I'm Tess Truelove with Atlas Rose Design." And then she looks at the camera. Looks straight at him. Her bright smile socks him in the gut as she says, "Remember Atlas Rose Design. Los Angeles's number-one celebrity design firm."

A commercial pops on. Toothpaste.

"Shit," Howler hisses. "I knew she was fucking trouble when she took that shot with a straight face."

Solomon, frozen, can only blink.

"Maybe she's married." Howler gapes, slack-jawed, up at the TV, the cocktail shaker held, forgotten, in his hand. This is his friend's worst nightmare. Knocking up a one-night stand.

He curls his fists on the bar top. "She's not married."

"I thought you used a condom."

"We did."

"Bullshit."

Solomon lets out a growl, and Howler instinctively takes two steps back.

Guilt and confusion twist like a tornado in his gut. He hasn't seen or spoken to this woman in six months. But now he's found her.

Beautiful.

Blond.

Pregnant.

Go get her, Sol. Serena's voice sounds in his head. *Go.*

Chapter Five

Solomon hates LA already. Hates it with a fiery passion he usually reserves for tourists who don't tip or people who kick their dogs. Since he's arrived, he's seen someone walking a vibrator down the street on a leash and a woman pushing a ferret in a stroller. He wants to be back in Chinook, back in his cabin with his dog and his carpentry tools. Back on his mountain.

For the hundredth time since he saw her on the news, he thinks of the girl. Tess. Sophisticated. Sharp. A far cry from the goofy, vulnerable girl he met in the Bear's Ear bar.

Who is Tess Truelove?

One thing he knows—it's the second time this girl's pulled him from his quiet life in Alaska. Of fucking course they live on opposite ends of the world.

Get a DNA test, Howler proclaimed. *Could be anyone, man. Don't let her shackle you* down.

His sisters—especially Evelyn, a cutthroat family attorney—are shitting bricks. His parents told him to do the right thing, and was that a smile he detected in his father's voice? Goddamn. He's thirty-five years old. It's not like time's-a-ticking, but what if the kid's his? As the oldest of four, he always wanted a big family. He and Serena had planned for it, eventually, but back at twenty-two, it seemed so far away. Like a dream of a plan. Only now...he's not getting any younger.

But a baby? A baby blows up his life. But hell, he hasn't had much of one since Serena died.

He's here for answers. If he's the father? He doesn't know what it will mean for him and Tess. He walked away from his family. His career. But walking away from his kid, being a deadbeat dad—absolutely fucking not. It'd haunt him forever if he was that kind of man.

Pausing on the sidewalk, he digs his phone out of his pocket, double checks the text from Evelyn, comparing the address with the one on the crumbling stucco apartment building in front of him.

The late afternoon sun makes slanted Rorschach-like shadows across the gated entrance. He frowns, not liking what he sees. The garbage cans overflow. Graffiti mars the side of the building. This is where she lives? It seems unsafe as hell.

Stepping up to the keypad, he hovers a finger over the buzzer. One push and he'll get answers.

He could be a father.

He'll see Tess. The girl he's thought of nonstop for the last six months.

Nerves churn in Solomon's gut. This is real. He's here, about to see her in person.

"Fuck," he mutters, rolling out his shoulders to ease his aggravation. "Get a goddamn grip."

"Excuse me. I'm just gonna wedge on in here. . ."

The voice, coming from behind him, has Solomon turning. A tall, dark-haired girl in combat boots and a black leather jacket slips in front of him. A bag of Chinese takeout propped on her hip. The scent of lo mein wafting between them, she punches in a code on the keypad. She tilts her head as she evaluates him, looking him up and down with laser-like precision. And then she sucks in a choking gasp that has Solomon jerking to attention.

"Holy shit. It's you." Her gray-green gaze pins him down. "The bearded baby daddy."

He scowls at the nickname. "You know Tess?"

"Know? She is my lifeblood. My force. My personal pan pizza." Before he can search for a retort, she flaps a hand. "She's my cousin. How'd you find her?"

"TV."

"So you saw."

"Oh, I saw."

The girl crosses her arms. Draws herself up. "And you're here to what?"

He shifts, not liking the way her eyes have narrowed in suspicion. "You her personal bouncer?"

"I am all the things to Tessie. But most importantly, I'm Ash." He extends a hand. "Solomon Wilder."

She cocks her head, a shock of black hair slicing across her face as she runs her gaze down to his black logging boots and up to his red flannel shirt. Attention back on his face, she lifts her brows. "Are you a lumberjack?"

Chef, Serena says in his ear. *You're a chef.*

But he can't say it. Hasn't since the day she died.

He lets out a tired sigh. "No. Why?"

"Because you're so. . .I mean. Just like. . . jacked. Like a bear." Her smile is feline. "Broad."

Jaw ticking, he runs a hand down the length of his dark beard. "Listen. I'm here to talk to Tess to see if. . ." He clears his throat, the hard rock that's settled in it. "How is she?"

Ash chuckles. "Oh, she is very pregnant. And you are the culprit." An arc of a dark brow. A stamp of a hard finger against his chest. "She's got your DNA in her, dude."

"I'm aware of that," he grits out.

First time he has sex after a seven-year drought, he gets the woman pregnant.

Christ.

Ash takes his elbow and pulls him off to the side to stand in a bed of rocks and rose bushes. "Listen," she says, holding up a finger as she frowns. "I've been with Tessie for every doctor's appointment and pukefest and frantic late-night Googling session, and if you're only here to make her feel bad or yell at her, you can just skedaddle back to Hulk Island or wherever the hell you're from."

He flinches, hating that this woman assumes, right off the bat, that he's a world-class asshole. "I'm not here for that," he says, inhaling a steady breath. He shifts in his boots, ignoring the perspiration that runs down his spine. The late September sun has no damn right being this hot. "I'm here because, if the baby's mine, then I want to be involved."

Ash's eyebrows skyrocket. "You do?"

"I do."

She chews her lip, considers him carefully. "Really? You won't leave?"

He frowns at the strange question. "No. I don't do that."

Nose wrinkling, Ash leans in. Solomon's entire frame tenses as she looks him up and down and then does a full-torso sniff. She shudders. Smiles. "Hmm. You pass the smell check."

He groans, sick of the interrogation techniques. All he wants to do is see Tessie. "Can I just talk to her?" he asks, taking a step toward the gate.

The girl lunges, grabbing his arm. With surprising strength and a bruising grip, she yanks him back. Before she lets go, she squeezes his rock of a bicep, an under-her-breath squeal barely contained.

"Oh no, no, no. Don't go in there. She will rip your face off. Hormones, you know."

Solomon scowls, looking up at the crumbling façade of the building. "You have a better idea?"

"I do actually." Ash's brows shoot up. "I have a plan. I have all the plans, and this plan is *the* plan. Do you understand me?"

"Not really, no."

"You gotta ambush her where she can't get rid of you. You have to be sneaky."

Sneaky. He's never been sneaky, not once in his goddamn life.

He crashes around his old cabin like a pack of marauding wolves. "What are you talking about?" Solomon grits out, frustrated as hell.

Ash throws him a grin. "I'm talking about a babymoon."

He draws back. "A baby what?"

"A babymoon. It's where frazzled working mothers escape to a tropical island paradise to relax before their heathen spawn make their way earthside."

With a frown, he clarifies, "Are we still talking about Tess?"

Eyes dancing in amusement, she bounces on the toes of her combat boots. "Yes. She leaves for Mexico tomorrow, and you should surprise her." She pulls out her phone. "I'm supposed to go, but you can take my place."

He cocks a brow. "Sounds like it'll piss her off."

"Tessie is already pissed off," Ash says, then sighs. "Look, Solomon, there are three things you should know about her."

"What's that?"

"The first—she's wound. Tight. She doesn't get stressed. She snaps like a fucking Kit Kat."

He frowns. That doesn't track with the easygoing girl he met in the bar. "And the second?"

Her face softens and her hands drift to clasp against her heart. "She really needs this. Not just the vacation but. . .*this*." She moves a hand between the two of them. "She doesn't think she does, but she does."

Though Ash hasn't said the words, he hears them anyway. *She needs you.* A hard swell beneath his ribs has his chest tightening. A protective primal instinct short-circuiting his heart.

He clears his throat. "And the third?"

Ash's eyes turn murderous. "Don't break her preggo heart, you hear me?"

Solomon grunts and lifts his chin, trying to ignore the small fraction of softness needling him in the gut. "I'm only here to talk about the baby."

"Then say yes." Ash regards him with a pleading expression. "Please."

He hesitates. Catching Tess off guard seems like a dirty move, but then, he's here to do that exact thing, isn't he? The only difference is he'd be ambushing her in a different country. Stuck together so they can hammer this shit out with their kid.

"Christ. Fine." Solomon blows out a breath. "If you think it'll work, I'll go."

Relief flashes across her face. "I'll see if I can transfer my ticket to you." Her fingers fly across her phone.

With one last glance at the drab stucco building, he wonders what in the hell he's gotten himself into.

Ping. Ping. Ping.

Her phone is blowing up her goddamn brain.

Tessie closes her eyes and breathes through the sound. Hand on her swollen stomach, she crosses her studio apartment, letting Bear's reassuring kicks take her mind off her job.

Apparently, she's not off the clock yet. Atlas is bound and determined to squeeze every last bit of work he can from her before she leaves the country.

Ignore it. She fights the urge to jump to attention, to be Atlas's yes-sir girl.

For seven days, she will not work. She will, as they say in *The Art of Raising a Baby*, take a load off.

Mountain man's flannel in hand, she buries her nose in the soft fabric, and inhales. Hard. She lets the scent drift down to Bear, like they both need a hit of calm.

Then, with a growl, Tessie sets the shirt back on the nightstand. No time to relax. She's behind schedule as it is. Lips pursed, she picks through a pile of clothes on her bed, wondering if there's a Hail Mary prayer she can send out into the universe that will make her bags magically pack themselves. Because she's tired. Dead tired. Dog tired. Pregnancy is wreaking havoc on her REM sleep.

As if her prayer has been answered, the front door opens. Ash slips inside, fluttering dark-painted nails as a hello.

"Oh good, you're here," Tessie says, tossing her laptop and planner on top of her suitcase. "I'm bringing Bear's doppler and my record player and earplugs for when you have that fourth margarita even after you tell me to cut you off. . ." She trails off, evaluating her cousin.

Ash looks like the cat that ate the canary.

She squints at her cousin and props a hand on her hip. "Where have you been?"

Ash sets a plastic sack on the counter and unpacks cartons of Chinese food, peeking over her shoulder. "Flirting with strange men outside your apartment."

Tessie rubs her stomach at the scent of sweet and sour chicken, Bear's impatient kicks echoing her own hunger.

"How goes packing?" Ash asks, licking oyster sauce from her finger.

Tessie sniffs. "Debilitating."

"It's the beach," Ash says, swooping over to intercept a blood-red kimono. "Pack the skimpiest shit you own and prepare to be mauled." Her face lights up as she snags a flimsy leopard print fabric as thin as a piece of floss from the pile. "How about this hot little number?"

"Are you kidding?" Tessie shudders and swipes the bikini from Ash. A hollow ache spreads through her stomach. "I'm pregnant. No one wants to see me in that."

More like she has no one to see her.

Ash tilts her head and snatches the bikini back. "You're not dead. Your body is banging. Pack it. You're a sexy mama."

"No. I'm not." Warmth stinging her eyes, Tessie blinks fast to keep away the traitorous tears. These days, all it takes is one minor inconvenience or kind word to send her into a breakdown.

"You look beautiful." Ash loops her arms high around her waist and pulls her in for a hug. "I mean it."

Tessie fills her lungs and nods, forcing her face into some semblance of a believable smile. She wishes she had her best friend's fierce confidence. Nothing's ever wreaked havoc on her self-esteem like pregnancy. Being single and pregnant is way worse than being just single. It's lonely as hell. Her body aches for a tender touch, for a foot massage, for sex. God, she *craves* sex. It's like the minute she reached the third trimester, her body launched itself into hyperactive horn dog speed. She wants to *fuck*. She wants someone to *want* her. To tell her she's sexy. She hasn't been touched, been held, since that night at the Bear's Ear bar.

And the happy couples shopping for baby gear or strolling in the park only compound the ache. Reminders that she doesn't have that. A partner. Someone in the shit with her.

A person to share it with.

She doesn't need a man to be happy, and she doesn't need a man to have a family, but at night. . .

Nights are the worst. Nights are when the hard reality of her situation grand slams her in the fucking face. She's alone. Single. Pregnant. Her baby's coming in three months. An actual human being who will be fully dependent on her. Can she do this?

Will her job suffer? Can she afford daycare? What if she's a shitty parent like her own deadbeat dad? Or worse, what if she gets sick and leaves Bear like her mother left her?

A part of her can't wait to hold her son in her arms, but another part—that paranoid, panicky piece—wants him to stay inside, stay safe, so she can protect him always.

Nights are when she wishes she had someone to hold her. To tell her it'll all be okay.

Blinking back tears, smothering her emotions, Tessie untangles from Ash and snatches back the bikini. Their tug of war finished. "Fine. I'll take it. Let's hope it still fits."

Ping.

Thankful for the interruption, she lowers herself to the bed while supporting her belly and checks her phone. "Ugh, it's Atlas. He wants a revision to the Jacobson mood board."

Ash scowls. "You're on vacation."

Typing out a message, she reassures her boss that she'll send it over tonight. "Not until tomorrow."

"*Tesssieee.*" Ash crawls across the bed, crumpling silk dresses and wraps. "Promise me you won't work this entire trip."

She wants to promise. But she can't. Slowing down isn't an option. People are relying on her. Her baby. Her job. Her clients.

"I just got this new account, Ash. The promotion. I can't drop the ball."

"Drop the ball? You're working eighteen-hour days. You always put your job first. You put Bear first. But what about you?"

Tessie laughs without humor. "What about me?"

Ash purses her lips. "It's not healthy to run like you are. You're freaking pregnant. You can't pour from an empty cup." Her cousin places a hand over hers, her voice softening. "You're gonna crash and burn. You only have three months left."

Tessie shakes her head, not wanting to deal with her anxieties about parenting right now. Or the blunt life lesson Ash is dealing. Her cousin has this uncanny ability to know exactly what she needs. Typically, she loves her for it. But right now, it scares her. Everything about this pregnancy scares her.

Scanning her small apartment, she chews her bottom lip. She worked her ass off for this. Anywhere else, she'd be well off. Not LA. The majority of her money goes to rent. Soon, daycare. That she scraped enough together for this vacation is a miracle.

Still, her apartment's her sanctuary. Pops of pink. An emerald-colored wingback chair. Funky antique store frames. A vintage record console beneath the window. A three-foot stack of vinyl beside her bed. A happy, harmonious, positive space.

It's why she became an interior designer. So she could give people safe spaces of their own. Even on a tight budget, she and her mother made their own comfortable space in their little home, decorated with thrift store trinkets and cans of spray paint. Tessie has always had a good eye for a steal, for the vibrant and unique. She knows how to make a room feel special and beautiful. Everyone deserves that.

And Bear will have it.

Only he doesn't.

Not yet.

Because she's been so damn busy with her job, she hasn't had time for her son.

All she's done so far to prep for the baby is clean off a spot on the wall where a crib will go. Hell, she still needs to get a crib. A baby monitor. And what else? She has a long list, a baby planner, and she hasn't even opened it since she got this promotion. More evidence that she isn't ready. A great, overwhelming hopelessness rises in her chest, and she has to blink back tears for the second time today.

She almost acknowledges her worries, her fears, aloud: What if I can't do this? What if I'm a bad mom?

But she doesn't have to. Her cousin, her best friend, knows them.

"We'll get everything done." Ash squeezes her hand. "Don't worry."

"We better." She laughs bitterly. "Or Bear will be sleeping in a dresser drawer."

"How very old-timey." The bed creaks as Ash hops to standing. "What you need to do is finish packing, then we'll eat." She nods at Tessie's stomach. "Feed the little urchin."

That's right. *Vacation.*

Inhaling a rallying breath, Tessie grabs her planner off her suitcase. "You ready to hear tomorrow's game plan?" she asks, ticking off checkboxes with her pen. "I'll do a quick Peloton ride in the morning, and then we'll meet for brunch at El Diablo before heading to the airport—what? What is it?"

At the counter dishing out Lo Mein, Ash waves a spoon in the air, sending oyster sauce splattering across the counter. "I might have had to change my flight."

Tessie deflates. "What, why?"

Ash presses her lips into a line and focuses on the food in front of her. "I'm so sorry. An emergency funeral came up. They're paying me double. Think how many virgin margaritas that can buy us." She lifts her head and offers an apologetic smile. "I booked the next flight. I'll be right behind you."

Tessie sighs, setting her planner aside. "I wish we could fly together."

"I know." Her cousin's lips twitch into an expression Tessie can't place. "You're going to have the best time."

She is. She really is.

With a fresh manicure, five new bikinis, and the best suite at the resort waiting for her, she is so ready for this vacation. She scrimped and saved for it. Finally, finally, she's treating herself. Finally, she's relaxing.

No stress.

No interruptions.

Just her and Ash.

Paradise.

Chapter Six

LUXURY.

Sanctuary.

She is here, for seven glorious days, ready to bask in her champagne dream of a vacation.

Heart fluttering, hands clasped to her chest, Tessie click-clacks her way through the glossy lobby of the Corazón del Paraíso Resort. Already, she approves. Mightily.

The resort is gorgeous. Upscale. Lush and tropical. A lesson in everything she loves. Breezy accents and neutral dreamscapes. Funky yet sparse without being cold. A pleasing palette of soft pinks, golds, and creams. Marble floors. A huge gold bowl of fresh flowers sits on a circular table in the middle of the lobby. Floor-to-ceiling windows showcase the beach outside. Palm trees sway in the breeze. A burbling waterfall behind the reception area evokes a sense of peace and calm. There's not a thing she would design differently in here.

"Oh, hello," she says to a terra-cotta-uniformed man who's popped up beside her bearing a tray of bright green drinks that look like smoothies. "Are these—" She points, and the server nods at the drink, at her belly. "Thank you," she says, taking a mocktail. "Gracias."

Reinvigorated, drink in hand, Tessie inhales the scent of the ocean. Salt and sea. A recharge of her soul.

An escape.

A kick.

Smiling, she rests a palm against her stomach. "You like it too, huh?" she murmurs to Bear.

As she sips the cucumber fresca drink, excitement wiggles into Tessie's heart. An excitement she rarely allows herself to feel. When was the last time she did something like this? Escaped? Had *fun?* She cannot wait for Ash and her pale-ass skin and surly attitude to slither in. She's ready for the sun. Ready to work on her tan and wrangle one of those freakishly garish pineapple drinks fancified with a little neon umbrella and towers of fruit garnishes. And the room. Oh God, she cannot wait to see the room. Against the advice of her budget, she splurged on a suite. A way to say thank you to Ash for putting up with her, for helping her with this pregnancy every step of the way. She couldn't have done it without her.

Tessie turns on her phone to check the time. Stiff from the plane ride, her hips ache, and all she wants is a power nap. Or two.

The device immediately pings in her hand. She groans. Is she insane? Turning it on is only asking for Atlas to harass her. Still, her fingers itch. To work. To fix. When she sees the first text, a heavy weight settles on her shoulders.

Suddenly, the time isn't important.

After a beat, she shoves the phone into her purse.

Juggling her bags—the travel record player in her hand, the duffel slung over her shoulder, the suitcase rolling behind her—Tessie wobbles in her heels as she navigates her way to reception.

Midweek, the lobby's mostly empty except for a couple arguing about whether lobsters feel pain when they're boiled alive and a—

Tessie stops. Gawks.

Holy shit, there's a bear.

A big burly bear in the lobby. And it's turning. It's lumbering. It's coming her way and—

It's bearded.

Tessie gulps.

Oh God.

It's him.

At first, the sight doesn't compute. Her brain scrambles, then locks up. And then it screams bloody murder.

Here, here, the mountain man from Tennessee is here.

"What—why—" Her mouth is permanently unhinged, emitting nothing but a steady stream of gobbledygook. "What—are—you—how—what—"

His eyes clash as he stalks up to her. All six foot four of him in blue jeans and a thick red buffalo plaid flannel fitted over broad shoulders.

"You took my shirt," he grits out.

"I did not." Tessie presses a hand to her mouth, stumbles back. Her heartbeat is off the charts. Stratosphere status. "Don't come any closer," she warns. Then, noticing his attention on her belly, she twists her hips, moving her duffel bag in front of her stomach to block his view.

"You're accosting me." She looks at the lobster-fighting couple for help. "This man's accosting me."

They ignore her, still locked in a heated battle PETA would approve of.

He grunts, an unhappy look settling across his rugged face. "I am not."

"Look up here," she says, jabbing a neon nail at him to direct his gaze away from her stomach. She doesn't like the way he's looking at Bear. Like he's here to put a claim on him. "Not here."

"Where else do you want me to look?" he mutters.

She draws herself up and pulls her shoulders back, refusing to be ruffled. "What are you doing here?"

"I saw you on TV."

She cringes. Oh God. That damn interview.

"I'm here to talk to you," he says, sounding as if he's already irritated with his decision.

She shivers at the dark timbre of his voice. It's what she imagines a forest would sound like if it could talk. Rugged. Low. Husky.

"Where's my cousin? Where's Ash?" Narrowing her eyes in suspicion, Tessie cranes her neck and pops up on her toes, peering around his linebacker frame. Then she gasps, an awful thought coming to her. "What did you do to her?"

He scowls. "I didn't do a damn thing. She asked me to come."

Tessie shakes her head like there's water in her ears.

No. No. No. This can't be happening.

Abashed, he runs a hand through his thick shock of black hair, then reaches for his back pocket. He holds out a crumpled piece of paper. "She, uh, gave you a note."

A note? A fucking note?

Snatching it from him, she rips it open.

I'm sorry.

I love you.

You need this.

Have fun.

Have fun?

Tess stands there, frozen, rocked in her high heels. Fuming, she balls the note in her fist, her tightly wound emotions de-corkscrewing.

"I'm gonna kill her. Straight-up cousin-cide her. She's the one who got me in this position in the first place. Because I listened to her dumb advice. *Get lit, get loose, get laid,* she said. Well, nowhere in that did it say, get knocked up."

She's very aware she's muttering to herself in the middle of the lobby, vowing cold-blooded murder under the scrutiny of a complete stranger, but she's too pissed to care.

The man spreads his hands, his expression uncomfortable. "I was trying to check in for you, but they, uh, need your ID."

She bristles. This is her vacation. *Hers.* Nowhere in the fine print did it mention she'd have to share it with this mountain man who looks like he just hopped a moose to travel down to Mexico.

She shoots him a glare. "We'll see about this."

BABYMOON OR BUST | 55

Whirling around, she spins on her heel and marches toward the reception desk. The hard thump of boots follows her.

"Excuse me," she says, coming to a stop at the reception. "I need to check in, please." She stiffens as the bear of a man settles beside her, his scent floating between them. He smells like fresh pine and icy air whipped by the wind.

One sniff, she thinks, willing her nostrils to close. *Only one. For her baby.*

The receptionist, a girl wearing funky geometric glasses, beams. "Of course. Last name?"

"Truelove. Tess."

As the receptionist checks on the room, Tessie stabs out a threat of a text to her cousin.

> **Tessie:** You. Are. Dead.
>
> **Ash:** The real question is—will you attend my funeral?
>
> **Tessie:** Hard pass. Because I will be in prison for your murder.

"Ah, yes. You're in the Villa Bonita suite with an ocean view. However, I am sorry, miss," the girl says, causing Tessie's gaze to snap up. "Your room is not yet ready." She inclines her head toward the large windows showcasing a balcony overlooking the ocean. "Perhaps you and your husband can wait in our Cielo bar."

Tessie sighs and pinches the bridge of her nose. "Great. Already it begins." Another sigh. "He's not my husband." She dares a glance at the man whose face is set and stiff. Very unsmiling. "What do I call you anyway?"

A weary light flashes in his eyes. "Solomon. Wilder."

Solomon Wilder. *Solomon*. She rolls his name around in her head like a marble. He looks like a Solomon. More like a Solemn Man. With a sigh, she turns her attention back to the receptionist. "Is there anything you can do?"

"I'm so sorry. But the wait won't be long." An apologetic smile. Another tap at the keyboard. "I have your number on file and will text you as soon as your room is ready. If you like, you can leave your bags here and we'll bring them up."

"Fine."

After dropping her bags and record player with the valet, Tessie turns on her heel and stalks past Solomon, through the lobby, and out onto the balcony. She chooses a seat at a table overlooking the beach. The ocean is a cool blue roar against the sizzling backdrop of the bright orange sun. For a second, she's at peace. Calm.

Then a nearby seat scrapes against the concrete floor, the sound needling her brain.

Solomon sits across from her. Bearded. Serious faced. She fumes. She can't even enjoy the moment because she's got some burly bearded mountain man blocking her ocean view.

Narrowing her eyes, she leans across the table. "You're sweating."

He grunts. His discomfort is obvious. "I know."

"Did you maybe pack anything other than flannel?"

"I wasn't exactly planning for a tropical beach vacation," he grumps.

Good. She settles back in her chair with a smug smirk. Maybe he'll tuck tail when he realizes the sun's the boss down here.

His gruff rumble of a voice rolls out. "Tessie, listen." *Tessie.* Dammit, her name in his mouth has her going soft. Like a hot knife running through butter. "I didn't mean to freak you out. Or catch you off guard."

Tessie smooths her blond hair, trying to look saner than she feels. "Well, you did both."

His enormous fingers dig into the edge of the table, a clear effort to stay calm. "I saw you on TV. Saw. . ." He waves a hand up and down her torso. "I came to LA to talk to you and ran into Ash. And then—"

"Hola. Can I get you anything from the bar, señor?"

A server waits, ready for their order.

"Beer," Solomon says, and their gazes meet.

"Liquid courage?"

"Can't hurt."

"Do you maybe have one of those mocktail pineapple man drinks?" Tessie asks the server hopefully, aware of Solomon's dark eyes checking her over.

"Apologies, señorita," he says. "Not at this bar. The tiki bar on the beach has them."

"Club soda, then."

God, how she wishes for a shot of tequila, a glass of rosé, anything to take the sting out of this conversation. Beneath the table, she holds her stomach, feeling the thump of little feet peppering away impatiently.

"So... you're here," she says, examining her neon-pink beach nails. "What do you want?"

"You're pregnant." Solomon's attention drifts to her belly. His throat works the words out. "Is it... mine?"

It'd be so easy to lie. To tell him no, to get him out of her hair. But she's not a monster.

She lifts her chin. Meets his eyes dead-on and says, "It is."

He grips the armrests of his chair.

His world-off-its-axis reaction is obvious. She stays quiet for a beat, letting it sink in.

Solomon leans back in his chair, jaw slack and body rigid. Exhaling, he runs a hand down his dark beard. "Shit."

He sits like that for one, maybe two minutes, until the drinks are delivered, and then he swallows half his beer in one gulp. As he does, Tessie takes a second to evaluate him. She's seeing him for the first time in six months. Up close. Too close.

Too dangerous.

Too handsome.

Her mouth waters. Her heart flutters. There's a distinct twinge down below that comes from a long drought. From want.

His eyes are still that same deep blue she remembers. Pantone color 19-4045 TCX Lapis Blue. A hue so dark it could have come from the depths of the sea. Under the sleeves of his thick flannel, his brick-like biceps bulge. His black beard is close-cropped. His shoulders have their own zip code. Massive. Massive. Everything about him is massive. She could surf on his collarbone. His hands—broad, callused—could engulf her.

Oh God. She holds her belly, wincing at the thought. The baby will be explosive. It'll rip her in half.

"Jesus fucking Christ." The curse has her focusing on his face. Twisted into a grumpy frown. "How'd this happen? We used a condom," he insists, voice hoarse, wrenching a hand through his thick black hair.

"It failed. Not everything is foolproof. Hindenburg, Titanic, MySpace." Her phone gives a melodic ping, but she ignores it, picking up her glass, soaking in the cool condensation. "We can get a DNA test if you don't believe me."

Here it is. He's gonna walk. He's only here to make sure I won't sue him for child support.

He gives her a look like she's stupid. "I believe you."

She blinks. Her heart thumps against her ribs. "You do? I mean, good. You should. Because I don't have sex."

He arches a brow.

"All the time, I mean," she stammers, rushing to clarify. "I mean, not with strangers. Not with just anyone. That one night, it was..."

"A mistake?" Solomon asks in a low voice.

Swallowing, Tessie looks down at her swollen stomach. "No." She turns her attention back to him. "I wouldn't call it that. Not anymore."

Nodding, he lifts his beer to his lips and finishes it. His expression is thoughtful, his eyes on her face in that broody glowering way of his.

She purses her lips. "If it makes any difference, I did try to find you. I called the bar. I even had them put up posters."

A smile, all but hidden behind that dark beard, twitches the edge of his lips. "Like wanted posters?"

She flushes, her face going hot. "Like missing persons." She clears her throat. "Anyway, what I'm saying is, I thought you should know about Bear."

A grunt. "Bear?"

"The baby. That's what I call him."

"Him?" This time Solomon's fingers tighten on his empty beer glass.

She claps a hand across her mouth. "Shit. I'm sorry. I didn't—I—"

He holds up one mitt of a hand. "It's okay."

A muscle twitches in his bearded jaw. A smile? Grimace? A combination of sorts? A smimace? A grimile?

Brows knitted, he asks, "You found out?"

"Of course I did. I've had enough surprises to last me the entirety of my thirties." She tosses her hair, ready to get her disclaimers over with and get Solomon Wilder off her island. "Look. You're under no obligation with this pregnancy, okay? I don't want anything from you. I don't need money or child support. I'm prepared to do this alone. I *can* do this alone."

A deep frown furrows his brow, his irises twin blue flames.

She peers over her shoulder to make sure she's the source of that angry scowl.

"Let's get one thing straight," Solomon says in a gruff tone that brooks no argument. "I want to be in my son's life."

"Oh." Tessie straightens, his decisive words doing something twisty and warm to her insides. "Okay. Good, then." She gives a firm nod, her gaze ticking to his. "Despite what people may think, I'm not that terrible. I'd never keep him from you."

"Terrible?" He frowns. "Who says that about you?"

"No one. Everyone." *Ping.* This time, she scrambles for her phone. "Oh, thank God," she breathes. "The room's ready."

He's still studying her. Still frowning.

Seeing that the conversation isn't over, she wilts. "What do you want, Solomon?"

She knows what she wants. A bed. A pillow to scream into. A pregnancy compression stocking to strangle Solomon Wilder with.

"Look, I don't know anything except that that baby's mine and I'll do the right thing." He pins her with a look. "You're here for a week, right?"

A pit of dread forms in her stomach. "I am."

"Let's make a deal, then. Let's take three days to get to know each other." He holds her in his unwavering gaze. "We'll talk. Hammer this out. Figure out how to raise our kid together in peace."

Momentarily caught off guard by his offer, Tessie fixates on Solomon's face. His serious blue eyes with faint crinkles at the corners. His solemn expression. Is he truly as good of a guy as he claims to be? Will he really stay? Try to have a relationship with his son? It seems too good to be true. But then, he's here, isn't he? He followed her all the way to Mexico to talk. Maybe he is a good guy.

Maybe.

But she doesn't need to know. Doesn't *want* to know anything about him. He is an inadvertent sperm donor who gave her one of the best nights of her life. They have nothing in common except an agreement to figure out how to raise their son.

"You good with that? Three days?" Solomon spreads his large hands on the tabletop. "Then I'll leave you to the rest of your vacation."

No, she is very much *not* good with that.

As selfish as it is, she doesn't want to be stuck with Solomon Wilder. Or share.

Her vacation.

Her baby.

She's done this pregnancy thing by herself for the last six months, and to have this stranger, this man, elbowing his burly body in the way of her perfectly crafted plans is a pain in her ass.

Still, the sooner she agrees, the sooner she can get this over with. Get her vacation back. Get this brooding Buffalo plaid-clad mountain man out of her life.

Three days.

She can tough it out for three days.

Tessie shrugs and tosses her long blond hair. "Fine."

A grunt. "Good."

They shake on it.

Chapter Seven

Solomon follows behind Tessie as they're guided to their room. Along the way, the porter goes on about resort amenities like champagne bars and dedicated concierge service and nightly themed parties. Tessie's nodding along, but Solomon's brain feels like it's going to explode. All kinds of thoughts roll around in his head.

The first: *You took my shirt.*

Jesus Christ. *That* dumbass remark is what left his mouth after seeing her for the first time in six months? At the time, it was all he could think of. He saw her standing there in that lobby, stunned, and it knocked him off balance. Christ, he *growled* at her.

The second: A son. He's going to have a son. He's going to be a dad. The thought doesn't scare him as much as he thought it would. *Bear.* He repeats the nickname silently. He likes it. In fact, he goddamn loves it.

The third: Tessie and what to make of her. Uptight. Guarded. A far cry from the easygoing wild girl who bared her soul to him outside the Bear's Ear bar. The smile that hit him straight in the solar plexus that night is replaced by a scowl that—does he dare say it—has her looking even more beautiful than he remembered. All long blond hair, ruby-toned lips, and delicate, elfin features. And the hell of it is he can't keep his eyes off her. Her body's slim and toned, her stomach a small hard ball of baby.

His baby.

The thought does something to his senses. Overrides all rational thought and replaces it with hardwired primal instinct.

"And here we are."

The chipper announcement has him stopping in his tracks. The porter's paused at the foot of the stairs leading up to a suite perched at the lip of the white-sand beach. The ocean churns, choppy. Basking on the sidewalk in the sun is a comatose iguana. Far off, the shrieks of seagulls. Percussive music swells in the distance.

It's all too bright and too foreign. It's not home like Chinook. Familiar. Steady. Still, he's here, and he'll make the best of it. If he can live in a cabin in the woods for seven years, he can stick it out on a beach for three days.

Every muscle in Solomon's body locks when Tessie slips as she takes the first step, her heels sliding across the wet cement. He moves fast, darting forward to wrap a protective arm around her waist. She tenses as he yanks her close but holds on to him as she gets her bearings.

Close. So close her scent wafts between them, a mixture of coconut and sea salt. With her damn near in his arms, it's easy to register how petite she is. Maybe five foot four without heels and all legs and belly.

"You okay?" he asks gruffly, doing his best to ignore the sweep of her stomach against his. The bat of her long, dark lashes does something insane to his brain.

"Fine. Damn heels," she says, looking up at him with wide chocolate-brown eyes.

"Shouldn't wear heels."

She scoffs. Then she's pushing off him and making her way up the flight of stairs.

Solomon shakes his head.

Stubborn. Good to know.

It pisses him off that she's annoyed by his presence, but she'll have to deal with it. Suck it up like all that LA smog she lives with on a daily basis.

He has to duck all the way up the stairs, and when he finally squeezes his way around the corner, the porter is waving the room key against the sensor. "There are sixteen gourmet restaurants on resort property, unlimited meals and premium drinks."

"Wait," Solomon says. "Everything's included?"

Tessie gives him a withering look. "That's what all-inclusive is, Solomon. It's unlimited."

Unimpressed, he crosses his arms. "Sounds wasteful."

"It's not wasteful, it's—" She breaks off as the door swings open to reveal the room with a flourish. "Five fucking stars," Tessie gasps and then lunges inside.

The porter grins. "She's fast, señor."

Solomon nods, fighting his own grin. "She is."

"Shit," he says, following her in, rubbing suddenly sweaty palms on the thighs of his jeans. Instantly, he's out of his element.

Just like Tessie—the room's a stunner. A large luxurious sitting area with an L-shaped sofa, a coffee table that looks like a concrete slab, and velvet chairs. A master bedroom with a plush king-sized bed. Marble tile. Art deco palm tree prints hang on the wall. Their bags are already on baggage trays in the bedroom.

Amused, Solomon watches Tessie flit around the room, running her fingers over every surface. Metal. Silk. Wood. She's like a run-on sentence in heels. She turns in a circle, practically levitating as she drinks in the room. Barely able to stay in one place before rushing over to examine a new piece of décor. His breath catches as he watches her. Hands pulled to her heart, her mouth open in awe as she drinks in the glossy room.

It means something to her. This vacation.

She pauses at the bar where bottles of Tito's beckon. "Oh, would you look at this live edge slab?" Her neon-pink nails tap out a beat along the veneered countertop. And then she's off and moving again, a chorus of *oohs* and *ahhs* trailing in her wake.

"Are you..." He pauses. "Sniffing the pillows?"

Her cheeks flush pink, a round pillow clutched in her hands. "It's my thing, okay?"

Amused, he shrugs. "Whatever you say. Do your thing, Tessie." He thinks on it. "Design, right?"

"That's right."

He's reaching into his pocket for cash to tip the porter when Tessie lunges in front of him, beating him to it. She glides back to the sitting area, drifting toward a large swath of curtains that Solomon can only assume hides the terrace from view.

"Interiors." A toss of her long blond hair. "Transforming spaces. Making them pretty."

Solomon watches her brown eyes metronome across the living room. "What are you doing?"

"I'm thinking about colors."

"Colors."

"Like matching colors." She pauses, explains. "In interior design, we have a palette. Like there's blue, the base color, but it doesn't stop there. There's blue with green undertones or yellow, or—" She snaps her mouth shut. Smiles. "I'm losing you."

"A little."

"There are these things called Pantone colors. Standardized colors that ensure that the color you want is the color you get. No surprises." A smug smile grows on her face. "I can assign a color to anything."

"Then what's this?" He points at a gray faux fur blanket draped over the sofa.

Without missing a beat, she says, "Lava smoke."

He can't help it. "What about my eyes?"

Nostrils flaring slightly, Tessie tosses her hair. "Haven't thought about it." With a little shimmy, she makes her way to the button on the wall beside the linen curtains. "Should we see what this does?" She sends him an excited look over her shoulder and then presses it. A squeal tears out of her as the curtains slice open to reveal a spacious terrace overlooking the Pacific.

With another gasp, Tessie shoves open the sliding glass doors, a blast of salty sea air gusting past.

Even Solomon has to admit: the view's goddamn great.

The ocean's practically in their backyard. Mangrove trees hang on either side of the balcony. The sound of crashing waves drifts up over the beach. Hammock. Jacuzzi. A seating area with beach furniture and chaise lounges.

As Tessie moves to the wrought-iron railing, every muscle in his body goes on red alert. The sight of her and his son on the edge of the balcony, perched next to the mid-hip railing, scares the ever-loving shit out of him.

She's safe, Sol. Serena's quiet voice swirls around him. *She's safe.*

To calm his nerves, he joins her. Relief washes through him the second he's beside her. Steadying his heartbeat, the panicked tripping of his pulse.

"Damn good view."

"It is." She raises her phone for a photo, then lowers it, wrinkles her nose. "It never looks the same in photos."

"That's why you should enjoy it in the moment."

Her lips quirk up. "How very Buddha of you, Solomon."

He chuckles wryly. "You want a good view, you should come to Chinook."

She tilts her head, her long blond hair waterfalling around her shoulders. "What's Chinook?"

"A little town outside of Anchorage. Where I live. Chinook, Alaska."

"Alaska." Side-eying him, she fakes a shiver. "God. That's like opposite ends of the spectrum. What, is it snowing there right now?"

"Could be." September's early for snow, but it's been known to happen.

She arches a brow, a faint smile on her lips. "Still the best place for stars?"

His heart stirs at the memory of that night. "Damn straight."

Ping.

Ping.

Ping.

"Does that thing ever stop?" Solomon grunts. Her phone's been going off since he found her, stirring a real urge in him to toss it off the terrace.

Chest heaving, she gives an exaggerated sigh, breaking eye contact with him to scrutinize her phone. "If only."

The catch in her voice has him giving her a closer look.

Her words are laced with the same despondent tone she used when she said, "I'm not that terrible." And it makes him want to hit something. Most likely the person on the other end of that phone.

She raises the device, taps out a frantic text, then turns on her heel and flounces off.

Solomon tracks her movement, watching her petite frame disappear into the bedroom. He runs a hand over the back of his neck, a strange helplessness bobbing around inside him like a lost buoy. He's wondered about this girl for the last six months—her name, where she's from, why she ran out on him the next morning—and now she's here, but all he can do is make stilted conversation.

Everything about this is awkward. He's stuck with her for three goddamn days. One part of him wants to stick to business, figure out how to raise their son, then hop the next plane back to Chinook. Another part, the part that can't deny that night between them, wants to know more about her. Wants to tell her she shined a light on him, and he hasn't been the same since.

Turning back to the water, Solomon inhales deeply, breathing in the scent of salt and surf. Mexico doesn't have snow or mountains, but at least it's not a cement city. He scans the horizon. A catamaran floats lazily across the ocean. The waves crash on the beach. The—

Shrill scream coming from the bedroom.

Alarm has him bolting, has adrenaline instantly coursing through his veins.

"Tessie?" he calls, charging into the bedroom.

She stands next to the plush king-sized bed, wearing a terry cloth robe over her jumpsuit, a stricken look on her pretty face.

He grasps her arm, pulling her away from the invisible threat. "What is it? What's wrong?" Heart pounding, he searches for the culprit. A rodent he can shoo; maybe a bug he can pound with his boot.

"This." She gestures, her arms cartwheeling frantically. "Holy shit. This is my worst nightmare. There's only one bed. *One* bed, Solomon."

"Christ. That's it?" He breathes hard, his pulse doing some strange herky-jerky beat. This woman's making him sweat, making him lose his shit, and he's only known her for a few hours. "I'll sleep on the couch, okay?"

Her tight expression relaxes a bit, and she blinks. "You will?"

"I will."

"Fine," she sniffs, moving for her suitcase. "Then I'll unpack."

"Let me," he says, intercepting her before she can grab the overpacked duffel bag. "I don't want you lifting anything heavy."

The way her eyes widen, the look of surprise on her face gut him. Like no one's ever offered to take care of her before.

He takes the suitcase from the floor and places it on the luggage rack next to the bed. "Jesus, what's in here, bricks?"

She steps around him, a small smile on her lips. "No. Baby stuff."

Solomon watches as Tessie unpacks a thick stack of baby books, all with horror movie-sounding titles that make his blood pressure skyrocket: *Laboring Your Way*, *Breastfeeding Like a Boss*, *The Quickening*. Then comes prenatal vitamins, sheer leggings, and an odd-looking contraption that has a wand attached to a long cord.

"It's a fetal heartbeat monitor," she offers, seeing his look of confusion. "A doppler. So I can listen to Bear's heartbeat." The tips of her ears turn an adorable shade of pink. Her hand drops to cradle her belly. "We're on an island, and since my doctor isn't here... I wanted to make sure he's okay. Just in case, you know."

Solomon's mouth goes bone dry. There's a stab of overwhelming appreciation in his chest at the thought of Tessie taking such damn good care of their son before he's even born.

"You, uh, plan for everything," he says, his voice extra gruff as he forces the words out around the boulder in his throat.

He's rewarded with a shy smile. Just like the night they met. A callback to the girl, the night, that changed his world. "I try to." She flicks her hair, beaming. "It's my job."

Before he can think of a response, she jerks away from him, her expression closing up, like she regrets giving him that much.

As she busies herself unpacking and neatly arranging her things like she's moving into the room for the next two months, Solomon takes a second to study her, like he can peel off the layers and get to the bottom of Tessie Truelove. Fatigue dulls her chocolate-colored irises. Her spine is ramrod straight as she covertly checks her phone.

She turns. A long, colorful dress in her hands. "What?" Her eyes narrow in suspicion. "You're staring."

Overcome by the urge to sweep the hair from her face, he shoves his fists in the pockets of his jeans. "You tired?"

She blows out an aggrieved sigh. "Why? Do I look that awful?"

Awful, no. Beautiful. Fierce. Exhausted. Every yes in the goddamn book. Solomon fights an itch to make her sit down. Take off her sky-high heels. Put her in that plush bed and prop her up on silk pillows like a queen. But he holds his tongue. It's not his place. They had one night together six months ago. This is temporary, the two of them in the same room.

They have nothing in common, except an agreement to figure out how to raise their son.

"No," he grits out. "You look fine."

The minute the words are out of his mouth, he inwardly groans.

Fine. Fucking fine.

Real fucking smooth.

Her expression flattens.

He sighs. "Listen, let's get some dinner and then we can each do our own thing."

"Dinner," she echoes, her expression faraway.

He scrutinizes her belly. "You both should eat. Room service?"

"No way," she argues, straightening her shoulders. "It's my first day of vacation. We are not staying in the room. We're going out."

The last thing she looks like she wants to do is go out, but he holds his tongue. He's still brooding over the dark circles under her eyes. Over the phone that's now on mute but lights up every minute or so. A flare of annoyance has him clenching his jaw. Who the hell is bothering her on her vacation?

Tessie scrambles for her planner. A pen appears in her hand like a wand. "Let's see. . ." Tongue poking out of the side of her mouth, she scans the page. "Tonight, we have. . ." An unearthly groan rises up in her. Plopping herself on the edge of the bed, she balances her elbows on her knees. Chin in the palm of her hand, she meets his gaze and says, "We have dinner reservations."

He frowns down at her. "You say that like it's a bad thing."

"It is." With a sigh, she drops her face into her hands. "A very bad thing."

Chapter Eight

A CANDLELIT DINNER UNDER THE STARS. A TABLE decorated with a stunning tropical floral arrangement and twinkling candles. Fresh ocean air, the roar of the waves, the moonlit sky above. Perfection.

Nothing could ruin it.

Nothing, that is, except Solomon—sitting across from Tessie, his big, broad shoulders blocking her view of the ocean for the second time today. To add insult to injury, he's still wearing that same damn flannel shirt. Clearly, the man knows nothing about chill beach vibes and instead plans to glare at her all night like a grumpy sasquatch.

It's bad enough they're sharing a child. Now she has to share a five-star dinner.

Tessie shifts in her seat, smoothing a hand down her belly over the neon blue maxi dress she's changed into. She resists the urge to check her phone, nestled discreetly near the edge of her plate.

As the server adjusts the silverware, Solomon's brow wrinkles in consternation.

Tessie inhales a breath and holds up a hand, getting ahead of his criticism. "Before you say anything, there was limited seating, okay? I paid in advance. I couldn't cancel."

His lips twitch. "I didn't say anything."

She scowls. Already, she can see those hulk-like muscles racking in silent laughter.

A whisper of annoyance flits through her. Ash was supposed to be here with her, not Solomon. Sure, it's cheesy—candle lights lining a path and rose petals scattered on the sand—but when she booked this, she was dying for cheesy. For romance. Even if she was planning to share it with Ash.

Three days, she reminds herself. *Three damn days.*

Trying for casual conversation, Tessie asks, "See something you like?"

Solomon, evaluating the menu with bored scrutiny, grumbles. "At least the catch is fresh."

She rolls her eyes to the starlit sky. Here she is with the Debbie Downer of the hour when she could be with Ash. She grips her napkin in her fist. She's going to strangle her cousin. Preferably after the baby is born because she needs a birthing coach, but definitely, a strangling will happen.

A white-gloved server in his early twenties appears, a bottle of prosecco in his hands. *Louis* the gold-plated name tag on his starched shirt reads.

Before she can say anything, Solomon rumbles, "She can't drink that."

A shiver runs through her, Tessie's toes curling in her heels at the authoritative tone in his voice.

The server pauses mid-throttle of the bottle, jerking his head at Solomon. "For you, señor?"

Solomon crosses his arms, his buffalo plaid sleeves squeezing his biceps. "I'll drink what she's drinking."

Tessie pulls in a surprised breath at his show of solidarity. "You don't have to do that."

He gives her a long broody look, his expression flat. "Tess."

Tess. Firm. Stern. She kind of likes it.

No. Absolutely not. Because liking anything about Solomon Wilder means developing an attachment, and the only attachment she has is Bear, literally hooked up to her via umbilical cord, and that's how it will stay. At least for the next three months.

"Oh, uh, okay." Louis and Solomon both watch her. "Do you have those pineapple drinks? With the sunglasses and the cute umbrella?"

"No, señorita. I am sorry. They are only at the—"

"Tiki bar, got it. A mocktail, then." Flustered, she looks around for a drink list. "I don't—do you have a menu or—"

"Ginger ale, lime juice, mint leaves, simple syrup," Solomon tells Louis. But he's looking at Tessie. "That okay with you?"

She blinks. "Yes. Wait! We'll start with the crab cakes," she blurts before the young man can disappear. Before she can wither away from famishment. She is not meant to go this long without eating. Rubbing her stomach, she sends a silent apology to Bear as the server strides away.

Impressed, Tessie looks at Solomon. "You know your drinks."

"I do."

She pulls her shoulders back, resisting the urge to roll her eyes for the second time tonight. Is everything about him a grunt? Is this how he communicates? In monosyllabic sentences? "*Well,*" she drawls, lifting a brow. "How do you know your drinks?"

Another grunt. God, it's like trying to drag a confession out of a death row inmate.

Shifting in his seat, the mountain of a man clears his throat. "A buddy of mine and I—we own a bar."

"Really?" She tilts her head, trying to imagine a bar in Alaska. Igloos. Icebergs. Whale blubber. "That's... cool. You're a bartender?"

"A chef." A muscle twitches in his bearded jaw, his cool blue eyes dropping to his plate. "I was."

She frowns. "You don't cook anymore?"

"No. I don't."

Shame. She takes in his colorful tattoos. His hands. Broad and callused, big as bear paws, they look like they could do some damage in the kitchen.

And in the bedroom.

Nope. Nope. Not going there. Went there once, not again.

Flushing, Tessie takes a sip of her water to chase away the inappropriate thoughts. "What do you do?" she asks. "You have a job, right?"

Not that she wants his money, but it would do wonders for her self-esteem if her baby's daddy were employed.

"I make furniture. Sell it when I can."

"What else do you do in Alaska?"

Solomon pauses at the appearance of the server. Once the drinks are set down, colorful mocktails in coupe glasses, he sits silent. That's when Tessie realizes he's waiting for her to take the first sip.

So she does.

"Mmm," she says. Light and refreshing on her tongue. "It's perfect."

It is. Just enough to make her feel fancy. Feel normal.

Solomon dips his chin, that beard twitching again. He seems pleased with her answer and lifts his own glass to his lips. Tessie has to smother a giggle at the sight of this burly, bearded mountain man lifting a flashy drink like it's no big deal.

"So, in Alaska," he says, picking up the dropped conversation, "I fish. Hunt."

"You eat meat?"

"Christ." He sets his drink down, his handsome face pained. "Are you a vegetarian?"

"Only on a full moon after sacrificing a virgin."

He blinks.

"I'm joking." She gives him a teasing smile. Propping her elbows on the table, she rests her chin in her hands and evaluates him. "You're a very solemn man, you know."

Some of the tension leaves his expression. A smile, faint but real, tugs at the corner of his lips. The burn of his dark blue eyes on hers has her stomach taking a tumble. Has her mind flashing back to the Bear's Ear bar. Solomon, handsome, too damn handsome, the way he listened, showed her the stars. His strong yet gentle hands over her body, a drunk, desperate need arcing between them as they crashed through that motel room door.

Only tonight, there's something different about him.

She squints. He's like a strange frowning zodiac cipher she can't puzzle out. Every six-foot-four, glowering, broad-shouldered piece of him. She's curious. A part of her wants to keep digging. This is her child's father. She should know him. And yet...

Another part of her doesn't want to get to know Solomon Wilder.

Sure, they shared one night...one perfect, glorious night, and now they share a kid. But more than that? Off the table. Getting close, getting attached, getting sentimental? It's not in her cards. All her energy needs to stay focused on how to keep her life together. How to be a good mother to her son. The last thing she needs is a man to mess things up.

And that's when she sees it. What's different.

"Your ring," she blurts.

He flinches.

A heartbeat of silence.

"You took your ring off," she says again. Softer now.

A tight nod. The words wrench from his mouth. "I did."

"New girlfriend?" Tessie tries for nonchalance. Though she shouldn't care. Shouldn't be holding her breath waiting for his answer.

"No. No new girlfriend." Pain creasing his features, he opens his mouth, then snaps it shut just as abruptly as the server appears with the appetizer. They place their orders, the table falling into an awkward quiet with the disappearance of the server.

"So there's...no one?"

Silence.

Tessie stares down at her stomach, biting her lip, wanting to apologize, to search for something innocuous to say, to shake away the relief that's suddenly hit her heart.

Noted. Dead wife. Sore subject.

A grumble from Solomon.

"What's wrong?" she asks, scooping up a flaky piece of crab.

"I can't even see my food," he grumps, poking at a crab cake.

"Here," she says, grabbing up her phone to turn on the flashlight.

He winces at the bright blast of the light. "Jesus. Do you have to do that?"

"Well, you wanted to see it," she argues, then sits back in her chair with a frown.

Screw small talk and Solomon's surly attitude. It's time to get down to business. Time to get this over with. Time to feel this man out before she agrees to anything regarding their son.

"Let's talk about Bear," she announces, chin held high.

Solomon glances up, looking surprised.

She waves her fork, swallowing a pillowy lump of crab. "That's why we're here, right?"

"Right."

"I have one question for you."

"Ask away."

"What if you get cold feet one day and try to leave?"

"I won't."

"People leave, Solomon."

"I'm aware of that," comes his gruff response, "but I won't."

She regards him for a long moment, gauging his truth. How can she believe him?

Her own father hadn't wanted her. He walked out, left her and her mother when Tessie was two years old. Like they were bags of trash on the highway. She barely remembers him. The scent of cigarettes. Crinkled brown eyes like they'd been sandblasted by the desert.

He had a wife. He had a child, a daughter. And he *still* left.

Even people with ties break them.

Which is why she's wary of Solomon. If Bear's father plans

to walk away one day, he better do it now, because he won't get another chance.

"I have a question for you." Solomon jerks his bearded chin at her. "Where do you plan to raise Bear? In that apartment?"

She scoffs at the distaste on his face. Her home isn't much, but being insulted by a man who wears flannel to the beach is rich.

"I would. And where do you live? A cave?"

"A cabin."

"Let me guess. In the woods?"

A muscle flexes in his bearded jaw. "That's right."

"Well," she says, spearing another bite, "if you want to be involved in his life, you'll have to make time to come to LA."

"What about Alaska?" he counters.

"I have a job. I can't leave." She stabs a hunk of crab. Solomon's sits untouched. "I have everything planned." She ticks a list off on her fingers. "Hospital birth at Cedars-Sinai. Nursery colors, dolphin fin and banana. His name—"

Solomon's fork clatters to the table, his face pinched like his crab has gone bad. "Name?"

"No." She flattens her lips. "I'm not telling you."

His hard gaze is an interrogation spotlight. "*Tessie.*"

She bristles, suddenly defensive.

Her life. Her baby. Her *sanity*.

Letting someone else in to bulldoze her best-laid plans? Absolutely not. She won't allow it. She's trying to figure out how to do this working mother thing, and now this grumpy mountain man is here making all these demands, throwing a wrench in her life, stressing her out. This is her world, and it doesn't include a burly lumberjack throwing her off balance.

"You haven't been around. Don't blame me for making plans."

He rips a hand through his hair. Murderous energy wafts off him, blue eyes lit with anger. "I haven't been around because I didn't goddamn know."

"Well, I didn't know where to find you," she flings back.

They stare at each other until the server appears.

"Cracked pepper?" Louis asks, elbowing between them with a three-foot pepper mill that looks like a gigantic bong. Or a dildo.

Tessie can't be sure which is more appropriate for the situation, because she and Solomon, they're both getting fucked here. How did they get here? When did they veer away from pleasant conversation and dive headfirst into glowering silence?

Still eyeing Tessie, Solomon grits out, "No." His hands, resting on the table, are pulled to fists, the knuckles white.

Tension cuts the air like a knife.

Rolling his shoulders, Solomon tries again after the server leaves them be. "What if. . .every summer—"

She gasps and palms her stomach. "I am not giving up my child every summer."

"*Our* child," Solomon corrects her quietly.

Shamed, Tessie blinks back hot tears, worry curdling her stomach. Her lower lip trembles. "But. He'll be small for a long time. He just can't be without me." Her hands tighten on her belly, and she drops her gaze to the picked-over crab cake on her plate. Panic steals her breath, has her weak in the knees. The thought of losing Bear. Of ever being apart from him.

"I don't want him to be without you, Tessie. I want—*fuck*." The harsh blast of Solomon's curse has her looking up. He rips a hand through his black hair again, his go-to reaction when he's frustrated, she supposes, and clenches that steel jaw. Expression chagrined and angry, he asks, "How the hell do people do this?"

She shakes her head. "I don't know. But we will, okay?" Leaning in, she puts her hands out. "No lawyers. Please? We'll figure something out."

Lawyers mean they fight. They mean Bear's dragged through a nasty custody battle. They mean someone's trying to take him from her.

The thought churns her stomach.

This is her son. She can't understand the love she feels for

Bear. Maybe because it's innate. Unconditional. Hers. He is hers. She can do better than her father. She will. No one will take him away from her. And she sure as hell will never leave.

A grunt of affirmation from Solomon has her exhaling a long breath.

Slowly, she sips her mocktail, taking the time to analyze his facial expression. She can't read him. And why would she? She barely knows the man.

"Are you mad?" she asks after a moment, quickly setting her drink down. "You look mad. Your face...it looks like it's...melting."

He shakes his head, a muscle twitching in his stern jaw. "I'm not mad, Tessie. I'm frustrated."

A scoff pops out of her. "Well, me too."

Solomon doesn't respond. He's silent. Studying her face. But before he can say anything, her phone goes off.

She jumps, startled by the loud vibration of an incoming text.

Peeking at the phone where it sits next to her plate, Tessie swears. She asked Atlas to give her the evening before she finished her mood board, but apparently, he couldn't even do that.

Warmth behind her eyes.

Suddenly, she's not hungry anymore. Dividing up her child like he's an appetizer has left her with a sour ache in her stomach.

Gathering her napkin, she tosses it on the table and stands. Truce. No more. Not tonight. Between her boss's demands and Solomon's, she's done. She'll take a hard pass on crabby men cramping her island vibes. She wants to leave. She wants her compression socks and her record player and eight-hours of uninterrupted sleep.

"I'm going back to the room."

She turns, tears spilling down her cheeks.

But suddenly, Solomon's standing. Electricity snaps as he runs a broad, callused hand down her bare arm to snag her wrist. He stops her, turning her into him. "Tessie."

She sniffles. Tips her chin so she can see him. "What?"

His dark blue gaze scours her face, lingering on her tears.

Swallowing, his throat bobs with unsaid words, a conflicted look on his rugged face. "Your food."

She forces a smile and wills the tears away. "Box it up for me, okay? I'll eat it later."

After giving her one last, long once-over, Solomon lets go of her wrist, and Tessie turns. Phone in her hand, she starts across the beach, not even bothering to try and keep her tears at bay.

They talked, they tried, but what if it's hopeless?

What if they're nothing more than perfect strangers who hate each other?

Chapter Nine

Something warm and raw simmers in Solomon's chest as Tessie hurries away from him.

She doesn't want him around.

But who can blame her? He made her cry. He made a *pregnant woman* cry. Christ. He's an asshole.

Yes, he snapped at her, and the conversation got tense. He'd ground his teeth the entire time. Not fuming over Tessie, but over the way they couldn't make one damn decision, because nothing about their situation is normal.

And he saw it on her face too.

It's pretty damn clear Tessie Truelove wants nothing to do with him.

To her, he's an interruption. A threat. A grumpy bastard.

Worse, she thinks he'll take the baby away from her.

The thought has him feeling like an asshole of the highest variety.

Not for one damn second would he entertain the notion of taking that baby away. She's strong as hell and determined to raise the baby alone. He respects her for it. But he wants to be in his son's life. How does he reconcile that? How does he merge his easygoing life in Alaska with Tessie's rat race in Los Angeles? None of this is easy, but there's no question about it; they have to figure this out.

He's got two days left.

He feels even worse as the server slips past him to deliver their meals. At the sight of the fresh fish, Tessie's uneaten meal, Solomon frowns. She should have eaten more. All of a sudden, he aches to be back in Chinook, in his own damn kitchen, cooking her something healthy and delicious, instead of that shitty, anemic-looking salad on her plate.

In the distance, Tessie pauses near a palm tree to slip off her heels. He can make out her form, her long blond hair, the bright blue dress hugging the small bud of her stomach. Even in the dim moonlight, she shines gold like that night they first met. Beautiful.

Solomon smears a hand down his face and groans, half-tempted to go after her. He doesn't like her wandering around in the dark. It's too close to that night. That damn night that spun his world off its axis.

It's a resort, Sol. It's safe. No snow. No ice. No cars.

Still, he can't help it. It's nature to follow. Cursing himself, his overprotectiveness, he trails down the boardwalk after her, feeling like a creeper in the shadows. His body automatically drawn to her; his racing heart unable to rest until she gets to her destination safely. He keeps his pace smooth and efficient, keeping tabs on her while giving her distance.

A stab of regret knocks the wind out of him. He wishes he had asked her more about herself. Wishes he had grunted less. That he hadn't chased her away. Christ, could he have come off as more of a grump? He wants to know the girl he's raising his kid with. What puts that sad smile on her face. And who the fuck is blowing up her phone.

She's not glowing. Aren't pregnant women supposed to glow?

Solomon stops next to a gazebo when Tessie reaches their villa. Her phone practically glued to her hand, she takes the flight of steps gracefully, and then when he's sure she's disappeared safely inside, he turns and doubles back to the beach.

Guilt eats at his insides. Why the fuck did he let her walk away? He had stopped her. Almost. Felt the fast hammer of her pulse in her wrist as he ran his palm over her slender arm. He had found himself wanting to hug her. Touch her. Make her feel safe.

Kiss her.

Fuck.

No.

That's the last thing he wants. His son's his focus, and nothing and no one else. Even if her earlier question rings through his skull like a bell.

So there's. . .no one?

No one except you, he had wanted to say.

A goddamn idiotic notion. He barely knows her. Even if she's occupied space in his head for the last six months.

His ass is vibrating.

Solomon reaches into his back pocket and pulls out his phone. Evelyn. No doubt calling to check in on the situation. Tipping his head back to the sky, he blows out a hard breath. He's not in the mood but knows he better answer before his sister alerts his entire family.

"Hey, Evy." Sandy beach replaces the sidewalk as Solomon drifts down to the shoreline.

"Sol?" comes Evelyn's droll voice. Like she's amused at the world. "Are you in Mexico?"

"I am."

"Mmm. Good reception down there."

"Just finished dinner with Tessie."

"What's she like?"

"She's cranky and ignores me." He comes to a stop at the lip of the surf. "She's perfect."

"She's pregnant."

Not a defense. Just an observation. There's no one more pragmatic than his oldest sister. Evelyn's the only Wilder who worked her ass off to get out of their small town. Now a big shot family lawyer in Anchorage, Evelyn only returns home a few times a year, like she's too big to come back to the town that made her.

"Did you ask about a DNA test?"

He drags a weary hand down his face. "It's mine."

"Is she fighting you?" Evelyn's adopted her war voice, reminding Solomon of just how she got her nickname. Evil-yn. She'll go to any lengths to win a case. "Because if she is—"

"Evelyn, it's mine."

"Sol. How many times have we been through this?" she asks, exasperated. "It's important to establish paternity. If you don't, you give up your rights. You make it easier for her to keep you out of your child's life."

Christ. He should have screened the call when he had the chance.

He clenches his teeth. "She won't do that."

"How do you know, Sol? You barely know her."

He bristles. That's the whole damn point of this vacation.

"I just do."

A sigh. "If you want full custody—"

He shakes his head even though Evelyn can't see him. "Stop right there. I don't want full custody. Tessie and I are working on handling things."

She scoffs. "That never works. You live in different states. What if she sues you for child support?"

With a growl, he presses the phone tight to his ear to hear over the crash of waves. He walks the length of the beach, swearing as water rushes over the tips of his boots, soaking the hems of his jeans.

"Whatever my son needs, I'll provide it. I'm not worried about money."

Though he's told him to cut it out, Howler still pays him a salary. That, combined with what he makes selling his furniture, means Solomon's got a healthy six figures stashed in the bank. More than enough for his son.

"I know you're not. But I don't want you to get taken advantage of. I had a client . . ."

Solomon groans inwardly and looks toward the ocean. Contemplates tossing his ass in.

"He paid child support for eighteen years. And then do you know what happened?"

A bullet lodges itself in his chest, and he shakes his head to clear away the nagging thought. "Let me guess. He wasn't the father."

"That's right, Sol. He wasn't the father." His sister's voice hitches. "After all you've been through, I want to protect you. I don't want you to get hurt. You lost a wife. Losing a child. . ."

Jaw tightening, he looks out over the ocean. A hollow feeling settles over him.

He appreciates his sister's fierce protection. Out of everyone, she understands his grief the best. Serena was Evelyn's best friend. When she died, he and Evelyn got drunk on whiskey and wine for a week straight, talking gibberish and telling stories about her. Then he sold his house and built his cabin; Evelyn channeled that icy cool, and he hasn't seen the sister he knows since.

"Right now, you don't have many rights, but we'll fight for all we can." His sister's voice rattles his temples like a jackhammer, bringing him back to the present.

"Evy," he grits out, shaking his head like there's water in his ears. "What the hell are you talking about?"

"I'll do some research into her past. Meanwhile, pay attention to everything while you're there. Is she a drinker? In debt? Irresponsible? Smokes? Get me some dirt, Sol, and I'll run with it."

A ripple of annoyance runs through him at the thought of someone—hell, his own sister—digging into Tessie's past without her permission. Evelyn thinking Tessie hasn't given her all for their son is bullshit. The one thing he knows truer than day—Tessie loves that baby more than anything.

He refuses to let anyone—especially Evelyn—paint her as unfit or unloving.

"Evelyn, listen to me, and listen good. You will not dig," he growls. "You stay out of the dirt and away from Tessie. Do you understand me?"

A long silence. Then, "I understand." Evelyn's voice is contrite but not weak. "I just want the best for you."

Solomon stares off into the dark, in the direction of Tessie's villa. "I do too."

It's the longest day ever.

And Tessie's still up.

Working.

In bed, she lounges in a hotel robe, her laptop balanced precariously on her belly. Hair twisted up in a messy knot. Heels strewn on the floor.

She managed to put off Atlas all day by claiming bad reception, but now she has no choice. She needs to update Penny Pain's kitchen remodel with new specs. Change the stained wood to a herringbone mosaic tile so sexy it gives her goose bumps. This way, the contractors can get in there tomorrow and smash the shit out of the space.

One more project, one more update. That's what she keeps telling herself. She fought so damn hard for this promotion. She loves pushing the envelope with her designs, loves her clients. But Atlas and his toxic bullshit are making her miserable.

But she can't quit. Not now. Looking for a new job, especially while pregnant, sends her resolve scurrying. Time is ticking down. She has so much to accomplish for herself, for Bear. She just can't stop now.

She scowls at the Pavlovian ping of her email. Another email from Atlas. Marked URGENT.

This is my vacation. My only vacation in five fucking years because I've been your lapdog, she wants to scream.

Not a single message from Atlas contained an apology about

making her work on vacation. It infuriates her that she's not able to take this time off for herself. She should say no. Tell him to fuck off. But slowing down, jeopardizing her career, isn't an option. As a pregnant woman in a cutthroat industry, she has to be bionic to succeed. The harder she works, the more she boosts her portfolio, earns new clients. Plus, this job is her life. It gives her purpose.

Nothing—sleep, sex, social life—has ever measured up to the way she feels in her career. Maybe because she won't let it. Maybe because it's all she's ever let herself have. Maybe because her job saved her.

After her mom died, she went to college. She was worthless, attending classes during the day, waitressing at night, crying her eyes out in the cheap minivan she and Ash shared during her breaks. That was for two long years.

It was only when she graduated, got her first design job, and started staging homes that the stabbing pain of grief turned to a dull ache. Meeting with clients, staging furniture, pulling Pantones restored her mojo.

Her job was a gift, and even all these years later, she's still holding on to that.

Clicking into a reply box, Tessie sighs, thinking of the romantic candlelit dinner she left on the beach. The five-star gourmet meal wasted. She's managed to stave off her hunger with a pack of unimpressive hummus and pretzels from the minibar.

God, she needs this vacation.

"Don't we?" she coos to Bear, rubbing the curve of her stomach. Inside, her belly's peppered by soft kicks. Punches. He's up late, the sugar from the mocktail giving him an unwelcome energy boost. "We need a break."

Her only consolation is that she has six days left. What's one day of work, when tomorrow, she'll be on that beach, a pineapple man drink perched on her belly, a book in her hand?

Her phone vibrates on the nightstand. When she sees it's a call she actually wants, she scoops it up.

"You bitch. I'm going to get you back one day. So hard."

A husky laugh. "Just say thank you and tell me about that handsome mountain man."

Tessie needles her brow and sets the laptop on the bed. "Tell you about what? How much he hates me?"

She saw it all over his handsome, grumpy face. He thinks she's a bitch. A far cry from the silly dancing girl he met in that bar. Not to mention she brought up his dead wife. What hope do they have of even having a cordial conversation without it dissolving into chaos?

"He doesn't hate you," Ash says. "I mean, sure, you have the power to scare him away with your commitment issues and organic yogurt, but he came to find you, Tess."

"I wanted to be here with *you*, Ash. Not him." She glares at the door. Solomon returned moments ago, stomping around the living room like an ogre who's emerged from his cave.

"Believe me, I wanted to be there. But you needed this." She can practically hear the glee in Ash's voice. She's floating on a traitorous cloud nine high. "You have to finish it now."

"There is nothing to finish. It was a one-night thing. I was drunk."

"You weren't that drunk. You talked about him. Down to the color of his eyes. I've never heard you talk about a guy like that before."

Tessie cringes, a warm flush breaking out over her body. Ash's right. She did talk about him. Because what was the harm? He was hot, and she was a million miles away from him. He was a boost, a jump start, a memory she returned to when her spirits dipped.

Solomon was a perfect dream man of a one-night stand, but now he's here in front of her, and all she wants to do is pull the ripcord and evacuate. Sneak out on him like that first night. Because that's what she does when things get too close. She runs, she pushes.

Because turning down love is power.

Turning down love is safe.
Besides, she's had her three strikes at love.
Her dog.
Her dad.
Her mom.
Losing anyone else...

"There's nothing between us," she insists, twisting a rogue lock of hair around her finger. "We're handling business. Baby business."

A long silence. So long that Tessie pulls the phone away from her ear to make sure the call hasn't dropped.

Then a sigh. "Don't you think you owe it to yourself to see the what-could-be?"

"We're strangers."

"Not for long. You're having a baby together. You can't be strangers." Ash's voice turns soft. Inspiring. "Maybe you could be something."

Tessie's stomach turns to goo as she's suddenly hit by the feminine urge to take Solomon's lip between her teeth and kiss.

And kiss.

And kiss.

No way. Absolutely not.

They can't be something. Something is off-the-charts ridiculous. Because she and Solomon, they live in opposite worlds. He's hulking and lumbering and still in love with his dead wife, and she's—she's an uptight workaholic mess.

They'll share a child and that's it.

"Not everyone is your father, Tessie."

She groans as she struggles to sit up, her heavy belly a barricade to relaxation. "That's not it. Solomon and I—we are not into each other's life's rhythm. We're like snow and sun, okay?"

Tipping as far forward as her belly will allow, she taps her way out of her email, saving her design. Which is an immediate mistake. The click-clack of her nails on the keyboard has Ash gasping.

"Are you working? Unbelievable. I can hear you working."

She bites her lip, not even bothering to lie. "I'm almost finished."

"Your mom wanted you to see stars. Not work your ass off for them."

Tessie curls up in a tight ball against the pillow. The admonishment stings.

She knows.

She knows what her mother wanted for her.

Listen to more music. Find your stars. When you find that one good man, you better kiss him. Then keep him.

Her mother was barely lucid, dying in a hospital bed of a cancer that ate her quickly, but her words have haunted Tessie ever since. She's kept them close, heeded them like an X that marks the spot on a map. Like a spotlight to guide her life. Wise words from the best woman in the world. She had her mom for seventeen wonderful years.

And it still wasn't enough.

Tessie can only hope she'll be the type of parent her mother was. Happy and warm and safe. Her mother always said *I love you.* Never let a day pass without it. Was the role model of independence. Was both mom and dad. Taught her how to change a tire and how to walk in the highest of high heels.

If her mother were still here, she'd tell Tessie to trust Solomon. Because that's who she was. Kind and sweet and trusting. Everything Tess still wants to be.

Everything she's not.

Oh God. What if Solomon's a better parent than she could ever be?

What if she fails as a mother?

The thought is like a hurricane, thrashing her stomach with nerves.

"That's the point of all this, Tess." Ash's voice draws her back to the conversation. "You don't have to be alone in this. You can ask Solomon for help."

Never.

Because asking for help means letting him in. Once he's in, it means getting close. It means depending on him, loving him, only to watch him leave. Because life's a wash, and it all ends in loss.

She palms her stomach.

Except for her and Bear.

Her email chimes.

Her bladder beckons.

"I have to pee," she announces, scooting off the mattress.

"Fine." Ash snorts. "Change the subject. Have fun, you cranky pregnant thing, have fun."

After waddling to the bathroom, Tessie pauses by the bedroom door. Dipping as low as her belly will allow, she peeks through the crack in the door to see Solomon squeezing his big, burly body onto the couch. The blanket draped across his lap could double as a handkerchief.

A ripple of worry flits through her. What if they can't come to an agreement? Solomon wouldn't take Bear away from her, would he? He seems like a good guy, but she's been with good guys before. They're all good until they aren't.

Her eyes narrow on the water pitcher sitting on the bar. Maybe he'll get Montezuma's revenge and book it home.

She shakes her head and rolls her shoulders, pushing back at the building worry. Her emotions are making her crazy. She needs sleep. A clear head for the morning.

Tessie crawls into bed, turns off the light, and squeezes her pillow against her body, her son—her heart, a wild flutter inside her.

Chapter Ten

Six a.m. Coffee in hand, Solomon opens the sliding glass door to the terrace, a grudging appreciation flooding him when he sees the ocean. Though he feels like a traitor to Chinook, he has to admit that this hot, uncomfortable country is impressive.

Because goddamn that view.

The sunrise is a brilliant blast of pinks and yellows. The crash of the ocean and seabirds a symphony of noise. Salty sea air coats his skin in a damp dewiness as he takes in the rise of the morning. Despite the sun, there's a chill in the air.

He shrugs on his flannel.

Almost as peaceful as Chinook.

Back when he was a chef, Solomon counted on time. Time with his wife. Time in his kitchen. He worked long days and long nights, but he always got up with the sunrise and made sure he saw the stars at night. Waking and sleeping with the earth. A way to love and appreciate the land he grew up on. After Serena died, he kept to his routine. Waking. Rising. Breathing. Not dying. A reminder that life was still there. Spinning. Even if he didn't feel it at the time.

And now. . .

Now he doesn't know what he feels.

You do. You know, Sol.

Jesus, fine. He shakes off Serena's voice.

He's finishing the last drop of his coffee when the bedroom door blasts open. Dressed in a white off-the-shoulder dress that accentuates her tan and cork wedges, Tessie looks like a pregnant bronze ocean goddess who's just stepped off a yacht in Greece. The only things out of place are the laptop she carries and the phone tucked under her ear.

Solomon's mouth goes dry.

She's too fucking gorgeous for words. All he can do is stare like a fool. Christ. This woman's messing with his fucking heart rhythm. She has him on his goddamn knees like a dog with its tongue out. Has had him there since the moment he met her six months ago.

Tessie gives him a dismissive nod. Then her attention's sideswiped, her eyes back on the laptop she's heaving onto the room divider. Into the phone, she says, "But I have no control over DHL, Atlas, and you know that." She exhales hard and rubs the nonexistent wrinkle between her brows. "No, I told you—don't touch the design. Let a living room wall breathe." An under-her-breath mutter. "Jesus."

An explosion of words on the other end of the line—so loud Solomon can hear it from where he stands on the terrace—has her wincing. "I understand, Atlas, but"—she inhales, firmly—"this is my vacation," she says. "I paid for it." Her voice drops. Smaller now. "I saved for it."

Solomon frowns, a surprising stab of anger in his chest. A sudden urge to fling her laptop out to sea.

She listens for a few more seconds, then hangs up without a word.

He grunts, nodding at the phone. "Who's that?"

When she blinks, he mentally kicks himself. He's inserted himself into her business. Well aware he's been prowling in the background, brooding over who keeps bothering her. So much for not caring.

She chews on her answer a long second. Then her shoulders sag, the tips of her ears pink like she's embarrassed. "My boss."

"Sounds like an asshole."

"He is." With a toss of her golden hair, she turns toward him, her chocolate eyes clear again. "He's like laxatives and Klonopin rolled into one. He is not my favorite."

"Thought you were on vacation."

She nods, her focus drifting to the ocean. "I thought so too."

His fingers flex as she steps closer to him. Her perfume hits him like a drunk Friday night. The scent of coconut and exotic flowers calls to mind palm trees and little bikinis.

Goddamn.

Even with the dark circles under her eyes, she's the most beautiful woman he's ever seen. Tessie's all long legs and belly in that little white sundress. Suddenly, Solomon's hit by an insane urge to cup the curve of her stomach, to kiss her until her knees give out.

Christ, what's wrong with him? He's here to talk babies. Not make more of them.

"You're a rooster."

"I'm a what?" Solomon shakes himself out of his daze to focus on the woman in front of him. She's watching him with a scrutinizing frown.

She smiles. "A rooster. I usually do a morning Peloton ride. That's what they call us. Roosters. Because we get up early." At his silence, she opens her mouth again. "A Peloton. It's a—"

"I know what a Peloton is, Tessie. I'm from Alaska, not the Middle Ages."

"Mm-hmm." She apprises him, fluttering those long lashes. "A joke, Solemn Man. I'm impressed."

He grunts and turns away, but not before he's caught off guard by the ghost of a smile flickering across his face.

"I ordered coffee," he says, nodding at the pot perched on the coffee table. "Can you have some?"

Her face lights up. "I can. Exactly one boring twelve-ounce cup of coffee a day."

"Black?" he asks, moving to intercept before she can.

"Yes, thanks."

He passes her the full mug, their fingers brushing briefly.

Cup in hand, she heads back to her laptop. When she's stationed in front of it once again, her fingers fly furiously over the keyboard. Her coffee sits beside her, forgotten. Her mouth is pursed in an adorable pout, her brow furrowed.

A strange irritation sweeps over him at the protective instincts poking him in the ribs. Why in the hell is she still working? Where's breakfast?

She should be relaxing. The dark circles under her eyes bother the hell out of him.

Ash's words flood his memory. *She needs this, Solomon.*

She needs it, and he'll see that she gets it.

Jaw clenched, hands fisted at his thighs, he jerks his chin at Tessie. "You ever have coffee?"

Without tearing her gaze from the computer screen or her fingers from the keyboard, she tilts her head at her cup.

"That's not having coffee." He stomps to the terrace and pulls out two chairs, the sound a grating screech across the marble floor. He takes a seat. "This is having coffee."

Finally, she looks at him, a disgruntled look on her pretty face. "I get up early to work."

"I get up to see the sunrise."

She wrinkles her nose at the empty chair like it's a dare, then pulls her shoulders back, grabs her coffee and phone, and steps out onto the terrace. Gingerly, she lowers herself into the chair. She's tense. Shoulders stiff. Leg bouncing a mile a minute. Itching to get back to her computer.

He sips from his mug. Waits for her to do the same, and then he says, "You're working too much."

Working too much for a pregnant woman, he wants to add, but he stops there, because he likes his balls where they are.

Her brows shoot up, and she gives an exaggerated sigh. "You don't know me, Solomon."

"I'd like to." He smears a hand down his beard. "Last night. . .I don't like how dinner ended. I know it's a tough subject. I won't let things get that tense again. I promise."

Some of the fight goes out of her, her shoulders sagging. "Okay," she says warily. "What do you want to know?" Around and around, her hand moves over her belly, like she's channeling calm.

He thinks on it. Says the first thing that comes to mind. "Do you ever relax?"

Oh, Sol. No.

Tessie's eyes flash. "Do you ever *not* wear flannel?"

"Jesus, fine." He holds up his hands in placation. That probably wasn't the best conversation starter. Silence falls between them. Then, "I wear other things," he grumps, insulted. He'll never tell her he's baking in the sun. Breaking a fucking bead like it's nobody's business.

She snorts. "Like what? Overalls and trucker caps?"

Fuck. Her sassiness turns him on. Has him hardening. She's not like Serena. Serena was. . .well serene. Steady. Tessie's a girl on fire. He almost chuckles, imagining her in Chinook. Blowing through town in her high heels, blond hair whipping behind her. Feminine and fiery. A force he wants to reckon with.

If only she'd let him.

Ping.

Unable to help it, a growl tears out of him. "Your boss?"

She holds up her phone. Her eyes light up as she thumbs through the screen. "No." She rests her hand on her belly and gives him a bright beam of a smile. "I'm twenty-nine weeks today."

He glances at the swell of her stomach. "You are?"

Her lips curve. "Yeah. I have an app that tracks everything baby related." She scans the screen again. Giggles. "Bear's about the size of a butternut squash."

He chuckles. "Shit. They tell you all that?" Curious, he leans in, elbows on the armrests of his chair.

Tessie offers him her phone. A pastel-colored tracker is pulled up, with a baby diaper bouncing across the screen. Heart thumping, he reads the small blurb: *Baby now weighs three pounds. Baby can blink. Baby has lashes.*

"How, uh, long do you go?" he asks, handing back her phone, hoping she takes pity on him. Sure, he has three sisters, but kids and babies are about as foreign to him as long-term relationships are to Howler.

"Forty weeks. Nine months," she says.

He does the math in his head.

"I'm in the third trimester now. Almost there."

"You go to the doctor?"

She smothers a smile. "All the time. It's kind of what pregnant women do." After a brief hesitation, Tessie tilts her head. Bites her lip. "Do you maybe want to see a photo of him?"

Christ. The way she's chewing her lower lip, her sweet offer, has him catching a glimpse of the girl he met that night. Vulnerable. Kind. Open.

"Yeah," he rasps around the knot in his throat. "I would."

She perks up. "Okay." He waits while she swipes at her phone, and then she's scooting her chair closer to his. "Here," she says, putting her phone in his large hands once more.

Solomon examines the gray and white Rorschach-like blurs, frowning to figure out what he's looking at.

But then he sees.

He sees his son.

His.

It's real and it's happening.

The thought has his chest tightening. He wants this. With everything he has. Wants to be a father, to take his son back to Chinook, teach him how to fish, how to cook, how to be a good man—hell, a good person—every damn thing his own parents taught him.

Tessie's slender finger traces the screen. "That's his head, and this is his spine, see? And that's his..." Her eyes flick to his, a faint smile on her face. "You know." She laughs. "Penis."

Solomon's heart thumps in his ears as he drinks in the photos. As he swipes through, he's hit by a flare of worry. "And Bear's good. He's healthy?"

"He is." She taps the screen, angling in close to him. If he turned his face, her lips would be inches from his. *Stop. God damnit.*

"He's perfect. Ten fingers. Ten toes."

Sunlight falls over her face, illuminating everything beautiful about her. Honest happiness in her expression he only sees when she talks about their son. Their gazes catch and hold. She cradles her belly, her voice turning soft. "Now all he has to do is just stay in there until December."

"And what about you?" he asks gruffly, the thought tearing at him.

She blinks, caught off guard, then her face resets. "I'm fine now," she insists, drumming a finger against the edge of her coffee cup.

He swallows. "Now?"

A casual lift of her hand. "I was sick so much the first few months. Like barf-in-a-plastic-bag-while-I'm-driving sick."

"Christ," he says, frowning.

"But I got through it. Now it's easy sailing."

Solomon stares.

In awe of his child. In awe of this woman.

These last six months, she's been alone, doing all this herself. Protecting his son, putting her body through hell, going to doctor's appointments, balancing it all with a demanding career. Regret needles him. He's missed so much. Missed it by no fault of his own, but damn. It still stings.

"You have family in Alaska?" Tessie asks, straightening in her chair.

"In Chinook," he says. "Parents. Three sisters."

"*Really?*" Then she covers her mouth. Her cheeks turn beet-red.

"Oh, God, I'm sorry. I just thought. . .you lived on a mountain. I pictured you. . .never leaving. Like some sort of Yeti hermit."

He presses his lips together to hide a smile. She's not wrong. "For a long time, I didn't."

"Because of your wife?" she ventures carefully.

"Serena."

"Serena." She repeats the name like she wants to get it right. To memorize it.

His gut clenches as the thoughtfulness of the gesture sucker punches him.

A contemplative expression on her face, Tessie angles her head, studying him. "How long were you married?"

"Six years."

"Oh."

He wants to say more, to tell her about Serena, but the words stick in his throat. Admitting what happened. . .he's not there yet. He's not proud of it.

"So. Your parents," she prompts, clearly reading into his silence and deciding to change the subject. "What do they think about this mess?"

He looks at her sharply. "It's not a mess, Tessie." Wanting her to know where he stands, he locks eyes with her. "Not to them, and especially not to me."

She gives him a small, grateful smile, her hands automatically moving to her belly. "I really appreciate that, Solomon," she says softly.

A silence that's easy falls around them. He sips his coffee, shifting in his chair as hot rays of sunlight filter over the terrace. Yet he says nothing, makes no move to remove his flannel. He doesn't want to interrupt the moment by letting on that he's hot as hell.

They're finally getting somewhere, and he wants to pull her in closer.

So they sit, watching the ocean. Watching the sun rise higher and higher in the sky, until they see the white pops of umbrellas on the sand. The faint strains of mariachi music signaling that the beach has woken up.

"You were right." Her soft lilt of a voice floats between them. She offers him a dazzling smile. "This is nice. The sunrise."

It is. While he's done it every morning in Chinook, it's been a long time since he's enjoyed it. He likes sitting here with her and their son.

"Good," he says, happy she's happy. "I'm glad."

A hand on his arm.

He turns to her. Tries to ignore the jerk of his heart.

Tessie's studying him with eagle-eyed intensity. "You're hot?"

"What?"

She swirls a finger around his face, his damp brow. "Are you hot?"

A drop of sweat slides down his temple. He clears his throat. "Not too bad."

Amusement settles across her face. "We should get you some clothes." At his blank look, she arches a brow. "You know, go shopping."

He twitches at the word. "No."

She laughs. "You're at the beach, Solomon. You shouldn't suffer. You should be having fun. Surfing a wave."

An unbidden smile curls his lips. "I don't surf."

"I am well aware of that."

With a huff, she plants both hands on the armrests of her chair, ready to shove herself up, but he's there, taking her hand in his so he doesn't have to watch her struggle.

She stands, and he stiffens as her hand wraps around the swell of his bicep. His pulse races at her touch. He looms over her like a huge man-beast. She presses up on the tips of her toes to lean into him, her heated brown eyes on his face. The swell of her belly, the smallness, the nearness of her, sends a bolt of desire licking through his bloodstream.

"Shopping," she says again. "Nothing too painful, I promise."

Say no. Like all the times his sisters tried to dress him up when he was a kid. No when Serena brought home that falcon with the broken wing, because if it died, she'd cry, and Solomon never wanted to see his wife cry. No when Howler thought it was a good idea to buy a mechanical bull for the bar; it wasn't a rodeo, goddamn it. Put his boot down and say no.

Goddamn it. No.

But as he gets lost in her big, brown, pleading eyes, he's a goner. There's no fight left in him. He's over the edge. Done.

Tessie lets her hand linger on his arm before dropping it, and then she smiles. "C'mon, Solemn Man. Clothes."

Chapter Eleven

Tessie leads, and Solomon follows.

Next to the hotel gift shop is Seaside Escape, the upscale beach-inspired fashion store. As she winds her way through the aisles, a thrill of excitement shoots through her. It's been ages since she's been shopping. Scratch that. Since she had time to shop. All of her pregnancy clothes were ordered online between bites of food scarfed as she sourced furniture for her clients.

Glancing over, Tessie bites her lip at the sight of Solomon bumbling his way through the racks of clothing. He looks lost, confused. Like he'd rather be back in Alaska tossing polar bears around. Picking up hangers with his big hands. Scowling at the cheery yet cheesy slogans like *Beach, Please* and *Life is Better in Flip-Flops*.

"Don't worry," she says, sending him an assuring look over her shoulder. "I'd never make you wear slogans."

Solomon edges away from a macrame kimono like it's on fire. "Never been to a place like this," he grits out.

Instead of making a teasing remark, she moves close. Looks up at him. "Do you want help?"

Out on that balcony, she saw it. He looked out of place and uncomfortable in his red flannel. It hit her then, that she wasn't the only one feeling awkward with this whole arrangement. She wanted to help him.

Oh shit. Does this mean she cares?

No. It's a nice gesture.

Clothes. He needs them, and she can help. She is fashionable, and he clearly is not.

He gives an almost imperceptible nod. "Whatever you think."

"A wardrobe for the season." She tugs at his lapel, the fabric velvety between her fingers. "Because God knows you only have one."

She squints at his lips. Is there a smile beneath that beard? She can't tell.

As she wordlessly picks through the racks of clothes, Solomon looms like a quiet giant behind her, watching close, careful. Her hands move fast. Searching for what she likes, what will look good on him. That is, if they have his size.

Enjoying herself, she drapes garments over her forearm. Linen shorts, swim trunks, polos, sleeveless T-shirts, and, to top it off, a fun, floral Hawaiian shirt. Every item curated with a true Solomon vibe. Masculine, no-bullshit, sturdy.

She turns, pleased with her finds, and her stomach bumps into Solomon's hip. He's so close she can smell him. Desire prickles in her stomach.

Clearing her throat, she takes a step back. "What do you think?" she asks, lifting the hanger.

His dark brows shoot to the sky. "Pink?"

"Dusty rose. Pantone color 17-1718. It'd be a bold fashion statement. You could pull it off." Somehow, despite his Alaska zip code, the man has a tan. So very unfair, it should be illegal.

He rolls out his broad shoulders.

"Fine." She sniffs. "I'll add a black one too."

A disgruntled sound escapes him.

"As you can see," Tessie tells the salesgirl who's stepped up to help them, "he needs clothes."

The young woman takes the pile of clothes and waves at Solomon to follow her to a fitting room.

He frowns, looks down at Tessie. "I have to try them on?"

"Yes." She laughs at the mild panic in his eyes. "Go."

He grunts unhappily but obeys.

Amused, Tessie perches on the wide arm of a dark blue bench painted with light blue waves. Solomon's so tall, the back of his dark head pokes above the changing curtain. Her stomach growls as she waits. "I'm sorry," she whispers, rubbing her hands across her tight stomach. She forgot all about breakfast. She needs to feed Bear.

Once again, her attention strays to Solomon.

She huffs a sigh. She enjoyed this morning. Bonding over their baby. Learning more about his father. Peacefully coexisting without that awkward need to fill the silence. It was strange. It was perfect. Strangely perfect.

With a sigh, Solomon pushes back the curtain. His big body emerges from the fitting room wearing warm gray swim trunks and a black tank. "Well?" He extends his massive arms. "What do you think?"

Tessie shoots to her feet. Her mouth drops.

She thinks a lot of things.

Like no man should be allowed to look this good.

Like is it wrong to openly fan herself?

Like if she goes into labor here and now, she has no one to blame but Solomon Wilder.

Because Solomon's the most beautiful specimen of a man she's ever seen. He's built like a wall of solid steel. His broad chest, the bulge of his biceps in the tank top, the shorts clinging to his muscular thighs have Tessie's core sparking, and she wonders if the baby can feel it. Solomon's thatch of dark chest hair is barely visible, but Tessie knows it's there. She remembers curling her fingers in it the night they met, smelling his masculine woodsy scent, running her tongue along the veins in his forearms.

Oh God.

Weak-kneed, she sags against the wall, clenching her thighs together. She pulses down below. Holy shit, what's wrong with her?

Horny, her mind says. *You're horny as hell and staring at a great big burly body isn't helping you any.*

"Tess?" Solomon's frowning.

She shakes her head, clearing her daze. She's supposed to be critiquing; not objectifying.

A toss of her hair. "It looks. . .fine."

His frown deepens. "Fine?"

"More than fine," a flirty voice opines.

Solomon and Tessie both swivel toward the salesgirl breezing their way. "It looks phenom. Except you need to go a size up in those shorts."

Tessie glowers. Watches as the woman practically floats over on a cloud nine high to deliver Solomon another pair of shorts.

Back into the fitting room Solomon goes.

Tessie walks slowly to a rack, absentmindedly picking through the shirts. "Where do you shop in Chinook?"

His gruff voice is loud behind the curtain. "I don't."

"Let me guess, you've worn the same clothes for the last four years?"

"Something like that."

The curtain opens. There stands Solomon in a T-shirt and the larger pair of swim trunks.

"Perfect," Tessie says. "Try the rest of the T-shirts."

Solomon rolls his eyes. Then he grabs his shirt by the back of the neck and tears it off. The cashier gasps. He stands in the open fitting room, half-naked. Body, abs, scowl on display for everyone to see.

Tessie gapes. "What—What're you doing?"

"It saves time," he says sensibly, reaching for another T-shirt.

"Stop. Don't. Just"—she pushes at him with her palms—"put those away," she hisses.

"Put what away?" Brow furrowed, he glances down at himself. "The T-shirt?"

"The abs." She gets close and knuckle taps his muscled chest. Huffs. "I mean, do you have to flaunt the fact that your body is just solid rock?"

He sighs, pained. "Tessie."

The salesgirl approaches, more clothes in her hands, her face giddy as her eyes light on a half-naked Solomon.

Tessie narrows her gaze and snatches the stacked pile from the girl's arms. Pregnant or not, she will lineback this bitch. "Thank you. I'll take those."

She shoves the clothes at Solomon, shoves at his enormous arm. "Go. Change. Inside."

He growls and pulls the curtain closed.

After a second glance at the fitting room where Solomon is busy changing, Tessie checks her phone. Earlier, she got the feeling that if she kept working, her phone would be at the bottom of the ocean.

At the sight of the blank screen, she breathes a sigh of relief. All quiet on the Atlas front.

Tessie relaxes. Today. Today is for the beach and then lunch. Oh God, lunch.

Tacos. Definitely. Maybe another mocktail. Solomon can choose. She supposes they'll spend the day together. And why wouldn't they? They still have to talk about Bear. It might not be so bad. She liked learning more about Solomon this morning. It felt right. Like their night at the Bear's Ear bar.

The shove of the curtain tears her from her thoughts.

Hands clasped to her chest, Tessie gasps. A high-pitched squeak of admiration falls out of her mouth. Solomon wears a black polo shirt and linen pants, making him look casual and sexy. If he looks this good now, what will he look like with a baby in his arms?

Stop.

Abort thought.

"Oh." She resists the urge to check for a pulse, because where she lost her heartbeat, she isn't quite sure. "Oh wow. That looks..." Finally, she gives up the fight on her emotions, choosing honesty, no matter how weak it makes her look. "That looks so fantastic, Solomon." She strides to him, adjusting the collar with a flick of her wrist. "There. Now you don't look so very serial killer with a forest fetish vibe."

His rumble of a laugh has her jumping. "That's my vibe, huh?"

"Oh, it is very much your vibe."

He regards her with a skeptical arch of his brow, concern flashing over his handsome face. "Suppose you want me to shave the beard."

"God no," she says without thinking. "I love the beard."

She can't resist pressing up on her tiptoes to run a palm down his thick black beard. The coarse strands tickle her palm. Her core fires, sparks, as she resists the very idiotic urge to lean forward and sniff. Just inhale Solomon like the best kind of bong hit.

He stares down at her, his expression tormented. With one massive hand, he palms the small of her back to steady her. To keep her close. "Tess..."

That's when she catches a glimpse of them in the full-length mirror. The juxtaposition is staggering. Riveting. He's at least a foot taller. The epitome of tall, dark, and handsome. And she— blond and petite. But they don't look mismatched. They look perfectly matched.

And then there's the bump between them. Their little link.

Their only link.

She drops her hand from his face and lowers herself.

Anchors herself.

"I think we're done," she says quietly.

"Yeah," he agrees after a moment, studying her face. "I think so."

Slowly, he retreats into the fitting room. Seconds later, changing so damn fast she can't be sure he isn't Superman, he emerges in swim trunks and an army green T-shirt that squeezes his biceps like a python. The remaining pile of clothes stacked in his arms.

Tessie gestures to a rack of brightly colored shoes. "We need flip-flops."

He rears back a little. "Hell no."

She purses her lips. "Solomon, you can't wear those boots on the beach."

"I can't run in flip-flops."

"You're planning on running?"

"Seagull attack."

His utmost seriousness has her smiling.

"A seagull attack, really?"

"It could happen."

She shakes her head. "Sunglasses, then." After hunting around, Tessie snags a pair of Maui Jim's and a baseball cap, and then she adds a pair of flip-flops to the pile anyway.

Tessie click-clacks her way to the register. She's about to pull her wallet from her beach tote when there's a hand on her arm.

"You're not buying clothes for me," Solomon says, stepping beside her.

She frowns. "I am. I suggested this. I—"

"Tess." His voice deepens, cutting off any further protest.

She shivers. There's that stern admonition again. Why does she like it so damn much?

"I appreciate the help. But you're not buying these clothes."

She pulls her shoulders back, ready to argue with him, but his expression—clenched, no-bullshit jaw, stormy blue eyes—tells her he'll fight her. Hard. End of story.

"Fine," she says, tossing her hair over her shoulder.

He pays, and when they're finished, they step into the glitzy hallway that leads back to the rooms. Brightly colored fish swim in a tank that takes up the entire wall across from them.

They linger in front of the elevator. A *what now* expression creases Solomon's handsome face.

Sure, they could split and do their own thing, but she wants to keep this day going. Wants to keep Solomon close. To talk about the baby. That's it. That's all.

Gathering courage, she wets her lips. Looks up at him, a warm flutter curling her stomach. "Do you maybe want to—"

From inside her beach tote, her phone seizes, announcing a flurry of text messages and missed calls.

Don't answer. That's her first thought. But the thought of relinquishing control, of saying no, has her going clammy. Fear of failure has fangs, and it clamps down. Won't let her loose.

Won't let her lose.

She scrambles for her phone and swipes the screen. Blanches at the all-cap text from Atlas. CLIENT EMERGENCY.

"Shit."

"Everything okay?"

She peers up at Solomon, who's watching her carefully. "I have to go," she says helplessly. "I have to fix something for a client."

His brow furrows. "Are you sure?" he asks, looking like he's on the verge of saying more.

No.

She's not sure.

Not at all.

"It'll be quick. Just..." She forces a smile, going for reassuring. Unbothered. Because that's what she is, right? About all of this.

Her baby, her career, her looming parenthood—unbothered.

She swipes at him like a gnat, aching to get him out of here before she combusts. "Go have lunch at the tiki bar. I'll meet you when I'm finished."

"*Tess.*"

"Please, Solomon. Go, okay? I'll be right there."

Then, without a second glance in his direction, she turns and strides into the open elevator, leaving the hot sear of Solomon's dark blue eyes on her and the rest of his questions behind.

Chapter Twelve

Solomon has to admit it. He's a hell of a lot cooler.

Resting the shopping bags on the seat beside him, Solomon settles into a chair at the tiki bar-themed restaurant overlooking the water. The place is quiet. A sign advertising the bar's famous pineapple man drink—the one Tessie's been talking about for the last two days—hangs on the turquoise wall. A gentle breeze floats in from the ocean. The bartender mixes a tropical fruit concoction that would have Howler wincing.

Solomon orders a beer and a burger, even though hunger is the last thing on his mind.

Regret tightens his chest as he inspects the empty seat beside him.

Tessie.

She should be here. With him.

A smile tips his lips before he can smother it.

Today has been damn fun. More fun than he deserves.

He didn't want to like their little shopping spree, but he enjoyed himself. Arguing over flip-flops, Tessie flushed and stammering, trying on clothes he never would have touched in a million years in Chinook. He hasn't had that much fun since, hell, the night he met Tessie. The girl's a lick of fire, burning up his bloodstream. Messing up all his plans, changing the way he thinks about life and himself.

And Christ, the way she touched him, running her small palm down his beard, the soft swell of her stomach pressing against him, the flush of her cheeks, had him sporting a hard-on the size of Texas.

He rolls his shoulders, annoyed by the thought. Annoyed by his attraction.

She's not his problem.

So why does he feel responsible for her? Why does he want to keep her close? He's here in Mexico to figure out the best arrangement for his son, yet since the day he met Tessie, she's been like sunshine dancing across his skin. He wants to bask in her.

Is she relaxing? Is her asshole boss giving her a break? Did she have time to eat lunch?

Frowning at the thought, Solomon checks his watch. It's well past one. If his stomach's grumbling, what about Tessie? He doesn't like the thought of her hungry. She's pregnant. She should be eating. Resting too. The dark circles under her eyes that makeup can't hide are still there. She was up until two last night, the telltale glow of a lamp shining from beneath her bedroom door.

He glances over his shoulder—well aware he's acting like an overprotective bastard—checking for Tessie, wanting to see her breeze through the door, her long legs striding straight for him. He scowls, hating the damn Pavlovian response he has to the click-clack of her high heels.

"¿Una cerveza más?"

"Si. Gracias." He nods at the server who's delivering his burger. "Can I get one of those to go," he asks, pointing at the chalked cartoon drawing of the pineapple. "No alcohol."

"Si, señor."

Solomon picks up his burger, puts it down. It feels unfair to eat when Tessie isn't here to enjoy it with him.

To pass the time, he grabs up his phone. His big fingers swipe across the screen, and then minutes later, he's downloading the baby app Tessie showed him. A pastel-colored app that blooms like a rose when it loads. He inputs the information he knows and is met with a variety of irritating chimes and chirps and coos. "Christ," he mutters, ducking his head as a server frowns in his direction.

Solomon keeps swiping, zeroing in on a cheery article about preparing for baby. The overwhelming amount of information has him rubbing at a sudden ache in his chest. He doesn't know how to do this. But he wants to do this. It's bad enough he's missed doctor's appointments and choosing a name. The idea of missing any other firsts leaves him with a bad taste in his mouth. But now he's here, he knows, and dammit, he wants to support Tessie.

He wouldn't have it any other way.

As he's scrolling through a post about off-limit foods for pregnant women, his screen lights up again.

Howler.

After a second of hesitation, he answers, thanking Christ his best friend isn't here to see him. He'd give him shit for days about the clothes he's wearing. But it would be worth it. Solomon fights a smile. The memory of Tessie laughing and clapping stirs something inside him.

Fuck.

"What?" he says, lifting the phone to his ear.

"Aren't we chatty. How's the sunshine state?"

"That's Florida. How's Peggy?"

Howler laughs. "Still a hound dog. Had to keep her inside the last few days, seeing as we're having a little wildlife problem."

Solomon tips his head back and groans. "You got bears again? I told you to put locks on those damn dumpsters."

"Yeah, yeah, I know. Miller's on it after he finishes prep."

"Miller?"

"New hire."

Solomon frowns. Yeah, Howler needs a chef, but hiring Miller Fulton, a kid who doesn't know the difference between margarine and butter, is just asking for trouble. "When did this happen?"

"Don't worry about Miller, man. When are you coming home?"

"A couple of days. We're still talking about the baby."

"You sure it's yours?"

He bristles. At every word. The *It*. The implication that Tessie's lying, leading him on.

Solomon grinds his molars. "Yeah, mine. A boy."

Here and now, he puts to bed any doubt. And he'll shut down anyone thinking otherwise.

"That's great man." But the comment is dubious. Teeming with doubt. "Claiming that offspring, Sol, it's a noble thing to do."

Solomon pinches the bridge of his nose. No doubt this would send his asshole business partner running. The only thing keeping him in check in life is the bar.

"You figure shit out with Goldilocks?"

He drags a hand down his face. "Not yet."

Howler's voice drops an octave. "You think she just wants money?"

"Don't say that about her," he barks.

"What?" The voice on the other end of the line is strained. "You crushing on your baby mama?"

Solomon snaps his mouth open, searching for a retort. Fuck. But what can he say? That Tessie's more than a woman carrying his child? She's—she's Tessie. Impossible to crack but impossible to ignore. He couldn't if he tried.

"That's none of your goddamn business," he growls.

"Whatever you say." Howler sounds amused. "So figure it out. Then come home. Easy."

A sinkhole opens in the pit of Solomon's stomach.

Easy.

Fuck. Nothing about this is easy.

He and Tessie don't have shit worked out between them. He should be ready to hop the next plane back to Chinook, and yet the thought of leaving his son, that baby, has him bringing a hand to his chest to rub at the tight pressure building.

And what about Tessie?

Stop.

He had his chance. With Serena. And he lost it. He lost her.

Hurting someone else... he can't let that happen.

The only connection between Tessie and him is their son. End of story.

Solomon has to figure this out and then leave. He has a home, family, friends, even if his own life has been on pause for the last seven years. Even if the thought of leaving Tessie has left him colder than the burger in front of him.

Shifting in his seat, he ends the call. His heartbeat is unsteady. So are his thoughts.

Time's ticking. Time to talk about Bear. To figure out where they stand.

One more day.

And then he'll get the hell out of Mexico. Before he does something stupid like fall for a beautiful blond in high heels.

One more hour. That's what she told herself three hours ago.

Tessie groans and rubs her brow, her wistful gaze on the ocean beyond the terrace. The late afternoon sunshine streams in, as if beckoning her outside. But the beach will have to wait. For now, she has a full-on office set up in the suite. Her laptop lies on the couch. Her sketchpad on her lap. Cell phone and headset perched on the coffee table.

She's almost finished with this unannounced project. Almost free. After this, she'll put it all away and enjoy her vacation. She needs food. Except for a hastily scarfed granola bar, she and Bear haven't had much of anything. She's starving. She could hoover an entire plate of tacos.

Her mind moves to Solomon. To what he's doing. Wishing she were with him instead of dealing with design disasters. She can't help but grin at the thought of him standing in the middle of the boutique like a big giant who let her dress him. The memory of his body obscene. Impractical. Distracting.

Her laptop chimes. An incoming Zoom call from Atlas.

She sighs and pulls her laptop onto her thighs. "Hi, Atlas," she says, accepting the call, ready to smile her way through another one of his inane power sessions. "I just sent off the sketch."

He wrinkles his nose in distaste. "I received it. Five minutes late."

She lets the dig go. "Good. So, if that's all—"

"Listen, Truelove. I just got a call from Ben Moreno."

She wrinkles her nose as she thinks on it. "The restauranteur?"

"You know it. He saw your segment on *Access Hollywood* and wants you to design his newest hotel."

Her jaw drops at his news, a sense of pride filling her up. "That's—that's great. I can start as soon as I'm back in LA."

"That won't work for him. He wants to get started yesterday." Atlas snaps his fingers, signaling for another coffee. "I set up a Zoom call for four p.m. I want you to do a virtual walk-through with him of the space."

"But. But that will take all day."

"And?" His glare dares her to say no. "Are you confused, Truelove? This is crisis mode. Crisis mode doesn't wait for vacation. You know that."

"I do, Atlas. But this was *approved*. This has been on the schedule for months." Aggravation pulses through her. This is her last trip without a child, before she becomes a mother. Plus, she and Solomon still have so much to work out.

"I need *you*, Truelove. I need my best designer on this. I need you to get this done. If you don't. . ." One well-plucked brow arches knowingly.

Tessie clenches her fists. Visions of violence dance in her head. Visions of hitting Atlas in his smug little face. Strike that. Hiring Solomon to punch him in the face with his hammer of a fist. Still, even with Atlas acting like an asshole, she isn't the type to complain about work. This isn't just her profession, it's her personality.

To let go...

She exhales, giving in. "Fine."

"Good. Four p.m., Truelove. Don't be late," he snips.

For minutes after he disconnects, Tessie sits, hands balled on her knees, knowing she should work, but her body won't move.

Frustration and anger have hot tears building in the backs of her eyes. This is bullshit. She can't even take a seven-day break to focus on her baby and herself. She's in Mexico, in a literal paradise, and yet, she's practically a caged animal. Unable to escape from her job, the pressure, the cutthroat fight to make it to the top, when she really isn't sure it's what she even wants anymore.

What she does want is to be outside enjoying the beach. But instead, she's working her ass off for the asshole of the century. A toxic monster who doesn't appreciate her hard work. Who will never understand what it takes to be a single working mother. Who's been calling her Terrible Tess for years, when in reality, he's the terrible one.

She can almost see her future conjured up in a crystal ball. And it's not good. It's not happy.

What's going to happen when Bear's sick? When he's in school and she needs time off for parent-teacher conferences or spring break? When he has a little league game and she's late? The thought slices like a razor blade, has her cradling her stomach. Panic and despair ripple through her.

She's so tired of working hard and never getting ahead. Of juggling. Her pregnancy. Her job. Her emotions. She's sick of rushing, of never living in the moment, of doing this all alone. All she wants to do is enjoy her pregnancy and her baby and her vacation.

A fire curls deep inside her. In her soul, she wants to be the woman she was the night she met Solomon. Take risks. Rebel. See stars. And her job most definitely is not her star.

Not anymore.

The only one who matters is Bear.

Palms to her stomach, she looks down at Bear. Determination fills her. "Fuck that guy," she tells her belly. "We're getting dressed up and we're going to go eat."

It's so right and so wrong at the same time: shutting her laptop. She's going out. She is.

She'll put on her most expensive dress, find Solomon, and then go to the most extravagant restaurant, eat three lobsters—because it's all-inclusive or bust, baby—and then walk and walk along the beach until evening comes and she can see her stars.

Scrambling up, Tessie rushes into the bedroom to change. She kicks out of the hotel slippers like she's doing the can-can and grabs up her dress, an expensive bodycon dress that she saved a month's paycheck for, a dress that makes her feel sexy as hell.

She steps into it.

Pulls it up. And—

Gasps.

She can't get it up past her bump.

Can't breathe. Can't move.

She's stuck.

"Shit," she swears, tugging at the dress that's now suction-cupped to her stomach like a pumped-up blood pressure cuff. She jerks her arms. Flails. But it's useless. "Oh. God. *Oh no, no, no, no.*"

A hot and panicky feeling overwhelms her. As she squirms to escape the fabric's constricting clutch, she catches her reflection in the floor-length mirror. A fumbling woman in unflattering hotel light, a stuffed sausage in a dress. Wild eyes, limp hair hanging across her shoulders.

The growl of her stomach snaps her out of her daze. Has her dropping her chin in dismay.

If she's hungry, her baby's starving.

Oh God.

She's starving him.

Already, she's traded work for her son. The rabid little beast inside her needs a meal, and she's forgotten all about him.

Hot tears spring to her eyes. She hasn't even fed her baby yet.

What kind of mother is she?

Despair and doubt well inside her like a flood. Months and months of fears and anxieties that she's stomped down deep with the toe of her high-heeled shoe claw their way up from the pit in her stomach.

She's terrible. Terrible Tess. And she's going to be a terrible mother.

How will she do this alone?

She can't even change her dress without getting stuck in it. She doesn't even have Solomon's number to call him for help. Because she doesn't have friends. She doesn't have people who stick around. She doesn't even have sex anymore, and she's so, so horny, even driving down an old dirt road could get her off.

What if she lived truly in the moment like Solomon? What if she loved like Ash? What if she let life be and participated instead of going through the motions? What if she never finds her stars?

The crying hits her like a flood. Hot tears stream down her cheeks as she spirals into a Five-Mile Island meltdown.

She tries to sit on the edge of the bed, but her dress is so tight she can't even have that little dignity.

Instead, Tessie collapses to the ground in a pile of fabric and lets out a wail. All she wants to do is cry. She doesn't feel glowy; she doesn't feel ready for this baby; and she certainly doesn't feel sexy.

She wants to climb off the terrace, run to the beach, hitch a ride on a buoy, and take it out to sea. Sail away.

Far, far away.

Chapter Thirteen

Pineapple man mocktail in his hand, Solomon opens the door to the suite and steps inside, only to be hit by the most terrifying sound in the world.

Crying.

Tessie's crying.

A broken wail comes from the bedroom. The sound has Solomon's pulse spiking.

"*Tessie?*" he shouts, barely having time to set the pineapple man down haphazardly before lunging into the bedroom.

He finds her slumped on the floor like a wilted Cinderella, draped in a mess of black fabric.

"Tess?" He kneels at her feet, his hands held out because he doesn't know where to put them. "What is it? What's wrong?"

"Go away, Solomon." Keeping her head down, still sniffling, she lifts a hand, shooing him.

"You're crying," he says, idiotically stating the obvious.

"So?" She wipes her wet eyes, still refusing to look at him. "I always cry. I love crying."

His focus goes to her stomach, cradled in her arms as silent sobs rack her shoulders. A rock builds in his throat, and he can barely get the words, words that threaten to strangle him, out. "Is something wrong with the baby?"

Fear fills him, unhinging him at the notion of anything terrible ever happening to his son.

"No," she says with a shake of her blond head. "It's me. I'm wrong. I'm a mess."

He frowns. "That's the exact opposite of what you are."

"How do you know? You don't even know me." She lifts her face. Her eyes are puffy and red-rimmed. "All I do is push people away. I don't know how to let anyone in." She hugs her belly. "What if I push Bear away? What if I do everything wrong? What if he hates me?"

"No one could hate you."

"You hate me."

His jaw drops. Jesus. Like a knife to his chest. "I don't hate you." Chancing it, he tucks a lock of her long blond hair behind her ear. Then he lowers himself to sit beside her. "Sure, we're still figuring things out, but. . .I could never hate you."

"All I've done today is work," she says. "I haven't even seen the beach. My feet hurt." In a smaller voice, "I can't get out of my dress. I'm stuck. I feel like a hippo."

He tries not to smile. "You are very much not a hippo."

"I am. I'm like a. . .wobbly babushka doll." A despondent look crosses her face. "I'm pregnant and alone, Solomon. No one wants me. No one wants to *touch* me."

His heart breaks at the honest anguish in her voice. How can she think she's anything other than beautiful? Any man would be lucky to be in her orbit.

"I'm trying to be okay, but I'm by myself every night and every morning, and it just. . .it feels so sad." Her voice snags on the word. "It's so lonely."

The doubt in her voice, the fear, the raw vulnerability, hits him like a sledgehammer. She's single. Doing this pregnancy thing alone. Christ, how long has it been since she's been touched? Since she's been complimented? Except for Ash, no one's been around to help her. Hell if that wouldn't take a toll on a person.

Scooting close, he nudges her chin up with a massive finger

until she's forced to meet his gaze. "You are beautiful, Tessie. The most beautiful woman I have ever seen."

Her brown eyes widen. "I am?"

"You are. And you can do this."

Tears sparkle on her long lashes. "But what if I can't?" She sniffles. "I work too much. I can't even keep an air plant alive."

He stays quiet, letting her get it out.

"I don't know what I'm doing. I pretend to all the time. I pretend to be brave. I'm not really like that. I just. . ." She drops her head into her hands. "I'm scared. I'm scared to give birth. I'm scared of what type of mother I'll be. I'm scared to lose Bear. Or leave him. What if"—a sob tears out of her and her face crumples—"I'm just scared."

There's so much he wants to unpack, but right now, it's not about him. Solomon gathers her into his arms, and she doesn't resist. She sags against him, the warmth of her petite frame a comfort he didn't know he needed.

"Listen to me," he rasps.

She peers up at him, her big, beautiful brown eyes filled with tears.

"It's okay to be scared. But the one thing I know is that you're going to be a goddamn great mother."

She smiles wanly. "How do you know that?"

"Because I've spent two days with you, and already, I see it." He palms her face, making sure she hears him. "I see it in all the ways you care for Bear. Hell, he's not even in the real world yet, and already, you're there for him."

Her body goes soft against him, relaxing. So he keeps talking.

"And I'll tell you another thing too."

"What's that?"

"You're not alone. I'm right here with you. I know you think I'm leaving, but I'm not. I'm going to be a father to my son and help you with whatever you need." He pulls her closer, smoothing her hair. "Tell me what you need, Tess, and I'll do it. I'll give you anything."

He's lost all control. Anything she asks, he'll be at her beck and call. He thinks of the pineapple man melting on the counter and knows he'll do all kinds of stupid shit to make her happy.

She considers him, then whispers, "I need to get out of this dress."

He nods. "I'm good at getting women out of dresses."

She laughs, and Solomon's chest tightens. He wants to make her laugh for the rest of her life if it'll take that sad look off her gorgeous face.

He heaves himself off the floor and helps her stand. She does so with a wobble and a quiet groan. Then she's in front of him, half-naked. Solomon tries not to stare, but it's impossible. Even stuck in a dress, Tessie looks beautiful. The top half of the bodice droops down her belly, exposing a lace bra. Her breasts high swells of creamy, lush flesh.

He slides a finger between the fabric and her belly. It's tight, cutting off circulation and making him frown. It's hurting her. His hands go to the small of her back, grazing her smooth skin, searching for a zipper, only to find none.

He clears his throat. "I'll have to rip it."

She pouts dramatically. "Oh God."

He cocks a brow. "Worth more than my life?"

She quirks a smile. "Something like that." Then she closes her eyes and inhales a tenacious breath. "Do it, Solomon."

He steps close, looping his arms around her small frame. For a second, they sway, holding one another, her body so warm against his. Then, getting a careful grip on the slinky fabric, he gathers it in his hands.

Then, muscles bulging, he tears.

Tessie squeals. Her hands grip his shoulders as she doubles over. Her entire body racks. But she's not crying. She's laughing. One of the most beautiful sounds Solomon's ever heard.

The dress splits down the back, relinquishing its tight hold on her stomach. He lets it drop to the floor, where the fabric puddles at her feet.

"There," he rasps, pulling back. "You're free."

She lifts her face, her full lips pulled into a wobbly smile. "Please never tell anyone about this. Ever."

"Your secret's safe with me."

She takes in the limp pile of fabric on the floor. Only Solomon stares at Tessie. Nearly naked. Pouty lips. Wild hair. Mouthwatering. In black lace panties and a sheer black bra, she's one goddamn stunning pregnant woman. Not like he's seen many near-naked pregnant women, but on Tessie, it fits. It's mesmerizing. The same lithe body he touched six months ago, with just a bump of a beautiful belly.

She holds her hands to her chest, something raw and vulnerable moving across her features. "Thank you, Solomon."

He evaluates her tear-stained face. "What else do you need?" he asks thickly.

Anything. Anything she wants, he'll give it.

She hesitates. "A hug?"

"I can do a hug." He hates the gruffness in his voice, a tight constriction that betrays nothing, when really, it's all he's wanted to do since he saw her in that lobby. Hug her. For a long damn time.

Her face shy and soft, she lifts a toned leg to step out of the dress, then shuffles toward him. He opens his arms, and she melts into his embrace with a content sigh.

Solomon's breath catches at the feel of her. Petite. Perfect. She fits perfectly in his arms. The curve of her cheek pressed up against the center of his chest. The soft swell of her stomach warm and heavy against him.

They sway, and it's like the night they danced under the stars at the Bear's Ear bar. Nothing existed except them. Nothing mattered. Only the girl in his arms and her heartbeat syncing with his.

Tessie shifts her hips, sinking deeper into the hug. He hides a smile when she inhales and buries her face in his shirt. Every fragile, vulnerable ounce of her is pressed into his large frame.

Instantly, he's hard.

Gritting his teeth, Solomon closes his eyes, willing away the steel rod in his pants. This girl needs an embrace, not a damn erection poking her in the stomach.

"Mmm." Tessie's voice comes muffled against his chest. "You give good hugs."

He grunts. Makes a note. "Good."

She pulls back and looks up at him.

Unable to help it, he cups her cheek, stroking a thumb across the high arch of her cheekbone. "What else do you need?"

She swallows. Then says, "I need sex."

His brain short-circuits into a *what-the-fuck* scramble, then comes back online.

"Christ."

"I know. I'm awful for asking." Two tears slip down Tessie's cheeks. Misunderstanding his ragged swear, she flattens her small hand against his chest. "Please. We did it once. We can do it again." She bites her lip. "I just. I need to get off."

God, does he want to. Take her to bed, fuck her quick and hard, and then long and soft. Feel every fucking inch of her gorgeous, glowing body against his.

"I'm so horny. I haven't had sex since. . .well, us."

There it is. In her eyes.

Wild desire.

She needs gentle and she needs hard and she needs someone. And damn if that isn't him. Fuck. It has to be him. The thought of her having sex with anyone else is like a bucket of ice water dousing his erection.

He takes her face in his hands, the curve of her cheek fitting like a key in a lock. "You need this?"

"I do." She presses up on tiptoes, her small palm on his beard. "I really, really do."

Her eyes, big, brown, beseeching. The way she's looking at him—he's got no damn chance.

And then he's seizing her by the elbows, hauling her to his chest, kissing her like she's man's last breath. Not tentative or timid. Needy. Desperate.

Her kiss ignites him. Every male urge long buried is lit up with lust.

He liked her kiss six months ago, and hell if he doesn't love it now.

A groan rips out of him, and he tightens his grip. She slips her tongue into his mouth, winding her slender arms around his neck. Flames dance around them, the sunset outside casting slanted rays through the windows.

"Solomon." Tessie gasps, whipping back. "Oh God, oh thank you," she says, her eyes wide and wet, her smile dazed and ecstatic.

Then she squeals and goes back in for round two. She's hungry. Desperate hands all over him, up his shirt, skimming his waistband. Pressing herself, her full breasts, against him like she can mold to his body. Sucking his lower lip into her mouth like some gorgeous feral creature.

He's ready for it.

He kisses her deeper, roughly, his hands roaming her ribs, the soft swell of her stomach, her slender neck. He shakes as he inhales her delicious scent. Coconut and sunshine. Like he's holding heaven in his arms. Gold. Stardust.

Tessie.

Bad idea? Maybe. But he wants her to have this. Wants to give her something that will make her feel better, and if that's him, he won't complain.

Because the truth is, he wants this as much as she does. It's all he's thought about since Bear's Ear. Her memory wrecked him, had him taking his hand to himself in the shower more times than he can count. And now she's here, asking him to pleasure her, and hell if that's not what he's going to do.

Strike that.

Worship her.

Because she needs this. He can feel the crave in the arch of her slender, naked body writhing against him. All kinds of hungry. Starved.

"Tessie, baby, hold up," he growls, using all the willpower in the world to pull back from her sweet mouth. "If we're doing this, we're doing it right. We're doing it for you."

He wants to show her she's the most gorgeous woman he's ever seen. Even pregnant. *Especially* pregnant. Because her body is like nothing else. Feminine and wild and lush.

Dazed brown eyes meet his, her lips plump and wet from kissing. She takes a step forward. "Then let's do it," she murmurs, reaching behind her to tug off her bra in one smooth move, leaving her breasts bare.

His throat closes up on him, shattered at the sight of her near-naked body.

Her breasts. They're fucking perfect. Dark nipples. Full and pink, like sweet peaches in June.

He takes two fast strides to her, letting out a growl that's both primal and protective.

He gets on his knees. In front of her where he belongs. With greedy hands, he grips her lithe thighs. She makes a little moan at the contact. Dipping forward, he sweeps his mouth against her skin, pressing a kiss against the swell of her stomach. Tessie shivers, giving a broken whimper.

"That feels good." Her hands go to his hair, fisting the dark strands. "So good."

At her ragged voice, his cock twitches like a son of a bitch. It wants out, wants more, but he wills it to play down-boy.

"Sit," he commands.

Without argument, she does, her face exultant.

On the edge of the bed, she positions herself, all regal elegance, slim lines, and small stomach. Her long blond hair drips down her shoulders. Solomon moves between her legs, gripping her hips to jerk her into him before taking her breast in his mouth. Tessie arches under his touch, going limp, and he palms the small of her back to hold her up. Her eyes are closed, a pink flush on her cheeks as he traces her breast, the hard bead of her nipple, with his mouth.

A moan of consternation falls from her bee-stung lips when he finally pulls away.

Placing a gentle palm on the channel of her chest, he lays her on the bed. "Stay," he orders.

Once more, he gets between her thighs, this time spreading her knees.

He plans to scratch every itch she has. Starting with this one.

He presses a hand against the sheer mesh of her panties. He feels her pulse against him, feels her slick wetness. Her juices drip down her thighs. Dipping his head, Solomon licks up a line of her sweetness, a soft mewl coming from the woman on the bed.

"Is this okay?" he asks, lifting his head.

Tessie props herself on her elbows and peers over her belly, eyes bright, her mouth a pink pulse of *yes, yes, yes.*

Solomon's cock surges in his pants as he presses his lips to her soft pussy. Jesus Christ. She's so damn wet. And goddamn, does she taste good. He shakes as he inhales her feminine scent. He wants it in his beard. The smell of her. The kind of scent that brands him, leashes him.

Hooking a thumb in the waistband of her panties, he drags them off and over her toned legs, groaning at what he sees. A waxed landing strip. Delicate blond hair. Slipping his broad hands beneath her ass, he briefly curses himself for the roughness of his calluses on her velvet skin. He pulls her closer, into him, and then glues his mouth to her pussy. Sticking a tongue into her sweet softness has Tessie whining his name. Her hands, her nails, tear at his hair, and at the rough sensation, Solomon damn near explodes.

Still, he keeps it together. She's a dream. His dream. And he's determined to make her enjoy every damn minute of this. She deserves it.

Tessie's hungry, and he's gonna feed her.

He works her over with his tongue, making smooth concentric circles on her clit. The rise of her body leads him. He takes her higher, brings her to the edge, and then pulls back. She cries out, the sharp sound snapping him like a whip. Her knuckles are white as she grips the sheet corner, her breath coming in small puffs of air, her lips a pink O of desire.

Solomon growls, her pleasure feeding his, and then molds his mouth to her clit and sucks.

A shocked cry rips from Tessie's mouth. Her hips arch, her body bucks, and she's rising off the bed, levitating, her form a tremble of ecstasy, before she goes limp on the bed.

She lies there for a few long seconds, her eyes closed, a smile on her face.

Solomon straightens up and waits for her.

Tessie, her expression glazed, sits up. She sways for a long minute. The flush she wears on her cheeks carries across her collarbone, her breasts.

A grin Solomon hasn't felt in a long time overtakes his face.

Then, looking like a hot-as-sin carnivorous angel, Tessie lifts her arms and reaches for him. "More," she pants. "More."

Solomon comes to her outstretched arms like a beckoning.

A beginning.

The sight of his six-foot-four frame looming over her has her nipples tightening. His eyes are dark and hungry; he's a man locked on a target. The veins in his arms corded wires she wants to suck on. To lick. Be electrified by. She's already halfway there.

As he approaches, his face is stoic, but the bulge in his board shorts is obvious.

She smiles. She's still got it. Pregnant or not. And she's never felt so sexy. The way he ripped that dress from her body. Like that Tessie she was searching for in the Bear's Ear bar. No inhibitions. Ready to ask for what she wanted—not just in her career, but in her life.

Now. Now she's pregnant, sprawled naked on the bed with the biggest, most bearded man she's ever seen.

Solomon dips, bracing his palms on the bed, his arms caging her in.

She shivers.

He's built like a tank. The words that work their way out of him are gruff. "Now what?"

An ungodly groan comes out of her mouth.

"We kiss. I need the dopamine," she gasps before attacking his mouth. The lips that meet hers are warm and full and taste of salt and beer and *her*. His broad hands tangle in her hair, gentle, ever so gentle.

Her body simmering with impatience, Tessie claws at his shirt like a horny pregnant hell beast. God. She can't get enough. He's like drinking water.

But hot. He's so hot and she's burning alive.

She moans, threading her hands through his dark hair, reveling in the way he kisses her down to her overworked and overwrought soul.

He tastes like the mountains. Pine and icy air. His kiss dry tinder igniting through her bones.

God. She can't wrap her spinning mind around it. Who'd have thought this mountain caveman would be all smooth moves and clever fingers? Hot tears threaten to fill her eyes. It's been so long since she's felt sexy. Cared for. Happy. She wants to break down and bawl like a baby. But she can't. Not yet.

Because she's horny as hell.

She came once, and goddamn if she isn't going to come again.

One night. Get him out of her system. Get laid. Because sweet horny Lord, if she doesn't, she's going to spontaneously combust.

Tessie pulls back and gets up on her knees. "Sex, Solomon." She tugs at his arm, writhes on the bed, desperate for him. Makes grabby hands. Always grabby hands for Solomon. Her body feels like it's on a paint shaker set at max speed. "Sex. Now."

A chuckle rolls out of him. "Easy, baby. I got you."

Eyes on her, he stands, straightens his broad shoulders, and then makes quick work of his clothes.

Off goes his shirt. His rugged frame looms in front of her. Tattoos cover his chiseled arms, like vines wrapped around taut, tan muscle. Brightly colorful, a strange contrast to his handsome, serious face.

Her jaw drops at the same time her gaze does.

His board shorts are gone. A painful-looking erection stands at attention like a yes-sir soldier. Her eyes bug. He's huge.

Hers.

She shakes off the thought.

Not hers. No.

This is just a favor. A really, really feel-good favor.

Her hands fly to her belly. *God, he's gonna split her in half.*

Solomon curses. "Shit. I don't have a condom."

"I can't get pregnant." She bites her lip, hoping he doesn't change his mind. If he does, she'll absolutely explode. "I'm clean. I've had all the tests."

He swallows, still staring at her. "I haven't been with anyone since you, Tessie."

She shivers at the weight of his words. They're just words. And yet, they're heavy. With possibility. Need. Reverence.

And against every anti-love objection in her body, she adores them.

Stepping up, Solomon clutches her tight in his arms. "Is this going to hurt you?" he rasps, his eyes soft as he watches her in concern.

"No. I don't know." She considers it, laughs. "I've never had pregnant-sex before." Wiggling in his arms, she extends a leg like a gymnast testing its flexibility. "I don't even know how. . ."

A rare half grin splits his lips. "We'll figure it out."

And then the bed's shifting and she's swaying, but she's steadied, caught by Solomon's big hands gripping her thighs and pulling her on top of him to straddle his waist.

"This comfortable, baby?"

On top?

A rush of a pleased breath tears out of her. "Yes," she says, scooting into a prime position. He makes a pained sound in the back of his throat as she runs her wetness across his thigh, like a mark of her territory. A claiming that breaks all the rules, all the boundaries.

Just tonight. Just sex.

Tessie tips forward to kiss him but is stopped by her belly. A laugh bubbles out of her. "So no foreplay, then?"

Solomon chuckles.

Reaching back, she strokes the hard length of his cock. A strangled growl erupting, he grits his teeth and shakes his head. "This is about you."

About her? God, could this man be any more perfect?

A dark husk from Solomon. "Stop me if I hurt you."

She meets his worried eyes. "You won't."

Then, lifting herself, she sinks onto his cock, the hard length of him making her whimper.

A guttural moan rips out of Solomon. His dark blue eyes dusky with desire, his hands tremble as he grips her hips and yanks her tighter against him. He holds her steady. Like he'll never let her go.

"*Christ, you're gorgeous,*" he grits out. "Goddamn woman, what you do to me. . ."

Her body humming, Tessie throws her head back, sucking

him in, taking him in deep. Small palms pressed against his broad chest, his thatch of dark hair, she rocks, undulating against him.

Solomon keeps his dark gaze locked on her. The sheer ache. His handsome face, his tender expression...he's starved. Been hungry for so long. He needs this as much as she does.

She spreads her thighs and rocks. His hips grind and pump in solidarity, his slow and measured thrusts sending jolts of pleasure to her very core. He's so deep, hitting all the right angles that have her body singing like a song.

"Oh God, Solomon...yes. Like that. Keep going. Don't stop. Please. *Please.*"

She's pleading, moaning like a lovesick girl, but she doesn't care. She wants everything he can give her, and she wants it now.

"Rough or soft, Tessie? You call it. You tell me, baby. Tell me what you need."

Her eyes practically roll back in her skull.

"Harder," she demands. "Fuck me harder, Solomon."

He all but growls his approval.

Pumping deep, he plows into her, nearly lifting her off the bed, but he grips her thighs, keeping her secure. She pushes back, grinding against him. A white-hot current arcs between them as their movements sync up.

She drinks in the look on his face. Heated blue eyes, one corner of his bearded mouth lifting in smug satisfaction.

She's happy. He's happy.

Just like the night at the Bear's Ear bar. Two broken people with axes to grind.

And she sees him—straining against his release, holding on for her, and it only turns her on more. All he's doing, it's for her. No one's ever put her first.

No longer able to control herself, Tessie whispers, "Don't wait. I'll come with you. I'm ready."

A roar rips out of him. "*Tessie.*"

"Solomon." She whispers it.

It's his undoing. His name on her lips.

When Solomon's hoarse shout sounds, she lets herself go. She throws her head back, closes her eyes, and cries out. Every limb, every organ tremors. Warmth builds in her, bursts of color spark in her vision. A delicious, glorious euphoria racks her body. Saps every last ounce of her energy.

Down for the count, Tessie sways.

Solomon moves quickly, gathering her up in his arms before she topples over. Every muscle in his toned body flexes as he rolls her over, easily maneuvering her into a more comfortable position propped up against the pillows.

His rugged voice rakes over her. "I'll be right back."

Tessie lies there, eyes on the ceiling, her heartbeat pounding in her jugular, as she comes down from her high. Her emotions jump ship. Straight-up overboard. Tears pool at her lashes. It's been so long since she's felt sexy. Cared for. Happy. And Solomon did that. He keeps waking her up. Making her live.

She lets out a sob, and then she bursts into tears.

Oh God. Oh shit. She's crying again.

Solomon returns with a warm washcloth, the bed shifting as he eases onto the mattress beside her. "Tess?" Worry stains his gruff drawl.

Even the gentle way he cleans her up has hot tears blurring her eyes again.

"I'm fine," she says, wiping her cheeks, but she's a leaky faucet that won't stop. She sits up. Takes in his beard, disheveled and wild. "I'm fine. I'm happy. You're the first person to make me feel sexy in a long time. I needed that. Thank you." She sniffles. "I'm sorry for the hormonal monster meltdown."

"There's nothing to be sorry for," he says firmly. "C'mere." Getting back into bed, he pulls a faux fur blanket around her and gathers her up against his broad chest. He lets her cry and he holds her. He doesn't tell her to stop or try to distract her.

How long has it been since she's let someone in? Let someone see her cry. Ache. Want. Has she ever?

And she's not embarrassed.

Because here, in Solomon's strong arms, she feels the safest.

She should get out of bed. Get out of his arms, snap out of it, and go back to work. She wants to regret it. But she doesn't. She can't. All she feels is incredibly grateful to Solomon for his...help? Understanding? Plowing into her like a freight train? Yeah. That.

Tomorrow.

She'll rein it in, pull it back tomorrow.

A graze against her belly makes her jump.

"Shit," Solomon mutters, his handsome face abashed. His hand held out and away from her abdomen. "Sorry, I shouldn't—"

"No. It's okay." A strange sort of softness opening in the pit of her stomach, she takes his large hand and presses it to her belly. "You can."

A breath shakes out of him like he can barely believe it.

Neither speak. They wait.

Tessie studies his palm splayed out on her stomach with curiosity. It's huge. Monstrous. Like a giant holding the world in his hand.

But for once, Bear's quiet.

She palms her stomach too. Side-eyes Solomon. "Think we scared him off?"

"That's a good sign. Kid knows when to lay low."

She laughs. "Yeah."

Despite his easy tone, he looks crestfallen.

"Now what do you need?"

Her breath catches. She turns her head to find him peering at her.

He keeps asking her that, and she's going to turn into a puddle pretty damn quick.

Nothing. Everything. Should she say it? She hesitates.

But then her traitorous mouth blurts, "You?"

He nods, his face going soft with an emotion she can't place. "You got me." He presses a kiss to her forehead, pulls back. "But first food. You hungry?"

She sits up on her elbows, the blanket draped across her like a slinky toga outfit. "Starved."

Solomon gives her a stern look of reproach. "You should have eaten earlier." On his feet quickly, he picks up the phone and paces the room as he rattles off a room service order. His large body a solid wall of tensing muscle. "There," he says, hanging up. "Ordered everything off the damn menu."

She smiles. "As one should."

His attention moves to the record player. He lifts a big finger. "Can I?"

She nods. "They're in the case."

Solomon shuffles through the three records she brought, finally settling on Hank Williams. Lonely, melodic music fills the suite. A strange contrast to the bright sun, the cheery atmosphere of the beach outside.

"You're from LA," comes his soft rumble of a voice. He climbs back into bed and pulls her into his brawny shoulder. She sighs, not fighting it. Her legs wouldn't work anyway, thanks to the way he knocked the gravity out of her.

One night.

She can do one night.

"So why country?"

She adjusts herself in his arms. Instead of her go-to defense—walls up—Tessie relents. Softens. They're having a child together. He should know a little about her. It's only fair.

"My mom worked in a country bar when I was a kid." Tessie smiles at the memory. "We'd sing along to the jukebox at the end of her shift, and it just stuck." Then she laughs and covers her face. "I used to have a fantasy that my dad was George Straight. How cringe is that?"

"What happened to your dad?"

"I don't remember him. He left us when I was two. Walked out for cigarettes and never came back." A sad laugh tumbles out of her. "If that's not a country song, I don't know what is."

Solomon frowns, tracing a line down her arm. "Damn. I'm sorry, Tess."

"It's fine. He didn't want my mom, and he didn't want me." She burrows into his large body, letting the faint strains of "I Saw the Light" chase away the pressure building behind her eyes. "We were better off without him."

The frown hasn't left Solomon's face, the wheels in his brain turning. "Your mom raised you alone."

"That's right." She nods. "She was a single mother, and she rocked that. She really did. Never missed a spelling bee. Or a recital. We always had enough money. I don't know how, but we did. She always took care of me. I always felt safe. I want to do that for Bear."

"You will."

"You're so certain." She cups his unruly beard. "So solemn."

He smiles, a small smile, but it softens his gruff demeanor. She likes them both. The soft Solomon and the hard. Because with him, either way, she feels safe.

He's quiet, listening. Waiting.

Tessie blows out a breath, pushing past the pit in her stomach. Even all these years later, it's not easy to talk about. But she wants to learn, to practice, so she can tell her son about one of the best people in the world. "My mom died when I was seventeen. Right before I went to college. She had breast cancer. She didn't catch it until it was advanced. One day, she was there, and then she was gone. It happened so fast. Sometimes I think she held on until I went to college so she knew I was set, and then she felt she could move on. Is that stupid?"

"No. That's not stupid." He strokes her hair. "Earlier today..." Solomon's body has gone still. "Is that why you said you're afraid to leave Bear?"

She swallows, her eyes burning. "The last words my mom said

to me were *I'll always be here*. And then she wasn't. She left me. It's not her fault but. . ." A tear drips down her cheek, and Solomon's powerful arms tighten around her, banding her to him. "I just love him so much. What if something happens to him? What if something happens to me?"

He kisses her hair, his reassuring rumble vibrating through her. There's a tenseness to his body she can't puzzle out. "Nothing will happen to you, Tessie. I won't let it."

For some reason, his words soothe her.

For some reason, she believes them.

"Your tattoos." Attention drifting, wanting to get away from the sad subject, Tessie dances her fingers up a mountaintop strikingly etched on his massive bicep. Dark crows over soft snow-white peaks. With a nail, she traces his colorful ink and the veins in his arms. "Is this Chinook?"

"Yeah." His voice takes on a proud tone. "Alpine mountains. There's a ridge right behind my cabin. We have everything. Ocean, beach, glaciers." He chuckles. "A paved road."

She snuggles against his shoulder. Her slender fingers curl into his dark chest hair. She loves that this serious, stern mountain man literally wears his heart on his sleeve. "Mmm. Sounds pretty."

"It is. I want to take Bear to Chinook." He looks at her close and amends his statement. "One day."

"You can," she says, slowly considering it. She sighs, reality settling on her like a lead weight. "We still have a lot to talk about before you go."

A harsh hitch of Solomon's breath, and when she glances up, that muscle's ticking in his jaw again.

Go.

A tumbleweed rolls in her stomach. One more day, and he's gone. But that's what she wanted, right? To figure this out, send him on his way, then enjoy the rest of her vacation in peace.

And when he goes—she'll what?

Be alone.

It's better this way. To not get attached.

A soft ping draws her attention. She groans as her phone's hit by a blast of light.

Atlas.

Perfect fucking timing, asshole.

She pushes against his chest, ready to roll out of his protective grasp, but he snags her wrist. "You're not getting that."

She looks up into his eyes, soft but intense.

"You need to rest," he orders. "It can wait."

She drops her hand. "Okay." She likes being bossed around by Solomon. There's something primal about it.

Not dropping her gaze, he says, "We'll figure it out. Your job and Bear."

"We will?" she whispers, trying to ignore the hard thump of her heart at the way he makes it *their* problem.

He runs a thumb across her cheekbone. "We will."

A knock on the door has Solomon leaving the bed, shrugging on a robe that barely fits his massive frame.

Tessie watches him go, a warmth churning in her stomach.

It's only six. Early. But God. Lounging in bed naked, watching the sunset with the roar of the ocean in her ears, ready to have a room service feast is the most decadent thing she's ever experienced.

She eyes her shredded dress in the corner of the room and presses fingertips to the smile that ghosts her lips.

She owes everything to that dress.

Chapter Fourteen

H*E DOESN'T HEAR HER. OR FEEL HER.*
Serena.
Only it's not Serena.
It's Tessie.
Tessie.
Solomon wakes with a jolt, his heart pounding. The bedroom is cast in dim gray light, that weird place that exists in the margins of time, telling him it's not yet morning, not yet night.

Beside him, rumpled sheets. An empty bed.

Groaning, he roughs a hand over his beard.

God damnit. It's the second time she's done that. Snuck out on him.

Disappeared.

Left.

Fear comes, creeping, running the length of his spine like a ghost.

A fear he dealt with after Serena died. That he didn't do enough. That it's his fault. He was the stubborn asshole who let her walk off after their fight.

He was supposed to protect her, and he failed.

He lost her.

After she died, everything bad crept in. Loneliness. Guilt. Fear.

It was why he moved to the cabin. He thought he could hide from the past. Because he couldn't stomach the memories, the road where it happened, that road he had to pass every damn day. So he got a dog, bought a punching bag, grew out his beard, drank bourbon by the bottle. Trying to find his way out of his pain. Shutting down. Shutting off. Woodworking. Worrying about his sisters and his parents. Hell, even Howler. Guy was going to get shanked by a one-night stand one of these days.

It's been his crutch—worry.

And now Tessie.

This girl, the baby she's carrying, trigger his protective instincts. Give him a whole new set of worries.

From the bed, he can see the light in the living room. Tessie's up.

A strange need-her-beside-him feeling wiggles its way into his bones. Made even stronger by their earlier conversation. Tessie's story about her mother, her worry about their son, the forlorn hurt in her voice when she told him about her father. He gets it. She was hurt. She burns because she's afraid to get burned.

There are so many layers to her. The little glimpses she keeps letting him see—he feels honored and sucker punched at the same damn time.

Fuck her father. Some sorry sonofabitch walking away from his own daughter—he doesn't deserve her.

Solomon shakes his head. He can't figure out what happens next. Why being with Tessie does something to him. She's in his bloodstream. A shot of sunlight waking him up.

Sleeping beside her, being with her tonight. . .he doesn't regret it.

Teeth gritted, he exhales and swings his feet off the bed, pulling in a deep breath to steady his pulse. He runs a hand through his hair, glances at the clock.

Three a.m.

Christ.

If she's working. . .

He tugs on gray sweatpants and storms into the living room,

only to find Tessie sitting cross-legged on the couch. A bottle of coconut oil beside her, her gaze on the open terrace doors.

Beautiful. So goddamn beautiful.

Stop. Stop looking at her like she's yours.

But why not, Solomon? Why can't she be?

"Hey," he says, squinting against the light. "Everything okay?"

Her big brown eyes widening at his appearance, she smiles up at him, and for a minute his heart stalls. She looks gorgeous as hell sitting there with messy bedhead and wearing nothing but a nightshirt open at the belly.

"Oh, yeah." Her hands make circles on her belly, spreading the coconut oil over her skin. "Thought I'd come out here to do my counts."

His brow furrows. "Counts?"

"Kick counts." She pauses. "You want ten kicks a day to make sure the baby's still, well, kicking in there."

A breath whooshes out of Solomon. *Fuck.* Day after day, he's realizing he knows less than he thought. Everything about pregnancy seems so tentative. Fragile. Christ, what if something goes wrong?

Bear and Tessie—not untouchable. Anything could happen to them.

Fear. Goddamn fear. It's doing something to his chest. Has his heart sputtering like a carburetor.

Why does it worry him so damn much? The kid's in there, and he's healthy and happy and safe. Thanks to this gorgeous woman. He looks at her, a strange feeling of tenderness overtaking him. All she's done for his son; he can't thank her enough. Doesn't know how to tell her, but he'll try.

"Well," he asks, aware he's been holding his breath. "Did you get them?"

"An hour ago." She peeks over her shoulder and nods at the pineapple man. The side of her mouth quirks. "Had a sip of juice. That always wakes him up."

He nods, says gruffly, "Thought you wanted one."

"I did." She studies his face. "Thank you, Solomon."

He shifts awkwardly. "You talked about it enough."

She rolls her eyes, but a smile plays on her lips. She sees right through him. Then, after a second, she scrunches up her face and hisses a breath.

"Does it hurt?" he asks, coming to sit beside her. "Bear moving around in there?"

He studies the curve of her belly. It looks like a glazed donut, glossy with coconut oil. A memory of earlier tonight, planting kisses on her smooth skin, running his tongue across the arc of her stomach, has his heart turning over in his chest.

"No." She sits up straighter, long blond hair waterfalling down one slender shoulder. "Most times it's fine. Other times, it feels...gross." She pulls her lips to one side, like she's searching her brain for an explanation, then continues. "When he rolls or tumbles, it's like he's scraping my spine." She laughs, probably at the face he's making. "I know it's weird. Everything about being pregnant is weird. It's like having a parasite inside you." She smiles and looks down at her belly. "A wonderful little parasite." From under her dark lashes, she regards him. "He's moving now. You—you want to feel him?"

The offer undoes him.

That girl. That damn sweet girl from the bar is still here. The pissed-off girl who bitched him out in the lobby two days ago is still there too. He's getting more familiar with both sides of Tessie Truelove. And he's liking them.

His throat works, but the words won't come. Instead, he makes a gruff sound of acknowledgment. He places a hand on the side of her smooth belly. Tessie's watching him, waiting for his reaction, and then he feels it. A bump, a flutter. Hell, a goddamn punch against his palm.

He laughs, and she jumps, blinking like she's never heard the sound come out of him before.

"Holy shit." He leans forward, staring in awe at her stomach. He watches, fascinated, as Tessie's skin ripples.

His kid.

His son.

There's a tiny miracle growing in there, kicking and moving around.

Rendered speechless, he stays like that, cupping the hard ball of her belly. The curve, the swell. His heart feels like it's getting the pulse bashed out of it by a wrecking ball.

In that instant, everything feels different. Real. Meant to be. The lines of his easygoing small-town life rearranged. And Solomon's finding the light on the other side of the tunnel and chasing it down. But instead of feeling like this strange new world is a bad tux he wants to shrug off, because Solomon and tuxes don't mix, he feels, well, fine. This is all fine with him.

Bear.

Tessie too.

"Kid's a powerhouse." He chuckles, his attention shifting from Tessie's face to her stomach when Bear does what he swears are three roundhouse kicks in a row. "Aren't you?"

She nods. "He is. He's got your muscles already."

"Next time you get up, wake me," he grunts, the closest he can come to voicing his fear of her sneaking off in the middle of the night. "I'm always awake."

She smiles. "You don't sleep? What, are you a vampire?"

He clears his throat, distracting himself from the mental image of his mouth on Tessie's throat.

Settling back into the couch, Tessie stretches, the shirt lifting to bare even more of her stomach. "Well, I have news for you, Solemn Man; I don't sleep either."

"That so?"

"Oh, it's very so." As if she's conjured it, a yawn pops out of her mouth. "It's the way of the pregnant woman. No sleep, fat feet, peeing every ten minutes, and copious amounts of crying."

He tucks a lock of hair behind her ear. "I can survive all of those, Pregnant Woman."

Tessie makes a little humming noise and curls up against his shoulder. "Tomorrow," she murmurs, drowsy. "We have to talk about Bear."

"We will," he says quietly, wrapping his arm around her. "Of course we will."

Minutes pass, and her eyelids shutter. Her breathing softens, evens out. He pulls her closer. The ocean crashes steadily in the darkness as Solomon's brain comes alive. He doesn't know what he's doing anymore. All he knows is he's got a gorgeous woman in his arms and tomorrow is going to come too damn soon for his liking.

Temporary, he reminds himself.

This vacation.

Tessie.

Everything—with the exception of his son—is temporary.

The sounds of mariachi music and the chaos that comes with a breakfast buffet blur the edges of Tessie's reality.

She sits across from Solomon at a white-tablecloth-covered table. Prim and proper and perfectly ignoring last night.

This morning, this breakfast, is all business. Not the memory of Solomon barging into her bedroom, panicked and out of breath, thinking she was in danger. Especially not the memory of two toe-curling orgasms.

She is on a tightly planned schedule with her career and her baby, and there is no room to pencil in a very hot, protective mountain man.

Not like she has to worry about him much longer. Because tomorrow, he's out of Mexico and bound for his mountains.

At the thought, her heart twists. She scowls down at her empty plate.

Stupid traitorous heart. Stupid tongue jumping down Solomon's throat.

Still. She refuses to be embarrassed. Refuses to regret it. She needed sex. Like water. Like air. A simple human need, and Solomon helped her out.

Just two people swapping body fluids with no strings attached.

But before baby talk, business talk.

"There." She extends her phone across the table.

Solomon takes it in his big hands. He reads the email. A politely worded missive to Atlas that states she will not be working on her vacation, when all she really wanted to type was GET FUCKED redrum style.

As Solomon reads, she surveys the restaurant, hoping to see the server with their meals. She's starving. Bear too. He kicks her stomach, just as impatient for a chocolate croissant as she is.

"You forgot something."

At the rumble of Solomon's deep voice, Tessie arches a brow. "What?" she asks, taking back her phone and scanning the words again.

"The line that says if he bothers you, I snap his legs."

She laughs, unable to help the delighted thrill that sweeps over her. "What are you, my personal bodyguard?"

Solomon grunts but doesn't disagree.

Still, she can't help but check her phone one last time.

Nothing. No message from Atlas.

"Tess," Solomon says, the scowl on his handsome face deepening.

"Okay, okay." She waves a hand, sticks her phone in her purse. "See? The phone's going away. You can't grump all day."

Not even this grouchy caveman can get her down.

The best sex of her life showed her the hallelujah light. Showed her the *why the hell is she working on vacation?* light. Showed her the *Atlas needs to be flung from a very high cliff* light.

Was she nervous sending the email? Of course. It's like detonating an atom bomb on her life.

But Solomon is right. It's what Ash has been trying to tell her. She can't go on like this. And now is the time to put her foot down.

And if Atlas dares fuck with her, she'll send the LA Times a lengthy manifesto about one of LA's most famous design firms firing a pregnant woman.

A rumble from Solomon. "No phone. No work." His blue-eyed gaze is so fierce she doesn't dare argue with him, or else her phone will be in the ocean. "Just you and me."

"And Bear," she adds breathlessly.

"And Bear."

His handsome face softens, has Tessie already regretting her no-more-kissing vow.

Straightening up, she sips her coffee and inhales a determined breath. "Now that that's done," she begins, determined to do this. Determined to work together for their kid. "You ready to talk about Bear?"

Solomon's eyes get dark and dusky. "Ready."

"Okay. Go with me on this. Obviously, we'll have to figure things out as we go, but. . . we don't have to complicate things. You go back to Alaska. I go back to LA. I have the baby. He lives with me in LA." She watches Solomon's face for any kind of disagreement, but there is none. Hard to read. Just like the man himself.

"When I travel for work, you could come out and stay with him. And when he's older. . .you could take him back to Chinook." Though it pains her to give up Bear for even the tiniest morsel of time, Solomon's his father. She won't and can't take that away from him. "You can come out to see him whenever you want. I won't ever stop you from seeing him. We share birthdays and holidays. Switch off."

She glances up as the server sets their food on the table. Platefuls of eggs and hash browns and fruit and chocolate croissants.

"I only have one condition."

His brows draw together. "Name it."

"You can't come and go," she says resolutely. It's her deal breaker. "You can't stop calling, miss birthdays, or go MIA and then show up one day unannounced." She juts her chin. "You're either in his life or out. You have to pick one."

The man stares. The muscles in his jaw and throat work. And Tessie waits. Waits for him to walk away, to say it's too hard, hell, to get up and leave.

Instead, after a long silence, he nods. "I'm in. I'm in it for the long haul."

His words have her shivering. The look on his face. So damn intense.

God, if it's true...

Beneath the table, she cups her stomach. Her son could have everything she never had. It means so much.

It means Solomon Wilder's a good man.

And she's never had a good man before.

Ugh. Why does he have to be such a good guy? It has her on edge. Jumpy like a squirrelly Chihuahua that doesn't know what's stomping its way. Because she keeps expecting him to leave like her father. Like all the losers she's dated.

She wonders, what would it take to make this man walk away?

What would it take to make him stay?

Stay for Bear, she reminds herself.

His son.

Not her.

"When he's born," Solomon says, breaking the momentary spell her thoughts had put on her. "I'd like to be there."

She nearly spills her coffee. God. Oh God. Imagining Solomon Wilder on the receiving end of labor, watching her bearing down on a hard exam table, has her breaking out in a cold sweat.

Mouth agape, she sets her coffee on the table. Picks up a fork. "Really? You do?"

"You'll need help, right? When you bring him home?"

"How come you know so much about babies?"

"My sisters," he says, cracking a rare smile. "I was the oldest. Saw how my parents scrambled to survive every time they brought a new baby home. They weren't exactly easy. Evelyn especially."

Tessie keeps a straight face, trying to shake off the girly, warm feeling that's settled down below. Indigestion, she tells herself. She's sick. She drank the water. Only in Mexico, right?

Scooping up a forkful of eggs, she floats him a teasing smile. "It could happen fast, though. You might not make it."

"I'll make it."

"Okay," she breathes, and the two of them share a smile. "If you want."

"I do," Solomon says with a stern nod. "I'll be there, Tessie."

"I'm glad you want to be in his life," she admits. "That's a good thing. Really. I just...why? Why are you doing this? Sticking around?" She can't help the question. She props her chin in her palm and considers him. "You don't have to. You could go back to Chinook, easy and free."

Brow furrowed, he locks his piercing blue eyes on her face and doesn't let go. "I don't walk away from things that are mine."

"Oh." A soft, uneven exhale. "I see."

Her entire body's a tremor. A warm pulse down below. A sudden image of Solomon cradling their son in his burly arms pops into her head, and Tessie goes molten.

After stomping down her gooey feelings in a box labeled *Ignore Them*, she decides to focus on eating. A safe, neutral, non-horny activity. As she's about to bring her fork to her mouth, Solomon launches out of his chair. He grabs her wrist, sending her fork clattering to the plate, the eggs slipping off to the tablecloth.

Diners rubberneck, the buffet line squeals to a halt.

"Solomon, what—" Tessie gapes at him. His face. She's never seen a face like that. Pissed off. So damn pissed off.

"Don't eat that," he says softly, letting her wrist loose. "The eggs are raw."

Tessie examines the food on her plate, her stomach lurching. Oh God. He's right. The eggs are slimy and runny, straight out of the shell.

Then Solomon's scooping up her plate. The ground thunders beneath his feet as he storms over to their server.

"Listen. I know it isn't on you." He nods, regarding Tess. Though his voice is calm, it's laced with a hard edge of anger. "But you tell the chef that the next time you serve something like this, to anyone, especially a pregnant woman, you make sure it's fucking cooked."

The server stammers out an apology and bustles off, plate in his hands.

"Are you okay?" Solomon asks, coming back to the table. He settles across from her again, searching her face.

"I'm fine. I'm just—" Her voice shakes out in a wobble. "That scared me."

"I know," he says hoarsely. "Me too."

She examines him curiously. "How'd you know that? About the eggs?" It has her sick to her stomach thinking about what could have happened. The bacteria could have sent her and Bear to the hospital.

"I downloaded that app," Solomon grumbles, looking none too happy about admitting it. Rolling out his broad shoulders, he runs a hand down his dark beard. "Read some of it while you were working yesterday." His blue eyes burn bright. "They shouldn't serve raw eggs to anyone. Especially you."

"Oh," she says, stunned. Heart thundering away in her chest, she presses a hand to her stomach to quiet the butterflies. She loves that he cares. That he's taken the time to download and research. It says a lot about him as a man. A partner.

Because they are partners.

When it comes to their son.

"I suppose you could cook me something better, Solemn Man," she teases, wanting to wipe that wild, worried look off his face.

He arches a confident brow. "I would." Interest lights his expression. "What are you craving?"

"Chocolate. All the chocolate. And hot sauce."

"Hot sauce, huh?"

"Potatoes with salt. Chicken sandwiches with pickles. Oh God, I'm drooling. Am I drooling?" Her laugh echoes around the restaurant. "Sounds like you should get in the kitchen, Solemn Man."

A muscle jumps in that chiseled square jaw of his. "Sounds like I should."

Suddenly, Tessie's hit by an urge to know more about Solomon Wilder. She wants to be in his kitchen, watching his massive hands work, watching him whip up gorgeous dishes that can feed her and Bear.

His gaze falls to hers, watchful. "Here. Have mine," he says, pushing his breakfast plate forward. "You're hungry."

"You're hungry too."

He crosses his arms, biceps bulging, and leans back in his chair. "I'll survive." His lips twitch. "I'm not sure you will. I saw the way you devoured that sandwich last night."

She gasps and stabs a spear of melon. "That is an act of war, and I won't have it."

She chews the fruit, studying the man across the table. He wears the cargo shorts and T-shirt she picked out for him. Handsome.

But.

She frowns.

Holy shit. Is it possible she actually likes him better in the flannel?

She shakes off the inane thought.

"So," Tessie says, searching for a topic to intercept the ridiculous thoughts inside her head, "after this, I was thinking…beach?"

"No."

"Please?" Dropping her fork, she prayer-palms her hands, trying not to laugh at his disgruntled expression. "C'mon, we have to put your swim trunks to good use. What if I get swept out to sea and need something burly to hold on to?"

His frown deepens. "Tessie—"

"You can be my anchor. Besides, it's your last day, Solomon."

"My last day," he repeats.

Is it just her, or did a look of disappointment cross his face?

And why does she feel disappointment too?

This was their deal.

Come up with a solution and then move on with their lives.

Tessie's stomach churns.

Indigestion, she tells herself.

It's all just indigestion.

Chapter Fifteen

Tessie's laid out on a lounge chair. A coconut drink balanced on her belly. Two straws, hooked together, feed into her mouth. In her hand, a fuchsia-colored book with two cartoon characters embracing on the front.

She looks happier than Solomon's ever seen her.

It's about damn time. At breakfast, he decided it was his personal mission to make sure she had fun. To make sure that asshole she calls a boss gives her space. Right now, Tessie doesn't have a worry in the world, and that's how it's going to stay.

Truth is, Solomon's settled in and enjoying this vacation too. Sand between his toes. Beers that magically refill themselves. The soothing crash of the surf in his ears. He's never been to a place like this before, but he's warming to it.

Tessie rolls her head to look at him. They've been at the beach the entire day, wasting away in the late afternoon sun. She makes a sound of contentment, slurping the last of her coconut water. "Why do all drinks taste better in the sunshine?"

"I like beer in the mountains."

"Of course you do. I, for one, would love to be reincarnated as a swim-up bar in my next life."

He chuckles. "Having fun?" he asks, hoping like hell she is.

She sits up, surveying the beach. "Oh yes. Bound and determined." With a waggle of her brows, she lowers her sunglasses.

"You should try it. Take off that shirt. Show a little rippling pectoral. I know you got 'em."

"Tess."

"Solemn Man," she teases, her flirty tone making warning bells go off in his head. Christ. This girl's dangerous. For his head and for his heart. And yet. . .that raging want inside him has him perpetually losing it.

A beam of a smile curves her lips. "Anyway. It's perfect. The drinks are perfect. The weather is perfect. Everything is perfect except my hair, which is a frizzball."

"Looks good to me."

She huffs. "Well, we can't all have your perfect beard."

He grins. "Perfect, huh?"

With a small sigh, Tessie scans the horizon. Solomon redirects his gaze to the magazine in his hands, damning the flexing of his cock. He's got a hell of a view, and he's not talking about the ocean.

Tessie wears a string bikini that shows off her long legs and the small bump of her belly. The sun has her lithe body glowing. Her sea-damp hair melts over her shoulders like honey. Her nose is tinged pink, dotted by a W-shaped constellation of freckles that have come out with the sun. Solomon's mind flashes to last night. Just last night, he was kissing her, his hands in her tangled hair, her—

Her phone.

Her phone is fucking *pinging*.

Every muscle in his body tenses.

Cringing, Tessie lifts herself up on her elbows to inspect the cell phone on the side able. "It's Ash," she says as she types back a reply. "Relax, Rambo."

Relax. Right.

The tightness in his shoulders ebbs—barely. He's still on edge from the scare at breakfast. Those goddamn eggs. Sure, he overreacted, lurching up from the table like a goddamn madman but,

Christ. He wasn't taking any chances. Food poisoning can be serious for anyone, let alone a pregnant woman. Let alone his—

This girl who gives him heartburn on a daily basis.

His mind moves back to their conversation at breakfast.

They worked out a solution, but it doesn't feel like enough. Yet, what are his choices? Move to LA? Ask Tessie to move to Chinook? He can't do that. She's got a job and a life. He'd never ask her to give that up. They're two people from two different worlds, who both have to move on.

But do they? Is that what he wants?

Time's ticking down. It's his last day in Mexico, and though it should be a relief that he'll be back in Chinook tomorrow night, relief is the last thing he feels.

Leaving Tessie... he doesn't like it.

Movement beside him has his thoughts clearing. Tessie's kicking her feet off the lounger and standing up. Her hands cradle her sunscreen-oiled belly. "Going for a swim. Want to come?"

Hell yes, he wants to come. Wants to follow her around the beach and keep his hold on her if there's a wave.

"Record high. Might as well." He stands, finally giving in and reaching behind him to tug off his shirt. He grabs a beer from the bucket, ignoring Tessie's hoot, and then, together, they stride down to the beach.

As they trade the sand for the surf, Solomon has to fight the urge to drape a towel around Tessie's shoulders.

She's pregnant. She's got a man by her side, and still, heads are swiveling, *Exorcist*-style. It pisses him off and makes him proud all at the same time. Because Tessie's hot as hell, so goddamn sexy, and she's not even trying.

Fucking let them rubberneck. Let their tongues drag on the sand like cartoon wolves. Because he's the one by her side, and damn if that doesn't have him hard as hell.

He takes in her pretty profile. Every atom in his body wants to kiss her again. Wants to take her to bed and keep her there, moaning in his arms. It turns him on so goddamn much to see her carrying his son. Solomon clears his throat, dragging his mind out of the gutter. She's made it clear what she wants, and it's not him. And she's got enough problems without adding a slavering man to the mix.

"You know, I like having you here," she says, bumping her shoulder against his arm as they stroll down the sand for the surf. "You're like my shield."

His eyes flick to hers. "How so?"

"Now I can point at you when people ask who the father is."

He bristles at the thought of nosy assholes invading her privacy. "Who asks that?"

She flaps a hand. "Oh everyone. Perfect strangers. They even try to feel my stomach without asking. Like it's their right or something." The edges of her lips turn down.

Solomon doesn't like it. Not one damn bit.

"You have no privacy when you're pregnant."

"Guess I'll have to get you a T-shirt that says baby daddy with an arrow," he teases, wanting that gloomy look off her face. Wanting to break the hand of anyone who tries to touch her belly without her permission.

A squeal bubbles out of her. "Did you make a joke? Are you joking about this?" She laughs, a delighted expression crossing her face. "Solemn Man jokes. He lives."

He halts. "Okay, that's it. You're going in."

Growling, he lunges for her, and she squeals, running down to the surf. When he catches up, he hooks an arm high around her waist and scoops her into his arms. She twists gently in his grasp but doesn't try to escape. He holds on to that. On to Tessie, carrying her out into the sun-warmed ocean. Lowering her into the water, he turns her loose in the waves. Not too far out, though; losing Tess in the ocean isn't happening today.

Beer held high above him, Solomon dunks his head in the cool water. "Fuck," he exhales when he surfaces, shaking water from his face. "That's cold."

Tessie laughs and dives under. She arcs in a circle, then pops up out of the water.

Waves slap on the beach, music from the DJ booth and muffled conversation from the swim-up bar float on the air. But for Solomon, nothing exists but the two of them. The water so clear he can see her lean legs kicking.

She lets out a content sigh and extends her arms, her legs. His heart settles at the sight. Tessie bobbing in the water. Her swollen belly like a slicing shark fin in the surf. He could watch her all damn day.

She swims toward him, her head angling.

Drifting like the moon to a tide, he reaches for her. After a second's hesitation, she reaches for him too. Their fingers link under the waves, tangle.

And then, slowly, he pulls her toward him.

When her body meets his, they lock together, and all Solomon can do is tighten his grasp. She's meant to be here, in his arms. Imprinted, melted against him. The warm curl of her petite frame into his has a protective, primal instinct revving up inside him.

Tessie watches him for a long minute, then she loops her arms around his neck and relaxes into him. Her bare legs hooked around his waist. Her brown eyes all kinds of searching. With trembling fingers, she palms the side of his face, his beard.

Then—

Her warm lips land softly on his. They taste like sea water, like coconut water. Solomon drinks her in. Her scent, heady, has his cock flexing hard against his swim trunks as reality drifts further and further away. The kiss builds slow, a smooth dance of tongues, a sync of heartbeats.

Tessie whimpers and then pulls back. "I'm sorry," she breathes.

"Don't be," he rasps.

"I mean..." She chews her lip, her attention locked on his mouth. "Should we be doing this?"

"What are we doing?"

"I don't know." She tilts her head. All kinds of questions lighting up her soft brown eyes. "Solomon, what are—"

"Oh my word, Rick. Isn't this the sweetest sight?"

Slowly, they swivel their heads. Bobbing beside them in the waves is a couple wearing bright fluorescent flowered visors and oversized sunglasses.

"Lovebirds, true as can be."

The woman, zinc oxide smeared haphazardly across her nose, wags a finger. "Let me guess. Babymoon?" She zeroes in on Tessie's stomach in a way that has Solomon scowling. "Look at you. Fit as a fiddle. First one?"

Tessie's smile drops, resets. "You got it."

Solomon grunts, adjusting Tessie so her stomach is out of their eyeline and drifts farther out, but the couple follows. Chattering, oblivious. "Twentieth anniversary here. Believe you me, we needed a break from the little urchins."

The man raises his hand. A snap of a Wisconsin accent. "Rick and Roni Zebrowski."

Roni splashes closer. "Where ya from?"

Fuck no. Getting drawn into a conversation is the last thing Solomon wants. Not when he's got Tessie in his arms and his name on her lips. No fucking way.

"Oh, uh, Alaska," Tessie says, shooting Solomon a look, warning him not to volunteer any more information.

"We were on an Alaskan cruise once." Rick bobs his head. "Now there is a beautiful state." He pats his full belly. "Let me tell you, couldn't stomach the food, though. Ate McDonald's the entire time."

Solomon glowers. Fucking tourists. Doing everything but experiencing Alaska the right way. He wishes for a shark right now.

A tsunami. Anything to escape this conversation and get back to what Tessie was going to say.

"Sol?" A hand on his arm. Tessie bats her lashes at him. "You need another beer?"

He frowns. "No, I—"

"Oh, you do." She snatches up his full can and looks at the couple. "He drinks 'em like water. Straight up guzzles them." Her lips twitch as she turns her gaze to him. "I'll be right back, okay?"

Oh, hell no.

He grabs her wrist. "Tess, I think you need to let me—"

She smirks at him, gently untangling herself. "Pregnant women can do hard things, Solomon." She looks at Roni, sharing a smile of camaraderie. "I swear he has such first-time daddy jitters." A very un-Tessie-like giggle pops out of her as she looks at Solomon. "I'll get it, *sweetheart*. You just relax. Enjoy the Zebrowskis."

You're fucking cold, woman, he thinks, watching as Tessie and her bikini shimmy off with his full beer, her shoulders racking with laughter as she runs up the beach to the bar. But he's smiling.

For the first time in a damn long time.

Chuckling to herself, Tessie hoofs it up the sand. The look of betrayal and agony on Solomon's face as she left him there to fend for himself will live rent-free in her mind for the next decade. She'll let him sweat a bit and then go back and rescue him. Meanwhile, it'll be good for him to come out of his grumpy mountain man shell.

Pausing by her beach chair, water dripping off her salt-drenched hair, Tessie checks her phone, casting a guilty glance over her shoulder in case Solomon's watching.

A breath looses in her chest.

So far, nothing. No emails, no texts, no missed calls. It seems too good to be true. Atlas scurrying off in silence. She'll have to enjoy it while it lasts.

Today's been a perfect slice of paradise. Not a worry in the world, all the coconut water she can drink. This is what she imagined when she pictured her babymoon. Slothful laziness that could put a cat to shame. Maybe she didn't imagine having Solomon around, but he hasn't been so bad.

A slow heat creeps over her already flushed cheeks.

He's been wonderful, in fact.

Keeping her sane.

Keeping her safe.

Keeping her sexually satisfied.

In his strong arms, bobbing in that water, going against everything screaming at her that a relationship is not within a ten-mile radius of her heart, she kissed him. It was so perfect in that moment. Like his kiss was the true slice of paradise she wanted.

She had been close, so close, to asking, *what are we?* The question was on her lips, dripping slow like molasses.

Because she thought she knew. She and Solomon—they are Bear's parents.

But she's also starting to get a sense of who the real Solomon Wilder is. Fierce. Protective. Loyal. In his presence, she's found a comfort. With her upcoming birth, with her job, she doesn't feel so unsure. All her problems go away when he holds her in his arms. She feels steady. Because that's Solomon. That's her—

Child's father.

That's it.

That's all.

But what if—

No.

Her chest strains.

She has to stop. She has to get her head on straight. All she and Solomon are, will ever be, are friends. Co-parents. End of story.

Settling for each other because of their son would be ridiculous. They'd end up miserable, resenting each other. Besides, he's made it clear he's only here because of Bear. Tessie wants a man to want her for her. Not like the men are lining up to date a soon-to-be single mother who works eighteen-hour days. Not like she wants anything anyway. Heartbreak and loss are not on her agenda.

It's easier this way.

Soon, they'll return to the real world.

But why does she feel sick to her stomach when she thinks about him leaving?

Because she's hungry, that's why.

Trekking up the beach to the tiki hut, Tessie tosses the beer can in the trash. She stops next to an ice cream cart and snags a scoop of vanilla perched on a waffle cone.

Food. She needs food to distract herself from the crazy train of thoughts ripping through her mind.

As she licks the ice cream, she meanders down the beach. Scouring the crowd, she pinpoints Solomon striding out of the ocean like a hunky Poseidon, rivulets of water cascading off him. His muscles flex in the sunlight. The deep V-lines by his hips, the dark thatch of a happy trail, have her staring.

Shamelessly.

She never thought she'd want to climb a mountain, but Solomon is one she'd eagerly scale. Ripped and chiseled. Dangerous terrain if one doesn't know what they're doing. A challenge Tessie wants to best. In bed. Again and again and—

"Shit!" she swears as she stumbles into a trash can. The hot singe of metal on her skin has her jumping back, only to have a piercing pain stab her foot. She swears again.

Propping one hand on a water station, she lifts her left foot, only to end up hopping around on one leg like a very pregnant flamingo, trying to balance her belly and the ice cream in her hand. As she cranes to examine the damage, the ice cream avalanches off the cone, hits her belly with a splat, and then lands on the sand.

"Damn it," Tessie says, staring forlornly at the sticky white trail on her stomach.

"Ma'am, are you okay?" She looks up into the blinking eyes of Ice Cream Cart Guy.

"I'm fine. I just need to sit d—oh, wow, okay," she says as Ice Cream Cart Guy takes her elbow and waves off a couple occupying a nearby bench. Wincing, she holds her stomach as she lowers herself. "I stepped on something, but I can't see what it is."

"Here. Let me look." Ice Cream Cart Guy crouches beside her.

That's when she hears the voices.

"Is she okay?"

"Does she need a doctor?"

"Is she in labor?"

Oh God. She wants to sink into the sand.

This is ridiculous. This is mortifying. A crowd has formed around her, people passing her water and concerned glances, all because she's seemingly a fragile flower of a woman carrying a gigantic ticking bomb in her body.

Ice Cream Cart Guy whistles. He dips his visored head, examining her foot. "It's a shell. Got you pretty good." He stands and takes Tessie's elbow. Then, in a bold move of overconfidence, wipes at the ice cream dripping down her swollen belly with a fat stack of napkins.

She cringes at the clammy, intrusive touch of his hands.

"No. That's okay. You don't have to—"

"Let me get this cleaned off, then I'll help you back to your room—"

"Move," a deep voice rumbles from somewhere high above. "Now."

Oh, thank God.

She sends a look of relief up over her shoulder.

It's Solomon, approaching in a quiet, dangerous stride. He kneels beside her, a muscle jumping in his bearded jaw as he stares the guy down and says in a cool growl of authority, "I got her."

"He does." Tessie grips Solomon's hard bicep to hold him back, her lips fighting a smile. He's watching the guy like he'll kill him if he touches her again. "Thank you for your help."

As Ice Cream Cart Guy skedaddles, nearly tripping over his own feet in an attempt to get away, Solomon turns his attention to Tessie. The beach bags hang off his broad shoulders. Worry burns in his blue eyes. "What happened?" His voice is low and ragged.

"Pregnancy brain," she lies, keeping her face even. God, she can't tell him she was daydreaming about scaling his body like Everest. "I crashed into a trash can, and I think there's a shell in my foot."

His dark brows draw together. "Let me see if I can get it out."

She flings an arm across her face, covering her eyes dramatically. "Do it."

His expression determined, Solomon props Tessie's leg up so her calf rests on his massive thigh. After snagging a bottle of water from a nearby vendor, he pours it over her foot and cleans out the sand the best he can. He works gently, his big hands careful as he examines the injury.

Tessie hisses a breath when he pulls the piece of shell from her heel. Then Solomon takes his shirt from the beach bag and wraps it around her cut like some sort of mountain man makeshift bandage.

"Got it," he says, lifting his eyes to her. He tucks a lock of hair behind her ear. "We'll find a first aid kit back in the room. I don't want that to get infected."

She bobblehead nods, feeling lightheaded at his worry. "Okay."

Shoving up, he stands. She holds out a hand, waiting for him to pull her up beside him. Instead, he simply scoops her up in his arms, one hooked under her knees, the other looped behind her back.

"Solomon." Embarrassed, she ducks her head against his chest, a hot heat in her cheeks. "Everyone's watching."

"So? You're hurt." He says it like nothing matters. Except her.

"I am not hurt." His grave, bossy tone has her smiling. "Besides, that shirt was eighty dollars."

"So?"

"And you're carrying me. It's kind of redundant, you know. To clean and wrap the foot and then carry me."

He tightens his hold. His face blazes with protectiveness. "I like carrying you."

Resting her head on his mile-wide chest, she bites back a grin. She likes it too. Likes the way she looks beside him. Bright and blond and petite next to this giant of a dark, brooding man. Likes the way eyes widen at Solomon's appearance. People practically dive out of his way as he storms down the sidewalk. But best of all, she likes the way he treats her. Like she's precious. Like he's her bodyguard, and she is. . .

She is his.

Stop.

Stop.

Tessie lifts her head to look at him. "You escaped from the Zebrowskis."

His eyes blaze with humor and something else she can't place. "No thanks to you."

"I was letting you brush up on your communication skills."

A grunt.

"See?" She pokes his chest. "They need work."

When they get to the room, he sets her gently on her feet to retrieve the hotel key from the pocket of his board shorts. But he doesn't let her loose. He keeps her tucked protectively in the crook of his arm, staring down at her, the expression on his face one of primal need. Agony.

Tessie clears her throat, twisting into him. "Solomon, the key—"

Before she can process what's happening, his mouth is colliding with hers. She whimpers, her hands, her nails clawing at his shoulders, wanting more. Her body crackles all over, fireworks sparking as Solomon's tongue strokes over hers, fierce and eager and hungry.

Tessie gives a broken moan.

Fuck it. It's his last night.

Might as well live a little.

Live.

Because that's what she's been doing with Solomon.

Pressing herself up on tiptoes, she deepens the kiss. Opening her mouth and sucking in his tongue, because this man's kiss is one of her favorite substances on the face of the planet. In response, a growl tears out of Solomon. He grabs her by the ass and slides her up his body until her trembling legs are slung around his waist and her arms are looped around his neck.

Back in his arms.

Where she belongs.

Fumbling. Solomon's fumbling for the key, cursing, holding on to her with one arm. The sight would be hilarious if she weren't so hot and bothered. Because all she can think about is: *Inside. Bed. Sexy times.*

"Find the key," she gasps against his lips. She licks the side of his face, his bristly beard, tasting the salt on his skin. "Now. *Now.*"

"Fuck, I'm trying," he hisses, pained.

If the glint in his eye, the rock of an erection in his shorts are anything to go by, he's dangerously close to kicking down the hotel room door. But finally, he finds the key, swipes the sensor, and gets the green light. He slams inside. She clings to him like a howler monkey in heat.

Their kisses are frantic. Like time's ticking down. Like they're starved and feral and everything will burn up in the end. A low moan rips out of Solomon's throat as she pulls back and cups his face in her hands. His scruff tickles her palms.

"Goddamn, Tessie," he growls, giving her hips a squeeze. "I can't stay away from you. That guy touching you. . ." A shudder works its way out of him. "You're in my fucking mind, my veins, my—"

He doesn't finish the sentence.

He doesn't need to.

My heart.

He was about to say *my heart.*

Tessie kisses him to drown out his words. The ache in her soul. "One more time," she chokes out. "Please."

Doubt, disagreement flash in his eyes, but he slams his mouth to hers anyway.

With frenzied fingers, Solomon peels her sticky swimsuit from her body, emitting a growl that has her toes curling. And then Tessie's naked, except for her tan lines, and Solomon lunges for her, ferocious. "You're beautiful," he grits out. "So damn gorgeous, Tessie. *Perfect. Fucking perfect.*"

One broad hand grips her hip while the other slides up to cup the heavy swell of her breast. Her head falls back at the sensation. Her entire body's a tremor. She feels so damn worshipped. Under Solomon's attentive touch, she feels like a goddess.

Mouth fusing to hers, he backs her up against the bed.

"Get on your knees," he orders.

Bossy. She loves it.

"Okay," she breathes and flips herself over on all fours. Peering over her shoulder, she takes him in, riveted, as Solomon strips out of his swim trunks. Finally free of the constricting fabric, his cock surges and comes to life. Tessie savors the sight of the tower of strength that is Solomon Wilder. He's a wall of chiseled muscle, washboard abs, dark dusting of hair across his chest, colorful tattoos winding themselves around his biceps and forearms.

The thought comes to her sudden and ferocious—*this mountain man; he is the only one she will ever want.*

No. That's a horrible thought.

A forever thought.

And then his massive fingers are all over her, toying. Teasing.

Running down her curves, smacking her ass, gliding gently through her wet folds. He slips a finger into her, then another, and at the feel of him inside her, she nearly comes undone.

"Solomon." Eyes shuttering, she trembles at his touch.

Then his hot mouth kisses a trail down her spine, one hand caressing the curve of her belly, and her body goes molten.

This man. He's going to be the death of her.

"Please, Solomon," she gasps, lifting her head to plead with him. "I can't wait anymore. *Please.*"

His eyes flare at her words.

The bed shifts as he settles his weight behind her. His fingers dig into her curves as he makes sure she's steady. Then, slowly, he eases into her. Tessie gasps, her body igniting with hot urgency. Her fingers dig into the sheets. She's so tight and he's so large and hard, and it's the most overwhelming sensation. The best sensation. The two of them. Together. Tonight.

She's faint. Faint from having too much, from this strange, warm fluttery feeling in her chest, from the way their bodies-brains-souls-hearts are hardwired for one another.

"Tell me if I hurt you," he grits out.

"You won't. You can't."

Together, they rock. Solomon moves in and out as Tessie sinks onto his length, her warmth sucking him in.

Nothing but labored breaths, Solomon's deep rumble of contentment, fill the sunlit room. Faster and faster, he pumps against her, his giant body covering hers with tenderness and care. A delicious tension creeps over Tessie when he speeds up, pistons his hips forward and thrusts hard.

Her body buzzing, Tessie cries out as Solomon's hand slips between her legs. His callused thumb sweeps over her clit, making slow, smooth circles. "That good, baby? You tell me what you need."

"More," she says on a moan. "More. Oh God. Oh, Solomon. Yes. Right there."

He drives deeper, no more teasing. The hard rack of his solid wall of muscle a kick-drum against her own fragile form. With a skilled hand, he runs his thumb over her clit and, driving his hips hard, slams into just the right spot to make Tessie scream.

The orgasm kicks her in the teeth at the same time a rumble explodes in Solomon's chest. Rhythmically, she pulses and squeezes around him, her orgasm a Pantone burst of color, and then she's gripping the sheet corner, crying out to a God she never appreciated until now, all before going limp.

Before she can collapse, Solomon has her in his arms. Gripping her high around the abdomen, he pulls her down with him in bed. They settle in the cool sheets, their bodies still joined, locked together, burning bright like shooting stars that will never come down.

Solomon strokes a line down the curve of Tessie's tan arm. Sand in the bed, sand in the sheets, but he doesn't care. The end of the world couldn't get him to move right now. Not with Tessie curled up in his arms like an ocean goddess he doesn't deserve. The thin bedsheets cover the curve of her hip, the swell of her stomach. He can't tear his damn eyes off her.

"You got some sun," he murmurs, pressing a kiss to her pink shoulder, tiny freckles popping on her smooth skin. She tastes like sunscreen and sex. Coconut and salt.

Tessie, naked, pregnant, stirs lazily against him. A swirl of blond hair, a hum of contentment. Then, her voice drowsy, her eyes heavy lidded, she strokes slim fingers over his beard. "Life's a beach, isn't it?"

"Shit." Solomon sits up, jarred by the reason they're back in the room.

She leans up on her elbow. "What is it?"

"Your foot."

"It's fine," she says, turning to reach for him, but he's already up and off the bed, cursing himself. The ground thunders as he stomps for the bathroom.

He comes back with a first aid kit. Sits on the edge of the bed and places her foot in his lap. Tessie, propped up on a mound of pillows, looks small and vixen-like, her blond hair swirled up behind her.

"We should have done this first," he grinds out, swiping her foot with disinfectant. Guilt spears him in the stomach. Shame for taking care of himself before Tessie. She's hurt, and all he could do was think with his dick.

Tessie sits patiently, both palms on her stomach, her expression one of amused confusion.

As he wraps a bandage around her heel, she wiggles her pink-painted toes. "See? All better." She tips forward, a teasing smile on her face. "Better than the ice cream guy, for sure."

Solomon scowls. That guy, with his hands on her stomach, tugging on her arm, had flipped a switch inside him, kicking his protective instincts into overdrive. In that instant, he saw his future in one fell swoop. Or, should he say, Tessie's. Dating. Passing Bear to another man. Needing someone who isn't him. A random guy living with his son, seeing him and Tessie every day. The vision is like a fucking knife to the chest.

"Solemn Man." Tessie's soft voice floats between them. "Relax."

He startles, his thoughts clearing as he finds Tessie's concerned gaze on him. Then, like she knows just how much he needs it, she takes his large hand in hers and rests it against her stomach. "He's kicking."

At the feel of his son fluttering in her belly, Solomon unclenches. He doesn't know when they started doing this, touching each other like it means something, but he likes it. Too damn much for his own good.

"There," he says, setting aside the first aid kit. He gives her bandaged foot a once-over. "That should do it."

Tessie tilts her head, the sheet falling away to reveal a flash of pert, pink nipple. "You can cook, you can build, you can wrap a bandage like a pro. What else don't I know about you?"

He thinks on it. "I have a dog."

A smile graces her face. "You do?"

"I do." He settles next to her on the bed, drawing her hand into his. "Peggy Sue. She's my hound dog. I got her after—" He pauses and clears his throat. "After my wife died."

He doesn't know why he stops there. Why he doesn't say more. It would be so easy to tell her about Serena. But tell her what? That he became a hermit after she died? That he was celibate for seven years until he met Tessie? That her death was his fault? What would she think of him, learning how far he'd sunk?

"I love dogs," Tessie says, picking up the dropped conversation. Her expression says she won't press. "You know, I used to have a dog. Mr. Bones. He was the best. A ratty little troublemaker we got from the pound. Scruffy, kinda like this." She puffs a laugh, leaning forward to rub a hand over Solomon's disheveled beard. "My mom trusted me to take care of him. And one day, he ran off. I was so nice to that dog. As a kid, I never understood why he left. Now, of course, I realize he probably got hit by a car or picked up by someone else." Gaze drifting to the sheets, she wets her lips. "Dogs leave. People leave. And they especially leave me."

She doesn't say it in a sad way. She says it in a this-is-how-it-is way.

Like a snap of realization, Solomon gets it.

This.

This is why she's a wall. Why she's so dead set on him being all in or all out. Because she was hurt. Because every time she trusts, every time she brings someone into her life, they show her she's better off alone.

The thought leaves Solomon with a hole in his heart.

"I don't run off, Tessie," he says, nudging her chin up so he can search her soft brown eyes. "I don't leave. Especially you."

A little shrug. "That's true. You haven't."

Only Solomon hears the unsaid. *Yet.*

Because tomorrow, he has to go.

Gaze drifting, he takes in his duffel bag on the dresser.

Misunderstanding where his mind has gone, Tessie scoots out of the bed, the covers slipping off her slender body. All tan lines and bronze flesh. "I'm going to shower." The smile on her face drops. "You should pack." Her voice is high, strained.

"Tess—"

"Come join me when you're done?" she offers, her smile tepid.

With a stiff nod, he watches her shimmy off toward the shower. The wiggle of her supple ass, the sway of her hips have him hardening, the hand on her belly has him softening.

Christ.

He's fucked.

Once again, Solomon's gaze drifts to his duffel bag. When the sun comes up, they'll part ways. He got what he came to Mexico to get. An arrangement that works for them both in regards to his son.

His heart pounds in his jugular.

But it's not what he wants.

Forty-eight hours ago, he was so sure that everything—with the exception of his son—was temporary.

Only, he doesn't want temporary anymore.

He wants Tessie.

Chapter Sixteen

THE BRIGHT SUNLIGHT AND THE HARD THUMPS IN her belly call Tessie awake. She blinks, unable to move. She looks around for the cause of her stranglehold, only to see that it's Solomon. His arm wrapped high around her waist in a protective, claiming embrace, pressing her tight against his muscled body.

A smile tugs at her lips. It's nice. Being held. This is so much better than wrapping herself up in Solomon's stolen shirt at home, the one she hides beneath her pillow. She sighs and, unable to help it, snuggles closer to him. So much better. The real deal.

Which is why he needs to go.

It was during a middle-of-the-night pee break that she came to this conclusion. She wants him to stay, which means he should leave. Because she's getting attached. It's getting harder and harder for her to keep her distance. The way he took care of her yesterday...

Her body ignites every time she's within two feet of him.

Still...

He's nice to look at.

Silently, she examines Solomon Wilder. In sleep, he looks like a calm, slumbering giant. With gentle fingers, she traces the sun on his tan skin, the glance of light lingering across his brow. She angles in to huff his wiry black beard. Then she lifts the sheet and ogles. Damn right, she ogles.

"Got something you want to tell me, Tess, or are you just gonna stare at me all morning?" The deep rumble of his voice shakes her.

She jumps and grabs his shoulders. His grip on her tightens. She scoffs. "You sleep like a predator."

He cracks an eye. A smile.

Her heart flips.

A broad hand slides over her bare hip as he says, "You just tell me where you want me to prowl."

Swallowing, she imagines Solomon prowling around her like a growling forest creature. Her gaze flits to the clock. Her jaw drops. She gasps. "Solomon."

"What is it?" He leans up on an elbow, his concerned gaze flying to her stomach. "Tessie?"

"It's ten. We slept in."

He raises his stunned face, smearing a hand across weary eyes. "Fuck. First time in a goddamn long time."

Sighing, she flops onto her back and stretches out her limbs, enjoying the freedom, the slice of warm sun. A lazy decadence she's never allowed herself. She smiles at the ceiling.

This. This is what she came here to do.

A loud pounding on the door has Solomon's face screwing up. "Did you order food?"

"No. Maybe it's coffee," she says hopefully, scooting out of bed. If there's one thing that will get her moving, it's that bright kick of hope that is caffeine.

He tries to reach for her. "Stay. I'll go."

She slips on a robe. "I got it."

Eagerness a bright bubble in her step, she makes for the front door. But what she sees through the peephole has her mouth dropping.

Holy shit.

What the hell is he doing here? One thousand miles away from LA.

Heart pounding, Tessie adjusts her robe over her bump and wipes her face, wishing she were in her go-to heels and pencil skirt. Greeting her boss with bedhead and dried drool on the corner of her mouth isn't exactly a career-making moment.

Another pound on the door.

She pulls it open.

"Atlas, what—"

Without waiting for an invitation, he strides in. "What am I doing here?" He spins on his heel in typical dramatic fashion. "I am here, Truelove, because after your little email yesterday, I figured I'd need to come and talk some sense into you personally."

She frowns. "So you flew down here to what? Scold me?"

"I flew down to bring you back." Glancing over his shoulder, he scans the room. His lips curl up. "Glad to see we pay you too much."

She resists the urge to snort. To search for a high heel to throw at his stupid, smug face. That's the fucking lie of the century. Pays her too much. She had to beg for a raise even with her promotion.

"Truelove." Atlas claps, the sound echoing in the quiet space. "We are swamped. Like I told you, Ben Moreno wants to redo his Beverly Hills restaurant. He's requested you. Personally."

She blinks. It's an honor, but it isn't going to happen. She inhales, steels her spine. "And *like I told you*, that's wonderful. And I will do all that when I get back to LA. Right now, I'm on vacation."

"Then consider your vacation request denied." The dismissive flap of his hand has her blood boiling.

She grinds her teeth, presses hands to her belly to steady herself. "But—"

"The client doesn't wait. You know that."

"Then he's not *my* client," she says with a bitter laugh. "This is my first vacation in years, Atlas. *Years*. I need this."

He sneers. "I need *you*, Truelove. You're my best designer. Even if you are—" And then he waves a hand in the vicinity of her stomach.

Oh.

Oh hell fucking no.

Anger worms its way inside her. Suddenly, Tessie's seeing her future at Atlas Rose Design bright and clear. Unrealistic expectations. Late hours. Working every weekend. In the past, she was willing to overlook the demands of the job to build her career, but this is not what she wants anymore. At all.

If he's asking this of her now, what will he ask when her son has a baseball game, when she has to pick him up early from daycare? God, what about when she's on maternity leave and breastfeeding and weepy and leaking from every orifice? The answer resounds, loud and clear: a big fat no.

Sure, she can work hard, be a single mother, and raise a child. Her mother did it; she can do it. But if she stays at her firm, she'll be wrecked. She doesn't want to just survive a job; she wants to thrive. To have a life with her son. To put him first.

To put herself first.

Atlas runs a short finger down a bristly black sideburn. "Don't make me regret giving you this client, Truelove."

"So don't," she says, straightening her shoulders. She crosses the room to open the sliding glass doors to the terrace. When she pulls one open, the sound of the ocean fills the room. She inhales the calm, the surf and salt. "Keep Moreno yourself."

That has Atlas frowning. His bravado knocked down two pegs. "Truelove. C'mon." He takes a step toward her, stubby hands out in a placating gesture. "We both know this job is your first love. You've worked so hard these last few years. I hate the thought of you throwing all your hard work away." A sneer curls his lips. "All for a little sand and sun."

Atlas runs a finger across a fat stack of coffee table books. "You eat and breathe this shit, Truelove. I know you. You can pick a Pantone color out in the dark, transform a room blindfolded. This job is your life."

Oh God.

Oh gross.

Tessie deflates like a balloon, only to have an epic hollowness fill her up.

This job *is* her life. Putting the client first. Coming home to an empty bed. No time for anything but work, never letting herself have any fun. Take risks. Live. Fucking live, which is what, in the end, her mother really wanted her to do.

Find stars. Take risks.

Suddenly, she's so tired. Exhausted. She sits on the arm of the couch and stares up dully at Atlas.

Taking her silence as acquiescence, he softens his tone. "Listen, I recognize that you need a break, but that will come. Later. Right now, what we need to do is buckle down."

Liar, she thinks. He has no intention of giving her time off. Not now, not ever.

Her boss lifts a palm in supplication and edges farther into the room. "I brought your sketches. We can sit down together and nail this out. It shouldn't take too long. One or two days. It won't be a problem."

"It most definitely will be a problem."

The deep rumble has Atlas turning, has Tessie's heart soaring. Her stomach tightens at the sight of a shirtless Solomon standing in the archway of the bedroom. Sleeves of ink and muscle. His grizzled beard, overprotective stance, and large steel frame the best kind of backup there is.

Atlas chuckles, then he turns his attention back to Tessie. "Been enjoying yourself, I see."

Fire snaps her spine, snaps her to standing. "I have been, thank you." Lifting her chin, she crosses her arms, letting them rest on the high arch of her belly.

Stepping close, Solomon drapes a protective arm around her shoulder. Tessie revels at having him by her side. The way he says nothing, doesn't try to take over, simply letting her know he's here, that they're a team, is hot as hell. She sees it in his eyes. He won't let her fall.

Ignoring Solomon, Atlas sets his man purse on the bar and unsnaps the latch. "Now if you'll remember what I said about the—"

"Don't per-my-last-email me, Atlas," Tessie snaps, sick of his shit. Bear kicks in her stomach like *give him hell, mom*. "I don't think you heard me. I. Am. Not. Working."

Atlas scoffs, a smug sound that has her hackles rising. "Unbelievable. Here's that Terrible Tess we know and hate."

Her eyes narrow. Fucking gaslighter.

"That was you?" A dangerous edge stains Solomon's voice. "You gave her that name?" His eyes flash. His hands pull to fists. "Now we got fucking problems."

The deep rumble of warning sends a smile to Tessie's lips. An overprotective Solomon Wilder is a sight she'll never get enough of.

Tessie sticks an arm out, stopping him before he can move for Atlas.

She's got this.

"I'm not terrible, Atlas," she says, taking a step forward, keeping her head held high. "You're terrible, and I am not taking the shit you give anymore." She inhales a breath. Steels her nerves. She'll worry about mistakes later. Because right now, she's going to worry about her and Bear.

"I quit."

The words have her lightheaded. Ecstatic.

Atlas gapes at her. Then he shakes his head. "I knew this pregnancy would make you weak."

A growl from Solomon.

She scoffs. "Fuck you, Atlas. And get the fuck out of my room." When he stands, frozen in disbelief, she flings an arm. "Go."

"Now," Solomon snarls, advancing. His big body a hard stomp of a warning. "Before I toss your ass off that balcony."

Tessie smirks as her unwanted guest takes a step backward, tripping over his own feet in his haste to dodge Solomon's combustible glare. Red-faced, Atlas grabs his man purse and stiffly walks out, slamming the door shut behind him.

Tessie stands there in disbelief, nerves and excitement crashing over her like a rogue wave.

Holy shit. She quit. A job she bled for, fought for, screamed at interns for. Well, no more.

"Tess?"

She turns.

Solomon's there, gripping her elbows to pull her close. "You okay?"

"Yeah." She nods. "Surprisingly, I am." She looks up at his handsome face, creased with concern. "I don't know what the hell I did, but that wasn't the right job for us." She glances down at her belly, smooths a palm around it. "Was it?"

"I'm proud of you."

Her heart skips a beat. "You are?"

"I am." A muscle works in Solomon's jaw and he pulls her another inch closer to him. "I wanted to punch that asshole."

She laughs. "I did too."

Solomon cups her face, his eyes gentle blue waters, but steel laces his quiet voice. "He disrespects you like that again, and I will."

"I'll let you."

A feeling of freeness she's never felt before settles over her shoulders. She's on vacation. An actual vacation.

"We have to celebrate," she says, clinging to Solomon's broad shoulders to bounce on her tiptoes. "Beach all day, lunch at the taco shack, and then we have to—oh." She sinks back down to her heels, her stomach plummeting, crestfallen, as reality sets in. Her hands fall to her sides. "You leave today."

Solomon swallows hard, his Adam's apple bobbing. "Tess, listen..."

His face is so intense she draws back.

"What is it?"

"What if we changed our deal?" His voice comes out rough. His blue eyes quickly hardening, piercing hers.

Her breath hitches. Worry flutters in her belly. "Changed our deal?" she echoes. "About Bear?"

"No." He runs a hand through her hair, cups the back of her neck. "About us."

"Us?" Suddenly, her knees are weak, and she has to press both palms against Solomon's broad chest to hold herself up.

"What if I stay for the rest of your vacation? To help you relax?" he asks, his words a strange staccato beat. Like he's trying to keep it together and failing epically.

"Relax." She hums. "Is that what we're calling it now?"

His eyes lock on hers and hold. "For Bear."

"For Bear."

She inclines her head, considering his words. As long as Solomon wants to be here for Bear, why should she stop him? Bear's his son. His offer to change their deal changes nothing between them.

She wets her lips, something warm and soft surging inside her. "Alright then," she whispers. "Four more days."

The hard lines of his handsome face soften. "Four more days."

And then Solomon dips his face to kiss her, his arms locking tight around her like he'll never let her go.

The thunder of heartbeats, of breath pulsing between them, has every cell in Tessie's bloodstream lighting up.

She keeps doing unplanned, impromptu things while this mountain man is around, and she kind of likes it.

In fact, she kind of loves it.

Swinging for the fences, taking big risks, winging it.

She's winging it.

With Solomon Wilder.

Chapter Seventeen

"What's your middle name?"
"Jack."
"Jack, huh? It fits you."
"What about you?"
"Anne. Tessie Anne Truelove. Truelove was my mom's last name."

Sitting up, best she can, Tessie eyes Solomon. The two of them are piled lazily in a hammock by the beach. "Moment of truth. Favorite color?"

"Green." His brow wrinkles. "Like a spruce tree."

She laughs, delighted at his attempt to describe the color, and claps her hands. She never imagined she'd be lying in a hammock playing twenty questions with a bearded mountain man, but here she is.

She likes it. Learning more about the man that is Solomon Wilder.

He says nothing, only pulls her into his arms and kisses her temple. She curls up against him, tossing a tan leg over his hip to accommodate her bump.

Yesterday morning, his offer to change their arrangements had her wanting to stomp on it with the toe of her high heel shoe. . .but she didn't. She couldn't. Because, against everything, she wanted him to stay too.

Now, she and Solomon are in sync. It happened wordlessly,

without discussion, a come to Jesus, a come together moment. The way he backed her up, the way he's staying. She's never felt so calm, so confident in her decision to *just be*.

The only checklist she wants to make is a list of places where Solomon's mouth needs to be.

She should be petrified, terrified, shitting her type-A brains out, surfing the internet for a new job, but all she can think about is free. She's free. And wild. That girl she was six months ago, who gave no shits, who swung like a boss and took risks. It thrills her.

No Atlas breathing down her neck, no worries. Enjoying her baby, her body, and damn good sex.

But quitting her job doesn't mean she can just throw caution to the wind and shirk her responsibilities. Sure, she and Solomon have a perfectly nice, perfectly easy arrangement, but it's only for four more days.

They're friends with tropical vacation benefits.

This, them, whatever it is, is off limits.

"What about you?"

Tessie startles and raises her head to find Solomon scrutinizing her, his brows lifted in expectation.

"What about me?"

"Favorite color?"

"Ugh." She wrinkles her nose. "How much time do you have? Okay, okay. . .if I had to choose, it would be—No, I can't. I can't choose." Bottom lip stuck out, she pouts dramatically. "Ask me something else. Anything else."

An evil smile appears on his bearded face. "Tell me Bear's name."

"No!" She pokes a finger in his side, earning a grump of protest. "That's for me to know and you to find out."

He rolls his eyes. "Mature."

"Fine, fine, fine. If you want me to confess something, I will." She bites her lip. "But you might hate me."

"*Tess*," he growls, watching her with varying levels of worry and suspicion.

"I did it." She scrunches her nose and then laughs. "I lied to you. I stole your shirt."

His laugh is explosive, husky, and it shakes the hammock. "Tess, baby," he says, kissing her brow. "I had no doubt about that."

A shiver racing down her spine, she palms his cheek, admiring the rare smile gracing his face. "I like this."

"Like what?"

"Your smile."

With a grunt, he kisses her again, wraps an arm around her waist, and says, "Hold on."

Swiftly, Solomon moves, but before the hammock can flip, he steadies it. With his hands on her arms, he helps her carefully sit up in a swing-like position.

Tessie kicks sand in his direction. "Add that to the list of things you do right. Getting out of a hammock without toppling it."

"Precious cargo," Solomon says, giving Tessie a look so intense her heart puddles. "Got to."

"Oh," she squeaks, a dreamy sensation filling her up inside. Can this man go one single day without saying something that makes her melt?

There's a rustle of movement as a server appears. In his hands, a tray of sandwiches, fries, and ice-cold drinks—beer for Solomon and a virgin mojito for Tessie. Solomon tips the server, then, instead of reaching for his drink, reaches for Tessie's.

She smirks at him. "Are you like one of those Middle Ages tasters?"

He scowls, caught.

She leans forward, amused. "What if it's poisoned?"

"I'll take my chances," he says and then takes a giant gulp. After a second, he hands it over.

"My hero." She takes a sip. Bubbly and refreshing. She rests a hand on her stomach as the hammock sways. "Bear likes the rocking."

Solomon rests his broad palm on her stomach. His dark brows rise. "Kid's kicking like a ninja."

"He's a tiny little Wild Man," Tessie murmurs, tracing a finger over Solomon's muscular forearm. His dusting of dark hair has her wondering.

"Were you blond when you were a baby?" she asks, peeking up at him.

He chuckles. His craggy face breaks into a smile. "No," he says, lifting a fry in the air, offering it to her. "Everyone in my family is black-haired and blue-eyed."

"Like the Galway Girl." Tessie smiles and opens her mouth, accepting the fry he feeds her. As she chews, her brain churns, cranking out images of her son and Solomon. A beautiful baby boy with dark hair. Brown eyes or blue, she doesn't care. Just healthy and happy and theirs.

Her fingers trace the colorful designs on Solomon's beefy biceps. "Will you let Bear get tattoos?" she asks.

Solomon nods slowly. "When he's eighteen. Then he can go crazy like I did."

They eat in silence for a few minutes. The crash of the ocean, the burn of the sun, the slow sway of palm trees in the salty breeze.

Solomon's strong hand drops to her hip, palming the low curve of her stomach. "You feeling okay? About your job?"

She swallows hard, chokes down the nerves creeping up on her. "Oh, a freak-out is imminent, but right now, I'm all about in-the-moment." She tosses her hair over her shoulder. She's had other offers. Maybe finding a job she loves will be hard, but finding one less toxic than Atlas Rose Design should be a cinch. "Although getting hired while pregnant might be a bitch." She marvels at her stomach, palming her bud, and smiles at Bear. "But we can do it. Can't we?"

"We'll figure it out."

His voice, fierce, gruff, has her looking up. There's that *we* again.

"We will?"

No hesitation in his answer, he says, "Yeah. Damn right we will."

We.

Are they a *we*? Is she ready for *we*?

They finish their meals, their drinks, and then crawl back into the hammock. Tessie curls up on Solomon's chest. One of his big hands makes lazy caresses up her spine while the other is permanently glued to her belly.

His breath tickles her hair. "You feel like staying in or going out tonight?"

Staying in. The only activity she's game for involves a bed and Solomon. With the exception of the hammock, they haven't left the room since Atlas tucked tail and ran.

She stretches out on the mountain of a man's giant body, curling up like a cat in the sun. "Staying in," she yawns. "But we should go out one day, right?"

He chuckles, slipping a hand under her chin to bring her lips to his. His irises darken as he looks at her. Lust mixed with something she can't quite place. Does she want to place it? To name his feelings would give voice to all her fears. Everything she's been trying to avoid since her mother died. And she can't do it. Not yet.

"Anything you want," Solomon says with such solemnity that for a long second, it steals her breath, her heart. "You got it, Tessie."

And she believes him. Really and truly believes it. If she asked Solomon to slay, to kill, to steal for her and Bear, he would.

She inclines her head so she can study him. Her belly warms. She could study his chiseled face all day. Thick brows. Mussed dark hair. Square jaw. Stern. Solemn. Handsome.

She gives a casual shrug. "I saw something about dinner and dancing." An advertisement on the in-room television. A *fiesta extravaganza!*

His throat bobs. "Dancing?"

She wets her lips. "Tomorrow night at the Pavilions. We could go," she says, going for as uninterested as possible.

"I have two left feet."

"I remember." She rubs her stomach. "I'm not exactly a pillar of balance these days myself."

He smiles down at her, his dark blue eyes softening. "Whatever you want, Tess. You just tell me."

"Okay, then. Tonight, we stay in," she says, nodding decisively. "Tomorrow, we go out."

A grunt of affirmation. Then he links his fingers with hers, and Tessie stretches along the warm solidness of his hard body. Like they're growing roots, reaching for the stars. Like they're living for just one more breath. Like everything that's precious to her is contained in this hammock. This nine-by-twelve cocoon-like space of comfort and joy.

She wants to remember this moment. This perfect heartbeat in time. Her and Solomon and Bear.

"Solomon," she says, lifting herself up on her elbow. The hammock wobbles. "I want to take a photo." She smiles. "Documentation to prove I got you on a beach."

His throat works. "Sure. Why not."

Reaching behind her, she snags her phone. Her arms shoot up to the sky, the camera pointing down at them. Tessie, bright and sunny. Solomon, dark and brooding. The tiny baby in her swollen belly, stuck perfect and right between them.

Chapter Eighteen

"Did you get the photo?" Solomon asks the next evening as he steps out onto the terrace to watch the beach come alive. In the distance, faint strains of music. The lights of the pavilion lightsaber the sky, signaling the beginning of the event to come.

"We got it," his dad says, voice tinny over the speakerphone.

With a sigh, he rests his hip against the railing. If Tessie's ballsy enough to quit her job, then he can call the family he's been screening since he arrived in Mexico.

"So you're staying," Evelyn says, her voice flat and dry.

"You're smiling," Jo pipes in.

"You're smiling a lot," Melody adds. Ten years younger than Solomon, Melody's the baby of the family. "Oodles and oodles of smiling."

Solomon rubs his brow. Christ. He sends his middle sister Jo the photo of him and Tessie on the beach, and it's passed around the family like news down the AP Wire. He swears under his breath, picturing his entire family, minus Evelyn, crowded around the kitchen island, the cell phone passed between them. It's the way of the Wilders. Family dinners. Group phone calls. Group texts. Things he hasn't been part of in a long damn time.

He sighs. "You say that like it's a bad thing."

"No. It's a great thing," Melody says. "I haven't seen that smile since—"

Her voice cuts off in a strangle, but he knows what she was going to say. Hell, they all do. *Since Serena.*

His mother's voice now, edging in, chasing away the awkward silence. "So that's her? Tess?"

Solomon clears his throat. "Yeah." Unbidden, a smile hits his lips. "Tessie."

At the thought of her, he straightens, glancing over his shoulder to search her out. His heartbeat ticks up a notch as she exits the bedroom, her own phone pressed to her ear. She's fresh from the shower, wrapped in a fluffy white towel. They spent all day at the beach again, and tonight, dinner and dancing.

Before Tessie, it's the last thing he'd be doing. But now, by her side is where he wants to be.

Relief fills him. He doesn't have to leave her yet. He still has time.

A vacation he didn't know he needed with a girl he didn't know he needed.

Tessie glances up and gives him a small wave before disappearing back into the bedroom.

"I see her little bump," Melody coos, bringing Solomon back to the phone call.

Evelyn sniffs, unimpressed. "She's wearing a bikini when she's pregnant."

Jo now. "God, you're stale, Evelyn."

"I like her," Melody announces.

"You haven't met her," Evelyn snips.

Jo says, "Jesus, let the man live, would you, Evil?"

Mom sighs. "Girls."

"Listen," Solomon barks. "I wanted to call and tell you that I'm staying down here for a few more days."

"How long's a few more days?" his dad asks.

He paces. "Monday."

A yelp from Melody.

"Well, son. If that's what you need to do, you do it."

"Yeah, Sol," Jo says. "Keep that smile on your face."

Solomon appreciates how even-keel they are about this whole situation. Even after what he put them through with his disappearing and distancing act, they're loyal as hell. That's the Wilders too. They support, they don't meddle.

With the exception of Evelyn.

"What about the baby?" his mother asks.

"It's mine." His heart warms, heats like a bonfire. Clearing his throat, he tears a hand through his hair. "Hell, I forgot to tell you. It's a boy."

A chorus of gasps and a little scream from Melody assault him. Evelyn the only silent objector.

"Oh, Sol," his mom says, tears in her voice. He can practically hear her dabbing the corner of her eye. "That's wonderful."

"A *babyyy*," Jo singsongs. "He's gonna have a little beard."

"Sure can't wait to meet the little guy," his dad gruffs.

"And then what?" Melody chirps.

Solomon tenses, stopping his pace across the terrace.

Goddamn good question.

He hasn't thought about his future since Serena. His life was routine, rote, but without meaning or purpose. Hell, he didn't give much thought to the world beyond his front door. He lived in his memories and one moment at a time. Black coffee in the morning. Walked his dog in the woods. Made his money woodworking. Bourbon in the evening.

Buried in grief, he kept himself closed off from the world so that he couldn't have a future. He didn't want one without Serena.

But now...

Being here with Tessie has opened his eyes. There's more to his life.

More he could have.

The last six months—hell, the last five days—he's been picking pieces of her out of his soul. Blond hair in his beard. Her lipstick on his chest. Her bright smile when they sway to the record player every night, both of them pretending that time is on their side.

Nothing matters except waking up next to Tessie. His hand on her belly, feeling the little squirm of their son inside. Already, he loves that baby fiercely. With everything he has.

"Are you bringing her back here?" Melody chirps in his ear. "Are you two, like. . .together?" she asks, instantly earning a scoff from Evelyn. "Or are you going there? Or maybe—"

"Melody, sweetheart, I think Sol's just trying to figure out this whole baby business," his mother chides.

He chuckles. "Thanks, Mom."

"You have fun, Solomon," his dad says, tone hopeful. "Keep that smile on your face and bring it back home, you hear me?"

"I will." The words come out rough thanks to the brick stuck in his throat. He put his family through hell after Serena died. Made them worry about him. Made them think he'd never be the same.

A chorus of *I love yous* and goodbyes, and then Evelyn saying, "Sol, can you stay on the line?"

He sighs and waits for the rest of the family to hang up, and then his sister is hissing, "Why are you really staying?"

He frowns at her accusatory tone. "It was my idea," he says, not wanting Tessie to take the brunt of Evelyn's bad mood.

"You're getting attached."

He grinds his teeth. "It's my son. I think I have a goddamn right to get attached." He smears a hand down his beard. "Tessie needed this. She needs to relax. She quit her job and—"

"Wait." A frantic clacking on the keyboard. "She *quit*? When she has a child to feed? Unbelievable."

Fuck. He shouldn't have said anything.

"She'll find a new job. She's a senior designer."

Even now, Solomon can't help but marvel at the fierce force that is Tessie Truelove. It was so goddamn ballsy quitting her job like that. It took all he had to hang back, to not grip the guy by his throat and toss his ass off the terrace. But his girl stood her ground. And it was damn sexy.

"How is she going to find a new job? She's seven months pregnant." A sputter over the line. "I don't believe this girl."

"She'll find one. Anyone would be lucky to have her."

"Does that include you?" Evelyn asks. "Sol, she's still a stranger. There's nothing between you but a child. You can't commit because of that. Because of a one-night stand that got out of control."

He pushes away from the railing, opening his mouth, ready to tell his sister to butt the hell out, but the calm of the crashing ocean chases away his urge. Of course Evelyn's prickly, worrying about him moving on. He wants to tell her he does know Tessie, and he likes every side he sees.

A whole damn lot, in fact.

Tearing his eyes from the water, he strides toward the suite. "Evy, I'm not discussing this with you," he murmurs and then hangs up.

His shoulders settle as he stares down at the photo of him with Tessie and Bear set as his phone lock screen.

He has more important things to focus on.

"You haven't left the room, have you?" Ash crows as Tessie, phone tucked under her ear, pulls cocktail dresses from the closet. "All you've been doing is having hot, hot monkey sex with that steel cage on legs."

She has. She and Solomon are having so much sex that if she wasn't already pregnant, she would be now.

"We did leave the room," she argues. "We went to the beach yesterday and today."

"Wait. That's it? No cheesy activities like water aerobics, yoga, or beach limbo?"

"No." She cocks her head, frowning. "Is that bad?"

"Tessie, you planned nothing?" Ash gives a whoop. "You are fucking living chaos! I bow to thee, chaotic queen."

Tessie rolls her eyes but laughs. "Let's not go that far. We're going out tonight. To a dance." She appraises herself in the mirror and smiles. Long sultry waves waterfall over her shoulders, her makeup dark and smoky. On point, as always.

"You sound swoony," Ash says, breaking Tessie from her dreamy daze.

She huffs. "Swoony is the last thing I am. What's the point of falling for him? He lives across the world. Besides, he's staying for Bear. He doesn't want me."

Biting her lip, Tessie arranges a plethora of dresses on the bed. Bright, colorful pops of fuchsia, lime, and coral. Ignores the plummet of her damn dumb heart.

"Are you sure?" Ash prods. "Have you asked?"

"I can't worry about it." Shaking off her nerves, Tessie selects the coral gown. Then, putting the phone on speaker, she steps into the dress, hoping this time she doesn't need to be cut out of it.

"I have to find a new job." Her voice comes out muffled as she shimmies the slinky garment up her hips, her bump. Her only lifesaver is, thanks to a clause in her contract, she still has insurance until the baby's born. "I have to focus on Bear."

"Bear will be happy when his mama's happy."

"We barely know each other."

"Isn't that what you're doing? Getting to know each other? Face it, Tess. It's like you've been on five dates by now. By LA standards, you should already be divorcing." Ash's bouncy voice turns serious. "Wouldn't you want to be with Bear's father if you could? Isn't that, like, the ultimate goal of this whole thing?"

"No." Not wanting Solomon to overhear, Tessie picks up the phone, switching off the speaker. "The ultimate goal was to figure out how we raise Bear, and we have. We can't let it turn into more than it is."

A growl of frustration. "But what if it's already something? What if it's the most splendiferous occasion of fate in the universe? You met the guy for a reason. You slept with him for a reason. You came back to LA with him on your mind. And Bear happened. Solomon saw you on TV, a thousand miles away from him when you never even exchanged names, numbers. What are the chances? You know me, I'm cynical as fuck, but if that's not the universe, not your mom telling you to work it out, then we gotta get someone new in the big up above."

Tessie's breath catches in her throat. Her words of refute lost. Even as she tries to deny what her cousin is saying, her thumping heart screams its protest. That girl who doesn't believe in love, who's never had it, maybe, kinda, sorta, wants to dip a toe in. Because isn't that the point? To take risks? To live?

She could try for once in her life.

She could try with Solomon.

"You can raise Bear alone," Ash says. "I know you can. But do you want to?"

The question hangs in the space between them.

Does she want to do this alone? Would she do it with anyone else? The answer is no. She likes Solomon. So serious. Protective. His steady ways. She and him—they feel natural. Bear is his son. It fits.

It all fits.

Then why is it so damn hard to let herself give in?

She searches for her voice. "No," she admits. "I don't want to do it alone."

"So don't."

"Tess?" A knuckle rap on the door. "You ready to go?"

Her heart beats fast at the deep rumble of Solomon's voice. "Ash," she says into the phone, "I have to go."

Smiling, she crosses the room, grabbing her clutch and kicking on her heels. She rips open the door, a wisecrack on her lips, but the second she sees Solomon, her voice dies a quick death. A solid wall of chiseled muscle stands in front of her. His dark blue eyes flashing, Solomon wears a crisp white shirt with light gray chinos. His black hair and beard combed neatly.

Suave. Sexy as hell.

She ogles without shame, drinking him in.

A sizzle hits her in her core, and she pulses down below. All of a sudden, going out seems like a very bad idea.

His eyes brush over her face. "Tess, you okay?"

At her silence, Solomon moves close. A massive arm bands around her waist, holding her up. Her stomach takes a dive. Her legs promptly turn to gummy noodles.

Okay, now she's swooning. *Damn Ash.*

She shakes her head, clearing it. "I'm fine. I'm just—" Voice strained, she tucks a lock of hair behind her ear. "It's—I mean, you…"

His mouth flattens. Somewhere behind that dark beard, there's a grin tucked away. "You're looking like you like me, Tessie."

She sniffs. "I'm only mildly besotted."

"Mildly?" He threads a big hand through his dark hair, disheveling it, looking devilishly handsome. "Guess I'll have to brush up on my skills."

"Oh? For who?" The words leave her lips in a breathless rush. She feels the briefest sting of jealousy at the thought of Solomon with another woman. Because he isn't hers, not permanently, and there's a very strong possibility he'll meet someone in the future.

Oh God. The thought makes her want to hurl.

A half smile turns up the corner of his lips. "For you, Tess."

She swallows, forcing a wobbly smile, trying to ignore the way her galloping heart suddenly high-fives her chest. "Oh. I see."

Solomon's piercing gaze holds hers. He offers an arm. "You ready?"

"Ready," she whispers, her stomach tightening.

For this, yes.

For everything else, putting a lockbox on her feelings, saying goodbye in less than seventy-two hours?

Most definitely not.

Still, she links her arm with his. "Ready."

Chapter Nineteen

Tessie stops at the top of the pyramid of stairs that leads up to the entrance of the open-air beach pavilion and gasps. Every inch is lit up in a ball of brilliant bright light. A canopy of jewel-colored flowers and garland hangs from each beam. Scarlet lanterns flicker in the night, bobbing and dipping in the air. A swell of banda music—clarinets and trumpets and trombones—fills the dewy night air.

"It's so beautiful," she says, her mouth open in a kind of joyous awe.

"It is," Solomon murmurs.

It's all he can say. Because the rock in his throat has him in a stranglehold. The perfect fucking ten at his side has him damn near on his knees.

Tessie's drop-dead gorgeous. Her beauty white hot and searing. He's never seen her look so refreshed, so radiant. Streaks of gold shimmer on her eyelids, making her chocolate-brown eyes shine. Her long blond hair spreads around her shoulders like melted honey. Her bright coral off-the-shoulder dress is practically painted on, showing off her mouthwatering curves, her tiny bump, that perfect baby in her belly.

His son. Theirs.

He's never been so goddamn whipped.

"Should we go in?" she asks, peering up at him. A lock of hair falls across her face.

"Yeah." He adjusts her small hand in his. Somewhere along the way here, they unlinked arms, linked fingers.

"If I make it past ten, I'll be surprised," she observes, looking up to the moon.

He palms her stomach, murmurs, "We do surprises best, don't we?"

Her cheeks flush and her long lashes lower. "Yeah," she agrees, smiling bright, like they have the best secret in the world. "We do."

He holds her gaze for a long moment. His heart is going to explode out of his chest. Then he clears the boulder from his throat. "C'mon, Pregnant Woman."

Clasping her hand tight, he leads her to the hostess stand, and after Tessie confirms her reservation, they enter the pavilion. At the front of the room, a band plays on the small stage. High-tops decorated with vases of flowers, with reserved signs, are spread out across the floor. Servers pass cocktails and tapas.

"Oh my God," Tessie squeaks, tugging on his arm. "This is giving me millennial prom vibes. *Oh!* Here's our table," she says, setting her clutch on a high-top with a *RESERVED—TRUELOVE* sign. "Oh my God, look at that chandelier!"

He chuckles when she lets out a second gasp and releases his hand to take in the scene. Winding through guests with her rounded belly, she glows. She grins as she watches the band, examines the flowers, runs a hand down the linens and steals a canapé from a tray.

This is the girl he met back in that bar. Funny, sweet, always down for a good time. But the other side of her, the one he's gotten to know over the last week? Icy, ballsy, and brazen. Brave. A fighter. For her and her son. He loves that side too. That hard shell of hers is just that—a shell. To protect herself because she can't stand to have one more thing walk away from her. And Solomon knows how it feels.

A rustling of sound has him turning. A nearby server admires Tessie. And why wouldn't he? Her beauty casts its spell over everyone in her orbit. When he notices Solomon's eyes on him, the man adjusts the tray in his hands. Giving a small bow of acknowledgment, he says, "Your wife's beautiful, señor."

A knot tightens in his throat. Only rectified when he says, "She is."

Stop. Stop looking at her like she's yours.

Why not, Sol? She is.

It hits him then, hits him hard.

He wants her to be his.

And he doesn't just want to be in his son's life. He wants to be in Tessie's. Wants to *be* Tessie's. Because she's his. She and Bear, they're both his.

The night at the Bear's Ear bar cemented it.

His second life began the night he met Tessie.

He just didn't know it until now.

Solomon's stomach dips, a familiar sensation settling in his gut as the realization winds itself around him and won't let go. His heart is ticking like a bomb.

Fuck.

He loves her.

He loves this woman who's carrying his child. Not because of that, but in spite of it.

He knew he was falling for Tess, knew it was fast, but nothing prepared him for this.

It wasn't part of the plan.

And now. . .

Now he's going to do everything he can to keep her.

Moving gracefully, swaying near the stage, Tessie places a palm on the low swell of her stomach, and Solomon's heart hitches.

Everything right there, he can't live without.

Dance with her Sol.

Serena's spirit hovers. Nagging, cursing him.

Dance with her or someone else will.

Dance with her or I will.

For a long second, he scrubs his hands over his face and swears, assaulted by guilt. Guilt because he never danced with Serena to that old jukebox in Howler's Roost. How he sat on the sidelines, arms crossed, grunting, letting her have fun without him.

Second chance. New chance.

He can do better than he did with Serena.

A drum beats in his chest as he strides across the open space. When he reaches Tess, he cups her elbow. She turns, her beautiful face surprised—eyes shining, mouth an O—then she smiles.

"Dance with me," he says.

She arches a brow. "I thought you didn't dance."

"With you, I do."

Then he snags her hand and leads her onto the dance floor, where they melt into a small crowd of slow-swaying dancers.

"You're not so bad," she murmurs. The soft light illuminates the delicate features of her pretty profile. "I think you lied about having two left feet."

He peers down at her. Holding her in his arms feels so goddamn perfect. "Think I was nervous about the beautiful woman baptizing the bar floor with chardonnay," he replies.

She socks his arm, laughs.

"Think we were both pretending to be people we weren't," Tessie muses after a second.

"Maybe. But I liked the girl I met that night. I still do."

Her eyes widen at his admission. "I like you too, Solomon." A shy flush storms her cheeks. "I like your flannel. I like your grunts and your handsome beard. I like everything about you."

Fuck. If he thought he was done for before, he really is now.

"Are you frowning or scowling?" She palms his cheek. The touch of her singes. A rush of heat to his nether regions has him squirming. "It's just really hard to tell."

He laughs. "I'm smiling, Tessie."

"You are?" She reaches up to trace the edge of his lips, his beard, with a delicate finger. "Hmm. A smile. I must have done something right, Solemn Man."

He drops one hand to palm her stomach. "You're doing everything right. You're perfect."

"Sometimes I don't know about that," she says with a humorless laugh.

He shakes his head. "Tess, we're in this together. You're not doing this alone. And whether or not you believe me, I'll show you. I'll prove it."

She lifts a slender shoulder. They've stopped in the middle of the dance floor. "All I believe in is Bear."

"That's a good thing to believe in."

"I don't want to let him down."

"You won't. Hey." He touches her chin, hating the sad look on her face. "I'm not here to make your life harder. Or take him away. I'm here to help. To stay and be a good dad to Bear."

His stomach knots as her big brown eyes spear him. Slowly, she slides a hand up his chest to rest over the space of his heart. The heat of her hand radiating through his shirt. And he burns. Solomon burns in all the best ways a man can burn. Raw. Alive. In love.

"That's. . .the only reason you're staying?"

It's hard to breathe. Caught up in her question, what she's really asking him.

Say it. Say it fucking now.

Say that Bear isn't the only reason he's staying. That nothing matters except waking up in bed next to her. That he doesn't know what this is between them, but he's not ready for it to end. Not yet. Not ever.

Say that he loves her.

Sol, take a shot in the dark and tell her.

He moves closer, capturing her face in his hands. "Tess, listen. . ."

"Yes?" she whispers, her molten eyes locked on him.

"Tessie, baby, I—"

"Well, howdy. Ain't we so happy to see y'all here!"

Solomon's stomach plummets, his late-night confession gone up in smoke. He drags his attention from the girl in his arms to the intrusive source of the nasally drawl.

Fuck.

Rick and Roni Zebrowski stand across from them, ready to wreak chaos.

Tessie hides a smirk at the sight of Solomon's what-the-fuck expression, the way a rumble of a growl builds in his chest and how he works his jaw back and forth as Rick and Roni follow them back to their high-top. "We had the hardest time rustlin' up a table. Mind if we join you?" Without waiting for an answer, Roni drops her sequin purse on the table with a clatter.

"You had a hard time," Solomon says through gritted teeth, "because Tessie planned ahead and made reservations."

Placing a hand on Solomon's arm, Tessie conjures up the placid smile she gives clients when they ask her to design burial chambers for their pets. "Feel free to join us," she offers. "We're not staying long."

Not if she can help it.

She wants to get back to that conversation. Solomon had been about to tell her something important. She saw it in his eyes. The hard bob of his throat. Her big, tough mountain man was nervous, and she wants to get to the bottom of it. Because maybe it's what she hopes it is. Maybe he feels the same way she does.

"You want drinks?" she asks the table. "We'll get drinks," she offers, snagging Solomon by the bicep and dragging him over to the small bar.

"We can go," he grunts after they place their orders. His glare could fry the sun.

Ash's comment about her getting out of the room resonates in Tessie's mind. She didn't get dressed up only to be ambushed by two perfectly annoying strangers. This is what vacation is for. Meeting others. Expanding one's worldly horizons. Although, after a second glance at Rick and Roni Zebrowski, she's beginning to understand why Solomon stayed on his mountain.

"Ten minutes," she says. "Then we can bolt if it gets painful." She presses into Solomon. "Besides, admit it, you're mildly intrigued. They're wearing neon suspenders; how do you not want to know more?"

"Fine," he says with a flat chuckle. He leans in to press a kiss to her lips.

Tessie stiffens, a pleased shiver curling down her spine. Oh God. They're kissing now.

Spontaneous random kisses out in public.

Kissing like a couple.

She's suddenly breathless, her heart pumping hard, this gooey teenage feeling heating her up inside. And she knows—with every cynical love-adverse bone in her vibrating body—she's falling.

Too hard. Too soon. Too fast.

Wilding out for Solomon Wilder.

Internally, she groans. *Ugh. Heart and mind align; same page, please.*

She has to stick to her guns. No attachment.

Even if saying goodbye will hurt like hell.

"Code word," Tessie says, snapping out of her inane thoughts, "bananas." She flips her hair and snatches up two drinks, watching the amused smile tug at Solomon's lips. "I bet you the first diaper change you say it first."

Rick and Roni are deep in conversation when they get back to the table. Solomon hands a drink to Rick, takes a sip of his whiskey, and rests his large elbows on the table.

Rick raises his beer in a toast. "To new friends."

Roni gestures at Tessie's cocktail glass, her face puckering. "I didn't know you could have alcohol."

Tessie's body is a cringe. Here they go. Unsolicited advice. A never-ending part of her pregnancy.

"It's a mocktail," she says evenly, then takes a long sip.

"A what?"

"A mocktail. It's non-alcoholic," Solomon says, his voice as lethal as an injection.

Roni fans herself. "The fancy things they have these days. . ." she drawls, instantly launching into a menu of what she could and could not eat when she was pregnant with her firstborn.

As Tess tries not to zone out, she shifts on her heels. Wearing them was a mistake. Her feet feel like they're in a vise. But before she can turn to hunt for a chair, Solomon's placing a light hand on the small of her back and asking, "You need to sit?"

"Yes," she breathes, looking up at him. How he can read her, how he's so attuned to her needs, has her blood warming. He stalks over to the bar and brings back a barstool for her. With one hand in hers and the other on her waist, he helps her onto the highback chair.

When she's settled, Tessie shares a warm smile with Solomon. Beneath the table, she searches for his hand. His big fingers pull her hand into his. Offering comfort. Solidarity.

With a narrowed, sniper-like gaze, Roni asks, "Now, when did you say you're due again?"

"I didn't," Tessie breathes out, already tired of the inquisition. Already wanting to get back to their room. She hates that being pregnant is like open season for interrogation, perfect strangers dying to share their hot takes on her body, offering shitty criticisms, and asking personal questions that are none of their business.

When Roni waits for her reply, lips pursed in anticipation, Tessie sighs and gives in. "December twenty-third."

"Ooh, a holiday baby," Roni titters.

"Our oldest was born on Halloween," Rick adds with a goofy

laugh. "Never seen so many zombies in the delivery room, and I'm not just talking about the pregnant women."

Roni squeals like he's just told the best joke in the world.

Pained, Solomon sets his whiskey down and rubs a palm over his bearded jaw.

Roni sucks on the lime from her margarita glass, says to Tessie, "You look small for twenty-nine weeks. Are you sure—"

"She's sure," Solomon snaps.

Tessie squeaks and squeezes his muscular thigh under the table. A warning to keep it together. "So what do you think of the resort?" she asks Roni, desperate for a change in topic.

"Oh, it's beautiful. It'd be even better without all those birds squawking every morning." She waves a hand. "Don't get me wrong; I love nature, just not when it interrupts my vacation."

A strangled noise comes out of Solomon's throat.

Tessie leans in. "Say it," she whispers so low only he can hear. "Code word."

"Never," he grits out, stone faced. Every part of him a tense, rippling muscle. He's white knuckling his frosted whiskey glass.

"It's so good you two are doing this." Roni downs her margarita, leaving hot pink lipstick smeared on one side of her face. She swivels her finger between Tessie and Solomon. "Go to all the shows and concerts and vacations you can before the baby is born, because you'll never get a chance again."

A tremor of unease twists Tessie's stomach. With Roni's rambling, all her insecurities and fears and anxieties about giving birth have come clawing to the surface.

"Have you been to the spa yet?" Tessie asks, hoping to take the spotlight off her stomach. She adjusts herself in the chair, steeling her spine. "It's rated one of the best in the world. Their massages are supposed to be epic." She chuckles and looks at Solomon. "I should schedule a foot massage."

A small smile ghosts his lips. "Should stop wearing heels."

Gasping, she swats at him with her clutch. "I will wear heels, Solomon, and you will adore me every step of the way."

Eagled eyed, Roni chimes in. "Honestly, Tessie, I really can't believe you're still wearing heels. No wonder you're tired, wearing shoes like that." Her lips pucker. "I heard they can cause miscarriages, you know."

Tessie jerks back like she's been slapped. The words her worst fear served up on a platter—so cruel, so paralyzing that her eyes flood with tears.

She'll leave the baby.

The baby will leave her.

Rick closes his eyes. "Shit. Roni."

"For fuck's sake," Solomon growls, his hand balling into a fist. "What is wrong with you?"

The couple take a step back from the table, their faces pale.

Solomon looks at her, the bones of his handsome face rigid with rage. The hard line of his jaw moving over and over. "You want to go?"

Tears spill down her cheeks. She bobblehead nods.

She can't handle this with grace. Not anymore.

"Yes," she says. She's shaking, absolutely a tremor. Her heart beats so hard in her chest it could punch through the walls of her ribs at any moment.

Holding tight to her hand, Solomon helps her off the chair. Then he tucks her against his side as he thunders out of the pavilion, walking so fast that she has to hurry to keep up.

The sky's dusted with stars when they step outside.

Solomon turns to her, worry etched on his handsome face. "Tess..."

But she doesn't listen.

She can't.

Instead, she runs.

All she wants to do is get away. From the advice. From her

fears. From worries that have followed her all her life. That this sad kind of lonely will never leave her.

"Tessie, wait!"

Solomon's shout follows her, but she doesn't stop. Panic, fear fuel her forward, her heels click-clacking across the wooden slats of the boardwalk.

She keeps running. Over cement, past palm trees, onto soft sand until she reaches the surf. There she stops, kicks off her heels. Water crashes over her ankles as tears slide down her face to stain her stomach. A sob tears out of her.

"I'm sorry," she whispers to Bear, cradling her belly. "I'm so sorry. People are stupid. And you're going to have to put up with them. But I'll protect you. As long as I can, I'll be there, okay?"

She watches the ocean, wanting to shriek at the sky, wanting her mother, wanting to go back and slap Roni Zebrowski across her margarita-stained mouth, when there's a rumble from behind her.

"Tess."

She turns around. Head down, she walks straight into Solomon's open arms.

"Bananas," she gasps against his chest.

"You can't do that to me," he says in a gruff voice swollen with panic. Then his big fingers are against her cheek, in her hair, raising her face to meet his eyes. "You can't run." He kisses her lips, her temples, her throat with such desperation that for a second, she feels faint. "You hear me? Don't run. Not from me. Please. Please, Tess."

"I'm sorry," she whispers. She closes her eyes. Solomon's knock-out touch, his hug, is like a warm blanket. She smells the whiskey on his breath, his Solomon-scent in his beard, and she wants to live there forever.

"No, I'm sorry," he says in a voice that breaks at every angle. "And before you say it, you didn't overreact. They're assholes. Fuck those people." His callused thumbs whisk over the high arch of her cheekbone, sweeping away her tears. "You wear your heels, Tess. No one's got the right to say shit like that to you. You're going to be a great mother. And Bear's going to be fine. Do you understand me? Nothing will happen to him. I won't let it. Don't listen to her. Don't even give them a second damn thought—"

With a wild cry, Tessie throws her arms around his neck and smashes her mouth to his. The tight knot of fear inside her releases, and she presses up on tiptoes to melt into Solomon's body of steel. His strength.

Her Solemn Man.

"Thank you," she whispers against his mouth. She clings to him like she's dissolving. "No one's ever done anything like that for me."

"*Fuck*," he bites out, the intensity making her shiver. Like he's her shield, her bodyguard, and nothing and no one will ever hurt her. "You get used to it, Tess. You get used to me. Because, baby, I'm here." He holds her tight; he's trembling just like she is. "For you, anything."

A sob-laugh breaks out of her. "Does that include tossing Roni into shark-infested waters?"

He kisses her back, squeezing her tight against him, then holding her at arm's length. "You just say the word." Blue eyes sweep to her belly before moving to her face. "Are you okay?"

She nods. Sniffles. "I am. We are. Some night this was."

He bands the back of her neck with his broad palm. "It's not over."

"It's not?"

As she stares up at him, something inside her comes alive.

Sparks. Flames. A voice telling her she's right where she should be.

"No, Tess, it's not," he growls fiercely, his gaze drifting to the inky sky. "Because, baby, we got stars."

Then he's grasping her face in his large hands and leaning down to kiss her in the moonlight.

The ocean crashes over her bare feet, Solomon's boots, but all Tessie feels is his lips on hers, the warm surety of his touch, his *I am here for you* vibes. There's no question in his kiss; only an urgency. A hunger. A promise.

Tonight, all her doubts, all the tightly controlled lines she's drawn in the sand between them, are washed away by a single wave.

By a single kiss that has her losing her heart to Solomon Wilder.

Chapter Twenty

Solomon opens his eyes to bright sunlight, to the low croon of the record player, to an empty bed.

Another goddamn empty bed.

"Fuck," he groans, lifting up on one elbow.

One morning. Just one morning, he'd like to wake up to discover Tess hasn't run out on him. To find her beside him, sleeping, soft and safe. Resting. Especially after last night.

He flops onto his back to study the ceiling. His stomach has been in a knot since Tess ran out of the pavilion with tears in her eyes. The way she looked last night: pale, panicked, terrified.

He could see her, during the conversation with those people, about to crack. She needed him. And he refused to let her down. He could have controlled his temper better with Rick and Roni, but he was pissed as hell, and all his focus was on Tessie.

Tessie and Bear—they're his responsibility. It's his job to protect them.

And then she ran.

And every long-buried emotion he's been hiding from cranked on like a flood.

She ran from him. Like Serena. It had set him off, had him panicking, had him chasing her down to the beach and holding her in his arms like it was the end of the world.

Up until now, he's given her crumbs about his marriage, but that's it. Now it's time to give her the truth about his past. He has to give her an out before he gives her everything. Because he's ready. Ready to make that woman his.

Where is she anyway?

Frowning, Solomon sits up and checks his phone. A missed call from Evelyn, from Howler. Then he leaves the bedroom and goes into the living room.

Sun on her skin, Tessie's dressed in yoga pants and a black tank top that hugs her stomach. Her hair, in two loose braids, hangs over her breasts. A gorgeous flush of color rides high on her cheeks.

"Morning," he says, relief washing through him at finding her nearby.

"Hi," she says, pulling a lavender yoga mat out of the closet. Seeing his curious stare, she lifts the mat. "Exercise. I haven't done any since I got here. There's a combo prenatal and postnatal yoga class at noon. I thought I'd check it out."

He makes his way toward her. "You have breakfast?"

"Mm-hmm. Left you some coffee."

"Generous of you."

She laughs and rubs her stomach. "Bear was hungry."

Gripping her hips, he pulls her in to him. Rests a hand on her belly. "Blame the baby."

"I will. I have eleven weeks to do it." She sticks her tongue out at him and pulls back.

But he holds her tight. Close. "Listen, Tess. We need to talk about last night."

She flinches. "I know. I'm sorry for freaking out like that."

"You didn't freak out." Holding her gaze, he cups her cheek. "Never be sorry for that."

Her lips tip up like she doesn't believe him. "Okay. Thanks."

"Hold up," he orders when she turns to slink off. "Get your beautiful butt back here."

She looks startled by his tone but returns to his arms.

"I need you to hear something," he says, all his focus locked on her. "I need a favor from you."

"What kind of favor?"

"You can't walk out on me. You can't leave."

Her eyes widen at his words, but he continues.

"I get why you do it. But you don't have to run. Not from me. And if you need to. . .you tell me. No more dead of night slinking off—"

She scoffs. "I do not slink, Solomon—"

"No more leaving our bed, Tess."

It's a demand, and he won't apologize for it. He nudges her chin up with a finger, making her meet his no-nonsense gaze. "I don't ever want to not be able to find you. You understand me?"

"I'm—" She opens her mouth, ready to argue with him, then shuts it. "Okay. I won't leave." She tilts her head back as she appraises him, her brown eyes soft and curious. "Will you tell me why?"

"I will." He kisses her forehead, running his palms down her slender shoulders. "Later. I don't want you to miss your class."

Her lips flatten like she's unhappy, like she wants to say something.

He tucks an errant wisp of hair behind her ear. "Go, Tess."

After a second of hesitation, she pushes off him and tucks the mat under her arm. "You could come with me," she offers, pausing at the door. "Do some downward dog."

He chuckles. "I don't think I bend that way."

She gives a flirty little smile. "That's not what I remember."

His dick flexes; the urge to drag Tessie back to bed has real teeth. "Tell you what. Tonight, you pick what we do. Whatever you want."

"I chose last night."

"Yeah, but last night was bullshit. Your choice again."

Always your choice.

She narrows her eyes in suspicion. "Really? Anything?"

"Anything."

Her beautiful face lighting up, Tessie gives him a wicked grin.

"You're gonna kill it at water aerobics." She flutters her fingers. "See you later, Solemn Man."

Solemn Man.

His heart gutters as she disappears out the door.

Jesus, he's got to get his goddamn head on straight.

Call Howler and Evelyn.

Then he'll spend the day with Tessie.

And he'll tell her everything.

The yoga studio is on the other side of the resort. A spacious room illuminated by sunlight with floor-to-ceiling windows on one side, and mirrors on the other. The instructor, a woman with an electric yellow pixie cut, wears a headset and is gently ushering students to their spaces.

When she catches sight of Tessie, the instructor claps her hands in glee. "Oh, we have another little mama in the room."

A chorus of *oohs* and *ahhs* has Tessie fighting the urge to roll her eyes.

"I'm Devon," the instructor says, doing a sort of curtsy. Colorful bangles glitter on her arm.

"Tessie."

"Tessie. Beautiful. Have you taken yoga before?"

She smiles, adjusting the mat under her arm. "I have, but not while pregnant."

"Perfect." Devon gestures to the front row. "Please take a seat. I'll offer prenatal modifications for each move for you, mama. So ignore what everyone else is doing and just pay attention to me."

As she spreads out her mat, Tessie regrets the decision to put her body through exercise. Sweating her damn ass off is the last thing she wants to do today. But Ash's words keep goading her. She needs to experience this vacation to its fullest. When all she really wants to do is spoon with Solomon on the beach.

"Alright, are we ready to get started?" Devon's voice crackles over the speakers. A swell of flutes and bird chorus fills the room. She nods at Tessie. "You let your body do what it needs to do."

A woman decked out in Lululemon puts her mat next to Tessie. "When are you due?"

"I'm not."

The woman blanches, stammers out an apology.

Tessie keeps her face placid, but inside, she's smirking. After last night, she plans to adopt Solomon's take-no-shit strategy.

Which is what she needs to give to herself. A no-bullshit talk.

Last night was a clearing of the clouds in her head. In her heart.

Last night uncorked every feeling she's kept bottled up.

The way Solomon came for her, defended her...it's still curling her toes.

Last night, he showed her who he truly was. A good man. Who doesn't make her feel so alone. Who would always protect her and Bear. Who doesn't walk away.

Which is why the thought of him leaving in just a few short days has her freaking out. She can do this baby business without him, but she doesn't want to. It feels so right with him. They're good together. So damn good. She can read him. Sure, they're just getting to know each other, but what if there's more there?

She used to think the only thing she and Solomon shared was Bear.

But what about a heart?

Devon's melodic voice sideswipes Tessie's thoughts. "Your body, your womb, is heavy right now. We will lighten it up. Keep a straight line as we extend. Clear your minds. No brain power on jobs, on husbands, on babies. It's just us and the moment. Palms to the sky." Devon glances her way. "Mama, follow me, and I'll adjust."

Nodding, Tessie shakes herself out of her daze. She tries to focus, going through the languid motions, watching Devon inhale and exhale.

Tessie dips into a pregnancy-friendly version of cat-cow, enjoying the stretch. Her mind drifts.

Solomon.

Last night showed her they could make it. They could try.

Hell, she wants to try.

The universe has been screaming at her to try ever since it got her into this mess at the Bear's Ear bar.

It goes against every bone in her type-A body. Getting close to Solomon means opening herself up to get hurt, means he could walk away at any time. She should let them both go back to their respective lives. Los Angeles. Chinook. Getting attached only means heartbreak.

But it's too late, isn't it? All week, she's taken risks.

Is she ready to take another one with her heart?

Not one man she's been with can hold a candle to Solomon. He's more rough than smooth, like no one she ever imagined going for. All of those Los Angeles douchebags—she'd let them slip in, then she'd slip out, leaving before she could get attached. And she was still doing that to Solomon. Until he called her on it this morning. She liked that. Being put in her place by a stern-talking mountain man is hot as hell.

She's falling, she's in, but what about him? Why would he want her? Her life is a hot mess. She's unemployed. Lives in LA. She's neurotic as hell when he's about as chill as a rocking chair.

What would they even do?

How would they make their different lives fit the same future?

But instead of running from these questions, she wants to figure it out.

Figure *them* out.

Because she likes him. So damn much. She likes his flannels and his beard and his massive hands and his grumpy *hate the world* attitude.

Oh God. She's hopeless.

She's sunk.

Tessie sucks air, huffing hard as she props herself into a modified downward facing dog. Lululemon's grunting next to her, noises that should be banned in all public spaces.

Devon prattles on, her face rapturous. "Your body is an angel. Singing its praises. Extolling a virtue you can't live without..."

As Tessie propels herself upright, she glances at the clock on the wall. Then and there, she determines: exercise, bad; Solomon, good. She aches to get to the bottom of their promised conversation. What Solomon meant when he said she can't walk away. She wanted to stay and listen because something in his gaze was sad. Serious.

Later, today, she'll ask him what they are.

Throw caution to the wind, wear her burning heart on her sleeve, and ask.

What are we, Solomon?

Because she thought she knew.

But now...

It's fast; she knows it is. Falling in love with a man after seven days is chaotic. She's like an animal. Maybe she's entering her villain era, or it's the hormones, but she's certain it's love. She liked him that night under the Tennessee stars. She's held him in her heart and her brain for the last six months, along with his red flannel shirt. And she loves him now. There's no one she wants more than Solomon Wilder.

Tessie drops into modified plank, doing a few sets of pushups that have her cursing her pathetic upper body strength. How is no one else sweating? Her hairline, her underboob, her belly are all damp.

Once she's back on her feet, she brings her hands to prayer position and breathes through the motion. Calm. She is calm, inhaling short, shallow breaths. A smile touches her lips as the image of Solomon pops into her mind. Her big, bearded man doing a prayer palm has her chuckling.

"Remember, mama," Devon crackles over the headset; she's

frowning, "you're taking long breaths. Not short. You need to exhale through the nose or mouth. Not hold it in."

Tessie cracks an eye, feeling frazzled. Sweat drips down her brow. "Wait, what?" she huffs before a wave of lightheadedness washes over her.

"Tessie? Mama, you okay?" The words are garbled, oatmeal mush in her ears. Black spots dance across the room.

"I'm—" Her heartbeat accelerates, and she sways on her feet.

Tessie tries to say something, tries to hold herself still, but the head rush has her. Her eyes roll up, her legs crumple, and then—blackout.

Chapter Twenty-One

Solomon slips onto a stool at the outdoor cabana bar, ready to tick down the hour until Tessie's done with her yoga class. He orders a beer, because it's five o'clock somewhere, and watches the bartender do prep work for the day. A musician plays steel drums, the bright sound enveloping the beach in island vibes.

As he's taking his first sip of his beer, the door to the kitchen swings open and the chef pops his head out. The bartender turns, a grin on his face, and the two men fall into a rote bullshit banter. It's a familiar sight, one that leaves Solomon with a hard knot of regret in his stomach.

It's him and Howler. Years ago, in their bar. A dream they built; a dream he gave up after Serena died.

But now, with his son in the picture, he wants it all back. The camaraderie. His kitchen. Planning menus. Picking out local produce from the farmer's market. Creating dishes he can share with his town, his friends, his family.

He wants to go back to work. He wants a purpose, that fire in his gut again. He wants his dream back.

Why? Tessie. The way she looks at him—she makes him want to be a better man.

She's uprooted his world, and he likes it.

God, he fucking craves it.

Craves *her*. He's obsessed with her. Can't get the girl out of his head. The soft swell of her belly beneath the sheets. The earthy softness of her dark brown eyes. The long blond hair falling across her breast. She's taking over every damn part of him. He'd go to war over this woman. Because he wants her. Wants her in his bed every night, wants to cook her favorite meal, to show her around Chinook. Wants to build Bear a crib with his own hands. Be a damn good father, but beside him, always, Tessie.

Whether she wants him is another question entirely.

Hell, for all he knows, he's just a guy leaving her limp and satisfied at the end of the night.

Not to mention, she's sophisticated, gorgeous as hell. The champagne to his beer can. She could marry an architect. Not some chef who lives in Alaska. She's going places, and he's stuck in Chinook.

All he can offer her is a busted bar. A mountain. A hound dog that farts in her sleep. But he wants to. Goddamn, does he want to try. He loves this woman, and the thought of leaving her in two more days? It's a sucker punch to the chest.

Which means he has to sit his ass down and talk to her. There's so much still left unsaid. His tendency to not show his emotions, to stay silent, is what bit him in the ass with Serena. He needs to communicate better. Like last night.

He should have told Tessie how he feels, not just about Bear, but about *her*. That he loves her. Wants more than the memory of Mexico—wants a future with her.

Before his thoughts can get away with him, Solomon's pulled into the conversation happening between the bartender and the chef. *The posole's so oversalted it's inedible.*

Leaning up on his elbows, he says, "Add potatoes." When they say nothing, their expressions confused, he clears his throat. "They'll soak up the salt."

The chef nods, a smile breaking out on his face. "Gracias, señor." With that, he ducks into the kitchen, a flurry of Spanish echoing as the door swings shut.

Hit by a surge of determination, Solomon pulls out his phone. Howler answers on the tenth ring. Lazy fuck.

"I want to come back to the bar."

"What? Fuck, man."

A woman's voice, a rustle of blankets, a bark from Peggy, and then a door slams shut.

"Don't jerk me around."

"I'm not," he grunts, watching the clock tick behind the bar. He's already annoyed at himself for checking it more than he should, knowing that soon Tessie will be done with her yoga class and back in his arms.

A triumphant hoot. "Goddamn! When were you thinking?"

"When I get back to Chinook."

"Which is?"

His chest tightens. "Two days."

"Man, that's fuckin' perfect. You come back. We'll get the bar back in shape, then—"

"What happened to the bar?"

Howler's exhale is long and pained. "Me and Jimmy tried to patch some drywall. Let's just say we ended up with a few more holes than we started with."

Solomon needles his brow. "Christ. I leave you alone—"

"For seven goddamn years."

He flinches.

Though Howler's voice is easy, it's also laced with a tight sadness. Not only did Solomon distance himself from his family when Serena died, but he shut Howler out too. His best friend since stickball and sandboxes. Loyal as hell, Howler stuck around no matter how shitty Solomon was to him, but his friend still carries pain from the aftermath of Serena's death.

He gives an apologetic grunt. "I know."

"Well, you're coming back. So."

"What if I brought Tessie back?" The question rolls off his tongue. Feels right.

A beat of silence passes. Then a sigh. "Man, I ain't sure. If that's what you think you gotta do..."

His jaw flexes. "I do."

"You're not gonna marry her, are you?" Howler's voice is dubious. "Just because you knocked her up."

"No."

Yes.

Fuck.

Just the thought has his ribs cinching, his heart doing the fast palpitation dance.

Marry Tess. Damn. That thought. Those words.

This fucking woman who tears him up inside has him wanting to make vows, promises, declarations he hasn't uttered in years.

Why wouldn't he marry her?

He'd be crazy not to.

Not because it's easier this way. Not because he got her pregnant. But because with Tessie, he's no longer sleepwalking.

He's in love with this woman who's blown up his entire fucking world. Who's burned into every part of his broken soul. Who's about to give him a son, give him a life he never knew he wanted.

Tessie—all the stars in the universe point to her.

"Sol?" Howler whistles. "You still there?"

He swallows the knot in his throat. "Yeah," he chokes out. "Still here."

"Get your ass back home," his best friend says, genuine joy in his tone. "Your kitchen's waiting."

Solomon ends the call. His heart pounds in his chest. It feels like he's rolling away the boulder from the entrance of a dark cave. Letting sunlight shine. And that sunlight, that golden ray of goodness, is Tessie. His Tessie.

It's back to business, back to Chinook. Until this moment, he hadn't realized how much he truly missed it.

His goddamn life.

A quiet smile overtaking his face, Solomon inspects his beer, drains the glass dry, then rubs his sweaty palms on the thighs of his jeans. Christ, he's nervous, and he doesn't get nervous, but this woman's got a leash around his heart. And he wants to keep it like that.

Forever.

In his periphery, there's a flash of terra-cotta and white. The signature uniform of the resort staff. A short bald-headed man steps up and offers a timid smile. "Excuse me, Mr. Wilder?"

He rotates on his stool to face the man.

"I'm sorry to bother you, but we've had an incident at the health club with your wife."

"What kind of incident?" he demands, not even bothering to correct the man. He's two for two here, and that's how he's keeping it.

"During her yoga class, she...she fainted, señor."

The words jerk Solomon off the barstool. "Where is she?"

The man backs up. "She is still there, sir."

Panic twists in his throat like a knife. He feels like he can't breathe.

"Take me there," he finally manages to rasp. "Now."

Five minutes later, Solomon's pounding up the steps to the health club. His pulse unsteady in his ears. Guilt's a record on repeat in his head: *He should have gone with her. He should have gone with her.*

The second he slams into the studio, his frame locks. A circle of yoga pant-clad women hovers, their arms crossed, soft whispers floating between them.

"Oh, that poor thing. She just fell over."

A woman with neon yellow hair shakes her head. "I told her long breaths." She turns sad eyes toward Solomon. "She took short breaths."

"What?" The words are gibberish to him. Time stands still as he scans the room. No sign of Tessie. He needs to see her; he needs her like air, and every second he's far from her is like part of his life ticking down.

"Where is she?" he thunders, and when there's silence, he takes a step forward. "Where the fuck is she?"

A woman wearing bright-orange leggings gasps. He lowers his voice, trying not to act like a fucking lunatic, but his heart is a racehorse out of the gate. Desperate to get to Tess. To find her. To make sure she's okay. "Tell me where she is. Please. Now."

A man in a staff uniform emerges from the circle. "We moved her."

"Where?" His hands curl into fists. The thought of some Joe schmo manhandling a pregnant and unconscious Tessie makes his blood boil.

"Back here," the man says, leading him behind a curtain.

Solomon's heart leaves his chest, plunging into his stomach.

Tessie.

She lies on the floor, a pillow beneath her blond head. Her eyes are shut, her face ashen, her yoga tank has ridden up to expose the gentle moon of her belly. A second small circle of women surrounds Tessie, murmuring their concern, pressing a cool cloth against her brow. But to Solomon, they barely register. All his concern, all his focus, is on the unconscious woman in front of him.

"Move. Now," he says, elbowing his way through the crowd. "Get away from her. Give her some air."

He drops to his knees beside her, brushing his fingers over the golden hair stuck to her pale cheek, then looks up at the hovering attendant. "We need a doctor. Right now." He doesn't recognize his voice. It's ragged. Wrecked.

He nods. "Si, señor. He's on his way."

Turning back to Tessie, he rests a large hand on the hard ball of her stomach. God, he's dying. Fucking dying, and he won't recover until he sees the brown of her beautiful eyes. She looks so vulnerable, so still it scares the fuck out of him. He closes his eyes, rage and helplessness twisting his gut.

Too close.

Just like Serena when he found her on the side of the road. So lifeless, so cold.

The baby. Tess.

He wasn't here. He wasn't here to protect them.

The thought's enough to end a man.

Gently, he cups her face, and her head lolls into his palm. "Baby, wake up."

At his touch, his voice, she stirs. Her thick lashes flutter, a small moan escaping her parted lips, and Solomon nearly falls apart then and there.

Thank Christ. Thank God.

"Tessie, my Tessie," he murmurs, dipping his head to press a kiss to her brow. His heart feels like it's on its last beat. "Wake up, Tess. Baby, come back. Come back to me."

Tessie.

My Tessie.

Whispers halo around her head. Strong hands cup her face. Callused thumbs sweep across her cheeks. A desperate, haggard voice that says, "Wake up, Tess. Baby, come back. Come back to me."

And she does.

Her eyelids flutter open. Solomon's worried face, his dark blue eyes stare down at her. "Thank God," he rasps. He strokes a thumb over her cheekbone.

"Hi," she whispers, still held in a dreamy state.

His exhale is ragged. "Hi."

She blinks her heavy eyelids. "I took short breaths."

"Yeah," he says. His face is creased with relief and something else she can't place.

He strokes her hair, and she resists the urge to purr like a kitten. His big fingers against her skin are cool. His touch steady and grounding, like an anchor pulling her back to the present.

"Yeah, you did."

She squints at him, at the hard line of his jaw, the intensity of his deep blue eyes. She's never seen his face like this. "You look...weird." She tries to reach up, to touch that smile or frown on his lips, his dark beard. But instead, he captures her hand and holds it close to his pounding heart.

"I'm not the one lying on the ground right now."

She smiles. "Noted."

"How do you feel?"

She thinks on it, then gasps as it comes rushing back. "Oh my God. Bear."

"Easy," Solomon orders as she struggles to sit up. Quickly, he tucks a protective arm around her waist to keep her steady. Glancing down, she clutches her belly, aching to feel that little squirm inside. Immediately, hot tears fill her eyes. A fear, sharp and prickly, pokes at her.

She caught herself before she fell, rolled so she didn't hit her stomach, but what if it's worse? What if it wasn't her breathing? What if something's wrong?

She grips his shirt, clings to him. "Solomon, we have to make sure the baby's okay."

He blanches. Her fear echoed in his own eyes.

"Where's that damn doctor?" her mountain man growls, whipping his head in one direction, then the other. When he sees the attendant, his gaze narrows. "We need medical attention immediately. My"—a beat, Solomon swallows, then—"My Tessie needs a doctor."

Despite the gravity of the situation, she can't help the small smile that tugs at her lips. "My Tessie?"

He scowls, rips a hand through his hair. "Okay, this frustrating woman who scared the damn life out of me needs help. How's that?"

The man above them nods. "Apologies for the delay, señor. He should be here any moment."

Solomon swears, pale and stone faced, and tucks her tighter against his chest.

"Solomon," Tessie whispers, snagging his arm. A sudden thought coming to her. "If we go to the room, we can use the doppler."

At her words, he's already up and moving.

"Send the doctor to our room," he orders. "I'm taking her back to rest."

Then Tessie's being lifted, picked up in Solomon's strong arms. The world moves around her so fast she barely has time to grasp what's happening. She stares up at his stern face, his strong, square jaw, as he storms past a pack of whispering women, out of the studio, and into the fresh air and sunlight, and Tessie feels like she's falling.

She bites her lip, looping an arm around his neck, studying him through dark lashes. She covets Solomon's serious gaze like a love letter. "You're carrying me again."

He grunts, his gruff voice stained with a tenderness she's never heard from a man. "I'll always carry you, Tessie," he says, dropping a kiss on the crown of her head.

"Oh," she whispers.

Solomon might as well be carrying a molten mess of woman, because she's practically a puddle in his arms. She has no right to feel this cared for, but she does. This man is doing things to her no one has. Her emotions lit and wired.

With a soft sigh, she drops her head against his broad chest. Safe. She feels safe. She wants Solomon Wilder near her always.

Once they're inside the room, he sets her on the bed gently. Props her up with pillows.

Without words, Solomon brings her the doppler and drops to the mattress beside her. Tessie reclines and slips the waistband of her yoga pants down to bare the swell of her belly.

"It's my fault," Tessie whispers, her eyes flooding as she sets up the machine. "I forgot my water. I wasn't breathing right. . ."

God. Already, she's fucking up, and Bear isn't even out of her belly.

"Don't," Solomon says, his voice rough. "Don't do that."

With shaky hands, she runs the wand over the moon of her belly. She waits, her breath, her heart on standstill. Then a sound like a hundred galloping horses fills the room. A sound she's familiar with. Strong. Steady.

Bear.

The air rushes from her lungs. She sags back against the pillow in relief as Solomon looks to her. "That's his heartbeat." Tessie closes her teary eyes. Panic slowly ebbs its way out of her veins and a wobbly breath escapes her. "He's okay."

"Thank God." The desperate catch in Solomon's voice has her heart flipping over in her chest. Reverently, he places a hand on her belly and glues his worried eyes to her face. "Now we'll make sure you are."

She battles a smile. "Sounds like you're fussing, Solemn Man."

He gives her a look. "Sounds like I am." Handing her a bottle of water, he watches while she drinks it, then goes to get a cool washcloth. He's draping it over her brow when there's a knock on the door.

"It's about goddamn time." Jaw tight, he stomps through the suite.

Seconds later, a smiling man with deep brown skin and a shock of white hair enters the room. "Ms. Truelove, I'm Doctor Rodrigo. I'm the staff physician on site." He takes his place next to her while Solomon stands with arms crossed at the head of the bed like an overprotective bodyguard. "I understand that you fainted."

"I did." She palms her stomach. "I was taking short breaths instead of long, and I forgot my water, and then I—" She snaps her mouth shut, stopping her idiotic ramble and exhales. "I just want to make sure my baby's okay."

"I'm sure he is. Shallow breathing can make you lightheaded, especially when you're pregnant." The doctor opens his bag and smiles. "But let's check you over, just in case."

As Doctor Rodrigo settles into his exam routine, taking her vitals and asking general questions about her pregnancy, Tessie watches Solomon in amusement. He paces the room like a concerned, caged animal.

It's only when the doctor snaps his bag shut that Solomon comes to a halt. "They're okay, right?" he asks, his body a brick, his hands fisted at his sides.

The doctor chuckles. "They're just fine." To Tessie, he says, "There's nothing to be concerned about regarding your baby. It appears you just overexerted yourself." He gives her a reproachful glance. "Vacations are for relaxing, not exercise."

She laughs. "I know that now. Thank you so much."

He smiles and stands. Looks to Solomon. "Make sure your wife gets plenty of water and rest."

Solomon nods and extends a hand. "I will. Thank you."

The doctor heads to the door and closes it behind him.

Only Tessie stares at Solomon.

He turns, catches her staring. "What?"

She licks her lips. "You didn't tell him."

"Tell him what?" He moves to the side of the bed.

"That we aren't together."

He clears his throat. His piercing blue eyes sear into hers. "I didn't want to."

"Oh."

The blunt admission catches her off guard. Has her feeling like fainting all over again, only this time, in the best kind of way.

"Tessie?"

"I just. . ." She touches a hand to her temple, hoping to regain some sort of control of her hammering heart. "Feel kind of dizzy again."

Sitting beside her, he pins her with a serious look and says, "Rest. Now."

Exhaling heavily, she arches a brow. "Doctor's orders."

"My orders," he growls.

She shivers at his bossy tone. The one that tells her he'll take care of her and then some.

Without words, he helps her change. After removing her tight clothing, he slips a worn T-shirt over her head. She smells the beer on his breath, her scent in his beard. As she settles into the pillows, she's hit by exhaustion and relief. Coming down from the adrenaline, she rubs a tired hand across her face, then her belly, feeling Bear's reassuring kick.

Solomon places his hand on her forehead, and she leans into his cool, comforting touch, closing her eyes. And she feels it, his massive hand unfurling like a flower to cup her cheek in his palm.

When she opens her eyes, he's still staring at her. Still frowning.

"What's wrong?" she asks.

His throat works, then he finally forces the words out. "I was scared, Tessie."

She blinks. "You were?" She can't imagine anything scaring the guy. Well, maybe a supply chain shortage on flannel shirts. But not her. Not the object of his daily scowl.

With his index finger, he traces a line across her cheekbone. "I was."

Confused, she tilts her head. She's never seen his face like this. "The baby's okay. I'm okay."

"I should have gone with you today," he says, an edge to his voice.

She leans up on her elbows. "Solomon, you don't like yoga. It's fine."

He looks to the window, his expression far away, a muscle jerking in his jaw. "It's not fine."

"Yes, it *is* fine, and it's not your fault."

He scrubs his face and nods. "It feels like it."

The conversation from this morning dawning, she lays a hand on his arm. "Is this about Serena?"

He drops his gaze to where she's touching him, his expression pained. When he finally looks at her, he gathers her hand in his and swallows. "I want to tell you about how my wife died. So you know."

In that, Tessie hears his unspoken words. *So you understand why I'm like this.*

"Are you sure?"

"Yes. It's time I told you."

"Then I want to know," she says, squeezing his hand.

She scoots forward on the bed, closer to Solomon. Deep in her soul, she knows this isn't something he talks about. She wants him to know he can open up with her.

"Serena and I, we got married young. I told you that," he rasps.

She nods.

"We had lived in Chinook our entire lives. I had the bar, and she was a park ranger. We worked long hours, odd shifts. For a few months, she had been distant, more quiet than usual." He runs his thumb over Tessie's knuckles, glances to the window again.

"The night she died, we got into a fight. And Serena and I didn't fight. Our marriage was. . . good. Maybe not always perfect but. . ."

"What is."

He turns back to her, his voice rough. "Right. What is." Solomon drags a hand down his dark beard, quiet for a long moment. "She had these grand plans to see the world, and to me that's what they were. Just plans. But that night, she brought up the possibility of moving. She wanted to leave Chinook. She was bored, she wanted to travel, and who could blame her? But I had my bar, my family. I couldn't leave. I wouldn't." He swallows thickly. "She told me I was selfish. I told her if I was so damn selfish, then she could go by herself." He flinches. "And she did. She walked out. She was pissed at me, and hell, I was pissed at her."

Tessie sits quietly, listening, letting the man in front of her take his time to process his emotions.

"I didn't go after her." He raises haunted eyes to hers. "She was stubborn. We both were. It felt like she had dropped a bomb on me. I sat in that damn house and stewed. But then an hour passed. It was too dark, too cold, and she didn't have a jacket on. So I went looking for her."

Tessie holds her breath, waiting.

"I found her," he says, balling a fist. "On the side of the road. A car had hit her during her walk."

Tessie covers her mouth. "Oh my God."

"They drove off. They fucking drove off and left her there." A wave of fury rolls through his body, stiffening his posture. "I got her to the hospital, but it was too late." His throat works the words out. "She was gone."

It doesn't feel like enough, but still, she says it. "I'm so sorry, Solomon."

A muscle flexes in his jaw. His voice one of hard admonishment directed at himself. "I let her walk off. I let her leave, and she got hurt."

In that moment, Tessie understands Solomon better than she ever has. His protective nature. His secluded cabin in the woods. Why he's asked her not to run off, or at least tell him where she's going. The panic in his voice as he chased her down the beach. His worry as she came to today. It was too close. She was a reminder of his wife, a reminder of someone walking away from him yet again.

"Don't blame yourself," Tessie says, the tortured look on Solomon's face combusting her heart. "For any that."

He dips his bearded chin. "I didn't give the best of myself to her. I worked too much. I was a bad husband."

She shakes her head, refusing to let him do this to himself. "Did you hit her? Cheat on her?"

He lifts his head, pain flashing in his eyes. "No."

"Did you love her?"

"Yes."

"Then that sounds like a good man to me."

"I wasn't there for her when she needed me." His big shoulders slump. "Today... if you had been hurt..." His voice turns ragged, thick with emotion. "It terrifies me to think about losing you."

His admittance has her heart flopping like a fish on land.

"Me?" she breathes.

He chuckles. "Yes, you, Tess." He tucks a lock of hair behind her ear, his large fingers skimming the line of her jaw. "Nothing's more important than you and my son. I want you to hear that."

"Okay," she whispers. "I do. I'm so sorry about your wife, Solomon." She gives him a small smile. "At least that explains your handsome, grumpy face."

He cocks a brow. "Handsome, you say?"

"And grumpy." She smiles. "But mostly sad."

"Hell, I'm not sad." His dark blue gaze lands on her face. His massive hand palms her stomach. "I've been sad for so many goddamn years. But here, with you, I'm not sad."

His words leave her dizzy. "Then what are you?" she breathes, doing her best not to hold her breath after today's scare.

"I'm happy, Tess. *You* make me happy."

"I do?"

"You do." On a chuckle, he pulls her in closer. "Now stop asking me questions, Pregnant Woman, and kiss me."

He leans in, sealing his lips against hers. Whimpering, she grips his broad shoulders with her nails and hangs on. The kiss deepens. Emotions rise between them. Not wild passion, but something softer. Solomon kisses her like her air is his. Like he's a desperate man who's just been saved.

Saved. She saved him.

They saved each other.

When they pull back, they're breathless. Tessie watches him from beneath darkened lashes.

So much. So much more to say.

"Solomon—"

He cradles her face in his big hands. "I want you to rest."

She bites her lip. "Will you rest with me? I don't want to be"—she could lie, she could say alone, but instead she says what she's really feeling—"without you."

For a second, he's quiet. "You're never without me," he says softly. "You'll never be without me."

Cue heart into overdrive.

Nodding, she blinks back tears as Solomon settles behind her. Strong arms band protectively around her midsection as he tucks her small frame against his big body.

"Thank you for telling me about Serena," she whispers.

He smiles against the back of her head, but he stays silent, burying his face in her hair. Then, slowly, he palms her stomach. His warm clasp envelops her, and it feels like a claiming.

Tessie's heart thumps. She doesn't want rest.

Solomon.

That's what she wants.

Chapter Twenty-Two

Eyes on her reflection in the mirror, Tessie adjusts the hoop in her ear, then smooths a hand down the front of her multicolor maxi dress. She looks like a sunrise—vibrant pinks and purples and oranges—and feels more peaceful than she has in a long time.

It's been a perfect day of beach slothfulness, of all-she-can-drink coconut water and Solomon's lips on hers as they played in the sand and the surf. For the last hour, she's been confined to the room, Solomon claiming he has a surprise for her.

Still, as perfect as it's been, there's been an air of heaviness.

And it's not just because it's their last night.

Tessie's mind keeps spinning with Solomon's confession. He's loved before. Had a wife. Experienced a loss no one should experience. He's blamed himself for so many years for something that wasn't his fault. She's honored he shared that with her. It couldn't have been easy.

His honesty, his warmth, his vulnerability. It makes her like the man he is more and more.

Her attention drifts. Beyond the windows, the palm trees sway in the breeze. A brilliant symphony of reds and pinks and oranges light up the evening sky, almost as if it's determined to give Tessie the best sunset of her life on her last night in Mexico.

Last night.

Oh God. The idea of walking away from Solomon makes her stomach churn.

With a humorless chuckle, she thinks back to when she first got here. How all she wanted to do was get him out of Mexico, and now...now she wants to do everything she can to keep him.

She has to tell him how she feels. Before it's too late. But tell him what? And who's to say he even feels the same way? For all she knows, he's ready to get back to Chinook, and all she'll be is a distant memory.

Still, she has to try. She'll never forgive herself if this is one risk she passes up.

She cups her burgeoning belly. She's grown, bigger than she was when she arrived.

"Right?" she asks Bear. "We have to tell your daddy we want him. The both of us."

A quick knuckle rap, and then the door cracks. Solomon looms, his large body barricading the suite behind him.

She drifts toward him, magnetized, and then he has her in his arms. Sweeping a hand over her belly then up to cup her face. "You look beautiful, Tess," he murmurs, but his face is creased in concern.

"Is that okay?" she asks.

"It is. I just hope you weren't counting on going out, because we're staying in."

She arches a brow, impressed. "You planned something?"

"I did. Dinner."

"I don't need food," she teases, pressing up on her tiptoes to brush her lips against his. She could subsist on Solomon's kiss alone.

"Well, you're getting it anyway," he growls, holding her tight against him. "You need to eat more."

"I like you, Solemn Man. You know the way to a pregnant woman's heart: food."

He laughs. "Tess, baby, I got an entire loaf of bread with your name on it."

Then he's gone, his loud stomps echoing against the walls.

She slips on black sandals, giving her feet a break for once. Pausing at the mirror once more, she runs her fingers through her golden beach waves. She adds a pop of pink lip gloss and exits the room. There, she follows the faint strains of Johnny Cash drifting through the suite.

When she steps out onto the terrace, she freezes.

Her mouth drops at the setup that greets her. A table dressed for two. Elegant, white-tableclothed. Candles line the terrace. Flowers the color of fire bloom in a vase. Non-alcoholic sparkling wine for her and a bottle of Mexican lager for Solomon.

Speaking of Solomon...

He stands at a smaller table, a black apron tied around his waist. A burner and a chafing dish in front of him. Small bowls of already-chopped food covered in Saran wrap. Tongs, spatulas, and knives polished clean and shiny.

She gasps and claps in delight. "You're going to cook for me."

A muscle tics in his jaw. He's fighting that smile she so rarely sees. "Thought we could redo our first dinner here. You know, without the angry barbs."

"Yeah. I'd love that." She can barely get the words out. The lengths he must have gone to arrange this stun her. Absolutely take her breath away.

"Here." Coming to her, Solomon takes her hand. He pulls out her chair and helps her sit.

And then he gets to work.

In front of Tessie's eyes, Solomon comes alive. Deft, skilled, serious. His large, callused hands work dexterously as he slices into a challah roll. His forearms flex, colorful tattoos popping as he whisks a bowl of sauce. A pan sizzles as he adds the two halves of the bread.

He's in his element. Focused. Intent. Alive.

He looks up. "You like spice?"

She flushes at the question. "Yes. A lot."

"It won't give you heartburn?"

"No, it won't." She smiles at his insistence on making sure it's okay for her. "Stomach of steel, over here. What are you making?" she asks, leaning forward. It's thrilling watching him. Addicting.

His eyes glint as he picks up a knife. "You'll see."

She smiles, imagining his burly body moving gracefully in a kitchen. Her wild, solemn man, barking orders, creating beauty on plates. His brow is furrowed in concentration as he arranges a dollop of a white sauce in a pretty pattern.

Warmth curls Tessie's stomach, a soft pulse down below as she's hit with the irresistible urge to kiss him. Simply slam him up against the sliding glass doors and forget about this gorgeous dinner, forget that they both leave tomorrow. All she wants is to feel his hands on her body.

One last time.

Oh God. Are they really leaving? Is this slice of paradise really over? She's breathless, faint, heady with the knowledge that soon they'll part ways.

The clink of a dish snags her attention. "Tess." Solomon nods as he sets a plate in front of her.

What she sees has her heart beating wildly in her chest. Every craving she's had this pregnancy laid out for her on the plate. The most random meal, gourmet style—Chicken sliders with hot sauce and salted fries and bread and ricotta and candied lemons and strange vegetables and pineapple cream on meringue—but it's hers.

Heart in her throat, Tessie examines the plate with reverence. Solomon crafts a plate like she designs a house. With purpose. With love. Solomon cooking for her is more intimate than sex. He's letting her into his world. He's telling her something.

In that instant, she wants, more than anything, for Solomon to be the only one to ever feed her.

She picks up her fork, and when she realizes he's still standing, she shakes her head. Stretching out a hand, she says, "You have to eat with me. You can't stare at me like I'm a zoo animal or else I'll charge you admission."

With a husky chuckle, he sits across from her, but he doesn't touch his food. Solomon waits for her, his expression towing a line between nerves and an eagerness she's never seen from him before.

So she picks up her fork and digs in. First, a fry. Salty and herbed flavors burst in her mouth. Crispy, not greasy. Then the bread. Candied lemons smeared with ricotta on top of a tender grain bread. The soft dough has a perfect chew, a mellow sweetness, and it takes all she has not to devour it.

"Oh my God, Solomon."

He's grinning, his watchful gaze taking in her reaction.

"I take it back. You can't watch me eat. This is embarrassing." She laughs. Lifts her fork and examines a purple carrot drizzled in honey. The most beautifully strange color she's ever seen.

Solomon arches a brow. "What color is it?"

"What?"

A lift of his fork. "The carrot."

She laughs and appraises her food with a knitted brow. "Parachute Purple." Her nose wrinkles. "Or it could be Cactus Flower."

"Stumped by a carrot."

She gasps. "Never." She breaks off a piece of it, takes a bite. Then she looks up at him. "Solomon," she begins, shielding her mouth with her hand so she has some semblance of manners. "What made you want to be a chef?"

He scrubs a hand over his face, the bristly whisk of his beard rasping beneath his palm.

"Food was always important in my house. My mother had a garden, and she ran the agriculture program at our local high school. My father fished and hunted. We lived on and ate off the land. My parents taught us that." He pauses, taking a long sip of his beer. "I stumbled into it. Like everything in my life. I didn't want to go to college. I wanted to stay in Chinook. Do something local. Howler and me, our dream had always been to own a bar. But when we bought it, I figured out pretty damn fast I was a shit bartender. I couldn't move fast enough. I dropped every damn thing. Howler was better at it than I was. He wants to talk to people. I don't."

"You talked to me," she says.

He looks her straight in the eyes and says evenly, "I wanted you."

His directness has her core pulsing. Tessie takes a gulp of her sparkling wine to cool down.

"One day when we were young, we were hanging around after hours, drunk on beer. We were hungry. It was late, midnight, everything in Chinook was closed, so I went back into the kitchen and whipped up what I could from the herbs for the cocktails and leftovers we had in the fridge. I was twenty, maybe twenty-one. The food was good, and it was like a light went on. Having a job where I could hang with my best friend every day and try new things in the kitchen seemed perfect. I didn't take myself too seriously. Plus, I didn't have to talk to anyone if I didn't want to."

Solomon swallows a sip of his beer, says, "I don't have a degree. I never went to culinary school. But—"

"You're good at it," Tessie finishes.

"Damn good at it," he says, no arrogance in his tone, just confidence. It turns her on.

In the distance, the call of a seabird. The crash of the waves on the beach.

"Using the land to feed us is important. Making trips to the shore to collect scallops. Hunting wild boar. Using local produce and paying the farmer. If it's gone, it's gone. There will never be a dish like it again."

"I love that, Solomon," she says, scooping up a dollop of crema.

There's so much passion in his voice, so much heart. His love for his home is pure and tangible. Unlike Los Angeles, Chinook is not just a town. It's Solomon's soul.

"How long has it been since you cooked?" she asks after finishing a bite of chicken slider.

He cocks an eyebrow. "It's that evident?"

She laughs. "No. The food is delicious. It is. But the way you talked about it. . .It sounds like you haven't been in the kitchen in a long time." She shakes her head. "Not like I'm one to talk. I eat takeout most nights." She palms her belly. "Bear will have to get used to it."

Solomon's expression clouds, and a silence falls between them, an awkward reminder of their divergent paths in less than twenty-four hours.

"You're right." Solomon's gruff voice rumbles out as he picks up the dropped conversation. "I haven't been in the kitchen since Serena died."

"Do you miss it? Cooking?"

"I tried not to." He sets his fork down. "I sold our house. Walked away. From everything. From my bar, my friends, my family. I holed myself up in that cabin and made furniture. It was a living. But not a life."

Tessie's eyes light on his hands. Broad palms, long, callused fingers, veins standing out like lines on a map, dark hair on his wrists. Strong hands. Builder's hands. Hands that have spread her thighs and made her moan.

"I didn't wake up for a long goddamn time. But that's all changing." He inhales a breath. "I'm going back to the bar."

Tessie's head snaps up.

Solomon's eyes are glued to her face. "I called Howler and told him I want to come back to work." A grunt of a laugh. "He's in the shit with the Roost. It's falling apart and needs a revamp. Thinking food will help. Thinking it will help me too."

Her heart feels fluttery, dizzy from his revelation. Because she's happy. Happy he's happy.

"Oh, Solomon. That's amazing. What made you decide to—"

"Rejoin the land of the living?" he asks. With a shake of his head, he says, "I've been away too long. I needed to wake up." He takes a fortifying breath before continuing. "You did that."

She stills in her chair, unsure if she's heard him correctly. "Me?"

"Yes, you, Tess."

She shivers at her name in his mouth. Laced with gravel and fire and heat. Rugged and intense.

"You remember that night we met, I had a ring on?"

Slowly, she nods.

"I took it off because of you, Tessie."

His words have her heart dropping into her stomach. But she waits. Ready for his explanation. Because she needs to know.

"I barely knew you, but you did something to me that night. Changed my world, shook me up, opened my eyes." Solomon drags a hand through his dark hair, his expression tortured. "I couldn't stop thinking about you."

"Same," she breathes. "I thought about you all the time."

The admission leaves her aching, has Solomon's eyes closing, then opening.

"Remember what I said to you the night we met? About the stars?"

She nods. She'd never forget. "You said they shine the brightest in your hometown."

"Not anymore. You're my star, Tess." He places a hand over his chest. "You shine here. In my heart."

Before she can process what's happening, Solomon's out of his chair and kneeling at her feet. His expression filled with so much reverence she feels faint.

Wrapping muscular arms around her waist, he pulls her to the edge of her chair, toward him. "What if we make a new deal?" he rumbles.

"A new deal?"

"Yes. We try."

"Try what?" She scans the table, picks up a spoon. "The dessert?"

"No, Tessie." He smooths her hair away from her face. "We try us."

Her world swims. Her head spins.

"Wait," she croaks. "What does this mean?"

"It means I like you, Tess. It means I—" His face clouds, clears.

"It means if there's a chance, if there's a shot in hell that we could work it out, I think we fucking owe it to ourselves to try."

Tessie stares at him, every line of his rugged face. She wants it. Wants it so bad it aches. But still...

She closes her eyes, doubt sideswiping hope. "Try for Bear, right?"

"No." His voice is loud and clear, picking up on her hesitation. "Not just for Bear. We try for us. Because, Tessie, baby, I want *you*."

In a single second, gone is her heart, dropping off into the clouds. She gapes at Solomon, at this man who's done more for her in seven days than anyone has since her mother. Protected her. Made her laugh. Forced her to relax. Showed her what a partner is. He makes her better than when she's on her own, and she's pretty damn great on her own.

"Come back with me." He straightens up, cupping her face in his hands. "Come home with me to Chinook."

Bear goes wild in her belly, as if he likes the idea.

Tears fill her eyes.

Is this real life? Is this what love, what a relationship could be? She doesn't know. She's never had something that's lasted. Stayed. But now she has this man, here in front of her, asking her to take a chance.

A risk.

Bracing herself, she puts a hand on Solomon's shoulder. "I need..."

She licks dry lips. What does she need? She doesn't know, but with that, she disentangles from Solomon, stands from the table, and moves to the edge of the terrace. Her brain spins while she tries to process everything he's just said. The view of the ocean soothes her shaky heart. She looks up. The sky's inky, clouds obscuring the stars, but she knows they're up there. Blinking bright like a celestial roadmap to her life.

And she swears she hears her mom's voice, her words of wisdom.

Bumps in the road are just bumps, Tessie, not holes. We can get over them.

And this...this is a bump she never expected.

Now.

Now's the time to give in, to give up her fears, to toss them into the ocean. She has nothing waiting for her in LA. So what does it matter if she takes one more risk?

Finds one more star.

She drops her hands to her stomach. A flutter and then a tumble. Her son telling her to trust her gut.

"Tess?"

From behind her, Solomon's worried voice carries over the crash of waves.

She turns to face him, bracing her arms on the railing. He's standing tall now, his body locked like her next words have the power to undo him.

She lifts her chin. "You promise you'll never try to take Bear away from me?"

"I swear it."

"Were you serious when you said you'd stick around?"

A nod. "I was."

"Well. Then," she takes a step forward, sniffs, "maybe we should."

He swallows, tracks her movement. "Should what?"

"Try this. Together." Tears spill down her cheeks. "I don't want to do this alone. Or with anyone else. Just you." The air leaves her lungs, but she finds her voice. For once.

For finally.

"My Solemn Man."

Because that's what he is. It's what he's always been.

Hers.

For a long second, he's frozen in front of her. Then he lets out a roar and lunges forward, practically shoving the table out of his way to get to her. Hauling her to his chest, he crushes her mouth with a kiss that's toe curling, life changing. A ragged gasp shakes his frame as he slides his hands up her neck to tangle in her hair.

"I can't let you go," he husks when he pulls back, his eyes misted. "I can't walk away from you."

She answers by kissing him again, losing herself in his woodsy scent. In her own explosive ache.

"Are you sure you're ready?" she whispers between breathless kisses, thinking of Serena. She doesn't want to push him.

She doesn't want to lose him.

"I'm ready," he murmurs, his voice cracking. "All my life, I've been ready for you."

Her eyes flutter. So does her heart.

"You're mine, Tessie," Solomon promises hoarsely against her ear.

Her head spins, her legs go weak, but he braces her against him, holding her up.

"You and that baby—you're both mine."

A sob works its way out of her. Those words. Primal, protective. Oh God. She's going to shatter. She's defrosting faster than the upper continental ice shelf.

She matters. She is someone's *someone*.

A hot tear rolls down her cheek. Her pulse picks up, looping through her like a soundtrack.

Love, love, love.

The word whispers between them.

Love.

But she won't say it first.

There's too much at stake.

Bear.

Her heart.

Better to see where this goes before making any reckless declarations.

"Do you promise?" The words leave her lips in a rush. "We're yours?"

Jaw flexing, Solomon blows out a steady breath. His shoulders shudder as a wave of emotion rolls through his big body. "I'll show you. I'll show you what we are."

Then he's sweeping her off her feet, slipping his wide palms over her ass and lifting her up until she wraps her legs around his waist. And by the time they make it to the bedroom, she knows there's no going back.

Cock surging in his pants, Solomon carries Tessie to the bed, bound and determined to show her that she's his only one.

He saw it in her face. No one's ever chosen her before.

He heard the worry in her voice. That he's not ready. That's she's not the one. Well, no more doubts. Tonight, he's gonna lay her down and prove to her just how damn bad he wants her. How much he fucking needs her.

She's his only one. And that's how it's going to stay.

Forever.

"No doubt, Tessie. Do you understand me?" he grinds out as he sets her on her feet. Then he takes her face in his hands and looks her in the eyes. He needs her to know. Needs her to believe him. "Get it through that beautiful blond head of yours. You're mine. You and that baby; you're both mine."

In response, she lets out a throaty whimper. Her head falls back to expose the graceful line of her flushed throat. Solomon's dick throbs painfully in his pants. Unable to handle it any longer, he spins her around and, with a smooth hand, tears her dress off her so fast her curves have scorch marks.

"Solomon," she gasps, surprised. But a delighted smile tips her lips.

"Oh Jesus." He goes molten at the sight of her, his chest tight with pride. That's his girl, gorgeous and glowing. Naked and pregnant with his son.

His.

God help him.

He's burning alive.

"Get on the bed," he growls.

Panting, Tessie scrambles onto the mattress. On her knees, she faces Solomon. Hands trembling, he cups her face, framing it, and then he slams his mouth to hers. Solomon's heart combusts as her tongue sweeps over his. He's at his boiling point. Overheated, undone. Fucking in it with this woman. It's insane the way she makes him feel.

He brings his hand down to her legs, sliding it between the sweet flesh between her thighs. Then he's groaning.

She's soaked, her wetness spilling over his fingers. Sweetness. Heaven. Leaning in, he brings a taste of Tessie to his lips, then runs a callused thumb over her swollen clit.

Her puffy pink mouth opens, her gaze going hazy as she watches him from beneath those long lashes. Going limp, she sags against his chest, her delicate frame trembling against him as he circles a finger over the bud.

"Oh, oh, *oh*." Her broken, breathy whimpers of satisfaction, her breasts plump against his chest, her nails digging into his shoulders, have him hardening.

Then desperate hands tug at his zipper, Tessie doing her damndest to get him out of his jeans. Solomon chuckles at her eagerness. "Baby, no," he says. "This is all for you."

She pouts, but he wants to take care of her like she's taken care of his son. Show her she's more than a mother; she's a woman, his woman, and he's damn sure going to give her everything she needs.

Tears pool in her dark brown eyes. "Then make love to me, Solomon." She bites her puffy lower lip and palms the front of his chest. "Please. I need you."

Her words send a lick of fire down his spine. Snapping him—and his dick—into action.

A hoarse growl rips out of him, has him grabbing her high

around the waist to pull her down on the bed. Anchoring her to him. Tessie writhes, mewling, a little wildcat in his arms.

He pulls her against his body, her tiny torso against his heaving chest, her supple ass flat against his abdomen. She gasps as he slips into her from behind. Reaching back, her slender arm encircles his neck, her fingers diving through his dark hair.

They undulate together, Solomon taking her body on his, and she practically levitates in his arms, the gorgeous bump on her stomach rising like a pale moon in the night.

"Ruin me," Tessie gasps, spreading her legs. With a little squirm, she wiggles, burying him deeper inside her.

Christ. He groans, slams his eyes shut. She's killing him. Absolutely a goner. Her long blond hair waves around them like a halo, like a goddamn angel.

It's unbelievable. How goddamn lucky he is for the second time on this earth.

He buries his face in her hair, inhaling her sea-salt scent, crushing her against him. Shaking. From the weight of what this means to him. "Fuck, but what I wouldn't do for you, Tessie."

"Tell me." She moans hoarsely. "Tell me what you'd do for me."

"Anything," he growls. The truest words he's ever uttered. Knowing he may not survive them. "Anything for you and that baby. Kill for you, burn the earth, fuck you senseless, name it. Anything."

His words have her crying out, have her pumping her hips in time with his hard rhythmic thrusts.

He slips his hand over her breast, the heavy weight of it filling his palm. A ragged groan escapes him.

"Don't stop, Solomon," Tessie pants. "Don't stop." Her voice breaks on a sob. "Please."

"Never."

He slams into her. Hard. A silent scream parts her lips. Her juices spill down the inside of her thighs. Wet. Coating his thighs too. She's so goddamn wet for him, bathing his cock in heat and fire. It only makes him harder. Has him driving his hips forward.

Anything she wants, she gets.

"God, you're beautiful," he groans, cupping her lithe form to him. He punctuates his statement with a kiss to the back of her head, her shoulder, her neck. "So damn beautiful, Tessie."

Mewling, she throws her head back against his shoulder and bucks. The needy writhe of her body sends a shockwave ripping through him. Solomon roars his release, shuddering violently as Tessie cries out, her small hands fisting his hair, as they come together.

Each pulse of her body has him holding her tighter, until finally, she goes limp against him. A content smile spills over on her face as she rolls over, collapses back, laughing into the pillow, her hand covering her pouty lips.

After pressing a kiss to her cheek, Solomon disappears into the bathroom, then returns with a warm, damp towel. Tenderly, he cleans off her thighs and then settles beside her in bed once more.

With a sigh, Tessie rolls over into his arms to meet his kiss. Satisfaction etched across her beautiful face—hooded eyes, pink cheeks, delirious smile.

For a second, Solomon can't breathe. Tessie curled up on his chest. Small, soft, his. Christ. He closes his eyes, letting the moment settle. Never in a million years did he think he'd have this again.

Opening his eyes, he takes in her delicate profile.

I love you.

He should say it.

But the words are frozen on his lips. He's ready—but what if she's not? He's asked so much already. A selfish bastard who asked her to go back to Chinook. If that's not a way to add to the pressure, he doesn't know what is.

With a happy sigh, she smooths a hand down his beard, then her focus drifts up to his face. "Perfect ending to a perfect vacation."

"It was. And it's not over." Palming the side of her face, he murmurs, "You and that baby. My whole heart. My stars. You fucking have me, Tess. Never doubt that."

She curls her fingers in his dark chest hair. "I won't."

She watches him, heavy lidded. Her long lashes flutter with the slow wave of a beckoning sleep. With one hand, he strokes her golden hair. Cups the swell of her belly with the other. A rush of emotion has him. In less than three months, they'll be holding their son in their arms.

"Will you tell me?" he asks, and Tessie's eyes tick to his. "Bear's name."

A long silence. Then a quiet smile appears on her lips. "Why don't we come up with one? Together."

"Tess." A deep rumble of disagreement. He doesn't want her to change it.

"I want to, Solomon." Leaning up on her elbow, she cups the side of his bristly beard. Her even gaze honest, vulnerable as she looks into his dark depths. "It should be *our* name."

An inferno ignites in his chest. Goddamn.

If he didn't love her now. . .

"Thank you," he says.

Her surprised gaze meets his, blond hair falling over her shoulder as she tilts her head. "For what?"

His throat works. "For making me a father."

Tears rush to Tessie's eyes, and a watery smile tips her lips. "You're going to be the best father, Solomon," she whispers, placing his hand over her bump. "Bear will be so lucky to have you."

Trying to get his heart under control, because it feels like there's an atom bomb in his ribs, Solomon pulls Tessie to his chest. Her tiny body tucks perfectly into his side. It's not long, with his hand on her belly and her breath against his shoulder, before she's asleep.

Bear kicks in her stomach, small pulses that have him smiling, and Solomon cradles Tessie closer. He's never felt this content. Tessie knows about Serena, his past, his darkness, and his guilt. And come tomorrow morning, he's taking his stars back home.

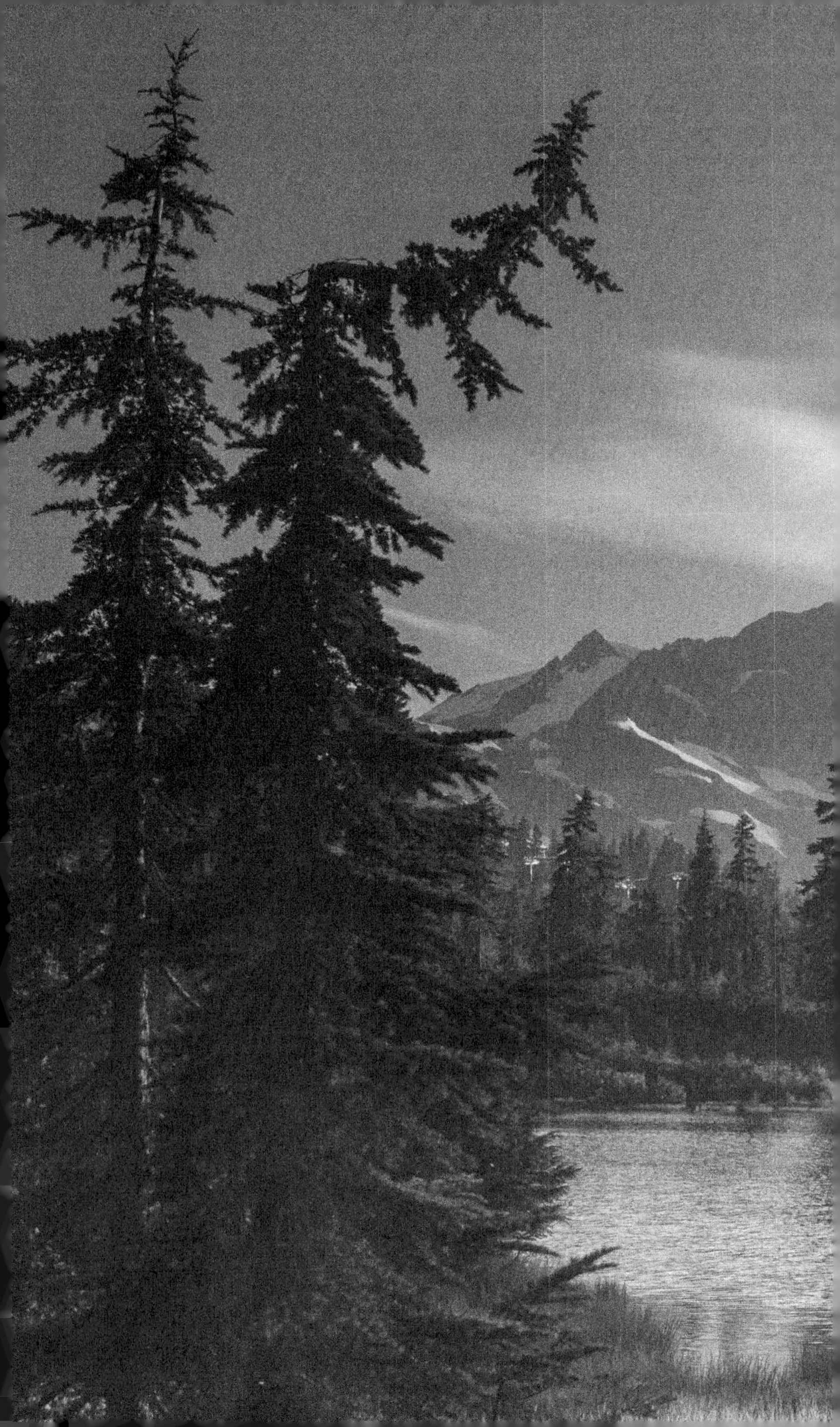

III.

Chapter Twenty-Three

Tessie bounces beside Solomon in his pickup truck as they take the long, winding road through dark green woods from the Anchorage airport to Chinook. Hand clasped in Solomon's, her Crosley record player safe in the back seat, her seat belt tucked low and secure around her belly.

Attention trained on the sights outside the window, she can't take everything in fast enough. It's a whole new world. A beautiful, icy, foreign universe.

She's traded sun for snow. Beach for mountains. Sanity for surprise. Because what she's doing is completely out of her wheelhouse. Even Ash had sounded astonished at her change in plan.

If there's one thing Tessie is not, it's confused. Nervous, sure. Exhilarated, yes. Hungry, always. But not confused.

Solomon claimed her. Their last night in Mexico, those urgent whispered words, *you're mine*. No one's ever done that before. Wanted her, fought for her, made promises with such conviction it broke her heart in the best kind of way.

She's giving up total control to go with the flow. To fly to fucking-off-the-grid-Alaska with this man, who's becoming like her left arm. She can't be without him. She won't.

Excitement swirls in her belly. The kind of wild freedom that comes with staying up all night. The thrill of extending a sleepover. Coming to Chinook feels right. Seeing Solomon's world. Meeting his family.

Bear's family

She keeps telling herself this is just an extension of the babymoon. To see whether she and Solomon click in the real world. She owes it to herself, and most importantly, she owes it to Bear to try. If they can come out of this together...happy, it would be better than she ever dreamed. The stuff of fairytales. The third act of a romance novel. Those happy, colorful, cheerful cartoon covers where a kiss is never just a kiss—it's a forever, a happily ever after.

Still, she can't let her heart go all in. Not yet.

Tempted as she is to say those three little words, she has to be practical about this. She and Solomon are talking; not committing.

Besides, she needs a job. Although her insurance lasts through the end of her pregnancy and she has a stable nest egg, the last thing she wants to do is rely on Solomon to take care of her financially. Here, in Chinook, she'll put out feelers in Los Angeles. She arches a brow at the woods. *If* she gets wi-fi reception.

Tessie gasps at the sudden appearance of what looks like a bird on steroids soaring above the treetops.

Solomon glances her way, then back to the road, a smile on his bearded lips. "Bald eagle."

Overhead, the October sky plumes with dark clouds. "When does it snow?" she asks.

He tenses, holding on tighter to her hand, but keeps his eyes on the road. "If we're lucky, November."

Tessie shivers and adjusts her shirt, scowling down at her unflattering attire. Finally, the joke's on her. She's wrapped in one of Solomon's flannels. They're warm, that's for damn sure.

Turning up the heat, he rakes his gaze over her, then drops it to the high heels on her feet. "We'll get you clothes, Tess," he says in that stern, gruff tone she loves. The one he uses only with her. A tone that tells her he cares, that he'll take care of her.

"You're about the same size as Melody, minus the stomach." He lets off the gas and flips on his blinker. "She's pulling together some stuff you can wear while you're here. We can get it tomorrow at brunch."

Tessie's stomach flips over, her easygoing feeling evaporating at the thought of meeting Solomon's family. What if they hate her?

At her sigh, Solomon squeezes her hand. "You tired?"

"I am. I'm running on exhilaration. And this baby is on my lung." She rests a hand on the high swell of her stomach. God, she's gotten so much bigger in the last few days. She shifts in the bench seat and arches a brow. "I'm thirty weeks today."

He glances over at her, eyes dancing with pride and affection. "I know."

"I feel huge."

"You're not huge. You're beautiful, Tess."

She flushes. Will she ever get tired of hearing him say that?

Just as quickly, she deflates. She has so much left to do. So much for keeping a content, worry-free brain space. It won't be long before she starts to itch, that need to plan, to organize, to fix. "I need to find a doctor too." She side-eyes Solomon. "Depending on how long I stay."

Before she left Mexico, she had a telehealth call with her obstetrician, who said it was fine to skip one check-up but recommended she find a local doctor if she stays, or to make sure she gets back to LA before thirty-six weeks because of flying restrictions.

Solomon grunts. His broody glower says he doesn't want to talk about her leaving. "I found you a doctor."

She sits up straighter, her heart warming. "You did?"

"I did." He's nonchalant, as if Tessie's heart isn't already boiling over. "We can go next week. See if you like her."

Smiling, she scoots closer, securing the middle seat belt around herself, loving the way he takes on responsibilities with her. Like it's their problem. Not hers. It's a relief. Not to shoulder everything for once.

"What else will you get me?" she asks, sweeping a kiss against the pulse in his throat. She drops her hand, trailing her fingers beneath the hem of his black Henley and up his warm, ridged stomach.

He stiffens. "Woman," he growls, doing his damndest not to throttle the wheel as they rumble across a narrow stone bridge, "Knock that shit off, or we're going in the ditch."

Tessie puffs a laugh and eases up on the kisses, but before she can resume her passenger-side position, Solomon wraps an arm around her shoulder, keeping her near. "You know what you have, don't you?"

Nestling closer to his big, warm body, she nuzzles her nose in his neck. "What?"

"The power to destroy me completely."

She laughs. "I'll use it wisely."

"Relax, Tess." His deep rumble vibrates through her. "I know your brain. No checklists. No worrying."

She scrunches up her nose, wishing she had some of Solomon's calm and contentment. "How come you know everything? How come you're so, so. . .steady?"

His lips twitch. "Because I come from the mountains," he says, pointing a large finger.

Tessie's gaze drifts upward, and she squeaks.

Rising up out of the clouds are dark, jagged peaks of earth. Mountains. Strong, ferocious, brooding. Like Solomon. Their snow-white domes, delicately scooped like ice cream, mesmerize her.

Tessie looks south out the window. Quaking aspens shake in the gusty breeze. A squirrel darts into the road, regrets its decision, and dives for the bushes.

They blow by the Welcome to Chinook sign, population, 8,000. The cheery town motto reads: Take a Look at Good Ole Chinook.

Turning, Solomon takes a paved road into town. At last, the landscape is civilized. Main Street. Boutique shops, restaurants, bars, coffee shops, a butcher. A man tinkers with his car on the side of the road, lifts a hand to Solomon, who does the same in return.

"Welcome to Chinook," her mountain man says softly. The glow in his dark blue eyes tells her all she needs to know. He loves this town, his community. And she wants to love it too.

"Where are we going?" she asks, laying her head on his shoulder.

"We'll swing by the bar to pick up Peggy and then head to the cabin."

"Mmm. I get to see the bar, the dog, and the cabin. I'm a lucky girl."

The apple of his throat bobs, an affectionate look crossing his face.

Nuzzling against Solomon, Tessie lets her heart ease her worries. It feels divine to give in to the now, to fully enjoy the present without worrying about what comes next.

She will worry.

Later.

Because wrapped tight in Solomon's arms, Bear safe in her belly, nothing else matters.

It's like the mountains knew he was bringing her home.

Solomon, pride in his chest and Tessie curled into his side, takes in the vast Alaska sky. Clouds as white as cotton set off against a great grove of trees that stretch the horizon. Being back in Chinook is like drinking from a fresh alpine stream. Will Tessie see what he sees? Magnificent beauty? The wild nature he's always loved? He hopes so.

Solomon pulls into the gravel driveway of Howler's Roost and leaves the truck running. "Stay here," he says. "I'll grab Peggy and we'll—"

But she's already unbuckling her seat belt.

Swearing, he cuts the ignition, then shoots out of the truck and over to the passenger side. He grabs her hand before her feet can hit the ground. Yes, he's acting like an overprotective asshole, but her center of gravity has completely changed. Not to mention she's wearing the highest goddamn heels he's ever seen. He isn't taking any chances.

"Easy," he soothes, his hands bracketing her shoulders, making sure she's steady on her feet. Eyes sweeping over her, he smothers a smile. She's damn adorable. Wearing black skinny jeans and Solomon's oversized black and white buffalo plaid flannel. Even pregnant, she's dwarfed by it.

"I'm not staying in the car, Solomon." Tessie squints at the bright red barns sandwiching the drab gray silo. Shifts her focus to the rusted chanticleer weather vane perched at the very top. "I want to see this place you've been talking about." She tilts her head and wrinkles her nose "It looks like a silo."

He rubs a hand over his beard. "It is a silo."

Hell, he's embarrassed to let Tess see it. Embarrassed that he let the bar get this bad, let Howler pick up the slack. Still, he can't keep her from it forever. Christ, it's his damn job. If she's sticking around—which, if he has any say in the matter, she is—it'll be a part of her life.

"Just . . ." Taking her elbow, he guides her carefully across the rock parking lot. "It's a wreck. Know that."

Her eyes drift to the neon sign, sputtering like it's on its last life. "I'm good with wrecks."

"You can't judge."

Her lips purse like the thought's a lemon. Then—

"Fine. I will internally scream my objections."

"Good."

As they approach the front door, there's a rustling in the bushes next to the trash cans. Solomon freezes and then shifts, putting himself in front of Tessie.

She digs her nails into the hard meat of his shoulder. "Oh my God, it's a bear, isn't it?" she squeals as the commotion gets louder.

He wants to tell her she's wrong. But he can't.

Fuck.

Howler's words about bears in the area send a hot rush of panic sweeping through him.

With a whip-quick hand, Solomon grabs Tessie—one hand on her back, the other just beneath her ass—and lifts her into the air. Pushes her toward the ladder on the side of the silo. "Climb," he orders. "Now."

"I don't climb ladders," she shrieks, palming his shoulders. "Solomon, put me down. I can run to the car."

"You can't run," he grouches. "Not in heels, Tess. What did I goddamn tell you—"

The bush explodes.

Tessie shrieks, a flurry of blond hair, as she climbs down his body like a wildcat.

Solomon lunges in front of her, only to be hit by a slobbering fool of a hound dog.

"Christ," he exhales. Relief nearly knocks him over.

Peggy gives a woof, and Solomon drops into a crouch, running his hands over her long ears and droopy jowls.

"Hey, girl," he says, giving a grunt of affection as his heartbeat resumes its normal rhythm. Hell, he missed his damn dog.

From behind him comes the sound of Tessie's laughter. Hands on her stomach, she's doubled over. "Oh my God. It's your dog."

"Great first impression," he tells Peggy drolly.

Tessie giggles. "She was coming to attack me. So vicious." She dips down and ruffles the hound's ears. Peggy, enjoying the pet, puts a paw on Tessie's thigh and tries to climb directly onto her lap, but Solomon puts a hand out, bracing the small of her back so the dog doesn't knock her over.

"Oh, she's so sweet."

Solomon's heart wrenches as Tessie dips her head to kiss Peggy's inky black nose.

Another rustle, and then Howler's stomping out from the back of the building, trash bag in hands.

He stops and gawks at the scene, then says, "'Bout damn time you got your ass back home."

Solomon pushes up to standing. "I'm back. Now you can stop bitching." He holds a hand out to Tessie, helping her stand, then tugs her close.

The bright grin on Howler's face drops off when he sees her. Solomon waits for his friend to say hello, frowning when he doesn't. Howler's attention drifts to her stomach, then back to Solomon. "Brought Goldilocks back, huh?"

Tessie arches a brow at the nickname but says nothing. With a flip of her silky blond hair, she pushes past Howler and into the bar. Peggy trots in after her, already in love. Solomon doesn't blame her.

Wincing, he follows them in. Tessie's tiny standing in the circular space. Bright and sunny up against the dark dankness of the bar. She considers the room, cocking her blond head, lips pursed and gaze narrowed.

She sees what Solomon sees.

Chipped bar top. A blinking neon sign. Two missing floorboards. The wood stove on the fritz.

Hands clasped on her belly, Tessie spins, smiles bright at Howler. "Solomon says you make a mean mocktail."

Howler crosses his arms. "Soda taps are broken."

"*Okaaay*," Tessie drawls. Her confused eyes dart to Solomon. "I'm going to scope out the kitchen."

Solomon frowns. It's not like Howler to be so tight-lipped. A goddamn asshole, if he had to call it. Luckily, Tessie's a pro, used to dealing with pricks like Atlas, and she lets the slight roll off her.

"What the fuck's your problem?" Solomon asks, voice low so Tessie doesn't overhear. "You're acting like a dick."

"Nothing," Howler snaps. Then he huffs. "Dude, I thought you were gonna go down there, figure your shit out, and come home. Not bring her back."

"She's not a fucking pizza," Solomon snaps.

Howler snorts. "What's she gonna do, move here?"

Solomon clears the knot in his throat. "We haven't talked about it."

"Haven't talked about it. . ." Howler mutters. "Well, you better, man. Soon too. She looks ready to pop."

Sobering, Solomon scrubs a palm down his face, his chest tight with worry. With reality. Maybe he was a selfish bastard asking Tessie to come back with him, but he learned his lesson with Serena.

Don't let her walk away. Go after her.

Tessie comes out of the kitchen, poking a finger at a stuffed squirrel holding a tip jar. "This really says taxidermy chic, doesn't it?"

"No judgment," Solomon calls out as she smirks at the nudie calendar behind the bar.

"I'm not judging. I'm observing with a critical eye."

Turning her attention to Howler, she asks, "What time do you open?"

Howler bristles. "We're open now."

"Doesn't look like it." She runs a finger over the dusty bar top, causing Howler's scowl to deepen. "What's your budget for the remodel?"

"We have a healthy budget."

Solomon smothers a smile, watching Tessie go toe to toe with his friend.

She walks out from behind the bar, then, stopping in front of them, she jerks a shoulder to the back corner of the room. "What are you planning to do with the space?"

Howler shoots Solomon a look of annoyance. "The space?"

"Just go with it," Solomon says.

An exasperated sigh. "Fine. Thought we'd make it more in line with what other popular bars are doing. Maybe add a pool table."

Tessie snorts.

Howler stiffens, his expression surly. "Think you could do better?"

Solomon's rubbing his brow, a headache already brewing. "Don't. Do not start with her."

Tessie draws herself up like it's a challenge. "Actually, I could." Done talking to Howler, she spears Solomon with a look. "This space could be spectacular." She flings an arm out. "I see wall-to-wall booths. Dark booths. The jukebox stays. Add mood lighting. Maybe a floor-to-ceiling window? Oh! Garage doors!" Stopping in the middle of the bar, she flings her arms out like she can hug the space around her.

Solomon nods. "It's a great space. We planned to do a lot of the work ourselves to keep costs down."

Eyes alight, Tessie lifts her brows. "*I* could do it."

He's already shaking his head. The last fucking thing he wants is Tessie on a ladder. Tessie hauling large objects around. Tessie smashing the shit out of sheetrock with a ten-pound mallet when she's seven months pregnant.

It's bad enough she's been on an eight-hour flight, stuck in the car for three hours. She needs to be home at his place, her heels off, resting.

"No," he says. "Hell no."

"Yes, Solomon. Hell yes." She grabs his arm, shakes it, and dances in place. "*Please*. Let me help you. I can order everything through my suppliers at cost. All you have to do is Hulk it around with your big muscles."

He opens his mouth to say no, but he can't. Because there it is. On her face. She's hooked. Pantone colors already flying around in that gorgeous head of hers.

"Fine, damn it," he growls, both amused and annoyed at how fast she's gotten him to cave.

She squeals and presses a kiss to his bearded cheek.

Christ. Is this what his fucking future looks like? Tying

himself up in knots, tripping all over to give her everything she wants? Jesus. He's a mess.

Still, he'll do whatever it takes to keep her in Chinook.

Howler shoots him a scathing look of betrayal. "It's my bar," he grouches.

"Our bar," Solomon shoots back.

"Oh, sure, you pull that card after seven damn years."

Eyes glittering with excitement, Tessie runs her hands lovingly down the brick wall. "We could Pantone the shit out of this."

"What the fuck's a Pantone?" Howler mutters, tearing a bothered hand through his sandy-blond hair. "You ain't painting that brick. It's an institution."

Solomon snorts at the theatrics. "We've pissed on that brick." He nods proudly at Tessie. "You want this done? She's your girl. She does this for a living."

"And I'll do it for free," she says with a smug smile. "Take it or leave it. Because I'm unemployed and I'm a sucker for a good Cinderella-story project."

"Fine." Groaning, Howler slaps a sticky menu against Solomon's chest. "You better come up with the best damn menu in Alaska."

"Damn right I will." Solomon's eyes snag on Tessie.

His heart clenches.

Goddamn, he loves the way she looks in his bar.

Tonight, he's going to love the way she looks in his bed.

Chapter Twenty-Four

Thirty minutes later, Solomon's whipping the truck down a winding gravel road. As they pass through a grove of dark evergreens, a cabin comes into view. Tessie sits up straight and turns to him. "Is that it?"

He noses into the driveway, kills the engine. "That's it."

A quick examination of the expansive yard has her smiling. Solomon's cabin isn't quite the dark and dilapidated shack she imagined. Instead, it's a quaint V-frame cabin nestled in the fringe of the boreal forest. Like a stylishly unfinished Colorado ski lodge. Chopped firewood is stacked in a pyramid pile next to an axe. A stone path winds its way up to the door. Blown glass wind chimes hang in the trees surrounding the yard. A large wooden deck perfect for reading or watching the stars welcomes visitors.

Her home.

For the next however many days, at least.

The slam of the truck door snags her attention. Solomon's out and rounding the front of the hood. With a grin, she takes the opportunity to ogle her handsome mountain man. He looks so damn good. So in his element with his beard and his muscles and his hound dog, who's howling in the back.

Her door opens. Then, gripping her hand with quiet intensity, Solomon helps her out.

Tessie stands in the wild woods, soaking it all in. This place Solomon loves. The heartbeat of this wild, wondrous country. A cool breeze whispers through the trees, ruffles the ends of her hair. Far off, there's the faint trickle of a creek or stream. Birdsong high in the trees. Rough, craggy mountains loom over the cabin like it's their solemn duty to protect it.

This sure beats the view of her apartment parking lot.

"What do you think?" Solomon asks, his gaze expectant. Nervous.

She inclines her head to look up at him. "Hmm," she hums. "It's not as grump as I imagined."

She's rewarded with a good-natured grunt. "Are you calling me a grump?"

"I'm calling you *my* grump."

His eyes soften, and the smile that appears on his lips sends her heart into a cartwheel.

Far off, the howl of a wolf. Tessie edges closer, gripping Solomon's comforting bicep.

As he regards the cabin, Tessie sees the knot of tension in his body fall away. He looks relaxed. Comfortable. At home.

"Did you miss it?" she asks softly.

With a heated look at her, he tugs her suitcase out of the back of the truck. "Not as much as I thought I would."

Her heart gives a little flip.

"C'mon, Pregnant Woman." He opens the tailgate of the truck and helps Peggy out, then twines his fingers with hers. "This way."

Obediently, Tessie follows him up the drive to the house. She pauses on the deck and nods at what looks like a storage shed on stilts set about twelve feet from the house.

"Why's it elevated?"

"To keep wild animals out," Solomon says, digging into his pocket for the key. He finds it and sticks it in the lock. "Better get inside." He lifts his brows, his tone foreboding. "We probably only have a few minutes until it gets dark."

"Wait, what?" Fear prickles the back of Tessie's neck, and

she scans the tree line. The sun's rays grow dimmer and dimmer through the foliage. "What happens when it gets dark?"

Turning back to Solomon, she catches sight of his smirk and slaps his arm. "Evil man," she hisses.

His smirk turning into a rare full-wattage grin, he kisses her temple, then swings the front door open. Peggy bounds inside with a woof. Cautiously, curiously, Tessie steps past Solomon. Instantly, the space is illuminated with a flip of the light switch.

"Oh, Solomon." She presses palms to her stomach and stops in her tracks. "It's so pretty."

Nothing she pictured did this justice. She had expected a stark, sparse space, but instead, she finds...charm. Beauty.

Solomon.

He keeps blowing all her assumptions about him out of the water.

Blowing up her heart.

The interior of the cabin is even better than the exterior. The living room, kitchen and dining room are open concept. In the elevated living room, two leather couches sit cozily in front of a stone fireplace.

Rustic yet chic. Something she would design.

Tessie walks the room breathlessly, pressing palms to the wood walls. Natural. No stain or paint. Just wild wilderness. She sniffs the wall. Looks at Solomon, who's watching her with an amused smile. "Pine?" she asks.

"Spruce," he corrects, setting her bag down and shutting the door.

She drops down beside the long kitchen table. Four chairs and a bench. Wood as smooth as silk. Running a finger over an elaborate leg, she peeks over. "Did you make this?"

He nods. "I did."

"It's beautiful."

Another gasp, the wheels in her mind spinning with

possibilities. "You should make the furniture at Howler's Roost for the remodel. Oh! The bar top. The stools!"

He chuckles. "Howler's already got me writing a menu. Don't push it."

She stands, giving a little wiggle, and Solomon's eyes flash in response. "What can I say? Chinook's inspiring me already." Tossing her hair over her shoulders, she arches a brow. "Except for maybe your friend."

The guy froze her out, clear as day. But she won't let it bother her. After her time in LA, she's used to cold shoulders and angry glares.

Solomon's face clouds. "Howler...he's just..."

"Jealous?"

"I'm not sure." He drags a hand through his dark hair. His hard jaw resets. "Don't worry about him. Focus on the bar, and we'll get it done." His serious gaze drifts to her belly. "It's gotta be fast, Tess."

She holds up a hand. "It will be," she promises. "I'm all about a challenge."

Excitement flutters in her chest. Fixing up Solomon's bar is pure adrenaline. A detailed vision of what the space could be came to her almost instantly. Industrial yet warm. Brooding but fun. Howler's personality melded with Solomon's. Because they're the soul of that bar, and it's important to reflect that.

This design—it's in her wheelhouse. It will give her something to do, help her feel not so lost at sea, put her restless anxiety to good use. Because before long, she needs to find a job. Before that old nervous energy comes calling.

When Tessie gets to the deep stairs that cut into the wooden wall leading up to the loft bedroom, she stops. There's no railing.

"Those stairs..." Solomon begins, looking adorably worried. "They're not safe for you."

"You weren't exactly expecting a pregnant woman to be huffing up them."

When he says nothing, his expression turning to a scowl, she goes to him, placing a hand on the front of his chest. His heart pumps fast beneath her hand.

She gives him a small smile. "Solomon, it's fine. I'll be careful."

He studies her, and then his mouth softens. "I'll help you."

With Solomon behind her, his palm on the small of her back, guiding her, she slowly and carefully climbs the stairs.

She gasps.

In the middle of the loft bedroom is a large bed. A faux fur-covered blanket is draped over one end, a leather bench at the foot of it. On one side of the room sits a wooden rocking chair and a small side table. An old claw-foot tub is opposite, next to the bathroom.

Delighted, she pulls Solomon by the hand. "Solemn Man, you have a tub."

He chuckles. "I'm not that off the grid."

Stepping toward the center of the room, she takes in the slanted walls that give the space a supremely cozy feel. She can't help but imagine her and Bear in this space. Because it's perfect. Perfect for a crib. For a family.

"This is beautiful." She bites down on her smile and locks her gaze with his. "I love it, Solomon. This is better than Mexico."

Something changes in his expression when she says the words. His throat works, his eyes stay on her. Then he lifts a hand. "Tess. Look up."

She does. And this time, she can't gasp. Can't even speak.

A skylight over the bed lets in the evening sky.

Lets in the stars.

The moment she sees the window, the first star twinkling in the majestic Alaskan sky, the floodgates open and her tears break free.

It all feels so fated. Like the workings of her life have slowly fallen into place. Like she has her beating heart in her hands and is showing it the life she was meant to live.

Because she's meant to be here. With Solomon. With their son.

In two quick strides, Solomon's beside her, wiping the tears from her cheeks. His big, strong hand cups her face, making her look at him. "Don't cry," he says in a low, rough voice. "You absolutely kill me when you cry, baby."

"I'm sorry." She sniffles.

"Don't apologize. What's wrong?"

"Nothing's wrong."

"Then why are you crying?"

"Because it all feels too perfect. So perfect." She shakes her head, hot tears streaming down her cheeks. Pressing palms against her bump, she looks down at Bear. "And I'm pregnant. And I'm stupid."

"You're not stupid." He touches her cheek, nudging her gaze to him. "I feel it too."

"You do?"

"I do. Something so damn right I want to lose it on a daily basis." His lapis lazuli eyes sear into hers. And she knows. The way he looks at her—he understands. Her fears. Her doubts. Her joy. Understands them and will hold them. "You, being here. . .it means everything to me, Tessie." He places his hand on her belly. "*You* mean everything."

Her lips part, but she doesn't say it.

Not yet.

Instead, she falls forward, and Solomon catches her like she knew he would, hauling her to his chest. His big body—warm and sturdy and safe—envelops her as she presses up on tiptoes to meet his lips.

And Tessie's pulse hammers out a melody in her bloodstream.

I love you. I love you. I love you.

Chapter Twenty-Five

Solomon and Tessie walk up the sidewalk to his childhood home. A cream-colored two-story house with a wraparound porch and a large oak tree in the front yard. Sunday brunch.

Brunch gives them an out. Two hours of conversation, and then they can go.

Inhaling a bracing breath, Tessie smooths out the front of her dress. "Okay," she says. "Go ahead. Knock."

The corner of Solomon's mouth twitches. His girl's got her game face on. He's noticed the signs. The way she chews on her bottom lip. The way she rubs three circles on her belly and then sighs.

"You're nervous."

She socks him in the arm. "Of course I'm nervous. I'm meeting your *family*." Apprehension stains her voice. "What if they hate me? What if they think I'm a trollop who got knocked up on purpose?"

He arches an amused brow. "Trollop?"

Her pretty face scrunches up and she palms her stomach. "This is Bear's family. I'm unemployed. I'm pregnant. I'm a *Californian*. I'm not exactly making a good first impression."

"Tess, baby." He takes her hands, stilling her. The sad look she wears has the power to destroy him. "None of that, okay? They're gonna love you."

No one and nothing will touch her. Especially while he's around.

She tilts her face up, her expression softening. "You promise?"

He kisses her brow. "I promise."

"No nerves?"

"No nerves."

Hell, he's the one who should have nerves. He hasn't brought a woman home since Serena. But he can't fucking wait for his family to meet Tessie. Being here in Chinook with her, his feelings have grown tenfold. Seeing her at his cabin, the way she loved it as much as he did, stole his breath away.

He doesn't have nerves. Not today.

Not with Tessie.

He doesn't want to hide her away anymore. He wants everyone to see her for the force she is. To know she's going to be part of his life.

That's how sure he is about her.

On the front porch, Solomon pauses before knocking. "You tell me if it's too much and we'll go. You understand?"

It's a lot for her; he gets that. She's out of her element, out of LA, pregnant, in his world, and now meeting strangers who are going to want to know everything about their plans, about the baby. Thank Christ that the only family member with the power to scare Tessie off is in Anchorage.

Tessie flicks her hair behind a slender shoulder, her expression adjusting to one of cool confidence. "I'll be okay."

"Just be yourself."

She snorts. "Be pregnant and grouchy. Got it."

He waits for her to give a small nod of assent, and then he takes her hand, and with his other, he knocks on the wooden door.

In seconds, the front door whips open, as if Melody's been waiting at the peephole, ready to ambush them. Ignoring him, his baby sister beelines straight for Tessie. Eyes bright, genuine warmth on her face. "Hi! I'm Melody."

Tessie smiles and extends a hand, her frame relaxing. "Tessie."

"It's so nice to meet you," his sister chirps. Her eyes fall to Tessie's stomach, then bounce to Solomon. "Oh my God."

He chuckles. "You thought I was making it up?"

"No, but. . ." Her lower lip quivers.

Solomon tips his head back to the sky. Tears from his family aren't on the agenda today.

"No crying," he tells his sister, who immediately squeaks her protest. "You cry, you do the dishes."

A scoff. "Fine." She extends an arm to Tessie. "Please come in. Everyone's so excited to meet you."

Tessie sends him a grateful smile, and they step over the threshold together.

Melody lifts a hand to her mouth. "Everyone, they're here!" Her peppy voice carries down the hall. Then she turns back to Tessie. "I personally would like to thank you for getting our brother out of his cave."

Tessie laughs. "It was my pleasure."

"Hell yes. You're here." Jo waltzes down the hall, her arms already outstretched. "It's time for all the hugs. I hope you're ready."

Solomon embraces his sister, the middle wild child of the family. When she pulls away, she homes in on Tessie. Belly. Tessie.

With a sigh, he says, "This is Tessie. And yes, this is her belly."

"Holy shit—can I—" Jo's hands hover a few inches from Tessie's bump, then she stops herself. "No, that's weird. I'm sorry. Like the first thing we want to do is feel you up. Oh my God, I'm awful. We are straight-up not respecting your body boundaries right now."

Solomon runs his hand down Tessie's shoulder, wanting her to know it's her choice. "You don't have to."

With a smile on her full lips, Tessie tilts her face up to him, taking his sister's awkwardness in stride. "Go for it."

An eruption of squeals has him chuckling. Four hands all pressing on Tessie's stomach. The image has his chest growing tight.

Has him picturing his son over here for family dinners, playing with his aunts, his grandparents.

"Solomon Jack."

A soft voice has him turning. His mother, long white hair streaming behind her, is rushing out of the kitchen. "Oh, it's so good to see you, son," she says, engulfing him in a desperate hug.

Throat tight, Solomon crushes her against him. It's been so long since he set foot inside his own house. In the years after Serena, he only swung by to help fix something or to drop off the casserole dishes his mom would leave on his front porch, never staying or enjoying his family. A mistake he made once, but he won't make again.

"Hey, Ma," he says, pulling back. "Where's Dad?"

She tuts. "Oh, you know that man. Fiddling with something on the grill. Figured we'd eat outside since it's the last nice day we might have for a while." She turns to Tessie, her blue-eyed gaze finding her. "And this must be your sweet girl. Hello, I'm Grace."

Tessie blushes and shakes his mother's hand. "Hi, I'm Tessie. It's so nice to meet you." She smiles at his sisters. "All of you."

"Stop standing around." His mother lifts her hands and makes a shooing motion. "We have drinks and appetizers on the porch."

In a loud chorus of voices, they follow his mother. But halfway down the hall, Solomon notices Tessie's no longer beside him.

He turns around.

Fuck.

She's taking in the gallery wall on the long hallway corridor. Photos of Solomon's family. Photos of him and Serena.

"Is that her?" she asks, pointing at one gold frame. "Serena?"

His mother's worried gaze moves to Solomon, then lands on Tessie. "It is," she says.

"Crater Lake," he says quietly, closing the gap between them to draw Tessie into his arms. "It was our honeymoon."

"She's beautiful." Twining her fingers with his, Tessie smiles. No trace of nerves on her face. "Should we go eat?"

Solomon lets out a breath he didn't know he was holding. Relief fills him. Tessie's taking it all in stride. Understanding his past and never asking him to choose.

Out on the porch, his dad, seeing Tessie, sets the tray of premade burger patties down and hustles over.

"Hi, Tess, I'm Jack. Nice to meet you." He kisses her cheek, then lifts his bushy gray brows at Solomon. "About time, son."

He rolls his eyes at his father's remark. But he likes it. He likes being back with his family, trading bullshit banter, being a part of the Wilder clan again. He didn't realize how much he missed this.

"You made a feast," he comments. Large trays of food are set up on the table. Fresh veggies and dip. Muffins. Fruit cut into star shapes.

"It's an occasion," Jo says, taking a swig from the bottle of champagne.

"A celebration," Melody chimes in.

Once they settle in, get small talk out of the way, the conversation turns to the obvious.

Babies.

"So..." Jo rubs her hands together eagerly. "Solomon's been holding out on us. We want to hear everything about this baby and your plans."

Solomon shoots his sister a hard look to go easy on Tessie. Sure, his family's excited, but that doesn't mean they have the right to ambush her with questions. Besides, she doesn't need to be worried. He's got her. Even if she doesn't yet know it.

Tessie smiles his way as he gives her hand a reassuring squeeze. "Well, it's a boy. We still haven't decided on a name, and he's due December twenty-third."

"When the baby's born," his mother begins, "what then? How long are you in Chinook, Tessie?"

"Oh, I..." Her hesitant eyes flick to Solomon and then back to his mother. "I'm not sure. We haven't planned that far ahead yet."

His heart dips at her answer. He needs to tell her. That he loves her. That her leaving will absolutely destroy him.

His mother leans forward and smiles. "I only ask because we'd love to give you a baby shower while you're here."

Tessie's face lights up. "Really?"

"Of course."

Almost shyly, she nods. "That'd be wonderful."

Jo kicks back in her chair, her blue-eyed gaze moving to Solomon. "No boys allowed."

Melody bats her lashes. "But you may come and help us set up."

Solomon cracks a laugh. "Ruthlessly used."

"Thought we'd ask Evelyn to come," his father adds.

At the mention of his oldest sister, he bristles. The last conversation he had with her was in Mexico. Her unwarranted admonition about Tessie leaves a bad taste in his mouth. "If she behaves," he says.

Tessie's lips quirk in a question. "Behaves?"

Jo tips back in her chair, gnawing on a baby carrot like it's a cigar. "The trick with Evelyn is to not make eye contact unless you want your pupils ripped out."

"Girls," their mother groans, laughing into her hand.

Tessie arches a wry brow. "Isn't she your sister?"

Melody shrugs, apologetic. "She's a little self-righteous."

Solomon chokes on a laugh while their father sticks his fingers in his ears. "I am not hearing this," he says.

Tessie stands from her chair, moving for the veggies and dip, waving him off when he rises to get it for her. "Tell me about Solomon when he was a little boy," she says, looking between Jack and Grace. "I want to hear everything about him."

A round of cackles erupts, and Solomon groans. This is just what he needs. His family dishing the dirt.

"Solomon was the wildest little boy," his mother starts.

Tessie listens, her attention rapt, her brown eyes gleaming with mischief.

"He was always into tools," his father adds. "Would sleep with them at night. Couldn't drag them away from him."

By now, everyone, minus Tessie, has had a few beers, and conversation is flowing. The sun is high in the sky, warming the chilly afternoon air.

"Laugh it up," Solomon says to Jo as he snags Tessie's wrist. "I'm the oldest. I've been digging up dirt on you since you were born." Slowly, he pulls Tessie toward him, settling her on his lap.

Instantly, the table falls silent. Jo coughs into her hand. Melody turns away from them, wiping a tear from the corner of her eye. The corner of his dad's mustached mouth twitches.

"Jesus," he mutters, cradling Tessie tighter in his arms. "You guys gotta knock it off."

Tessie, a red flush coating her cheeks, dips her mouth to his ear. "Solomon, they're staring."

"Let 'em," he grunts, and he kisses her in front of everyone.

Tessie laughs, burying her face in his chest as a round of chuckles fills the air.

"Oh!" Jo pipes up. "What about eighth grade?"

"Do not with the eighth grade." Solomon shoots her a glare. "Mom doesn't even know about that."

Jo laughs.

His mother arches a brow. "Know about what, Solomon Jack?"

"Yes," Tessie says, smirking. "I'd love to know."

Ping.

Tessie perks up. "Finally! I haven't had a single bar since I got here," she says, reaching for her bag as Melody passes it around the table.

Her sharp intake of breath has Solomon's attention dropping to her belly. "Everything okay?"

Tessie stares at her phone, a consternated expression on her face. "Fine. It's just my app." Her smile is thin as she looks around the table. "If you'll excuse me, I have to use the bathroom."

"Third door on your left." He gives Tessie a boost off his lap and watches as she disappears inside.

Seconds pass, and then his family turns to him.

"Oh, we love her," Melody says, a siren of a squeal emitting from her. "She's so..."

"Her resting bitch face is—" Jo raises a hand and smacks her lips. "*Mwah*, chef's kiss."

"Dishes," his mother says, pointing at Jo. Then she turns her watery gaze to Solomon. "You have to keep her, Sol."

He swallows the lump in his throat. "I intend to."

A dagger twists his heart. He's so goddamn grateful he's got the most supportive family in the world. Already, they love Tessie. His son. They should be angry at him for putting them through hell, for making them worry. Instead, they're happy for him.

His two worlds meeting—his hometown and his forever.

His father chuckles. "Have to admit, son. A baby. A new girl. It's a hell of a way to come back to Chinook."

Solomon nods and grins. He gets it. Because he feels back. And not just that. He feels found.

"There's something else you should know," Solomon says, grinning wider. "I'm going back to work at the bar."

Jo tosses up her hands. "Praise the Lord."

Voice cracking, his father clears his throat and adjusts his wire-rimmed glasses. "That's the best damn news in a long time."

His mother stands, walks around the table to kiss his cheek. "I'm so happy for you."

He takes her hands in his and swallows hard. Needing to get this out. "Listen, Ma. I know I wasn't there—"

"Hush," she says, squeezing his fingers. "There's no need for that. You're here now. For that baby and that girl."

"I am," he responds, no doubt. Never.

"That's all that matters, Sol." Grace smiles, pride and relief shining in her eyes. "You have a second chance with a wonderful woman. A family."

A second chance.

His mother's words nearly knock him over. And something loosens in his chest. The hard knot of regret, of guilt he's kept all these long years unraveling.

He has a second chance.

The future is wide open. He just needs to hold on to it.

Tessie sits on the edge of the Wilders' bathtub, leg bouncing a mile a minute, chewing on a nail. For the fourth time in the last twenty seconds, she rereads the text from Nova King herself. The woman owns the largest celebrity design firm in Los Angeles. A curt *can you spare a minute* that has her close to, if not, shitting her pants.

And then her phone rings. Explodes in her hands. Tessie nearly drops it in the toilet.

Fuck. It's her. Declining her call probably isn't a wise move, even if her career is already in the gutter.

She slides the Answer bar. "Nova, hi,"

"Tess Truelove, where have you been all my life? Clearly not at my firm." Nova sounds like an old-school Hollywood actress. Simultaneously bored and sultry.

"I've been out of the country. On vacation."

"I see." The designer's words are crisp, betraying nothing. "I heard you've parted ways with Atlas."

That's a nice way of saying she told her boss to fuck off. "I have."

"You're all over the news, Tess. The bungalow you did for Penny Pain is sending shockwaves through the community. According to *Architectural Digest*, you're the most requested designer since R.M. Matlin designed the Schumacher villa."

"Wow," she breathes, stunned. "I had no idea. I've, uh, kind of tuned out the world these days."

"Smart woman. Listen, I'm not calling to make small talk. I want to offer you a job."

Tessie's brain fizzes. She stands and paces from one end of the small room to the other. "What?"

"A job. I understand you're in need of one."

"I am." Desperately. "But. . ."

Is this what she really wants? Working for celebrities? Sure, she loves the glamor and the excitement and the challenge, but she wants to help people find their beauty. Not be barked at by whiny actors or decimate historic homes to make room for more stale open-floor plans. Going back to that same old tired world she wasn't a fan of.

She wasn't anything. Especially happy.

"Tess? You there?"

She inhales deeply. Time to take a stand. To do what she's been doing this last month with Solomon. It's time to live.

"Nova, I'm pregnant. And while I love designing, I won't do what I was doing when I worked for Atlas."

A long silence, so long she thinks maybe the call dropped, and then Nova says, "I understand. And I'm in the same position you are. We're working on making Nova Interiors an all-inclusive workplace, especially to mothers. Right now, we're only offering sixteen weeks of paid maternity leave, but we're hoping to adjust our policies in the near future."

Tessie's head spins. *Paid* maternity leave? Sixteen weeks?

"I understand your child comes first. Set your hours, be on the ground for your clients, but please draw lines. Our environment isn't perfect, but we understand a healthy work-life balance. I have no problem hiring you while you're expecting." A shuffle of papers. "If you're ready, I could email a contract to you."

Tessie stops pacing, dropping one hand to her belly like Bear's a Magic 8 Ball that has all the answers.

Because this job sounds like the answer to her dreams. A job. Money. Insurance. Potentially a non-toxic work environment. But...

But what about Solomon? What about Chinook?

A month ago, she would have snapped it up, no doubt, no question.

Now here she is, in a frozen world, far from LA. Taking risks. But are they the right risks? Is she being a flighty, irresponsible woman chasing a man halfway across the world all because she saw stars?

Doubt fills her up like a balloon. Her old worries of fear and abandonment crashing over her like a rogue wave.

She and Solomon agreed, when they left Mexico, that they'd try. But what are they to each other? They haven't committed. Neither she nor Solomon have said those three little words.

She's never done this before. Dating. A relationship. I love yous. What if she's bad at it? Solomon's been married before. What if he realizes later that she's not what he wants and he settles for her because of the baby? What if all she's done is quit her job, left her life, left her shitty apartment, left Ash, and run away to Alaska to live with a frowny, muscled mountain man who maybe considers this temporary? Who'll boot her the second she gets too neurotic.

She's trying to play it cool, trying not to care, but how long can she keep it up? How long can she go with the flow? She doesn't want to exist in limbo. She wants to exist in love. She wants Solomon. Her mountain man who smells like the woods. Wants his cozy little cabin with its wild mountains and stars.

Oh God.

How can she leave when she's desperately in love with Solomon?

And yet, if this all goes south, if they don't work, if she turns down the job, she's picking herself over her son.

Biting her lip, Tess glances down at her swollen belly. She doesn't have much time. She has to decide soon.

A shudder works its way out of her. "I just. . .I—can I think about it?"

A tap on the door. A deep rumble. "Tess? You okay?"

Shit. Solomon.

Nova's breath hitches. Like she wasn't expecting the refusal. "Of course. But I want you on my team, Tess. I will do all I can to persuade you." There's a smile in Nova's husky voice. "No less than one text a week. I promise you that."

"Okay, great, thanks," Tessie whispers, flattered. "Chat soon. Bye."

Tessie hangs up and then rips the door open. Before Solomon can say a word, she's gripping him by the front of his jacket and yanking him into the bathroom, into her lips. She slams the door shut and pushes him up against the floral-wallpapered wall.

She kisses him. Hard. Deep. Like she can ingrain his body, his tattoos into her soul as a reminder of what she has. Of everything she wants to hold on to.

They break away, breathless. Solomon's big hands cradle her face. "You okay?" he asks, his eyes sniper trained on hers. "I got worried."

"I'm fine." She kisses him again, hating to lie but not ready to tell him about the phone call. "My bladder's the size of walnut these days."

He lifts a dark brow, not buying it. "Or are you maybe hiding out in the bathroom?"

She flushes. "Maybe."

He grunts a laugh. "Well, you have to tell me. I don't want to be here either."

Tamping down her nerves, she smiles up at him. "Yes, you do. I love your family. Big and loud and all over the place. I didn't have that. You're lucky."

"I am."

"Bear will be lucky too."

"He will be." Solomon runs a big hand over her stomach. "And guess what?"

"What?"

"They love you too."

Tessie presses a hand to the center of her chest, relief slowing the fast flutter of her heart. "They do?"

"They do."

The words are a balm. Tessie had been nervous about meeting his family. Worrying about whether they would compare her to Serena. But she didn't feel that way at all with the Wilders. She felt welcome, all her fears put at ease.

For now.

Once more, Solomon pulls her into him, his steel-rod arms hugging her tight, and Tessie buries herself in his big body, like she can forget about the real world.

Like she doesn't have a very, very big decision to make in a very small amount of time.

Chapter Twenty-Six

Bossy. Beautiful. Pregnant.

Tessie.

Tessie, holding her thirty-two-week belly, sticking one high-heeled foot on a fruit crate to get a better grip on a lamp bulb.

"Woman," Solomon shouts from the bar top, fixing her with a stern glare. "Don't you fucking dare."

She freezes, a guilty look on her face. Then settles back on the floor. Gesturing at the crew of guys installing black booths in the back of the bar, she calls, "Okay, fine. You heard him. Help me or he will yell at me."

Solomon huffs a laugh. Woman's still wearing those damn heels, even after he bought her a perfectly nice pair of boots. Stubborn.

And he fucking loves it.

Tearing his mind from Tessie, he tunes back into what he's doing. Beside him on the bar top is a haphazardly assembled slider and a notepad filled with his chicken scratch. Local ingredients. Ten items for the menu. Damn good items. Upscale bar bites that will knock the socks off locals and tourists alike.

This is for Howler. A thank-you for putting up with his bullshit for the last seven years.

"Who did this?" Tessie's impatient voice carries. She's bent over a table, labeling new tunes for the jukebox. "You blocked all my sunshine. How am I supposed to work?"

Howler's dry scoff. "Can we just pump the brakes, Goldilocks? 'Love Shack'?"

"It's a classic."

Even if his best friend's dislike of his girl bothers the hell out of him.

Howler's Roost is currently a demolition zone, thanks to Tessie. He's never seen her look happier. Or more pregnant.

For the last two weeks, their lives have consisted of working on the bar and the baby.

They went to a doctor's appointment, where Tessie and Bear got a perfect bill of health. She's healthy, the baby's healthy, and Solomon can breathe easier.

Because Tessie's thrown herself into the bar revamp at lightning speed. Sourcing furniture for the bar, drawing up mood boards, beg, borrow, and bribing her connections for expedited shipping, hiring local contractors to help where he and Howler can't.

The working side of Tess turns Solomon on something fierce. He's loved watching her weave her design magic. She's a stubborn, take-no-shit woman. Working hellish hours no pregnant woman has any business working. And she's doing it for him.

Selfless as hell. They would never have gotten it together if it weren't for her.

Tessie's put her life on hold for him. He had no damn right to ask her to come to Chinook. Now it's up to him to give her everything she needs. His *I love you*. His entire heart. His home. A ring on her finger.

Shaking his head to focus on his food, he arranges arugula on top of the burger and frowns. Too pretentious?

Slender arms snake around his waist. "I like this look, Solemn Man. You cooking for us." Tessie's voice, the click-clack of her heels, is damn near Pavlovian. His dick jumps in his pants.

"Want to try?" he asks.

She nods eagerly. "Feed me."

He does, slipping a sliver of a slider into her mouth. A grin tips his lips as he watches her chew, her brown eyes closing in satisfaction.

"What do you think?"

She groans. "Next level." She splays a hand on her belly, which has Solomon doing the same, soaking in the slow roll of movements. "Bear's a fan."

"You got good taste, kid," he tells her bump.

Storming over, Howler grumbles, then slumps on a stool. "Can't believe I closed my damn bar."

"*Our* damn bar. And it's only for five weeks." Solomon gives his friend a look. "Deal with it."

"We should have a party," Tessie says, leaning over to type something on her laptop. "To celebrate the revamp."

Howler perks up. "Might work." The sly twitch of his mouth says he wants the biggest bash around to bring in all the out-of-town girls.

"Will work." Tessie flips her hair. "Half-price cocktails."

Going rigid, Howler glares. "Never."

"I'm done with you," Tessie huffs, flouncing away.

"She's moody," his best friend says, lifting his brows.

"She's pregnant," Solomon barks in a tone that says he better cut it out or else. Resting his elbows on the bar, he leans down and roughs his face. "Look, could you try to get along with Tess for five goddamn minutes?" The two of them working together has been like bleach and ammonia. Do not mix.

Howler picks at a corner of the slider. "You're raisin' a kid together. It ain't like she's staying. Right?"

Mouth open, Solomon's ready to tell Howler he's being an asshole, but before he can get a word out, the front door slams open, and a harsh gust of icy wind sweeps through the bar.

Solomon stiffens.

There, in the doorway, stands Evelyn, her black hair wound in a tight bun, her no-bullshit briefcase hanging off a stiff snow-covered shoulder. Barely moving her head, she scours the bar. The moment her eyes land on Tessie, her face darkens.

"Fuck." Solomon wipes his hands on a rag and slings it over his shoulder. His sister's expression could set ice on fire.

Howler perks up on his barstool. "What's ole Evilyn doing here?"

"Baby shower," he guesses. "For Tess."

A chuckle. "This'll be interesting."

Solomon ignores him. He's got enough to worry about with his sister in town. Judging by their telephone conversations, she's not here to make friends.

Pushing off the counter, he strides fast for his sister. "Hey, Evy."

"Solomon." She nods curtly. No hugs. It's Evelyn's stiff, keep-your-distance way. On rare occasions, he and his sisters have seen her let her tightly wound guard down thanks to a few glasses of chardonnay. That it will happen this visit, Solomon's doubtful.

"You just get in?"

"First stop." She holds his gaze, then swivels to Tessie. "Is that her?" Disdain coats her voice. "The pregnant blond thing shimmying with the broom?"

His hands fist on the thighs of his jeans. "Be nice."

"I'm always nice."

Howler, sneaking by with a ladder, coughs, "Bullshit."

Evelyn puts out a stop-right-there hand. "You bring up fifth grade again, and I personally detonate your bar."

His friend snickers, then says, "Goldilocks incoming," before loping over to a group of guys who are laying new floorboards.

With a sigh, Solomon glances over his shoulder, opening his arm up to Tessie and curling it around her as she reaches his side. "Tess, this is my sister, Evelyn."

"Hi," Tessie says, tucking a lock of hair behind her ear. Her cheeks are pink, flustered at the surprise visit. "It's nice to meet you."

"Hello," Evelyn says, her eyeline defiantly avoiding Tessie's belly. A clear line drawn in the sand. She isn't a fan. And she wants Tessie to know it.

It takes all he has not to shake his sister. To Tessie's credit, she picks up on the cold shoulder. Putting a hand on his chest, she looks up at him. Her expression cool, neutral, tells Solomon she'll give as good as she gets. "I'm going to get back to work. I'll give you two a second."

He tries to catch her hand. "You don't—"

But she's already off and running. He watches as she struggles to pick up a left-behind soda can. But since she can't bend over fully because of her belly, she toes it with her high heels, rolling it where she needs it.

Solomon looks at Howler. "Go help her," he barks. "Now."

"Christ. Fine," Howler mutters, flashing Solomon the bird before slinking off toward Tessie.

"How cute. You brought her back." Evelyn purses her lips. "Like a souvenir."

His mouth presses flat. "Stop."

She adjusts the front of her trim navy suit. "Is there somewhere less-Tessified we can talk?"

With a frown, he takes his sister's elbow and steers her back into the kitchen. When they're alone, he slams a hand on the steel workstation. "What's wrong with you? You're acting like a. . ." He trails off, at a loss for an inoffensive word to call her.

"I am aware of how I'm acting, Sol. I'm acting like a bitch. And I'm aware of how you're acting too. You're being an idiot. You don't know what you're doing with her. Which is why I'm here. To help."

Heaving her heavy briefcase onto the counter, she huffs out a breath. Then Evelyn pulls out a thick stack of papers. "You've done one thing right at least. Getting your job back. That'll help us in court."

"Court?" He rips a hand through his hair. "What are you—"

"I drew up paperwork," she says, sliding the documents toward him on the slick metal counter.

"What the fuck are these?" An acidic hole shreds his gut as he grabs the papers. Flipping through them, he sees a DNA order. A big bold headline that says *Petition for Custody*.

"I didn't ask you to draw up paperwork." Feeling utterly numb, he scans the paragraphs of legalese. "Neglect? Unstable living situation?"

Guilt twists his heart.

Christ, if Tessie saw these. . .

Solomon exhales roughly, battling the urge to toss his sister in front of a moose. "Evelyn, you got two seconds, so talk fast."

Blue eyes flashing, she begins. "She doesn't have a job, Sol. You're supporting her. How is she going to feed your son when she goes back to LA? Make it make sense. Better yet, *you* make a decision. Get custody; keep your son here with his family."

"Tessie is his mother," he grinds out. "We are his family."

She scoffs. "Just because she's having your child doesn't mean you have to settle."

Enough. Fucking enough.

"I'm gonna say it once, Evy, and I want you to hear it. First," he says with forced calm, drawing himself up to full height so his sister takes a step back. "You bring up these papers again and we're gonna have problems."

Scanning the kitchen, wanting this bullshit as far away from him as possible before a hole blasts open his chest, Solomon grabs a recipe book from the counter and stuffs the papers between pages. He shuts the book and puts it on the shelf before turning his gaze, once again, to his sister.

"Second—"

Say it, Sol.

Say it.

He inhales a breath, steadying his heart. "I love Tess. I'm planning to ask her to stay in Chinook with me. I want to marry her."

Christ.

The out-loud admission makes it that much more real. How much he wants it. How much he can't bear to be without her.

Hurt slams into Evelyn's big blue eyes, but then she's recovering, so quickly that he almost thinks he's imagined it. Then her gaze drops to his bare ring finger. And he knows. He knows it's because he's moving on from Serena. It hurts his sister. But Solomon refuses to feel guilty any longer. He's paid his dues. He has Serena's blessing. He doesn't need Evelyn's.

Refusing to be swayed, Evelyn crosses her arms. Juts her chin. "She shouldn't be here. She's not cut out for Alaska. Look at her. I bet she doesn't even own a pair of boots or a snowsuit."

"She doesn't have to own a fucking snowsuit," he snaps.

Because she's Tessie. She's Tessie in heels, she's sunshine, she's the woman he loves, and she'll never be Serena. Evelyn will never accept her. But he won't allow her to hurt Tessie.

His sister lowers her voice. "It's already snowing. Does she even know how to drive in the snow? Does she know it's twenty-four seven darkness here come January? What if she goes into labor and there's a blizzard? What if—"

"Stop. *Fuck.*" Anger and panic claw at his heart. He slams a hand down on the counter. "Stop."

Taken aback, Evelyn snaps her mouth shut.

But it's too late. Her words twist their way into his gut, ripping open a black hole of pain. Of fear. He has a second chance to be a good man, a good husband, a good father. But does he deserve it? Does he deserve them? What if he can't protect them?

Chinook is where Serena died. Where he brought Tessie and his son back. What if she slips, or they can't make it to the hospital in time?

Christ, if something happened to her...or that baby...

Suddenly, he can't get air. His pulse is a skipping record.

"Solomon?" The kitchen door pushes open, and Tessie's there, chewing her lip. "I'm sorry to interrupt but, we, uh, have a situation with the keg."

From the bar come the faint strains of Howler swearing bloody murder.

"I'll go." Evelyn turns on her heel, flapping her hand dismissively toward Tessie. "See you at the shower."

"See you," Tessie echoes. Then she drifts to his side, looking up at him in concern. "Solomon?"

"Let's go home," he says, tucking her safely under his arm, his heartbeat ramped up unsteadily in his chest.

She wrinkles her nose. "Are you sure? What about the menu?"

"I'll finish it tomorrow."

"What's wrong?" A hand on his chest. "What is it?"

Solomon turns toward the window, where a flurry of white dots the sky. His hold on her tightens. "I don't like the snow."

It's six by the time they make it home from the bar. A light dusting of snow fell when they were on the road, which had Solomon driving his old pickup at a geriatric speed. Practically strangling the steering wheel as he navigated the switchbacks to the cabin.

Ping.

With a tired sigh, Tessie sets her purse on the counter and sinks onto the leather couch. After giving Peggy an ear rub, she pulls out her phone.

Another text from Nova.

Time is ticking, Truelove. Say yes and make me a very happy woman.

The woman's killing her. The job offer hangs before her like an irresistible dangle of a carrot.

Tessie feels like the worst person in the world, keeping this a secret from Solomon. Like she has an escape hatch at the ready and all she needs to do is push the evacuation button.

She knows what she's doing. Knows it's wrong. Keeping an out in case this goes south. So she can leave first.

She can't wait on Solomon. He hasn't asked her to stay. And she won't push. She wants him to want her here.

Across the room, her Solemn Man stands at the living room window, staring into the dark. Ever since they got back to the cabin, he's been closed up like Fort Knox. Whatever has his face looking this dark and tense, she bets it has to do with his sister. Judging by the way Evelyn was staring daggers at her stomach, their conversation in the kitchen was about her. The air in the bar chilled the second Evelyn walked in. The first disconnect she's felt since she arrived in Chinook.

"Solomon?" she asks, watching the way the muscles shift in his back when she calls his name. "What's wrong? Are you"—*regretting us?*—"okay?"

"I'm fine, Tess," he says quietly. Then he turns from the window, crosses the space between them, and kneels in front of her. Without words, he slips off her heels and places her bare feet on his knee. Picking up one foot, he digs his thumbs into her arch.

"Feel good?" he asks.

"Hmm." She lets her body lengthen and relax. Closing her eyes, she tips her head against the couch, relishing the firm massage of her muscles. The strength in his hands. She needs to stop wearing heels. Not like she'll ever tell Solomon that.

"Today was too much." Solomon's deep, quiet voice breaks through her thoughts.

His words have her opening her eyes. His face is dark, his profile chiseled and cut in the sunset glow falling through the windows.

Tessie's heart flips at his overprotective nature. "Solomon, I'm fine. I'm pregnant. Not made of glass." She drops her chin and rubs her belly. "The bar is looking phenomenal. Don't you think?"

He sits, studies her, massaging her feet with his callused thumbs. "It is. We couldn't have done it without you."

Pride surges inside her. His compliment warms her from the inside out. Despite being dusty and dog tired, she's loved her time in Chinook. It feels like she's prepping for something she was meant to do all her life.

"Don't worry," she says when his expression doesn't soften. "Once we get the chalkboard wall in, I'll let you boys do the rest of the work."

"I worry, Tessie," he confesses, voice low and serious. "I want to keep you safe. Protect you and Bear."

She tilts her head, her long blond hair falling across her breast. "And you will." When he says nothing, instead staring down at her feet in his hands, she peers at him closely. "Is this about today? Your sister?"

An unhappy grunt.

Resolutely, Tessie cuts to the chase. "She doesn't like me."

His jaw flexes. Anger and wariness in his gaze as he finally admits, "You're right. She doesn't."

He continues to massage her foot, almost absentmindedly, then he sighs. "Serena was Evelyn's best friend."

Tessie gasps at the explanation.

"Seeing us—it isn't easy on her, but she has to accept it." He puts her foot down and pushes up to sit beside her on the couch. He wraps a blanket over her lap, her belly. "She'll come around. And if she doesn't, that's on her."

His words soothe Tessie. A bit.

"Forget about Evelyn," Solomon says, leaning forward and sweeping a kiss against her lips. "I don't want you or the baby stressed out when we get to the shower."

She blinks. "You're going? I thought it was girls only."

"Men will be in the garage. Drinking beer. Smashing shit."

"How very caveman of you."

He chuckles but still looks worried. "I'm not leaving you alone with my sisters without an escape plan."

Tessie wrinkles her nose at him. "Relax. It's a baby shower, not a Mayan sacrifice." She adds a smile, even though her stomach gives a nervous flip. "Everyone will be on their best behavior."

Chapter Twenty-Seven

The Wilder's roof is dusted with snow. Smoke plumes from the chimney. Despite the light layer of snow, the evergreens are strung with fuzzy pom-poms. A eucalyptus sign proclaiming WELCOME TO TESSIE'S BABY SHOWER hangs on the front door.

Tessie sits up straight when the line of cars in the driveway comes into view. Her stomach churns with equal parts nerves and excitement. A shower in her honor. And Bear's. A feeling of belonging, of joy, has her heart thumping hard.

"You excited?" Solomon asks, his voice low and rough.

"Actually, I am." Happy tears fill her eyes. Damn hormones. "No one's ever done something like this for me before."

"Tess." He throws the pickup into park and cuts the engine. His heated gaze sears her. "You deserve it."

She sniffs. "Don't make me cry."

"Remember. Come get me if it's too much."

Tessie laughs and squeezes his hand. "It won't be. I've worked with celebrities, remember? I can handle your sister."

Solomon climbs out of the pickup and opens her door. He helps her out of the passenger seat and then snags her hand to keep her steady on their walk to the front door. Which, really, in her puffy parka is more like a slow wobble.

"Oh my God, Solomon. I'm waddling. I'm actually waddling like a penguin. I can't do layers."

He chuckles, his eyes sniper focused on the ground, searching for patches of ice. "You look beautiful. For a penguin."

Scowling, she takes in her bump, ensconced in a bionic jacket that could double as a bullet-proof vest. "I am wearing the cutest outfit under here, I swear."

As they climb the porch stairs, a long whistle snags her attention. Ash stands in the doorway of the Wilder home, her tattooed arms tossed to the cloudy sky. "Woman, you are huge."

Tessie's mouth drops.

Stunned, she's frozen in place as her two worlds—LA and Chinook—smash into each other like oncoming freight trains.

"You," she blurts, poking a finger in Solomon's concrete chest. Watching her, he grins like he's kept the best secret in the world. And to her, he has. She swivels her stunned gaze to her cousin. "And you?"

"Oh yeah." Ash swaggers, stepping out onto the porch. "Solomon planned it all. Been camped out here since yesterday. Smuggled in like a good pound of cocaine."

Tessie stares at her mountain man, her hands clasped against her heart.

He did this. For her.

"You owe me," Ash says. "Hell of a flight."

Tessie cocks a brow and fixes her cousin with a stern gaze. "I owe *you*? In case you've forgotten, *you* owe *me*. This is all your fault. I never would have been here if it weren't for you."

Ash scoffs. "And that's a problem?" Her attention floats to Tessie's hand tangled up with Solomon's. "Looks like it's worked out pretty well for you."

Tessie strides, as fast as she can in her heels, toward Ash. Then, fiercely, she flings her arms around her cousin's neck. With a wobbly inhale, she buries her face in Ash's mess of dark hair. "Thank you," she whispers.

What Ash did for her—the thought has Tessie choking up.

She'd be missing out on her entire world if Solomon had never come on the babymoon. Ash gave her that push to change her world. She's never been more grateful.

Ash sags in her arms, smiling against her neck. "You're welcome." Lifting her head, she looks at Solomon. "I knew you'd get her to loosen up."

Tessie scoffs.

Solomon laughs and tucks her against his side as they squeeze through the front door.

Inside, it's commotion. The house smells of fire and cinnamon and pine.

"Sol?" Melody's voice, and then she's coming up behind Ash. "We put out the chairs, but you have to help us move the balloon arch."

"Who is *we*?" Howler drifts up from the hallway, a scowl on his boyish face. "Because I pulled at least ten muscles carrying that farm bench for you."

"Here, I'll take your coats." Jack claps Solomon on the shoulder and pulls Tessie into a hug. "Welcome back, Tessie."

"Thank you."

Melody drops a baby blue silk sash over Tessie's torso. It's emblazoned with the words BABY MAMA.

"C'mon," Ash says as Jo appears with a bottle of champagne. "Let's get this party started."

"Muscle. Now." Jo waves to Solomon while simultaneously giving Howler a shove that tells Tessie he used to pull her pigtails. "Then you boys scram."

Her heart's too light for her body. This show of family has her eyes threatening to fill with tears again. But Solomon's there, wrapping her in his arms and pulling her against his strong body. He bends down until his lips are next to her ear and says, "Have fun. And remember, the code word is Bananas."

She kisses him, smiling against his bearded mouth. "Never."

Solomon leans over an engine bay in his father's garage, connecting and disconnecting wires on a carburetor.

He's enjoying himself. Really fucking enjoying himself. Tessie's in the house, hopefully having a good time, and he's out here with his best friend and his father, sipping on a cold beer, working on a Jeep that hasn't seen a road since World War II.

"Hand me that wrench, will you, son?"

Solomon passes it down. He adjusts his jacket, shaking off the cold. Despite the insulated garage, the heat pumping, the temperature's dropped ten degrees in the last hour.

"Cold front's blowin' in," his dad says, as if he's read Solomon's mind. "Supposed to get snow soon."

Solomon frowns. "It's early." Too early.

"I think it's shot." Howler leans back on his stool, his arms crossed over his black leather jacket. "Jack, your best bet is to sell this rusted piece of shit."

His dad huffs a laugh. "It's not shot," he says, patting the side of the Jeep with affection. "I'll have this puppy on the road by next spring." He gives a craggy grin. "Maybe we'll drive Tess and the baby up to see Thunderbird Falls."

He says it so easily, but it has Solomon's breath catching in his throat. This time next year, his son will be here. And it's that easy. To see his future. Christmas, family dinners, road trips with his dad, cooking in the kitchen with his son, kissing Tessie on their front porch beneath the stars.

Bear's his.

Tessie's his.

Fuck, but he has to tell her. Tell her he wants her in his world, wants her in Chinook.

To stay. For good. Forever.

Christ. She is going to wreak havoc and cause chaos in his quiet world, and he can't goddamn wait.

Hell, he's already lost all control.

The look of sheer joy on her face when they walked up to the party meant for her made him dizzy, like everything's at stake. The way she lit up, the way she came alive—he wants to put that look on her face every damn day for the rest of his life.

Thinking of Tessie, of his son, has Solomon turning to Howler, has him saying, "When we get the bar open, I want to set a schedule. Especially once the baby's born."

He's putting his foot down now. Tessie is his priority. He won't make the same mistake he made with Serena.

Howler's face screws up. "She's got you on a leash already," he mutters.

"She doesn't," Solomon barks, causing his father to busy himself on the other side of the garage.

"Whatever, man."

He glances at his friend, who looks irritated and antsy. "You don't like Tess?" he growls, deciding to finally come out and ask it.

Howler chugs his beer, then tosses the can in the trash. "I like Goldilocks fine."

"Bullshit. You've been acting like a jackass since she got here."

Hesitating, Howler tugs a hand through his dirty-blond hair. Then he opens his mouth. "It's soon, man. Look, we're all glad you're coming out of your shell, but don't you think it's a little fast? The restaurant, the girl?" He grimaces. "You don't owe this chick anything. You knocked her up, and sure, it's too late to do anything about it—"

Solomon closes his eyes, his heart in a vise at the thought. "Don't fucking say that."

"She's just some girl, man," Howler says, anger in his tone.

He clenches his hands, the words hitting him dead center. "Tessie's not just some girl."

In his periphery, the garage door opens, closes. Jack disappearing into the cold to exit the boiling-point chat.

"She is." Howler punches a finger. "Admit it. She's the first girl you fucked after Serena. She's a goddamn rebound."

His patience snaps at that, fury igniting in his veins. "Howler, I swear, talk about her like that again, and I will punch you in the fucking teeth."

Nostrils flaring, Howler slips off his stool, puffs out his chest. "Do it then."

So he does. He slams his fist into his best friend's jaw. Swearing, Howler stumbles back into one of the rusted cars. Before Solomon can advance, he's up, bum-rushing him, dropping his shoulder, ramming it into Solomon's stomach as he tries to push him over. "Baby steps," Howler gasps. "You should be taking fucking baby steps."

"Fuck you," Solomon grunts. He shoves Howler hard in the chest, sending him sprawling across the floor.

The sight of his best friend on the ground has Solomon stopping. Has him balling his right hand into a fist and cursing under his breath. What the fuck are they doing? Fighting like assholes in his dad's garage like they're thirteen all over again. Christ. This isn't going to solve anything.

Breathing heavily, he rips a hand through his hair. Stares Howler down. "What the fuck's your problem?" he demands.

"You wanna know what my fucking problem is?" Howler says, pushing himself up to standing. "I'm scared, god damnit. I lost my best fucking friend once, okay? You shut down, man. We all lost you."

The admission, the pain that comes with it, sucks the wind out of Solomon, has him unclenching his fists. For seven long years, he put his family, his best friend, through hell. Their worry is well founded. He understands where Howler's coming from, even if it's not easy to hear.

Grimacing, Howler smears a hand down his face. "It doesn't work out with this girl, then what? You go back to the cabin? You turn into a fucking hermit again?" A ragged breath shakes out of him. "I just got you back, man. I can't lose you again. Your ma can't. Your sisters can't."

"You won't," he says in a low and steady voice. "I'm here. And Tessie's here, and that's how it's gonna stay."

"It fucking better."

Their eyes lock, drop.

Then Howler groans, doubled over. "Christ." He rubs his fingers over the bridge of his nose. "You punched me in the fucking face, Sol."

"Wasn't the first time," Solomon shoots back. "And you told me to."

And then they laugh. Big gut-busting laughs that fill the garage and dissipate the tension.

"Listen," he begins, roughing his hands on the thighs of his jeans. "It's bad enough I'm fighting with Evelyn about Tess. I don't want to fight with you too."

"What'd Evilyn do?"

"She drew up paperwork asking for sole custody."

Wincing, Howler lets out a pained breath. "Fucked up, man."

"Yeah." With a sigh, Solomon shakes his head and sits on a crate. He looks up at his best friend. "Tess is here to stay. She had my heart on a leash the night I met her, and you're going to have to get used to it. I love her."

His best friend blinks, jaw slack. "You do?"

"I do."

"Hell, why didn't you fucking say that in the first place?"

"Because I haven't told her yet." He winces and rubs a hand through his beard. "I'm an idiot."

"You gonna ask her to marry you or some shit?"

"Yeah. I fucking am."

Howler sinks beside him, stunned. "Well, shit," he says, soft and shocked.

Solomon looks at him sharply. "You got a problem with that?"

"No." He chuckles, a mystified grin spreading over his face. He claps Solomon on the back. "We're gonna raise a baby in a bar, Sol."

Solomon grins. They damn sure are.

When Tessie pictured her baby shower, she envisioned eating cake in the bathtub and crying into a bottle of non-alcoholic sparkling wine. Never this. A happy house filled with Solomon's family, Ash, and a few close family friends of the Wilders, who have long since left. The living room is cozy, thanks to the blasting fireplace. The coffee table is covered in unwrapped gifts and tissue paper. Trays of delicate finger foods, bottles of champagne, and a large bowl of nonalcoholic punch are set out on a sideboard. Baby pictures of Solomon and Tessie are strung on a long piece of eucalyptus garland.

If she had to pick a theme, it'd be vintage chic. And yet, she can't even turn on her designer critique. Because there's nothing to critique. It's perfect.

She never thought she wanted this. The stupid games, the small talk about babies and binkies and Boppies, the opening-presents-in-front-of-everyone schtick, the she's-currently-wearing-a-necklace-made-of-nothing-but-bottles, but she does. She wants it all, and most importantly, she wants Solomon's family.

She adores them.

Being around the Wilders has shown her who Solomon truly is. His parents raised him to be a good man. A man who takes care of the people around him. Who loves deeply and whose loyalty is fierce.

Bear has no idea the love that's coming his way.

Maybe with the exception of his Aunt Evelyn.

Evelyn sits on the loveseat, a permanent scowl on her face. Her posture says she's here as a favor to her mother and nothing else. Still, the woman hasn't cramped Tessie's style. She turned her nerves to ice in the presence of Solomon's oldest sister. She can be polite, but she doesn't have to fake it.

"I think that's a wrap," Jo declares with a victorious smile.

Melody scoots around the room, collecting gifts, stacking them in a neat pile. Most of the guests have already said their goodbyes, leaving just Tessie, Ash, and the Wilder women.

"It was fabulous." Smiling, Tessie looks at Grace. "Thank you so much for putting it together for me."

"It's our pleasure," the older woman says.

Needing to stretch, she stands from her chair. She smooths a hand around her stomach, feeling Bear thump and roll as she walks a slow pace around the living room.

Grace gives her a sympathetic smile. "It gets cramped in there, doesn't it?"

"It does. It is." She blows out a breath, pausing at the window to watch the snow.

"Round ligament threatening to take you out?" Ash asks, plucking a bow out of her hair.

Tessie grins. "You know it."

"How many weeks are you again?" asks Melody.

"Almost thirty-three."

Melody squeals. "So soon!"

As the women chatter, Tessie absentmindedly drifts around the living room, taking in the cozy décor. On the fireplace mantel, five wood-carved bears stand in a row. Photos of Grace and Jack at the Grand Canyon. Beside the fireplace, hanging on the wall, an acoustic guitar.

Smiling, thinking of all the classic country songs she wants to play for Bear on her record player, Tessie runs a finger over a string, pinging it. A mellow hum fills the room.

"What are you doing?" A sharp snap from Evelyn has Tessie glancing over. "That's Serena's guitar."

She retracts her hand, instantly feeling like an asshole. The back of her neck warms, an embarrassed flush coating her all over.

"I'm sorry. I didn't know."

"Well, don't touch it."

"Evilyn," Jo hisses. "Stop it."

An uncomfortable silence falls.

Tessie shifts on her sore feet, ignoring Ash's worried eyes on her. Suddenly, she wishes she had a glass of alcohol. She's too sober, too pregnant for this shit. For Evelyn's judgmental gaze, broadcasting clear as day: You're not Serena.

Ping.

"You need to take that, sweetheart?" Solomon's mother asks, giving her an out, a breather. A tight smile on her face, Grace looks like she's about to rip into her oldest daughter.

Tessie nods. "I do. Thanks."

"Here, I'll help you," Ash says, snatching Tessie's phone from the coffee table. Whip quick, she grabs Tessie's elbow and guides her away from the others. They scoot into the hall, where Tessie flattens herself against the wall, staring down at the phone in her hands.

Hot tears fill her eyes, the screen a blur of words she can't read. But she knows who the message is from. Nova.

She swipes wetness from her cheeks with a shaky hand and then groans. "Ugh, I'm crying. What is wrong with me? Why am I always crying?"

"It's hormones," Ash says, shooting a glare at the living room. "Hormones and one asshole of a woman." She runs a soothing hand down Tessie's arm, her expression softening. "Don't listen to her, okay?"

Easier said than done, because despite their hushed tones, the voices in the living room carry down the hallway.

"Why are you even here if you're not going to support Solomon?"

"You're scowling," Melody whispers. "You can't scowl at a baby shower."

Evelyn's strained voice floats from the living room. "Solomon isn't over Serena."

"He is," Jo argues. "You don't want him to be over her."

A scoff. "Serena was easy and this one she's...she's terrible."

Tessie's body is a cringe. Her cheeks on fire, her legs so shaky she could fall over where she stands.

Oh God. That word.

"Tess." A hand on her shoulder. Ash, nudging her, coaxing her in the direction of the bathroom, trying to spare her from the conversation.

But Tessie stays planted, frozen to the spot. A hot tear rolls down her cheek. She wants to disappear. The truth of Evelyn's words like a stinging slap.

She's still Terrible Tess. Not easy. She's never been easy. Never could escape that cold, closed-off world she's built for herself.

For the first time since she's been in Chinook, a sharp swell of self-doubt and despair rises up inside her. That old insecurity. Of never being good enough, of never being chosen, of always being left. Of wanting to run before someone else can ramble.

"She is," Evelyn continues, still on her Tessie tirade. "She's too flashy for Solomon. What's she going to do, wear high heels in winter? He needs someone down to earth. Like Serena was."

"You're acting crazy, Evy."

A withering sigh. "He hasn't asked her to stay, Jo. And you know it."

And so does Tessie.

What if she's not meant to find love because she's hard to love? What if the reason Solomon hasn't asked her to stay is because he's figured out that they don't click? What if it's because she's not Serena?

Solomon assured her he's ready. He's been widowed for seven years, but still...what if he isn't? What if she's not good enough for this great grump of a giant man?

Something tight and hollow grows in Tessie's chest. Maybe all that matters is her baby. Nothing else.

Evelyn's voice, louder now. "He's jumping into something he's not ready for. This is all temporary. I don't understand how you can support this."

"I know you loved Serena, Evy, but you're being selfish," Grace chides gently. "It's been seven years. We support Solomon because he is having a child, and Tessie is a lovely woman. And if we don't"—tears fill her voice—"he will disappear into that cabin, and we will never see him again."

Silence. The soft sound of sniffling.

Then a bright cry. A splat of something against the wall. And then Evelyn's storming out the front door without so much as a backward glance.

Ping.

Tessie's phone is still clenched in her hands.

Decision, Truelove? Don't make me beg.

Her eyes flood.

"What are you doing?" Ash's soft voice floats.

She sags against the wall and admits the terrifying truth. "I don't know."

Chapter Twenty-Eight

Solomon opens the door to the cabin, a frown tugging at his lips as Tessie slips off her puffy parka and hangs it on the wall hook before drifting to the kitchen island to set down her purse and kick off her heels.

There's nothing he hates more than the look on her face right now.

Ever since they left his parents' house, she's had those same sad brown eyes she had when they first met at the Bear's Ear bar. Vulnerable. Lonesome.

He's trapped by a need to figure out what's wrong. To fix it.

It's what he didn't do with Serena. His one mistake. He let *her* work it out, instead of working it out with her. This time, he's determined to be present, to be here for Tessie. If she wants to fume while he watches, done. Or if she wants to scream at him, he'll gladly take it. But no matter what, he'll be here.

He steps up behind her and presses a kiss to the back of her blond head. "You want to tell me what happened at the shower?" he murmurs, inhaling her sunshine scent.

Her slender form shifts against him. Tenses. "Your sister threw a canapé across the room."

"Jesus." Fucking Evelyn.

Wrapping an arm high around her midsection, he turns her so she faces him.

"What else?"

She's silent for a long minute, wetting her lips, and then she says, "They don't like me. No one likes me." Before he can rebut the statement, she untangles from his arms to pace across the floor. "Your best friend won't even make me a mocktail."

God, he hates how small her voice has gotten. How she's left his arms. He has to fight the urge to pull her back to him.

Crossing the room, he closes the growing gap between them. "Howler's acting like an asshole. But we settled it. And Evelyn needs to mind her own damn business."

"She said—"

She presses her lips together, looks out the window. Fear has Solomon clinched by the balls. Christ. If his sister brought up custody, he'll never forgive her.

"What did she say to you?" Reaching out, he takes her by the shoulders and gives her a soft shake. Her silence threatens to take him to his knees. "*Tess.*"

Lower lip trembling, Tessie tilts up her chin. "She said that I'm just temporary. That I'm not Serena."

Fuck.

If Solomon had known he'd be bringing Tessie back to fight with the ghost of Serena, he would have kept her away from Chinook. Leaving her alone with his family, with Evelyn, was a complete failure of a decision. He should have been beside her today, making sure she was okay. Make no mistake, the next time he sees his sister, they will have words.

Moving away from him, she shrugs. "Your family loved her. She was your wife. She's all over their house, which I understand." She turns to him, a fierce earnestness filling her voice. "She will always be yours, Solomon. I would never ask you to put her away."

He shakes his head. "No. You'd never ask me that."

"But what if"—her voice wobbles, the sound twisting a dagger in Solomon's stomach—"what if I'm not Serena?"

"You don't have to be Serena." His gaze rakes over Tessie where she stands, her arms clutched around her belly. Like she has to protect Bear. So much doubt and worry in her eyes it makes him sick. "I don't want you to be. You're Tessie. You're my Tessie."

He makes a move toward her, but she backs away, and the pit in his stomach grows.

"Today. . ." She bites her lip and tucks a long lock of hair behind her ear, her attention flitting around the room. "I felt out of place. I felt sad that you and Serena never had a chance. That she died. It doesn't feel fair." She sighs. "It doesn't feel like I belong here."

"You do."

"No. I don't."

"What are you saying, Tess?"

Her eyes glitter with tears, but she's finally looking at him again. "I got a job offer. In LA."

He freezes, his heart flatlining in his chest.

Fuck. He can't be too late. Not again.

He sucks in a breath through his nose. "What did you say?" he manages, his voice a ragged husk.

She tosses her hair, staring him down. "I don't know. What should I say?"

Don't let her go, Sol. Don't let her leave.

Taking his silence for hesitation, Tessie laughs dryly. Temper flares in her eyes. "What am I doing here, Solomon? I like plans and order, and you're this maniac mountain man who freeballs life into the wind. You have a bar, and I have a baby, and we're opposites in every way. We're worlds away."

"We're not. This world"—he approaches her and presses a large palm to her stomach—"is ours. You understand?"

"No. Yes. I don't know." She lifts her arms, lets them drop. Steps back again. Farther this time. "Why? Why am I here, Solomon? Why?"

Deep in the dark brown depths of her teary eyes, her worries shine loud and clear. That he'll leave them. That he doesn't want her.

Goddamn, he can't go another minute letting her believe that either is true.

Floorboards thundering beneath his feet, Solomon storms the room. He gathers Tess in his arms. "You're here because I love you," he says. "Do you hear me? I love you, Tessie. I loved you the night we met, and I love you now."

Tessie blinks up at him, looking shell-shocked, swaying in his arms. Her expression grows soft. And right as he thinks her stunned silence will break him, she opens her mouth, palms his chest, pushes up on tiptoes. Then she smiles the brightest smile he's ever seen, and says, "I love you too, Solomon."

Time stops.

It's been seven years. He never thought he'd be ready to hear those words from another woman. He thought he'd follow Serena to the fucking grave. But here he is. In love with a woman who loves him back. Like it's that easy. Like she's the best thing to ever happen to him.

"Tell me again," he commands. His voice shakes. His heart feels like it's a shooting star in his chest guiding him home.

Eyes watery, she blinks back tears. "I love you."

With a roar, he hauls her to his chest, cradling her close, crushing her mouth in a kiss, tasting her tears. Tessie whimpers, looping her slender arms around his neck.

"I love you, Tessie," he says against her mouth, trying to bring his breathing back to normal. He says it again. He has to. She has to know. "I love all of you." He holds her tightly. His hand goes to her belly. "And I love that baby."

Their lips meet as they crash into each other once again.

"What does this mean?" She laughs between breathless kisses. Tears spill down her cheeks.

"It means I want us all together," he says hoarsely. "Under one roof. I'll go to LA if you need me to. I'll be yours wherever we are, Tessie, because you're there."

He's ready. Ready to give his all to this woman. She's been so selfless; now it's his turn. If it means leaving the bar, his family, so be it. Because she is so much more than a second chance.

She is his eternity.

"No, Solomon. I don't want you in LA."

At her words, his heart hitches.

She bites her lip, her dark lashes lowering in that shy way he loves. "What if I want to stay here?" she whispers.

He gathers himself and cups her face in his hands. "Do you?"

Say yes. Christ. Put me out of my goddamn misery.

"I do."

"Thank fuck," he rasps, relief weaving its way through his heart. He pulls her in closer, like his last gasp of air. Tessie molds her sweet lips to his, a soft, savage heat building between them.

He loves every fucking part of this woman. Stubborn, sassy, sexy, vulnerable. He wants it all. Her in his bed, his heart between her teeth. He can't live without her. She is his soul. His star in the sky. North, south, east, west, down to hell and back. Any direction, he'll follow her light.

When they pull back, she sobs out a laugh. "I only have one deal breaker if I stay."

"Name it."

"I need my records."

"I'll buy you records, Tess. Stacks so high you'll never leave."

"Mmm, you will?"

"I will. Now here's my deal breaker," he murmurs against her lips.

"And what's that?"

"I'm going to marry you."

Her eyes pop open. Light leaps into her face, and she loops her arms around his neck. "I think I'll let you." A little laugh bubbles out of her. Joyous. Amazed.

What he'd give to keep that look on her face always. He wants to be responsible for her and his son, take care of them and keep them safe for the rest of their lives.

"I love you," Tessie says, running her small palms down his

beard, over his face, his lips, like she doesn't believe he's hers. "I love you, I love you, I love *you*."

"On repeat," he says with a grin.

"I've never said it." She smiles, her eyes misty. "You get it turntable style."

"There's no doubt when it comes to you," Solomon breathes into her hair. His heart pumps double-time in his chest. "Being without you, without our son, I can't fucking handle that. Not for one damn second. We click. You're mine. That's all there is to it."

She sighs happily. "We click."

"We do." He slips his hand up the hem of her dress. Her full pink lips part for him as he sweeps his mouth over the cool shell of her ear. "Remember Tennessee?"

She flushes. "I remember stars."

"Remember Mexico?" He drops his hand, catching the sleeve of her dress and slowly tugging it down her shoulder to bare her breasts. Her body is lush, all curves and bronze skin, still holding on to the last bit of tan from the beach, and his cock swells at the sight of her. Holding her firmly by the waist, he dips down, sucking the heavy swell of her breast into his mouth.

Tessie whimpers, stirring restlessly against him. "Oh. *Oh*."

He spreads her legs, sliding a finger along the edge of her lacey underwear to dip slowly inside her. "And this. Remember this?"

"Well." She sniffs primly, moans. "Solomon."

He grips her supple ass, running a rough palm over the smooth flesh, and pulls her into him. She gives a shocked squeal and rubs her sweet pussy against his thigh. The bulge in his pants is painful now, but Solomon persists.

Here and now, he ends all her doubt.

"Yours." A soft whisper from her pink mouth. "I'm yours."

"You are." Solomon lets out a growl both primal and primitive. "And if I have to fuck some goddamn sense into you, I'll do it."

Drawing back, she gasps. "I'm pregnant." But her lips curve, feline and pleased. She throbs down below. Her soft pulse beating against his fingertips.

"And you're gonna stay that way for the next twenty years if I have anything to do with it."

Tears shimmer along her lower lids. "Show me." Her voice is steady, eager as her palms ride up his chest. Her hungry eyes glitter. "Show me, Solomon."

"Goddamn right I will, baby," he grits out. This woman is slow torture. Fierce and delicate all at once. Fire and ice. "I'm gonna make you wet, and I'm gonna make you scream," he growls, trapped by her spell. "Then I'm gonna let you cool off and do it all again. Until you believe me."

Tess pants faster.

He leans down to kiss her lush mouth, easing her small frame up his body. With a whimper, Tessie twines her arms around his neck, loops her legs around his hips. With her cradled carefully in his arms, he backs her up against the wall. Angling forward, careful of her belly, he yanks her panties sideways, causing her to let out a gasp-like moan.

Then he's slipping into her, this perfect woman who loves him, this woman he'll never get enough of.

He strokes a hand over her golden hair, cups the nape of her neck, and pulls his hips back before pushing into her. Deeper than he's ever been before.

Tessie cries out, her head falling back.

"I love you, Solomon," she whispers, her eyes big and glassy. Her hips working little circles as he slides in and out of her. She sobs. "So much. Too much."

"I love you so fucking much," he says raggedly, dropping his face to her neck. Their limbs tangle, moans mingling in the small cabin. "From that first night I met you until the end of our days, Tessie, I'll love you."

Chapter Twenty-Nine

With Solomon's confession ringing in her ears, Tessie settles into Chinook.

To stay.

His *I love you*, him asking her to stay, means everything. In his choked voice, his haunted eyes, she saw her future.

Their future.

A man who wants her.

Who will fight for her.

Who loves her.

Solomon's held her in his calloused hands and let her into his tender heart. Dispelling her doubts, setting her on a course she doesn't question.

A risk. A star. A heartbeat.

Her mother's voice echoes in her ears. *If you take risks, Tessie, make them count.*

And this? This risk, it counts for everything. Bear's future. Her heart. Their family.

She's fallen into his world. Fallen fast and hard.

Mornings, she wakes in Solomon's strong arms, his beard tickling her belly as he kisses his way down her body. Afternoons are spent at the bar, throwing herself into work that saps every ounce of her energy. Evenings in the cabin, Solomon cooking for her, the record player spinning out country music as they dance slow over the hardwood floor.

She doesn't regret turning down Nova, not even for a minute. She'll find that one right path.

Tessie's stomach grows big and heavy. Thirty-three weeks. Thirty-four. Bear is busy in her belly, kicking and thumping and somersaulting. She plans for the nursery. She and Solomon take an online child birthing course that leaves her simultaneously excited and terrified. They argue about names. He likes Leo; she likes Lucas. At night, Solomon holds her belly and tells Bear about Alaska, and Tessie lies there, still and watchful, her breath held in her chest, feeling a love she has never felt before.

This little baby will be the best of both of them. Half her, half Solomon. And she will love him with every fiber of her being.

She never knew this much joy was possible.

On the last day of the bar renovation, Tessie walks the space, her heart bursting with pride.

The bar no longer looks worn and decrepit. But it's still Chinook; it's still in a silo. Still Solomon and Howler, but with a flourish. Long black booths line the south wall. A garage door has been installed in the front to open to a new exterior courtyard for the summer months. A tile floor that looks like rustic wood. Greeting guests is a wall of old hatchets, their handles spray-painted various masculine colors. Gone are the sticky menus, and in their place, a chalkboard menu listing food and cocktails.

Ash, who's lingered in Chinook to help, stands beside Tessie, watching Solomon plate a chargrilled burger and shoestring fries. The tattoos on his tan forearms flex and ripple in the bar light.

"Man," Ash says, pointing at Solomon with a retractable measuring tape. "He is going to look so good activating dad mode."

Tessie smiles. She already knows watching Solomon become a father will be one of her favorite pastimes. "He is." Hands propped on her hips, she turns to her cousin. "Do you think I'm doing the right thing? Staying?"

She has no reservations, but she hates leaving Ash. Ash is her gloomy soul sister, and the idea of being without her has her feeling not so together.

Ash shakes her head. "It doesn't matter what I think. It's what you think." A slow Cheshire cat smile spreads across her cousin's face. "But yeah. I do."

"I do too." Gray-green eyes drifting to Tessie's stomach, she says, "You know, preggo, having a baby is the most metal thing you will ever attempt. Are you ready?"

Tessie inhales. "I am. I really am."

She is. She's nowhere near the anxious woman she was in LA. Though birth, motherhood still have her nervous, she's calm. Steady. She can do this. She knows what she wants and who she is and who she loves.

"I'll miss you," Ash says.

Tears stinging her eyes, Tessie nods. Doesn't even bother wiping them away. She's thirty-five weeks pregnant, damn it, and she'll cry if she wants to.

At the bar top, Howler hangs up the phone with a hoot. "Roni LaPorte from *Thrillist* is coming up."

Impressed, Solomon lifts a brow. "How'd you manage that?"

Howler's grin is sly. "I have my ways."

The grand reopening of Howler's Roost is set for this weekend. Nothing fancy—just a signature cocktail, a local beer, and three appetizers, courtesy of Solomon. Friends and family and locals have all been invited.

As she always does once a space is complete, Tessie goes to the middle of the round room to take it in. She closes her eyes and inhales, then lets it all out slowly. "Look what we did."

Howler gives a grudging nod. "Gotta admit, Goldilocks. It looks damn good."

"Good," she mutters in response to the lukewarm compliment. Bantering with Howler has been the bane of her existence. She's quite enjoying it. "How about fabulous? How about spectacular?"

She stretches out a hand to the one person who always backs her up. "Solomon, would you look at this? Would you tell your friend he needs to work on his adjectives?"

A grin tugs at Solomon's lips. A tender protectiveness warms the intent gaze he keeps locked on her and his son. "I'm looking." Coming out from behind the bar, he slings an arm around her shoulders, tucking her against him. "But I'm also looking at a very pregnant woman who's dead on her feet."

Ash jerks her chin at Tessie. "Take her home. Tie her down."

"No more work," Solomon says in a stern tone that brooks no argument. "You're done working. You've been on your feet all day."

She palms his muscled chest. Looks up. "So have you." Between getting the bar ready and planning the new menu release, Solomon's been running himself ragged.

He grunts, shifting his enormous hand to her hip. "I'm not pregnant."

Dark brows waggling, Ash wags a finger. "We're officially putting you on maternity leave."

Tessie dusts off her palms and holds them out like she's being held at gunpoint. "Fine. I'm done." Between Solomon and Ash, they're like two very intense guard dogs. "I don't like the two of you together."

Ash laughs. "Deal with it."

Spinning around, Tessie points at Howler and grins. "Friday night. We're going to have a party."

Chapter Thirty

Solomon lingers silently on the staircase as Tessie unpacks a box of baby stuff. They've had deliveries all week, preparing for Bear's arrival. Dressed in a cozy sweater that hugs her bump, leggings, and winter slippers, she's on her knees. Long blond hair waves around her shoulders as she pulls out fuzzy blankets and bottles and small gilt-edged frames.

A smile tugs at his bearded lips. As sexy as she is pregnant, he can't goddamn wait to see her as a mother. She'll teach Bear how to be stubborn, she'll fight for him, dig her heels in when things go wrong, give him her good taste and love of Pantone colors. Solomon will be the muscle, the one to sling Bear over his shoulder and spin him until giggles fill their cabin. But one thing's for certain—their little boy will never doubt his mother's love for him.

Gripping the edge of the box, Tessie shoves herself up, wobbling once with that belly of hers, then steadies herself. She goes to the wall and hammers, humming along to a tune the old Crosley spins out. The slow sway of her hips, the bump on her belly, has Solomon's stomach flipping over.

Fuck but he loves her.

He'll never get used to the sight of Tessie in his home.

Their home.

That feeling of coming home to someone, of having someone always in his space—he didn't know how much he missed it until she was here. In only a few short weeks, they've settled into a routine. Natural. Normal, like it was meant to be. Like those stars knew something that Nashville night. Set him on a course for Tessie, and he'll never look back.

Because he wants this. Every damn day for the rest of his life. Go to work, come home to Tessie and his son.

His entire world.

Sensing him, Tessie startles and turns. "You're home."

Home. His chest swells at the word.

She inclines her golden head. "You like to lurk in the shadows, Solemn Man, and watch me wobble around?"

Solomon laughs softly. "You don't wobble."

"I do. But I wobble with style." She smiles. "How was work?"

He takes off his jacket, shaking snow from the sleeves as he climbs the last few stairs.

Peggy's curled up on the bed, giving a sleepy woof as he approaches. "Finalized the menu. Howler had a minor freak-out when his liquor order was delivered to the wrong address, but we survived, and the liquor is safely put away." He steps closer, studies the pictures on the wall.

She flushes. "Sorry, I hope you don't mind. I thought I'd decorate."

Shaking his head, he moves for her, dipping to kiss her, then pulls her to his side. "Not at all." He swallows, staring at the photo of them in Mexico. The one she took when they were stuffed in the hammock. "I love it."

Tessie waves at the small space she's decorated. The rocking chair with a knit baby blanket draped over the frame. "It's all ready." Her nose wrinkles. "Now all we need is the crib."

Solomon smiles when he catches the small yawn she's trying to hide.

"Tired?" he asks, running a hand beneath her hair and over her neck.

"You're like Ash's smelling salts." She nuzzles against him. "You keep me alive. Awake."

"You think you can stay awake for a surprise?"

Her chocolate-brown eyes light up. "I'm always down for a surprise."

Ducking his head, he presses a kiss to the corner of her mouth. "Stay here. Close your eyes."

With that, Solomon disappears into the small, sloped attic space and brings out what he's been working on for the last two weeks. His way to unwind in the dark, quiet nights with Tessie sleeping in their bed, the stars shining bright through the skylight.

"Okay," he says when he gets his surprise settled. "Look."

She does.

A soft gasp fills the space between them. Slices of silver flood Tessie's dark eyes. In front of her sits a simple gray-brown crib with arched ends.

Slowly, she approaches, running her hands along the smooth wood frame. "You made this?" Her voice has gone dreamy.

"I did. I wanted Bear to have a piece of Chinook. It's blue pine," he offers. "It meets crib safety standards. I made sure of it."

She smiles up at him, her full, pink lips trembling. Tears stream down her face. He swears she's trying to kill him. Tess crying is par for the course these days, but he still hates to see it. Her tears have the power to absolutely wreck him.

"Can we put it on the wall?" Tessie sniffles.

He lifts it easily, moving it beneath the sloped eave of the roof. The photo of Tessie and him in the hammock hangs overhead. When he lifts the blanket from the rocking chair to drape over the rail, a sharp inhale of air from Tessie has him turning.

"Baby, what is it?"

"You look like a father."

He swallows down the lump in his throat, her words threatening to take him to his knees.

At his silence, she touches fingertips to her lips. "Does that scare you?"

"No. It makes me happy." He takes a giant step to pull her

into his arms, loving how easily she fits. He sweeps the tears on her cheeks away with his thumbs. "Don't cry, Tess. You kill me when you cry."

She locks her shiny eyes with his. Places a palm over his heart. "The crib's beautiful, Solomon. I love it. Bear will love it."

"Rest of my life, I'm gonna take care of you and that baby."

"I know you will."

Her belief, her faith in him, is everything. To be the man she needs, the man she's chosen, it humbles him.

He smiles down at her, slipping a hand into her golden hair. In her face, her wide brown eyes, he sees his future. He sees everything.

And in his arms, shining like the sun, his world undimming, his eternity—Tessie.

The night the blizzard hits Chinook, Tessie wakes with a cramp in her belly. She's curled up in Solomon's arms, his steel frame draped over her like one of those calming anxiety blankets. A broad palm covers the top of her head, one arm curled protectively over her waist. Bear batters her from within, and she rests a palm on her belly, as if she can calm him. Then slowly, she inches her way out of Solomon's tight grasp. Not used to the cold, she pulls on furry socks and a flannel and pads across the hardwood to the rocking chair.

She sits and rocks and looks up to the skylight.

Snow flurries across the inky black sky. She knows what's out there, the jagged mountains, the alpine forest, a stream Bear will fish in, but right now, all that exists is darkness. The stars. Immediacy. The here and now. Maybe this is the lesson her mother wanted her to learn. That somewhere out there, the stars align, and a person finds their place.

A lesson she wants Bear to learn as well.

With a sigh, Tessie coasts her hand over the swell of her

stomach. Her breasts are heavy; her feet ache. Her belly is as hard as a rock.

Soon, she thinks, and her heart beats faster. *He'll be here soon.* All this hope. Their son. She can't wait to meet him.

"Tess." Solomon's urgent voice floats through the darkened room. He's searching the room, but he hasn't found her. Sitting up in bed, he's illuminated by the moonlight, his broad shoulders, the sinew of his muscular back.

"I'm still here," she says softly. "I didn't leave."

At her words, his tense shoulders relax. Then comes a swift rustle of sheets.

Solomon's hand presses on her shoulder.

Without speaking, they trade spots. She stands, and Solomon settles in the chair. Then he's pulling Tessie onto his lap. She curls up in his arms, resting her head between his collar and jaw. She closes her eyes, inhaling the woodsy scent of his beard. Solomon rocks. The motion is soothing, like a gentle wave stealing over her.

"Can't sleep?" he asks, palming her stomach.

"No. This baby's an absolute maniac." She sighs. "I'm sorry I woke you."

"You didn't."

He's right. She didn't. If she's not beside him, he'll wake. He'll come looking for her. She's learned this. She's learned so many things about her Solemn Man this last month, and she loves them all.

Voice hoarse with sleep, he asks, "What're you thinking about?"

"Lots of things."

"Tell me."

She smiles. That's Solomon. Always ready to listen. To fix. A man who is always there, who will never walk away. From her or from Bear.

She kisses his bearded cheek. "I have to get a job."

A grunt of disagreement. "You have to relax."

"But I have ideas."

"Until then, I make more than enough."

"How?" She tugs on his beard. "You live in a cabin. You own one flannel shirt."

A rumble of a laugh vibrates through his chest. Through hers. "I own the bar with Howler. It's not millions, but I make more than enough for our family."

Our family.

Oh God. If she wasn't already head-over-heels in love with Solomon, she is now.

He nudges her face up to meet his, silencing her protests with a kiss. "I want to give you everything, Tess. So let me."

She smiles, laying her head against his chest. "You make it sound easy."

"It is easy. Because you're mine." He pulls her closer. "Next?"

"I was thinking about food."

A chuckle leaves Solomon's lips. "First meal?"

She smiles. "Mmm. Champagne. Steak. Rare. A mountain of brie."

"Done. And done. Third thing?"

"I was thinking about names," she begins. "I don't know what will happen between us. . . if we get married—"

"When."

"Okay, *when* we get married, but however, whenever it happens. . .I want Bear to have my last name. It was my mother's."

She sits up. Her eyes flit to his, unsure of how he'll take it.

All Solomon does is nod. Intent. Serious. Then he says, "He should have it."

Tessie sighs and leans into his wide shoulder. Is it possible to be drunk on a person? Because every time this man opens his mouth, the world swims. In the best possible way. She continues, a sudden shyness setting in. Curling her thin fingers in his chest hair, she murmurs, "I was thinking we could name him Wilder."

The rocking stops. "Wilder?"

"Your last name."

He blows out a long breath. In the dark, all she can see are his eyes. Shiny with tears.

"Yes" is all he says, and then he kisses her.

Breathless, they pull away.

I love you, Tessie mouths in the dark of the room.

I love you, Solomon mouths back.

The baby kicks in her belly.

And then they sleep.

Chapter Thirty-One

COUNTRY MUSIC CUTS THROUGH THE CHAOS OF Howler's Roost. The booths are crammed with an assortment of wizened locals and curious tourists. People snag drinks, pluck Solomon's appetizers off trays. Behind the bar, Howler mixes cocktails with expert precision.

Over Tessie's head, a modern antler chandelier casts ambient rays of light.

Howler's Roost is hopping.

The bar is packed with friends and family. The whole town turned up for the grand reopening. A show of support for Solomon and Howler that has her heart doing a slow, spastic *thump-thump-thump*. The black dress Tessie wears hugs her belly tightly, earning her curious stares. She's shaken at least fifty hands tonight. Watched as the residents of Chinook pass by Solomon and squeeze his arm, congratulations spilling from their lips.

They see it. He's back and he's happy, and to Tessie, it's the most beautiful thing she's ever witnessed.

Which is fitting, because at least once every five minutes, Solomon has to stop what he's doing and make the same old introduction. "Yes, this is Tessie. Yes, she is pregnant. Yes, we're having a baby together." Not once letting loose of her hand, he hovers beside her like he's personally been sent to attack if anyone tries to touch her belly.

Spread out across the room is Solomon's family, including

Evelyn, who sits at the bar, tapping on her phone with her signature scowl. Tessie and Solomon circle the perimeter of the crowd, offering hellos and warm welcomes.

"Heels?" Melody asks, bouncing up to them, her eyes on Tessie's Manolos. "Of all nights?"

Solomon shakes his head. "I told her."

Tessie sniffs and swats at him with her clutch. "I've been wearing boots all month. Tonight, I wear heels. It's your party, Solomon. I have to look pretty."

A grin tugs at his bearded lips as he looks down at her with an expression of pure awe on his face. A warm flush coats her cheeks at his devout attention. "You look beautiful," he says, pulling her close.

Smiling, she rests her free hand against the side of her belly. It feels extra hard tonight.

"Tessie does look beautiful, but so does this bar." Melody runs gleaming eyes over the space. She props her hands on her waist. "Can we talk about the wall of hatchets?"

Solomon lifts his beer, pride in his voice. "Tessie's design magic in the wild."

"The most important part is that they're real," Ash says, prowling up behind them. "And can be used against Howler in a pinch."

Solomon booms a laugh that turns heads. Including Tessie's. She can't help but sneak a peek his way. In faded jeans that mold to his massive thighs, a wool-lined flannel, and a bearded jaw as chiseled as the mountains they live under, he looks every bit the rugged mountain man she fell in love with.

"Holy shit," Jo says. Still in her scrubs, her black hair covered in snow, she trudges their way. "It's blizzard central out there."

Outside, the wind howls. Beyond the glass windows of the garage doors, snow falls.

Solomon looks worried.

"Great," Ash says. "Just what we need. Serve them liquor and shove them into cars."

"Howler's going light on the booze," Melody assures them.

"But I'm not sure about Mom and Dad." Giggling, she nods at their parents, who are two-stepping their way across the floor to the twangy croon of Tammy Wynette.

When there's nothing from Solomon but a grunt, Tessie tugs on his arm. "You're not smiling."

"I'm glowering."

"I can see that." She scans his face. "What's wrong?"

"Nothing." He splays a wide palm over the small of her back. Tilting down, he kisses her temple. "Just counting the hours until I take you home to our bed."

"Mmm," she hums, shivering as his broad hand trails around the curve of her hip. The bar's nice, but Solomon's hands all over her body are even nicer. "Promise me we won't leave the cabin for days and days."

That, to her relief, brings a smile to his face. "Tess, baby, I can promise you that."

The night spins on. Two people ask for Tessie's business cards. One person goes in for a stomach rub but is blockaded by Solomon's big body and scared away with a growl. Howler gives a quote to *Thrillist*, a picture is snapped, a cheer goes up around the room. Soon there's talk of a speech as Solomon's mother and father spring a cake shaped like a cocktail on him and Howler.

"I'll get a lighter," Tessie says over the din, squeezing Solomon's arm to let him know she's headed to the kitchen.

Hands propped on her hips, she scours the kitchen for a lighter. Spying a box of matches on a shelf full of recipe books, a shelf so high it can only be meant for Solomon, she glances around for a solution.

Then, victorious, she spies a pair of tongs on the counter. If she can't use a stool or a ladder, she can be resourceful.

On her tiptoes and using the tongs as an extra-long arm, Tess clamps the box of matches and drags it toward her. Closer and closer. When she's sure she's got it, she yanks. But along with the than her corner, a recipe book, both crashing onto the steel countertop with a clatter.

"Shit," she swears.

Papers spill out of a book of recipes called *Cooking Alaskan*. Not wanting any of Solomon's notes to get lost in the mess, she picks them up, shuffles them into a pile. She's folding them neatly to return them to the pages of the book when she freezes.

Her name. Her name's on these papers.

Frowning, she reads.

As she does, every breath leaves her body. Her heartbeat slows, walking a fine knife-edge of panic. Her hands tremor. The papers in front of her feel like a sick, twisted joke. But they're really there. And they cut.

Words like *unfit* and *petition for custody* and *establish paternity* slap her across the face.

"Oh my God," Tessie whispers, bringing shaky fingertips to her lips when she sees the line for Solomon's signature. Tears flood her eyes. Rejection twists her gut.

Betrayal.

Like a needle dropping on a vinyl, she starts.

Turning fast on her heel, she exits the kitchen and runs straight into Howler. He steadies her by the shoulders. "Whoa, slow it down, Goldilocks. Where you going?"

She rips away from him, scowls. "Away from here."

"What're you—" His bright blue eyes drop to the papers in her hands. He pales. Swallows. Attempts a smile. "Would you sit, Goldie? I'll make you a drink."

"You don't want to make me a drink," she hisses, pulling the papers to her heart. "You never have."

Concern on his face, Howler raises his hand, gesturing to Solomon in the crowd. But Tessie's already off, storming to the coat rack. She yanks on her parka, sticks her hands in Solomon's coat pocket, and jerks out the keys to the pickup.

She needs to get out of here. Away from Solomon, away from

Chinook, from this town. Because it hurts too much. Losing everything because she was an idiot, a fool. Because she believed Solomon Wilder when he said he wouldn't get the courts involved. That they could work it out together. That they'd share Bear. But what he really wants to do is take him away from her.

On autopilot, she pushes through the crowd of people, past Evelyn, who's finally perking up on her barstool, and then she's tossing open the heavy front door and stepping out into the parking lot.

Tessie gasps as a blast of frigid November air hits her hard in the face.

She stands under the glittering sky, in the frigid cold darkness. Icy tears drip down her face. Snow gusts, sweeping over the tops of her feet. Overhead, a bright full moon illuminates the gravel parking lot.

Stars shimmer across the universe like when she and Solomon first met. A lifetime ago in that Tennessee Bar. Before Bear. Before this all blew up in her face.

With a shudder, she pulls her collar up around her neck and steps off the sidewalk. She hasn't made it far when the door slams open behind her.

"Tess, baby," Solomon growls, the sound of his voice making her body turn, as if it has no free will of its own. His chest heaves, his hands clenched at his sides. Ash at his shoulder. "It's not what you think." But his tone is guilty, like he already knows what she's found.

Lifting her chin, she strides forward and punches the papers against his chest. "Then what is it, Solomon? Because it looks like you're trying to take Bear away from me."

"I'm not. I swear it." He inhales a breath. "I know right now it looks unforgivable, but I can explain."

Shaking her head, backing away, Tessie covers her stomach. Solomon flinches. Suddenly, all she wants is for the tiny baby inside her to stay put.

"You don't want me. You just want Bear." Her voice breaks on the words.

"Tessie, no," Ash says, her hands clutched to her heart.

Solomon's handsome face crumples. "You don't believe that."

What should she believe? She's so confused. But she needs a game plan. An out. She needs to get away from Solomon. Now.

Drive back to the cabin and pack. Get on the next plane out of Alaska. Take her baby and her bad plans and go back to California and beg Nova for a job.

Tessie turns around and walks on shaking legs toward the road. Gravel and snow crunch beneath her heels.

Get away, get away, get away.

Her emotions, her hormones are all over the place. Running wild like a thundering pack of mustangs. From pregnancy. From the papers she discovered. From Solomon's frantic eyes staring her down.

"Where are you going?" he demands. He's beside her, his hand on her elbow. Trying to steer her back inside.

She shoves at him. "Away from you. I can't talk to you right now."

His hard bootsteps follow her. "Tess, get back here. You're gonna freeze."

Solomon's stern command sends shivers of fury down her spine. She crosses her arms and averts her gaze to the dark, hoping he doesn't see her teeth chatter.

A crowd is gathering on the sidewalk. Solomon's wide-eyed parents and his sisters. Ash. Howler. They gawk like they've come to watch Tessie combust. The thought only makes her feel more awful. More alone.

"Tess..."

She whirls on him. "You changed our deal," she shouts. Fear and panic and loss cloud her voice.

"Baby," he whispers, inching closer like she's an animal caught in a trap.

"You changed our deal on me. On us. You promised."

"I did promise," he says, sounding unsteady. Panicked. "And I'm telling you I didn't break that promise."

A clipped voice interrupts them. "Sol..."

Solomon's teeth snap together. So hard it's stunning he doesn't crack one. "Go back inside, Evelyn," he barks, no bullshit in his tone. "Now."

Shamefaced, Evelyn scurries off.

Inhaling a defiant breath, cold stinging her lungs, Tessie walks. The wind whips her hair, mixing it with her tears. Her face is frozen, but the only sensation that registers is the hot pump of blood in her veins, making her move.

"Wait. Tess. Listen to me." Solomon's voice breaks in the night air. He's beside her. Grasping her wrist, gentle yet firm, but she slips from his grip. Solomon curses softly, swearing at her, at himself.

"Leave me alone, Solomon."

"No fucking chance."

"I'm taking the truck back to the cabin."

He grunts. "Good luck finding it."

She stops. Swiveling her head, she searches the lot for the truck. Then remembers it's parked a half mile down the road. Shit.

Still, she moves, leaving the bar behind her, the bright light of the neon sign blinking in her periphery.

A silent stretch of seconds, and then—

"Walk, then." Solomon's deep rumble reverberates in the night air. Determination in his tone. "Walk off if you want."

"I will," she shoots back, holding her belly, not looking back.

"I'll be right behind you. When you want to talk, I'll be ready. I'll be right here."

His words have her heart two-stepping. Have her stopping. She turns around. "You don't have a jacket on."

She fumes at herself. Damn her for caring.

"Fuck a jacket."

"Oh yeah, that's a great idea. That's just what our son needs. His father getting sick and dying of pneumonia."

"I don't care, Tess. I'm not leaving you. And when you're ready to listen, I'll tell you about how I wasn't involved with drawing up these papers. Never in a million years would I fucking hurt you like that."

On shaky legs, she takes a step forward, to walk away. Only, the slow roll of Bear in her belly, Solomon's words, stop her.

Oh God. The realization kicks her in the teeth.

What is she doing?

She's walking away from him.

So damn worried about him breaking his promise, she didn't realize she was breaking her own.

"Tess, please." A strangled sound of anguish breaks in his throat, forcing her to turn back to him again. "I don't want you on the side of the road, baby."

Solomon stares at her with haunted eyes. His face devastated, absolutely agonized, and that's when Tess knows. She walks away, walks off, it'll kill him.

Here she is, a near-feral pregnant woman, melting down because of hormones while freezing her ass off. She's pushing him away, but he's staying. He isn't walking away or leaving her or letting her go. He's *staying*.

Clarity cracks inside her then.

Love stays.

She could walk away, she could end this, or she could face it and understand.

Her mom always told her to find someone who stays. Who doesn't walk away even when life is hard. Even when they fight.

This is what her mother would have wanted for her. Not money. Or a career. But love. A man who fights for her, fights with her and doesn't walk away, who fills her soul with peace and light and joy.

And that's Solomon.

Inhaling a deep breath, she forces her brain to leave its radioactive meltdown zone. And she finds Solomon's lapis lazuli eyes lasered on her in a way that has her stomach going molten and magnetic.

She steels herself, letting hope, love, break apart her shield. Praying that there is an explanation for the papers he's holding that won't break her heart.

She hisses, stabs a finger at him. Hating him but loving him too—too much—for the chokehold he has on her heart. "I'm pissed at you."

A hint of a smile graces his face. She knows now. Knows when Solomon is smiling or grimacing or scowling or laughing. All his bearded faces, she knows them.

They're hers.

The mountain of a man expels the air from his lungs in one long whoosh. "I know you are. And you can be." He scans the space separating them, and he takes a step forward. "Come with me. Let's talk, Tess. Yell at me. Hit me. Throw a heel at me. Just do it inside. Where it's warm."

She sob-laughs. Unable to help it. Unable to rein in the helpless, wild love she feels for this man. Even when he's infuriated her to no end.

"Fine. I will."

His frame sags in relief. Then the most beautiful grin lights up his rugged face as he holds out his hand to her. "Let's go, Pregnant Woman."

Tessie takes a step forward, reaching out for his steady hand, and then the worst thing happens.

She slips.

Legs shooting out from under her, she falls forward. Though her balance is nonexistent, she manages to twist herself, but she still lands hard on the cement. Pain ricochets through her hips, her elbow, her head.

"*Tessie!*" Solomon's panicked voice rings out like a shot in the dark.

The world swims. God. It hurts. Everything hurts. Like arrows needling her shoulder, her tailbone. For a long second, she lays there, gasping for air. Then, at the cramp weaving its way through her belly, she covers her face and lets out a wail.

In one fell swoop, she's in Solomon's arms, locked tight against his chest, her face buried against his racing heart. The only thing she hears is the wind gusting through the trees and Solomon's deep voice vibrating through her.

"I've got you. You're okay. You're both okay."

Chapter Thirty-Two

It's Solomon's favorite sound.

Bear's heartbeat.

He sits in the chair beside Tessie's hospital bed, his fists clenched tight on his thighs. Tears slip silently down Tessie's face, but she stares out the window at the falling snow as the doctor checks her over. She still won't look at him. Not since she discovered the papers. Not since she took that hard fall that spun his world off its axis.

When she fell, it almost ended him.

Driving like a madman in the snow, Solomon hauled ass to the hospital. The rest of his family and friends followed the minute he called them to tell them what was happening.

Now, her elbow bandaged, Tessie's hooked up to a myriad of machines that monitor the baby and her. The lines jump on the heart monitor, a steady pulse telling him their son's okay. Still, the fucking anvil in his chest, the fist wrapped around his throat won't let him loose. Worry for the baby, for Tess, eats at him.

Doctor Banai straightens up on her stool and says, "Right now, there are no signs of fetal distress or placental abruption. Or internal bleeding." She looks at Tess. "You said you had a cramp?"

"Yes," Tessie replies with a sniffle. "After I fell."

"Okay." The doctor turns a wise eye to the band strapped across Tessie's belly. "We're monitoring you for contractions. This could be the start of labor."

Solomon's chest tightens, and he can barely force his next breath out. "It's too soon."

Tessie presses a hand against her mouth to smother a sob.

"The survival rate for babies at thirty-five weeks is the same as that for babies born at full term." Doctor Banai smiles and stands, her dark eyes crinkling at the corners. "Rest, relax. I'll be back to check in on you."

Solomon's frozen, processing the news, when Tess's heart-wrenching voice says, "This is my fault."

"Don't," he grits out.

Tears streaming down her face, she rests a hand on her swollen stomach, her gaze still trained out the window. "I shouldn't have been wearing heels."

"I'm not going to do that, Tess. Blame you."

"Why not? I deserve it." Another sob rips out of her, shaking her petite frame. "I'm a terrible person. Bear could have been hurt."

He shakes his head, but she continues without even a glance his way.

"I know I overreacted." She swipes angrily at her tears. "But I saw those papers, and it was like my world blew up. All I could see was you leaving me. Bear leaving me. I saw everything I loved going away. Again."

He knows what she saw. And it guts him. Solomon doesn't blame her for her reaction. All Tessie knew about love her entire life was a disappointment, and this set her off.

She should be pissed. She should take hard and fast swings at him, aim straight for the balls, punch the living shit out of him, and he wouldn't stop her.

He blames himself. He made a promise to her about Bear. Whether or not Evelyn was behind it, it's still his fault. He should have come clean about those papers. Burned them. Instead, Tessie found them, and she got hurt. *He* got her hurt.

He scoots closer. "It's my mistake," he rasps. The words wrench from his clenched jaw. "I should have told you about the papers. You never should have found them the way you did."

Finally, she faces him. There's fear in her eyes. Wariness. She still doesn't trust him.

His stomach roils, nerves getting the best of him.

He has to make this right. If he and Tessie aren't okay—he doesn't know how he'll survive. Thinking about never holding her again, of watching her leave, going back to LA with their son, threatens to knock the wind out of him.

"Listen to me," he says, daring to take her slack hand in his, stroking a thumb across her knuckles. "This is on me. And Evelyn. You have to know that I never planned to take Bear away from you." He brings her hand to his mouth, pressing a kiss against her palm. "I'm so sorry, Tessie. I'm so fucking sorry."

When she finally speaks, it's like a glass of cold water after a drought, and the tension melts from his body.

"It scared me," she says, defeated and sniffling. "I went back there. When my father left. When my mother died. No one wanted me. All I have is Bear," she says in a small voice. "He's my son, my baby. Nothing can happen to him."

His throat works as he swallows. "You have me," he says raggedly.

Without a response, she looks away.

Christ, she's killing him. He slips from the chair, a desperate man, on his knees in front of her. But for Tessie, it's what he'll always be. "I love you, Tess. I want *you*," he promises, squeezing her hands in his. "You're my undoing, my entire fucking world. I'm not going anywhere. Baby, I'm yours." He closes his eyes. "Tell me you're still mine." His voice cracks; he can't go on anymore.

A long silence fills the hospital room.

His heart rate is off the charts. If he were hooked up to that goddamn monitor, alarm bells would ring. Christ. If she doesn't look at him, say something right this fucking instant, he's going to die. Shrivel into a broken husk of a man.

Then her sweet voice, his saving grace, says softly, "I'm yours."

His heart caves in with relief. "You are?"

"I am." She faces him, raising her gaze to meet his. "I want the cabin. I want Chinook. And I want you, my Solemn Man." Her beautiful brown eyes brim with tears. "I need you. Bear and I, we both need you."

"Fuck," he breathes, launching up. He can't get her in his arms fast enough.

Their mouths collide, his hands threading through her silky hair. Tessie exhales and gives a little moan, and Solomon tightens his hold.

Thank Christ for this woman.

"Thank you," he murmurs, kissing her hair, her cheek, her throat. "For not walking off. My heart couldn't handle that."

She closes her eyes, scratching her slender fingers through his beard. Her very touch licks through him like wildfire. "I know. Mine either."

Gently, Solomon lowers her back down against the pillows and tucks the blanket tighter over her lap. Splaying his hand over her belly, he waits for Bear's kick. Strong. Powerful.

Like Tessie.

Fuck. To think of how close he came to fucking it all up.

He's never letting her go again, so help him God.

"If it makes you feel any better," Solomon says, squeezing her hand, "I almost killed a whole flock of geese hauling ass to the hospital."

She laughs, then thins her lips at him.

"Baby, what is it?"

"I'm still upset." Her mouth quirks up. "I never got to throw a shoe at you."

He chuckles and traces a finger over her cheekbone. "You can throw a shoe at me later."

"I will. A stiletto. And you can't duck."

"Deal." Grinning, he leans down and kisses her. "I should tell everyone what's going on. You'll be okay without me for a few minutes?" At her nod of assent, he shoves up from the bed, already ready to get back to her.

When he's halfway to the door, Tessie gasps.

He rips around. His heart trips into his ribs and crashes down into his stomach. "Tess? What is it?"

Tessie looks up at him with wide, horrified eyes. Across her blanket spreads a dark stain. "My water broke."

Chapter Thirty-Three

The wave crashes down, and Tessie lets it take her. Lets it sweep over her in long, reassuring flushes of warmth.

Birth is wild. And she surrenders to the ride.

She wants to be worried, but she's too happy. Giddy with realization that it's happening, that Bear will soon be in her arms. Her son.

Their son.

She paces the room. The nurses let her walk, and where she goes, Solomon follows.

For hours.

Bear's heartbeat is strong on the monitor. Tessie has a plan, and Solomon's there to make sure she gets what she wants. Though nothing's gone as planned tonight, she is going to birth her baby her way, the best she can.

She breathes, focusing. Resetting. She isn't in a small-town hospital. She's in Chinook, in aspen and pine and cool air and nature. Her body is opening, flowering, readying to bring her son into the world.

She can do this. She trusts her body with all her heart.

She trusts Solomon.

"You got this." He strokes her hair as she breathes. "Tess, my brave girl."

Draped across his broad chest, she feels his heartbeat in

lockstep with hers. His broad, muscular arms band around her waist, roping her to him. Never letting her down.

"I love you," Solomon says. "I love you. I love you."

Tessie sags in his arms, her forehead dipping to his armored chest. "I love you back," she whispers. Over and over until another contraction hits and she starts pacing again.

She feels lovestoned. High like that time she and Ash smoked a joint in the linen closet and ate an entire bag of Cheetos and got discovered by Aunt Bev. Flying high, cackling like two old witches.

She's floating.

Hours pass. Outside, the sky is light, the snow still falling.

Pain now. Cramps in her belly. Radiating through her hips, her spine.

Her legs go weak. She doubles over with a groan she usually reserves for eating an entire pizza.

Solomon's there. Always that big, broad palm guiding her, helping her when she's not strong enough. His massive hands massage her hips, hold her when she needs support, release her when she paces.

She tries different positions. "These aren't working," she says, rising from the yoga ball.

"Handstand?" Solomon suggests, his beard hiding his shit-eating grin.

"Screw you," she pants.

Like all those women on all those TV shows, soon, she stops pacing and is in bed. She reclines against Solomon's chest. He holds her exhausted body in his arms. He gives her his strength.

She barely hears Doctor Banai instructing her to push. All she focuses on is Solomon. The jump of her baby's heartbeat on the monitor.

Focus gives way to frustration.

It's been hours. And she's tired. She's so damn tired. She couldn't push Bear out even if she was being poked with a cattle prod.

Her head falls back against Solomon's chest. Sweat drips down her brow. "I can't do it," she cries breathlessly. "It's too hard."

"You can," Solomon rumbles next to her ear. Kisses her sweaty temple. "You can do it, Tessie. My Tessie. My brave girl."

Inhaling the longest breath, she closes her eyes. Then she pushes.

She unravels.

A heaviness down below, a sharp burst, a relief.

Somewhere in the room, someone announces they see the head.

She sobs.

Solomon's deep voice reverberates in her ears as he whispers, "You're a rock star. You're so damn strong. I have you."

His trust in her bolsters her. Gives her strength. With Solomon here, she can handle anything.

The nurse commands her to give one last push, one last push, and she does.

Gripping Solomon's broad hands, she bears down. One long, last push, a howl like a wild animal, like Peggy Sue, like the Wilder her son will be, and then there's a slow sucking feeling and blessed emptiness.

Doctor Banai, head ducked between her legs, calls out what they already know. "It's a boy!"

Before she can ask if her son's okay, there's the sharp, bright cry. Steady and true. Strong.

Bear.

Tessie bursts into tears.

The baby's whisked away to be checked over. Solomon kisses her temple, smooths hair from her sweaty brow. He shakes beside her, whispering his joy, and then the nurses are placing a baby, a fat pink baby, in her arms.

Love.

It's immediate and heart-wrenching. Like her soul is in her

arms and she's holding it, only it's a better part of her. The weight of love.

Tessie only sobs harder when he wraps a finger around hers. They lock eyes, Bear's intent gaze never moving from hers, like he knows her already. *Dark eyes*, Tessie thinks. *Blue. Brown.* What Pantone color they are, she can't tell. It doesn't matter. It's all beautiful.

"Ours," she says, trembling. She turns her face up to Solomon, who's standing above her. "He's ours."

Her mountain man's throat bobs. His eyes shine with emotion, with tears. "You did so good, baby. So damn good."

"Look," she laughs. "No beard." Gently, she traces a fingertip across the curve of Bear's sweet pink cheek.

Solomon chuckles. Almost hesitantly, he runs a big finger over Bear's downy shoulder. The baby lies calmly in her arms, staring up at her. Tessie's gaze lingers on him, soaking in every inch, and then moves to Solomon.

She can't stop the rush of love. This man, who's been here for her since the beginning, who's never left her. Who taught her it's okay to be open and vulnerable. That he will hold her anger and sadness and fix it or sit with it. Whatever she wants. Her choice. Her heart.

It leaves her breathless, faint. There will never be enough time to tell him how much she loves him.

The moment spins on, nurses attending to her as she and Solomon drink in their son.

And then there's a tug down below. Sharp. Strange.

Suddenly, everyone in the room is moving, examining the monitors, talking in hushed whispers.

"What?" Tessie asks, lifting her head to see Doctor Banai frowning down at the space between her legs.

"What's wrong?" Solomon's gruff rumble has her trying to blink, to focus.

The world is heavier than it was only a moment ago.

Disconnected. Her head feels like it'll float away from her body. And she's trembling. Then a rush of something warm drains away from her. Like she's leaking.

She is.

"Call a Code Noelle," Doctor Banai orders. A flurry of movement, of sharp commands, erupts in the room. She looks at Solomon, worry lacing every word. "She's bleeding."

It's awful. The way Solomon's handsome face changes. Happiness to confusion to fear.

Tessie licks her dry lips. The very act draining. "Solomon," she whispers. Her heart is a freight train in her chest. The sheets beneath her are soaked. The blood running up her back and into her hair.

He's tense, standing tall, his worried blue eyes flickering to her, then the nurses. "What does that mean? What's wrong with Tess?"

"Solomon." Tessie's head lolls on the pillow. Her eyelids get heavier and heavier. "Take him," she whispers, trying to get his attention, rallying all her strength to get the words out. "Take the baby."

And then Tessie goes limp, eyes fluttering closed. Bear sags in her arms, only to be snatched up by Solomon before she loses grip completely.

Someone's yelling, the monitors explosive bursts of alarm, Solomon's shaking her, her name a desperate, ragged chant on his lips.

Stay awake. A woman's voice. *Stay awake, Tess.*

An endless sky of black in her dimming vision.

But no stars.

Chapter Thirty-Four

In a hard plastic chair, Solomon sits, every ounce of strength sapped from his body. His head buried in his hands. The waiting room is full. His family, Ash, and Howler sit in stunned silence, barely moving. No one speaks.

He's scared. More scared than he's ever been in his life. No matter how hard he tries, he can't shake the image of Tessie in that hospital bed.

Blood-soaked sheets. Her pale face. Her soft whisper of warning. She went limp before he knew what was happening. He barely had time to grab up his son before every person in the room jumped into action and hustled him out of the delivery room.

Now he waits. Fury, worry boiling over, his head and his heart already gone. He wants to hit something, kill someone. He can't see his son. He has no goddamn idea how Tessie is.

A squeak from Melody has him glancing up. Doctor Banai stands in the waiting room.

He rockets out of his seat. "How's my—" He stops himself. Hates himself. Hates that she's still not his wife. Getting over the lump in his throat, he manages, "How's my Tessie? How's my son?"

"The baby's fine," the doctor says, her tone soft. "We took him to the NICU to get checked over, but right now, there are no complications. You have a healthy baby boy."

Solomon sucks in a sharp breath, letting the news settle. "And

Tessie?" He barely recognizes his voice. Anguished. Ready for the grave.

Doctor Banai clears her throat, then says, "Solomon, her placenta tore after delivery. She hemorrhaged." A round of gasps goes up in the room. "Her blood pressure dropped. She's in shock."

"Fuck," Howler says, sounding panicked.

The frightened look Ash gives him has Solomon wanting to jump out of his skin.

"What does that mean?" he asks, tearing a frustrated fist through his hair.

"We need to take her to emergency surgery to repair the hemorrhage, but that means we need blood. Tessie's A-positive." Her face grave, Doctor Banai looks around the waiting room. "We're low on blood. With this storm, I don't know if we can wait for it to be flown in." After listing the types of blood Tessie can receive, she says, "We can test if you don't know, but we have to do it now. We don't have a lot of time. If we don't treat her quickly..."

Melody's sob breaks the stunned silence of the moment.

Christ no.

No.

Solomon hears the unsaid—what happens if Tessie doesn't get that blood. If they can't find it. If it takes too long.

The waiting room blurs around him. An awful roaring in his ears prevents him from hearing the low murmurs of his friends and family, while Solomon battles the urge to absolutely lose it.

Legs giving out, he collapses into a chair again, closes his eyes, and tries to breathe.

A hand clamps down on his shoulder. Howler.

God, he can't do this again. Lose the woman he loves. It can't happen.

"I'm A-positive," a crisp voice says.

When he opens his eyes, Evelyn is rising out of her chair.

"Are you sure?" Jo asks.

Their mother's eyebrows shoot up. "How do you know that?"

"Because I never failed to get less than an A plus in school," Evelyn replies. She looks at Solomon and then the doctor. "I have my Red Cross card in my purse. I'll go. I'll donate."

Relief rushes through Solomon.

"Go," Ash urges, her voice teary, her head buried in Howler's chest. "Please go now."

Evelyn pushes past Solomon, stopping only briefly to squeeze his hand. "It'll be okay," she assures, her voice cool with calm.

All he can manage is a numb nod.

"Drain me dry, doc," Evelyn says, and then she disappears around the corner.

He can't sit here. Helpless. Waiting. He can't fucking stand it.

With that, his heartbeat dangerously close to flatlining, Solomon shoves up out of his chair and moves in the direction of the exit doors and into the rising dawn.

Outside the hospital entrance, Solomon's breath puffs white in the air in front of his face. It's freezing, but he makes no move to warm himself. Doesn't stuff his hands in his pockets, doesn't hunker down against the frigid wind. He doesn't deserve warmth, not when Tessie's fighting for her life.

Hand smearing down his face, he tries to breathe steady when everything inside him is a tight ball of fear. It feels like he's falling off the edge of the earth, watching everything he loves slip away.

All these responsibilities he never thought he'd have—now they're all he wants.

Tessie woke him up. Made him love again. Gave him a son.

He can't exist without her.

Dawn is on the horizon. Only a few stars glitter in the early-morning light.

"Fuck you," he tells it, his face tilted toward the vast emptiness above him.

The universe is laughing at him. He didn't have time with Serena, and he won't have time with Tessie.

To lose her, after all this...

Unthinkable.

Fuck Chinook. Fuck the snow and his selfish self for asking Tess to stay. Fuck this small-town hospital when she could be in LA, safe and healthy and holding her son.

Her son. The mental image of Tessie not waking up, of never holding Bear again, of their son never knowing his mother...

Solomon squeezes his eyes shut, willing the dark thoughts away.

A rustle of noise behind him, but he doesn't bother turning.

"We drew straws." Howler settles beside him, lifting the collar of his wool-lined jacket to block out the wind. "To see who'd come piss you off."

Solomon drags a hand down his beard. "Go inside, Howler."

"And let you wallow all by yourself? Ain't gonna happen, man."

A long silence passes as they stare at the sky. The sunrise is a brilliant blast of pinks and purples that'd put Mexico to shame.

"I can't lose her." His voice cracks, pain lacing every word. "I can't."

"I know." Howler shoves his hands in his pockets. "You won't."

"I should've—"

"Don't," his friend interrupts. "You got that same look on your face as you did with Serena. You're blaming yourself. You do that, I take you out back and kick you into a snowbank." He claps a hand on Solomon's shoulder, squeezes. "She'll be okay. You can't keep Goldilocks down. You see her with that drill and those heels?"

Solomon chuckles, wipes his wet eyes.

"You got a son in there." Howler jerks his head toward the automatic doors. "He needs you. Tessie will too. Come on. Come back inside."

Solomon drags in a breath, sucking icy air down into his lungs. "I need a minute."

Howler watches him, releases his shoulder, and disappears inside.

"Please," Solomon begs the sky. Serena. "You got me into this mess. You fix it. Fix *her.*" Anguished, he buries his face in his hands, his breath a warm pulse against his palms. "Christ. Please."

Dropping his hands, he tilts his head back once more. "You're up there, and if you got pull, you save her. You save my Tessie."

He lets out one last breath. Says goodbye to Serena.

And goes back inside.

Chapter Thirty-Five

A day without Tessie, and Solomon's barely living. Running on fumes. Coffee. Visits from friends and family. His son.

Tessie's hand is cool in his. She's too pale, too small and fragile in the hospital bed. This bright, golden beam of a woman who lit up his life. Tubes feed into her veins. Her tan from Mexico is gone, her lips ashen. Christ, how he wishes they were back on that beach, Tessie cracking jokes about his flannel. If he knew then what he knows now, he never would have brought her to Chinook. He'd keep her safe and warm in the sun.

"You need to wake up, Tess," he says around the lump in his throat. "Meet your son. Come back to us."

Getting nothing but the chirp of monitors, Solomon sighs. He lifts her slack hand to his lips and kisses her knuckles. "Baby, please," he whispers against her cool skin. "Please wake up. I love you. I need you."

He's not above begging. Getting on his knees again like he's done so often in the last twenty-four hours. He wants to tell Tessie about their son. How the baby is strong and stubborn like she is. How despite being early, he's healthy as hell, has no need for the NICU. How he cries so much his tiny wail is the strongest in the nursery. How it's because he wants his mother. The baby knows it, and Solomon does too.

They need her back.

The soft crack of the door.

"Sol?" Evelyn slips into the room and drops into a chair beside him. "Has she woken up yet?"

He clears the boulder from his throat. "No."

Evelyn crosses her ankles. "You should go home. Rest."

He grunts. "I'm not leaving her."

"You have a baby, Solomon. You need all the rest you can get."

"I'll rest when Tessie is healthy and at home." Tearing his gaze from the woman he loves, he glances over at his sister. "Thank you. For helping her."

She gives a curt nod. "You're welcome."

"About Serena."

She shakes her head.

"Let me do this, Evy."

The line of her lips going flat, she crosses her arms, gives a small nod.

"You don't want me to move on, but I am. I know you don't like it. But you have to deal. I love Tess, and she isn't going anywhere." He makes himself believe the words, says them with conviction. Anything else? It won't happen.

Evelyn's lower lip wobbles. "I know." A shudder works its way through her rigid chest. Tears slide silently down her cheeks.

Solomon exhales roughly. "I'm going to marry her."

"I know that too."

"Every day, I'll do everything I can to be a better husband to her than I was to Serena."

Evelyn glances sharply his way. "Who said you were a bad husband?" She places a hand on his arm. "Serena loved you, Sol. And she would want you to move on. You *should* move on." She focuses on her lap, picking at the hem of her skirt. "Bringing you those papers, being cruel to Tessie. . .I'm a shitty shit of a sister. I was just. . .it's hard." She shudders a breath. "Even after all these years, I keep thinking it should be us double dating, sitting together at family dinners, you and Serena having a baby. It's hard to see someone take her place, but. . .it's time. I know it is." Her gaze drifts to Tessie. "I hope it's not too late for me to tell her I'm sorry."

"It's not." He runs a hand down his beard. "You'd like her," he tells Evelyn. "You should get to know her. She's a lot like you."

A snort. "What, a bitch?"

"No." He smiles, locking his eyes on Tessie. "She fights for the ones she loves."

"Serena would have liked her," Evelyn says, her expression stoic. The closest to an apology as she'll give. Better than.

"I know," he says hoarsely.

Evelyn stands and rests a hand on his shoulder. "Can I bring you anything?"

"Coffee." He settles back into his chair, the tightness in his chest easing a bit. "And my son."

Solomon stays with Tessie all night and into the morning. The nurses bring him Bear to rock and bottle-feed while he waits. Around midnight, the stars come out and the snow stops falling. And Tessie chooses that moment to open her beautiful brown eyes and save him.

Swimming through dark, through stars, Tessie blinks her eyes open to the broad-shouldered blur of Solomon Wilder. He's hunched over in a chair, elbows on his knees, his intent gaze on her.

She licks dry lips, tries to focus as the hospital room comes into view.

"Hi," she breathes, dazed. Like she's floating on a cloud that's about to dissolve.

Solomon's strong rumble fills the room. "Tess." He moves close and scoops her hand in his. Pain, relief break in his expression. "My Tessie."

"The baby," she whispers. Fog curdles her brain. All she remembers are bright bursts of images. Her son in her arms. Blood on the sheets. A strong hand in hers, squeezing desperately. "Is he okay?"

"The baby's fine," Solomon says in a voice she doesn't recognize. "He's healthy."

"He is?" Tears blur her eyes, her body limp with relief. "Oh thank God."

"You're who we have to worry about now." Her hand's lifted to Solomon's lips, his bristly beard scratching over her knuckles, a feeling she relishes. A sensation that tells her she is whole and back on this earth with Solomon and her son.

"Tess," he whispers, kissing her palm, the pulse in her wrist. Wet tears hit her skin. His large frame shakes.

Her eyes widen. Solomon's crying. This big, strong man, who always keeps her safe and protected, is crying.

"Don't," she murmurs, stretching her hand to palm his beard. "My Solemn Man. I'm here. I'm okay."

"You lost a lot of blood." His voice trembles. Leaning down, he cradles her close. Like he has to inhale her. Like if he doesn't touch her, none of this is real. A sob wrenches out of him as he takes her in his arms, hugging her the best he can. "I was so fucking scared, Tessie."

"Shh. I know."

They stay like that for minutes, pressed into each other as if it's the end of the world. But not for them. Tess knows it. Feels it. The entire universe in her hand, and it's Solomon.

"Can I see him?" she asks when they pull away. Her gaze searches his handsome face. "Can I see Wilder?"

At the baby's name, Solomon's eyes go misty.

"Yes," he says, shoving up from the bed. "God yes."

Tessie watches as he moves to a darkened corner of the room. Then, reaching into a hospital bassinet, Solomon lifts a blue bundle, cradles it in his arms.

"Here," he says, gently lowering the baby to her. He helps her hold Wilder, banding an arm around the middle of her back and lifting her up. His firm grip steadies her. She's so weak, all her extremities noodly, she doesn't think she could hold the baby on her own if she tried.

"Oh, Solomon," Tessie squeaks as she gets her second look at her sleeping son. He's beautiful. With a shock of thick black hair and plump, rosy cheeks, his face is peaceful and steady like his father's. "Hi," she whispers to Wilder, blinking back tears. She never even knew she was meant for this, but she does now. This moment. This heart. This baby.

This little baby who's the best halves of both her and Solomon. This baby who brought them together, but deep down, she knows she and Solomon were meant to be anyway.

Looking at Solomon, she smiles. "Baby of my dreams, right here." She traces the pad of her finger over his chubby cheek. "My little wild Bear."

Solomon settles beside her on the bed, keeping a steady hand on her back. "Look what you gave me," he husks, a muscle working in his jaw.

"He's beautiful." Dipping her head, she inhales Wilder's sweet scent, then kisses his shoulder. It's strange, magical, how the tiniest human brings out the biggest love. "Can you believe we made him?"

Solomon strokes her cheek. "He's perfect."

Tessie smiles, her heart beating out a content melody. "He's ours."

"You okay?" Solomon asks as he grips her elbow and helps Tess sit up in bed. His eyes don't leave her face.

She adjusts Wilder in the crook of her arm. "Better than."

With that, she brings her son to her breast. After a snuffling struggle, the baby latches and begins to nurse. A huge bottle of water sits on the nightstand next to her. The hospital gown draped low on her chest. Ash and Howler, perched on the couch in the small room, make low conversation.

Solomon levels a finger at Howler. "Don't stare," he commands.

Tessie laughs brightly, Wilder bouncing with the light movement.

Howler lifts his palms. "Dude, I'm not." He elbows Ash. "Did you see Wilder smile at me twice this morning? Clearly, favorite uncle status."

Ash scoffs, keeping her voice at a hiss-whisper. "You're fu—flipping insane. He's mine. And I will fight you."

"Will you both shut up?" Solomon growls softly, helping Tessie with the latch when Wilder slips off.

Tuning out the bickering family members, Tessie bounces her son in her arms, smiling down at him as he greedily drinks. Her heart melts watching her tiny human hold Solomon's giant finger. Even though he came early, Wilder's eight pounds of chubby baby boy. By now, she's spent three days in the hospital recovering, getting much-needed fluids, and is ready to go home.

If someone had told her she'd design a bar, plan a party, have a baby, and face death all in the span of five weeks, she'd have laughed in their face.

But here she is. Her son. Her mountain man. Her life.

Luckiest woman in the world.

"How do you think it tastes?"

Solomon rounds on Howler. "Get out."

Smirking, Ash pats Howler's shoulder. "We're working on his deep-seated Oedipus complex."

"I was talking about the hospital Jell-O." Howler shakes his head, his amused gaze drifting to Tessie. "Jesus, Goldilocks, rein him in, will you?" His eyes narrow on Wilder. "You think the kid's too young to learn how to bow hunt?"

"Oh God." A terrible thought occurs to Tessie. She looks up at Solomon. "He's going to be the one who buys our son a drum set, isn't he?"

The door cracks open. Melody, her face hopeful, peers into the room. "No," Solomon says gruffly, leveling a scowl of warning at his youngest sister.

Tessie hides a smirk. Ever since she woke up, Solomon's been an overprotective prowling bodyguard in flannel. He hasn't left her side. "No more visitors. Tessie needs her rest."

Melody arches an amused brow. "As much as I, the favorite aunt"—scoffs here from both Ash and Howler—"would love to see my new nephew, I'm here to take Ash to the airport."

Instant tears fill Tessie's eyes. "Oh no. I hate that you have to go."

"I know." Ash drops onto the edge of Tessie's bed, dipping to press a kiss to Wilder's downy head. A sad smile tugs at her mouth. "But I have a client who needs me. You know, that whole-death-waits-for-no-one schtick is a real bummer. I'll be back. Swear it."

Tessie laughs. "You're the one who needs a tropical vacation next."

Ash arches a brow, reaching out to take Tessie's free hand. "Me and sun? We'll see about that. Enjoy your mountain man." Her eyes sparkle with tears. "Your mom would be so proud of you, Tessie. You found your stars."

"I did," she whispers.

She stares at her cousin, her best friend who's done so much for her. Pushed her when she needed to be pushed, knowing what she needed when Tessie didn't even know. Who made her pull her head out of her uptight ass and find the man of her heart.

Tessie inhales a firm breath, squeezes Ash's hand. "I love you."

"I love *you*." Ash gives a proud, tearful laugh. "You've got this."

Tessie smiles at that.

She does.

Chapter Thirty-Six

Tessie jumps when she slides open the shower curtain. Solomon stands there, towel in hand and a frown on his face.

"Success," she sings. She waggles her brows at him, hoping to turn his grumpy face into a smile. "The biggest accomplishment a mama can have. A shower."

"I don't like you in there alone," Solomon says, tipping his bearded chin to look down at her.

She keeps her mouth shut. Sighs and lets him fuss. His favorite pastime since she and Wilder came home from the hospital.

Solomon's afraid. Afraid she'll fall. Afraid she's not getting enough rest.

She gets it. She's scared too.

Birth was easy, but the blood loss and hemorrhage pushed her body to its physical limits. That night left a scar on both her and Solomon.

Three units of her blood gone, two replaced. She was clinically dead for four minutes until the necessary bloods and fluids kicked in. For weeks after the birth, her body was weak and shaky. Like the new blood in her body hadn't kicked in yet. When she looked in the mirror, her face didn't match her memory. Her smile was like a runny egg that could slip right out of the pan.

Now, a month after bringing Wilder home, she's finally recovered. She and Solomon have hit a routine. They were like zombies the first few weeks. They'd look at each other like *holy shit, we're really doing this*, then laugh. These days, their shaky rhythm changes with Wilder, but it's a flow, the closest Tessie can get to a schedule. The baby sleeps all day and is up all night. Her boobs leak twenty-four seven. All modesty out the window. She's sure even Howler's witnessed a nip slip or two, but that's a worry for another day.

Tessie always heard the saying, *lean on your tribe,* but she never knew what it fully meant until she and Solomon brought Wilder home. To her surprise, Howler organized a meal train. Solomon's parents and sisters were over every day. Bringing food, walking Peggy Sue, rocking Wilder for hours so she and Solomon could sleep. Even the simple act of having someone hold her son while she peed was a lifesaver. It touches her immensely how many people have shown up for them. Even Evelyn sent them flowers and hired a housekeeper.

Baby steps. They're all taking baby steps.

Holding her elbow, Solomon helps her out of the shower. She dries off and steps into a pair of lounge pants and a baggy sweatshirt. "Now, food," he orders.

Instead of letting her walk, he scoops her up in his arms.

"I can walk," she argues, running her hands through his dark hair.

A grunt of disagreement. Bypassing the sleeping baby in the crib, Solomon carries Tessie down the stairs and sets her on her feet.

The small cabin is overtaken by flowers and food and diapers. A stale pot of coffee sits on the counter. The faint scent of breast milk hangs in the air. It's a mess. But it's her mess. And it's her home.

Solomon fills a saucepan with water and sets it on the stove. He busies himself, staying obstinately silent, but his back is tense. A deep kind of quiet worry in his eyes. She watches him in the kitchen, looking lost.

"Solomon." Tessie tilts her head, damp blond hair tumbling over her shoulder. She stretches out a hand. "Come here."

When he doesn't move, doesn't take his eyes off the saucepan, she sighs. He's been doing this lately. Keeping his distance. Like if he comes any closer, he'll break her. Hurt her.

So she goes to him.

Solomon frowns as she pads into the kitchen. "You need to rest, Tess."

She does. She's exhausted. But she also wants normalcy. A tiny slice, if even for a few seconds. They have to take these hurried grabs of love when they can. Because soon Wilder will wake, crying for his milk, and she'll be in her rocking chair. But she's grateful for it. Her life. The mundane. The new. Wilder on her chest. Solomon there. Always there. Never leaving her side.

Waving a hand, she gestures to the baby monitor on the counter. Bear sleeps easy in his avocado toast onesie. "Stop worrying. Let me live, Solomon."

He blanches. A tight fury has his jaw clenching.

"Shit," she says, realizing her mistake. She looks up, pressing a palm against his heart. "I shouldn't have said that. I'm sorry. I'm so sorry."

Without words, he takes her in his arms, squeezing her tight against him. Sighing, Tessie wraps her arms around his waist, resting her head on his muscled chest, inhaling his familiar woodsy scent. A scent that calls back memories. Mexico and his flannels. White-sand beaches and salty ocean air. Their hammock. Swims in the ocean. Sunsets. Sunrises. Afternoon sex. Solomon. Her Solemn Man.

She inhales deeper. Going back further in her memory. In time. Bear's Ear bar.

They've come so far. How they got here. . .it's almost celestial to Tessie.

"You should eat," he says, trying to step away from her hug, but she holds his massive frame tighter.

"We should stay here. Like this."

Solomon sighs, deep and low. Frustrated. But the tension goes out of his body, and he drops his face to kiss the crown of her head. "Tessie," he murmurs. His hands go to her hips. "My Tessie."

She looks up at him. "Tell me what's wrong."

"You should let me take you back to LA."

Since they got home from the hospital, Solomon's been on a kick about leaving Chinook. He has too many bad memories here. It was traumatic—losing Serena, nearly losing her—but leaving isn't the answer.

She shakes her head. "No. I don't want that. Our son doesn't belong there. This is our home. Wilder's home."

"You're giving it all up."

"I'm not. I'm getting it all."

Zero regrets about what she left behind in California. She's gotten so much more in return. There is nothing she wants more. No one she trusts more. No one she loves more.

Solomon just has to see that.

"Besides," she says, resting her hand on his bearded cheek. "That's not what's really wrong."

His handsome face clouds. His face, hard and controlled, makes her ache for him. She sees so much in those dark blue eyes. What will haunt him forever.

"What if you had died?" His gruff voice shakes with emotion.

She thinks about it. She does. What if she had died? What if her baby had died? What would Solomon have done? It had been her fear for so long, leaving her son the way her mother left her. But all she can do is live.

She's here for Wilder. She's alive. And for that, she only has her body to thank. The strange voice inside her head, a woman's whisper, telling her to stay awake. To hang on. For Solomon.

Life is precious, and she still has it. Giving those worries roots isn't healthy. For either of them.

"I didn't."

Solomon's large frame sags, and he gathers her in his arms. "What if—"

"No." She cups his strong jaw in her hands and forces his gaze to hers. "We don't do what-ifs. We do what now. What next."

They have to. This is the life they fought for.

Their fate all up in the stars from the night they met.

Nodding, Solomon slips an arm around her waist and holds her tightly. His face softens. "Then what next, Tess?"

"This."

Their mouths crush together, Solomon's beard tickling her chin. God, that beard. How she loves it. Urgent groans work their way out of both of them, and then Solomon is hauling her into his broad chest, careful with her yet firm, not letting her go. Never again.

A growl tears out of him, and finally, he kisses her like she's been needing to be kissed for so damn long. Primal. Forever.

Tessie whimpers, running her tongue over his lower lip. Her body arcs into his touch. Dissolves. His need echoes hers. Hungry. Gentle. He grips her waist, lifts her up, and places her on the counter. Tessie wraps her legs around his thighs, yanking him closer. Then his hands are tangling in her hair, his big palms cradling her face. "God, I love you," he murmurs between frantic kisses, his hand slipping up her shirt to cup her breast, heavy with milk.

Tessie gasps at the sensation and has no choice but to close her eyes. "I love *you*."

"Too much, Tess," Solomon growls, angling forward to press soft, hungry kisses down her throat. His voice shakes with emotion. "I love you too goddamned much."

They break away, breathless, as a faint wail sounds throughout the cabin.

She lowers her brow to his chest and laughs.

Solomon chuckles. "Right on time."

Then he picks her up in his arms and carries her upstairs to their son.

Epilogue

Four Months Later

With a sigh, Tessie rolls her chair away from the computer screen. She adds a last-minute note to her planner, adds a final Pantone color to the mood board, then shuts her laptop. Turns off the slow croon of her Crosley. Done. She's done for the night.

The first late night she's had since she started her new adventure. Over the course of the last four months, while nursing Wilder those long, late nights, it came to her. What she wanted to do. Really do with her life. Be a mother and have a career. But her way. While she's grateful to Nova for letting her take on a few virtual projects, Tessie took another great flying leap. She started her own online interior design firm. Truelove for your True Home. For all budgets. For all people. Not just celebrities.

Though her planner is still in use, she will do motherhood her way. Make time for a life, love. Her family.

Tessie finds Solomon and Wilder curled together on the leather couch in front of the blazing fireplace. An empty bottle lay beside them. Peggy Sue at their feet. Solomon's asleep, his son pulled into the protective cradle of his arm. It'd take a crowbar to pry the baby away from him. With Solomon's calm and steady nature, Wilder could not be an easier baby. Already long and tall like his father, Wilder has Solomon's black hair and Tessie's dark chocolate brown eyes.

The prettiest Pantones she's ever seen.

Watching Solomon grow comfortable in his role as a father these last months—it turns her on and makes her want to weep simultaneously. Because he's such a good man, a good human, and her son will be too.

Wilder will have what she never had. A home with both parents who love him. A father who will never leave. And Tessie will tell Wilder about her mother, how she was badass and brave, and introduce him to country music and a Crosley that will spin just for him.

For a long moment, Tessie watches them, her heartbeats, then smiles. She grabs a jacket off the hook and slips out onto the front porch.

The April night is bitingly cold. Though winter should be long over, it's near-blizzard conditions thanks to a relentless late season dump of snow. Each snowflake shimmers silver. Tessie's breath puffs white from her mouth, and she draws her jacket tighter around her. She's gotten used to the short days and the long nights. Because she always has her stars.

She was made for stars.

She and Solomon are stars. Existing wordlessly together, shining as a group, a team, just as they've done these last few months while raising Wilder. Learning how to be a mother hasn't been easy. A lot of sleepless nights. A lot of tears. Learning how to feel sexy in her new body. But Solomon has her. Never letting her doubt herself as a mother. Believing in her sometimes more than she believes in herself. Always letting her rage or cry. Always showing her how badly he needs her.

She could have done this without him, but she never wants to. She will never be without her Solemn Man.

The door cracks. A jingle of dog tags.

Strong arms band around her waist, and Solomon's there, pulling her into him as Peggy Sue bounds for the yard.

"You get your project done?" he asks, his deep voice a rumble against her hair.

"Mm-hmm." Relishing the sensation of Solomon all around her, she drops her head back against his broad chest. "How's your little sous chef?"

"Asleep. Finally. Drunk on milk." A glass of honey-colored liquid appears in front of her. "Thought we could have a drink of our own before dinner."

Tessie smiles and spins around to face her husband. "My hero," she says, accepting the glass of whiskey. She takes a sip, passes it to him, where he does the same. Then he drops his mouth to hers.

Tessie inhales him.

Heat, the buzz of the forest, builds around them.

This is their wild life now.

Days, Grace watches Wilder while Tessie works and Solomon opens and preps Howler's Roost. Late nights, they sip whiskey on the front porch, sharing conversation about their day, nothing around them but the inky black of the night sky, the stars.

Two months after Wilder was born, she and Solomon were married. They waited until she healed and then had an intimate ceremony at Howler's Roost. A wild and wondrous wedding, where Tessie rocked a short white dress and stilettos, and Solomon wore his flannel. They were themselves. They were in love. And they weren't waiting any longer.

That's one thing she's learned this last year. Waiting, delaying one's happiness, never works. She's so damn thankful that baby inside her pushed her to grow. Pushed her right into Solomon's arms. His kind heart. His beautiful soul.

She wants more babies with him. Wants to learn their life together, because so far, they've fallen into a blissful rhythm she never thought possible.

"This reminds me of when we first met." She lifts her chin to meet her husband's piercing blue eyes. "The stars. The whiskey."

His muscles tighten around her. "The gorgeous woman in my arms."

"Hmm. All that small talk about the stars worked."

"It did," he says, sobering. "I love you, Tess."

Her heart skips a beat, swells. He never fails to say it. "I know. I love you."

He dabs a finger on the tip of her numb nose. "Are you cold?"

"Maybe." She arches a suspicious brow. "Why?"

Solomon lets her finish the whiskey. He lowers his voice. "Because I could think of a few ways to warm you up." His words have her belly dipping and warming.

A mock gasp. "Solemn Man, are you trying to take advantage of me?"

The faintest of smiles tugs at his bearded lips. "What if I am?"

She presses up on tiptoes and whispers against his mouth, "Hmm. I think I'll let you."

He pulls her tight into his arms, dark blue eyes fixed on her, nothing but devotion in them. And love overflows inside her like a flood. Before Solomon, this would have felt too big for her. She would have pushed it away, run, but not anymore. She never imagined her life would take this turn. Taking risks. Learning to love. Making a family out of the strangest of circumstances.

Solomon sweeps a kiss against her lips, warm, searching, and it's like she's back in that Tennessee bar, only one year ago, meeting Solomon for the very first time. Then, with a quick growl and an even quicker hand, Solomon sweeps her into his arms. She rests her head against his chest, smells the forest on his skin, sees the undimming love in his eyes.

Her husband.

Her son.

Her life.

Stretched out in front of her forever, like the wild Alaskan starlit sky.

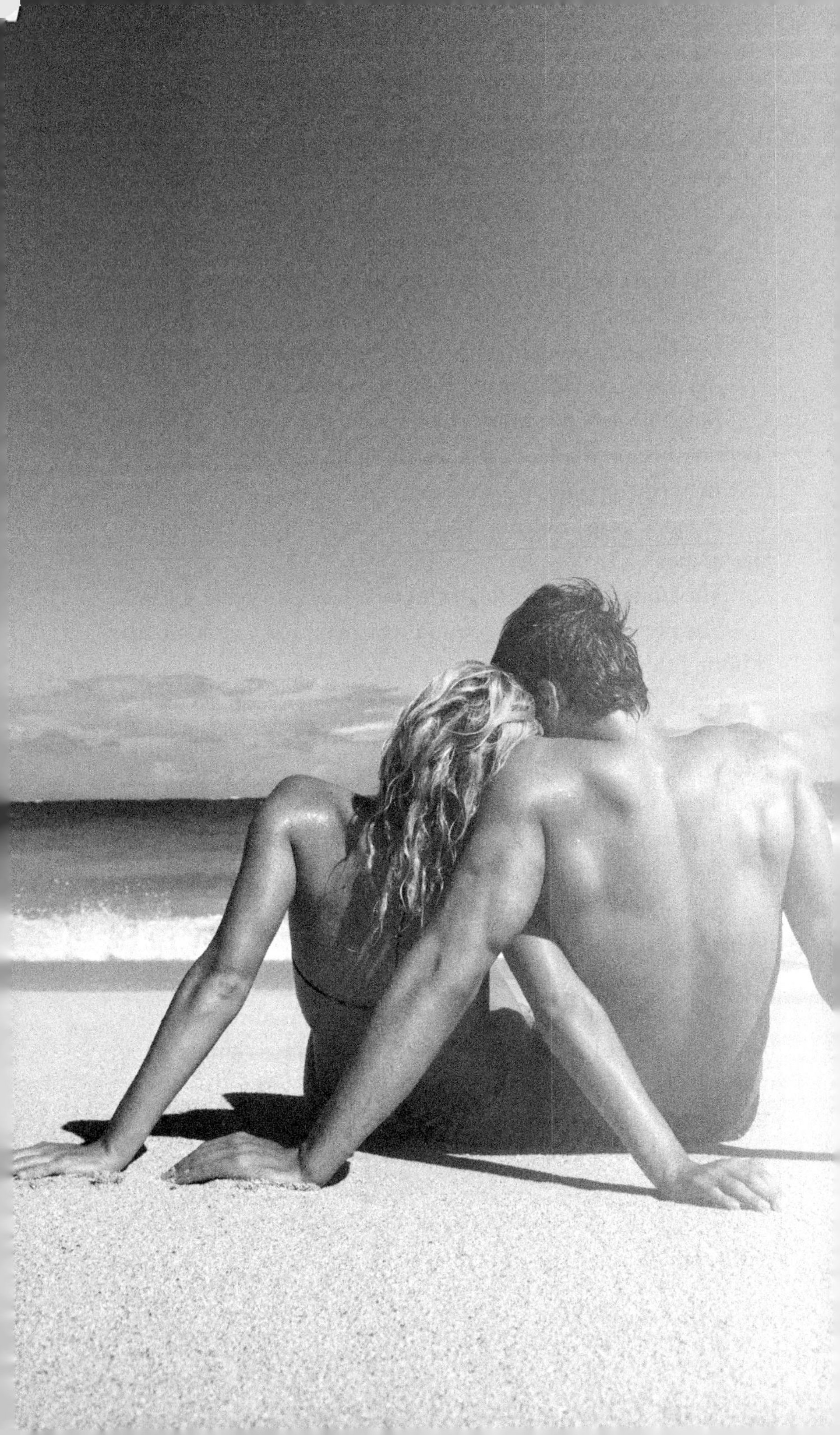

Bonus Epilogue

Two Years Later

WILDER GRIPS HIS HAND AND TUGS. "Here, Daddy?"

"Okay, little man."

Solomon settles on the sand next to his two-year-old son. Wilder's brand-new eyes take in the beach, wide with amazement, as he scoops up sand with his plastic shovel.

Scanning the horizon, Solomon runs white sand through his fingers. The crash of waves sounds on the shore. The late afternoon sun beats down. Damn breathtaking. He never thought he'd love the beach as much as he loves the mountains, but he does. He gives thanks to the sea for everything it's given him.

Because the beach is where his second life began.

He peers over his shoulder at the beach house, on watch for his wife.

But Wilder's bubbly laugh steals his attention. With jet-black hair and dark brown eyes, Wilder's the best combination of Solomon and Tessie. The child knows every lyric to every Hank Williams song, courtesy of his mother. He has Tessie's fierce mind and her fight. He's Solomon's little sous chef in the kitchen and the very best explorer of Chinook and its wildlife.

"Shells, Daddy, shells. For the castle."

"You got it." With a grunt, Solomon shoves up and gets to

work alongside his son. His big fingers collect creamy scotch bonnets, tusk shells, banded tulips. Then he and Wilder build. Soon, the sandcastle moat turns into one tower and then four.

"Can't do it." Wilder drops the shovel and collapses onto his bottom. The sand's stacked too high for him to scoop. His lower lip sticks out in a well-practiced pout. No doubt learned from Tessie. His wife still has him wrapped around her little finger. "Can't."

"You can, little man. You're strong," he tells Wilder, handing him the red plastic shovel and making him try again. "Like your mama. You can do anything."

"Mama!" Wilder squeals, tossing down the shovel to point a chubby finger over Solomon's shoulder.

Turning, he follows Wilder's joyous gaze.

Joy. That's been his life for the last few years.

Tessie's emerging from the beach house. The sight of his wife, gorgeous, glowing, tan-lined, and toned in a skimpy bikini, has him grinning. Then, his eyes move, lingering on the tiny bump on her belly.

They've been busy. Making more surprises. Building their family.

Between the two of them, they barely have any time—running a restaurant and a small business and chasing after a toddler—but they're doing it. Amid all the chaos, they managed to sneak in a second babymoon and leave it all behind for a week. The renovation to Howler's Roost was a game changer. Not only did it double income for the bar, but it got Tess a feature in *Architectural Digest* and Solomon a profile in *Food & Wine*. Tessie's business is kicking ass. She leaves Chinook every six months to check in with her clients around the United States. Their life is what they've made it. Solomon could never ask for anything better.

Everything he's ever wanted is right in front of him.

Shoving up, he meets Tess on the beach. Frames her face in his hands. "You get your nap?"

"Mm-hmm," she hums sleepily, pressing up on tiptoes to kiss

his bearded cheek. Her watchful gaze flicks to Wilder, then back to Solomon. "How goes castle making?"

"Serious business. No one's getting through that moat." He surveys her belly. "You feel okay?"

Chocolate-brown eyes sparkling, she nuzzles against him. "I'm fine. Just sleepy. Didn't you know, I'm in my house cat era? Sleeping more, lounging in the sun, hissing at interruptions."

"You sure?"

Tessie gives him a flat look. "Solomon, I will drown you in the Pacific if you keep asking me."

He grunts. No chances. None at all with Tess. His wife's four months pregnant, and after what happened with Wilder in the delivery room, he's a mess. He'll always be an overprotective mess when it comes to her. He'll never forget how close he came to losing her.

"Had a dream about names," Tessie says.

He splays a hand over her belly. "Did you?"

"What about Vienna?"

Solomon frowns. "Like the sausage?"

Tessie simply shakes her head and laughs. "I can't with you." She smiles up at him. "Checked in back home. Peggy Sue's alive, no thanks to Howler. Ash is actually going on vacation for once in her gloomy life."

"Oh yeah?"

"Of sorts. It's a job, but hey, she's off to Hawaii. She's gonna fry."

Solomon lifts his brows. "That's why you wear flannel."

"Flannel is nice, but this is better," Tessie says, tracing her finger over his muscular chest before dropping it to caress his tan forearm and then moving on to his hard bicep. His new tattoos, three stars added onto the inky black sky of Chinook, represent his family, and soon he'll add another. For their daughter.

He pulls her into his arms, kissing the tip of her freckled nose. "Feeling me up, Pregnant Woman?"

"It's only fair." Tessie laughs, the sweet melody lifting over the crash of the waves. "After all, this is all your fault." She rubs her swollen belly. "Look what you did to me."

"Do it again if you let me," he growls, fiddling with the thin string of her bikini bottoms.

Tessie gasps. "Don't you dare."

He kisses the top of her head, keeping one eye on Wilder playing in the sand. Slowly, he and Tess turn toward the horizon. A soft *oh* pops out of her mouth when she sees the sunset. A kaleidoscope of pinks and oranges. And then Solomon's hand finds hers, their fingers interlacing. As he holds his wife in his arms, his heart crashes around his chest like the highest wave. They stand in the sun, the screaming blue sky above, thinking of Mexico, almost three years ago, remembering how unsure they were of how to make their lives blend, but they did it.

He'll never have Mexico with anyone but Tess.

Solomon drops his mouth to her ear. "I love you, baby," he says, his voice ragged with emotion.

Tessie twists in his arms, curling into him. Her brown eyes soften. "I love you."

Sweet, warm, is the kiss. Soft and perfect. He drinks her in like a promise, this woman who's changed his life. Mountains or beach, good or bad, she's got him, and he's got her. Until the end of their days.

"Mama, up!" Tessie is launched forward by a squealing Wilder, who wraps his arms around her knees. "Up! Up! Up!"

Solomon chuckles, gently holding Tess's elbow to keep her steady. "Whatever happened to lying low, little man?"

Laughing, Tessie sweeps Wilder up in her arms. "You build your castle, Bear?"

"Oh, yes, Mama." Wilder holds her face between his hands. His expression serious, stern. "It will never fall down."

"I know it won't." Smiling, Tessie presses a smacking kiss to his cheek. Wilder coos and burrows his head in her neck. The way her love radiates, the happiness in his son's eyes, has Solomon's heart cracking open.

The best mother.

So damn lucky. He and Wilder both.

Clearing his throat of emotion, he says, "We need another picture."

Tessie arranges Wilder in her arms so he's locked tight between them, his small arms looped around both their necks. Solomon raises his phone, soaking up the smile on his wife's face. His son and Tessie right there in his arms, where they're supposed to be. Then, on the count of three, he snaps the photo.

After setting Wilder on the sand, Tessie appraises the photo. Turns and palms his dark beard. "If you ask me, the beach looks good on you, Solemn Man."

He tosses his phone onto a beach towel, turns to Tess. "It looks good on you too, Pregnant Woman." He glances down at Wilder. "What do you think, little Wild Man? Take your mama for a swim?"

"Don't you dare!" Tess shrieks, already backing away.

Solomon grins and makes a grab for her.

With a roar that sends Wilder into a frenzy of giggles, Solomon sweeps Tess up in his arms and rushes her down to the shoreline. Wilder runs after them, waving his arms. With Tessie's laughter ringing in his ears, his son beside him, love as warm as the sun above, Solomon rushes all three of them into the ocean, their laughter breaking up in the waves as they hold tight to each other.

Author's Note

Dear Reader,

    I first started writing this story in March 2022 while I was doing pelvic floor exercises to heal my abs and get rid of my tummy's little pooch. Turns out, I just needed to stop drinking wine. As I breathed deep, I started musing on all the things our body goes through, what we, as women experience during pregnancy and after birth. And like a screeching banshee Tessie and Solomon came flying into my brain. Bickering. Bantering. Kissing. The two of them kept me company in our little workout room while I practiced quick flick Kegels and stayed in the back of my mind until I got them out of it.

    Writing this novel has been a cathartic experience. I always wanted to write my birth story, but never had the time and/or was too emotional, so this felt like the next best thing. A bit of fiction, a bit of fact. Reliving and revisiting all the emotions that came with birth and pregnancy was like I ripped out a piece of my childbearing soul and slapped it on the page. Job security. Body insecurity. Wondering if you're meant to be a mother or a milk box. Trying to be a warrior when all you want to do is weep. And so, this book has a big, whopping piece of my heart in it.

    I hope you loved Tessie and Solomon's sweet, whirlwind love story. Because they're yours now.

As always, thank you for reading!
XOXO,
Ava

Thank you for reading!

If you enjoyed the book, please consider leaving a review on Goodreads and Amazon.
Every review means the world to indie authors.

Don't miss out on Ava Hunter's upcoming books! Sign up at www.authoravahunter.com to be the first to get the latest book news and bonus content.

Acknowledgments

Big thanks and love to...

Leni Kauffman for designing an amazing cover and bringing Solomon and Tessie to life. Working with you was an absolute dream.

Beth at VB Edits for your kick-ass edits and laser-sharp eye. See what I did there?

Chelsea, Tammie, and Rachel for being the best betas a girl could ask for. Thank you for your endless support and feedback.

Eve Kasey for being a world-class cheerleader. Your kind words, generous feedback and incredible support mean the world. You are a gem to the writing community.

The Trauma Fiction group on Facebook for their generosity and expertise in all things medical and babies.

My friends and family who put up with me and my writing angst.

And finally, my daughter Scarlett for making me a mama. Thank you for letting me mine your birth for traumatic writing material. See you in therapy. I love you, my wild child.

About the Author

Ava Hunter is a strong believer in black coffee, red wine, and the there's-only-one-bed trope. She writes contemporary romance with healthy amounts of angst where the damsels are never quite damsels, but the men they love (good, bad and rugged) are always there for them. Married to her high school sweetheart, Ava loves crafting strong, stubborn women that only make their men fall harder, adores all things pink, and can never ever get enough of protector romance.

CONNECT WITH AVA:

WEBSITE: www.authoravahunter.com
NEWSLETTER: www.authoravahunter.com
FACEBOOK: facebook.com/authoravahunter
INSTAGRAM: instagram.com/authoravahunter
TIKTOK: tiktok.com/@authoravahunter

Printed in Great Britain
by Amazon